Open Sea

MARÍA GUDÍN

TRANSLATED BY CYNTHIA STEELE

amazon crossing

Previously published as *Mar Abierta* by Penguin Random House in Spain in 2016. Translated from Spanish by Cynthia Steele. First published in English by AmazonCrossing in 2018.

Published by AmazonCrossing, Seattle

www.apub.com

Amazon, the Amazon logo, and AmazonCrossing are trademarks of Amazon.com, Inc., or its affiliates.

ISBN-13: 9781503903173
ISBN-10: 1503903176

Cover design by Shasti O'Leary Soudant

Printed in the United States of America

To my aunt Renata, who was like a mother to me.
To my uncle Pepe, who is always perfect.
To my cousin Eliana, who grew up with all my brothers and sisters.
To Alicia, who is always in my heart.

When someone inquired which were more in number, the living or the dead, he rejoined, "In which category, then, do you place those who are on the seas?"

Anacharsis, in Lives of Eminent Philosophers, volume I *by Diogenes Laertius, translated by Robert Drew Hicks*

Part 1

LEN

1

Oak Park

Santo Domingo, April 1655

Sometimes I wake up remembering the hundred-year-old oak tree at the top of the hill, right before the sheep pasture. Beyond the hill is Oak Park. The dream is always the same. I see myself running up to the tree that gave the estate its name. From there, you can make out the great stone mansion where I was raised, and to which I may never return.

In the back garden, next to the house, a distant figure anxiously scans the horizon. Piers . . . he must think I've snuck away from lessons again and that Mademoiselle Maynard will get mad and order them to lock me in the dark room in the cellar, where strange noises are supposedly heard. And where, to this day, a terrible secret is hidden.

Then Piers spots me and waves for me to come down. I ignore him. As he climbs the hill, I twirl around the tree trunk, spinning like a top, until I get dizzy and fall to the ground, laughing. Suddenly Piers is at my side, annoyed, but smiling just the same.

In those days, I was just a little girl, but the love that filled my heart was no less intense than it is now, when I haven't seen him for such a long time. Lately his face has become blurry in my mind, and I want to remember it clearly.

Back then, the sun that filtered through the oak branches felt warm, maybe because Piers was by my side. But now that I live in the distant, burning tropics, I realize that the sun of my English childhood was lukewarm, even cold.

I never speak about that time, which is tucked away in my memories like a bittersweet aftertaste. For a long time now, I've hardly mentioned it. People suspect I'm mad, that the British people I spent my childhood with mistreated me or perhaps cast a spell over me. They think I don't understand Spanish, with its harsh sounds, this language I learned so long ago from my mother. I haven't forgotten it, but I'd rather keep it to myself.

Since arriving here on Hispaniola, where my uncle lives, I am often lost in my thoughts, and when people speak to me, I tend to respond in monosyllables at most. My uncle is His Excellency Don Juan Francisco de Montemayor y Córdoba de Cuenca, principal judge of the Royal Audiencia of Santo Domingo, the first court of the Spanish Crown in America. At first, he called in doctors to bleed me, then Dominican friars with black capes who would sprinkle holy water on me, trying to make the devil leave my body. Not so long ago, my uncle even brought in a witch doctor from a nearby village, a mulatto hiding behind a mask, who started hopping around, beating a little drum. I managed to control myself for a moment, then exploded in laughter. That no doubt confirmed my uncle's fears about my sanity. He dismissed the man and sternly admonished me to pull myself together. I stopped laughing and started to cry.

I think it was Doña Luisa Dávila who suggested that it might help if I told my story to a good Christian woman—like her—my story of what happened long ago in the English lands, in that godless and schismatic nation. But the more she interrogated me, the quieter I became since I thought her obnoxious and repulsive. Perhaps she reminded me of Elizabeth Leigh, Piers's elegant sister, whom I can't help but blame for many of our misfortunes. My uncle, when he saw me withdrawing even more, asked her to leave me alone. And Doña Luisa, never content with sitting on the sidelines, offered to lend us Josefina, a black slave renowned as a healer.

My esteemed uncle was hesitant, but finally accepted. He didn't understand then or now what's wrong with me or just what to do about it. Sometimes I catch him gazing at me pensively, at this young stranger wounded by the sorrows of a secret past.

I wish I really had lost my mind, that I was demented and all my memories had been erased. Instead, they torment me, returning again and again like a toxic fog, forcing me to keep silent. My dreams are filled with blood, fire, shouting, and the smell of singed flesh and burning wood as the soldiers of Parliament, the terrible Roundheads, enter Oak Park, set fire to the estate, and destroy the Leighs' house. Once again, I wake up screaming.

They must have heard. Josefina comes in. I hear her scolding me under her breath as she crosses the room.

"Señorita Catalina, this darkness! Windows are meant to be opened."

Despite my protests, she flings back the curtains; a warm, humid breeze and brilliant tropical light flood the room. When she turns, her lion-like head is silhouetted against the brightness. She wraps me in an expansive smile; her eyes are so dark brown that they're almost black. She moves gracefully, like a slow boat on a calm sea, like the galleon that brought me here. Josefina comes over to the bed, chatting away in her Caribbean rhythm; I listen distractedly, though I'm always cheered by her warmth.

When Doña Luisa first brought her, I had reservations, suspecting she was a spy for our prying neighbor. But Josefina didn't let that intimidate her, and, since I wouldn't open my mouth, started telling me about her life. Her story touched something inside me: her childhood in a tribe in Africa, her capture, the horrors of the slave ship, her arrival at Cartagena de Indias and then Hispaniola. She sparked empathy in me, and the first syllables I spoke, after such a long silence, were words of consolation for her. After that, I began to talk a little more. When my good uncle noticed the change, he asked Doña Luisa to sell Josefina to him outright, but the lady refused, too accustomed to collecting fees for her slave's services as a healer and midwife. Still, wanting to please my uncle, she let Josefina stay on as our servant, though she often disappears on errands for Doña Luisa.

I have spent many afternoons with Josefina by my side; as I lie in bed, she holds my hand. We can stay like this for hours. I stare at the open-beamed ceiling, longing for Oak Park, my childhood games, and the love in Piers's hazel eyes and remembering the war that shook the house. She sits beside me, wrapping my slender white fingers in her strong black hands, perhaps thinking about the African lands where her family still lives. When we are together like this, my pain subsides, my desperation recedes into serene sadness.

Today, Josefina doesn't ask about the cries. She tells me news from the city, of the arrival of the new governor and the fleet. She coaxes me out of bed, combing my hair and sitting me down in the big rocking chair. She hums as she makes the bed, dusts, and mops the floors, one eye always on me.

Outside my window, a gray-crowned palm tanager unfurls its joyous song. In the courtyard, a parrot mimics my uncle's commanding voice. As I listen, I smile, and Josefina is pleased.

While Josefina keeps working, I venture out onto the balcony. Down in the courtyard, servants are coming and going from the stables, carrying buckets of dirty water, which they splash into the gutters. They notice my presence and look up at me, as you would look at a madwoman, with compassion but also suspicion. I return to my room, where Josefina has nearly finished. I peer out the window at the rushing blue current of the Ozama River, shimmering in the sunlight and ending abruptly at the ancient, massive fortifications of my uncle's home. Then a galleon appears on the river; I can make out its masts and semifurled sails. My mind wanders at the sounds of the port, but nothing remains of my world since my childhood love drowned in that now-sparkling sea.

2

Classes

Oak Park, Summer of 1640

I can see myself now, in the room where I used to study with two of
Piers's sisters, Margaret and Ann Leigh. I remember the big leaded-glass
window they'd open when the weather was fair, a cool breeze ruffling
the curtains. Mademoiselle Maynard would sit in front of it, dictating
lessons in her crisp French accent. I didn't listen to her, amusing myself
by looking out the window for Piers and his older brother, Thomas.
They often convinced Mr. Reynolds to let them out early so they could
go galloping through the fields.

At lunchtime, we always sat in the same places: the boys' teacher
and ours, face-to-face, with us children arranged beside them in order
of age. Piers had no choice but to accept me if he didn't want to be
bored and alone. We were both restless, made for one another—we
shared that sense of humor that lets two people communicate without
a word. We would climb trees, play hide-and-seek, laugh at funny stories, read books together. Sometimes we would quarrel, and that was
part of the fun. Sometimes, when we were reading, Ann would join us;
she was only two years older than Piers, but thought herself a young
lady and tried to behave with great decorum. In fact, she was still a

little girl and, when the teachers weren't there, would play along with our scatterbrained games.

Ann Leigh is fixed in my mind just as she looked then, when I first arrived at Oak Park. She had dark-blonde hair, with strands of gold shimmering in the sunlight, big blue eyes, pale eyelashes, and a long, slender nose. She was shy and liked quiet: long walks through the countryside, evenings spent reading next to the fire. The Leighs' library was well stocked, and Ann favored Shakespeare and John Donne's love poems. Sometimes she and I would sit behind the house, under a fir tree. From there you could see the magnificent silhouette of Oak Park, the moss-covered ruins of the abbey, the pond, and the gardens. We read many stories there and would often make up the endings.

Margaret, a year older than Ann, was livelier and more cheerful. She played the clavichord, was talented at crocheting, and would chatter on and on as she sewed. She adored gossip and rumors, especially about the court, and the only thing I ever saw her read were the scandal sheets she got from the servants. I can still hear her infectious laughter. She was a gemstone in the rough, gradually revealing herself, with her white skin, dark eyes, black hair, oval face, and aquiline nose.

Both sisters loved to sing and dance, and they taught me. They also watched over me, treating me like their little sister. In fact, most of my clothes and possessions came from them.

After lunch, we were required to rest. The teachers would retire to their rooms while the children would nap or do some homework. Piers and I would take advantage of those moments to sneak away. We warned Margaret and Ann not to tell. When it was hot, we'd run through the fields, climb up to the old oak tree, and explore the ruins of the Norman Tower, which they say was built in the time of William the Conqueror to guard the coast. We would even go to the river, crossing the sheep's ford or swimming as far as the cliffs and the beach.

When it was raining, as it usually was, we would snoop around the corridors, finding hidden passageways joining the rooms and even venturing into the no-man's-land of the kitchens, hoping to get something sweet.

The kitchens of Oak Park were spacious and thoughtfully laid out. In the middle, an enormous, perennially lit oven warmed the air. There was a separate room for meats, where a butcher prepared geese, deer, and for special occasions, veal or duck. The game came from the Leighs' property. In another room, a baker would vigorously knead dough for bread, pies, tarts, and other delicacies. I remember him well. Matt was a large man with an olive complexion. He seemed very old to me, practically ancient, but he could deftly lift the huge wooden paddle of fermented dough into the oven. They said he had been a sailor and now was lame, but that didn't interfere with the Herculean strength of his arms. He had thick, graying eyebrows over dark, defiant eyes. He guarded the baked goods from young servants and the household rascals. We were terrified of him.

One rainy afternoon when Piers and I were playing hide-and-seek, I climbed behind some sacks of flour in a little back room. When I heard the key turn in the lock, I didn't dare reveal my presence for fear of being punished. After a terrifying eternity, the door opened again, and someone came in. I held my breath and peered between the sacks. It was Matt, come to sharpen a knife on a whetstone. All I could think was, if he found me, he would kill me, and I would never see Piers, or Ann, or Margaret, or Thomas again; I would be reunited with my mother.

After a while, the noise stopped, and the baker started slicing bread, humming a sweet melody. Then the melody turned into words familiar to my ear, words with no relation to the language of this country; it wasn't English, nor the Spanish of my childhood. It made me think of my mother.

I slowly stood up, as if hypnotized. When he heard the rustling, Matt spun around, and I covered my face in my hands. Quick footsteps

came closer, and a strong arm pushed aside the sack I'd been hiding behind. He rested a big hand on my shoulder, then lifted me up into the
air. A guttural voice spoke to me in my mother's tongue.

"I'm going to eat a little girl raw!"

Suddenly, the arms holding me began to shake. I took my hands
from my eyes and looked at the man's olive-colored, laughing face.

"Miss Catalina! Everyone's looking for you."

He put me down gently.

"Why do you sing that song?" I asked.

He looked at me fondly, but didn't answer.

"Please," I insisted, "my mother used to sing that song."

The lullaby had soothed me in the house of my maternal grand-
parents, in Basque Country. It had always kept me company when my
mother was still alive.

"And I'm not Catalina anymore; now my name is Len!"

He was silent, and into his eyes crept a longing for something I
couldn't fathom. Then he said, "I see in your eyes the same anger I used
to admire in your great-grandfather's. You're the great-granddaughter of
Don Miguel de Oquendo, Captain General of the Guipúzcoa Squadron
and second-in-command of the Spanish Armada. You are Doña Catalina
de Montemayor y Oquendo."

"Did you know my family? Are you from my mother's country?"

"I'm Basque, from Donostía."

I had a thousand questions, but before I could ask them, he turned
those sparkling eyes, so dark that they looked black, on me. Then he
spoke to me slowly in a strange mixture of English, Spanish, and maybe that Basque language, from the place we both came from.

"I want you to keep this secret for me. Don't tell anyone you've
been talking to old Mateo de Aresti—and I won't tell Miss Maynard
what you and Mr. Piers have been up to when you're supposed to be
resting."

I heard Piers calling me in the distance. Matt nodded solemnly, and I ran out of the kitchens. I found Piers next to the pond behind the house.

"Where the hell have you been hiding?"

I told him all about my adventure.

"And he knows my full name: Catalina de Montemayor y Oquendo. Here, I've always been Kathleen or Len. I don't know how he could have found out."

Piers looked at me, amused, slowly pronouncing in the Spanish he was learning from Mr. Reynolds: "Dona Catalina . . . yes, I like it; it sounds nice. What's the rest?"

"De Montemayor y Oquendo. And it's Do-nya."

He repeated it in a British accent that made me laugh.

"Do-nna Catalina de Montemayor y Oquendo. That sounds impressive! Father says Spanish names are high-sounding, like their empire. With that name, you must come from an important family. My name is just Piers Leigh. Very short, very unimportant."

"Don't make fun of me! Now I'm Len, and I'm from here, Oak Park. I don't remember anything about where I came from."

That wasn't true. Of course I remembered where I was from, but after just a few weeks at Oak Park, I wanted desperately to be a Leigh, not someone from another family, another land. At first, I wanted to be Piers's sister, but later I would grow to love him in a different way.

I sulked and crossed my arms. Piers ignored me and kept talking, as surprised as I was by what had happened.

"How strange! The other servants say Matt is a madman."

"He was nice to me; he just laughed because I was afraid."

"He's been with us since before I was born. They say he arrived on a shipwreck and my great-grandfather took him in. Maybe he's a spy for the king of Spain . . ."

"What would he have to spy on, so far from the court?"

"The meetings in the East Room?"

In one corner of the house, there was a small office where Lord Edward Leigh met from time to time with local gentlemen or members of Parliament from London. Piers wasn't allowed in, so he was fascinated by it.

"I doubt it; he seems like a good man. Spies are bad."

"For you, there are only good guys and bad guys," Piers said, "but, from what I've learned, bad people are sometimes good, and good people aren't always up to snuff."

I reflected a moment. "Piers, do you think I'm bad?"

"When you run away, yes. Mademoiselle Maynard is looking for you. What will you tell her?"

"That I got lost."

"She'll want to know where . . ."

"I can't tell her I got locked up in the flour pantry playing hide-and-seek!"

"My La-dy Do-nna Catalina, I foresee that thou shalt be grounded to thy room for several months," Piers joked.

"Who cares?"

The children's bedrooms were on the third floor of a tower, from the days the house was a fortress. Our windows looked out onto some ancient battlements that formed a large terrace on the roof of the mansion. We could escape through them and then go back inside through another, unlocked room. So, being grounded in our rooms didn't frighten us. The only thing that really got our attention was when Miss Maynard or Mr. Reynolds would threaten to lock us up in a dark cell with a skull, underneath the cellars. They said it was an ancient dungeon from the time of Edward III. Thomas and Piers's sisters would tell us stories, saying you could hear all kinds of noises coming from there at night, moans and whispered words. They also said that, during the Reformation, monks from the ruined abbey next door had been tortured and executed down there in secret chambers. At night, especially when there was a full moon, their lost souls would wander, seeking revenge. The idea of going down there terrified me, and Piers felt the same, no matter how brave he acted.

With that threat in mind, I quickly returned to the classroom. Mademoiselle Maynard was fuming. She marched me to a small room on the third floor and locked the door.

Gorgeous afternoon light streamed in through the large window. If I hadn't gotten locked into the flour pantry and hadn't been punished, we might have made it to the coast, to the cliffs with breaking waves from the North Sea. Piers loved the ocean; he always told me that someday he would become a sailor and sail around the world. Once he had sailed on a merchant ship with his father, and he was very proud of that. It made me furious to think of Piers going alone to the coast, while I was locked in there and bored.

To distract myself, I reached for a book on the shelf next to the fireplace. It was a favorite of Piers and mine, a book with illustrations of ships of different shapes and sails. It was in my mother's language. I slowly turned the pages: an antique ship, another one with two sails flying the pennants of Castile, a little caravel with square sails, a Venetian *urca* or cargo vessel, a light patache, and the galley, with its long oars, a boat you never saw on the coast of the North Sea.

I turned another page, and there it was, the most beautiful of all. An enormous ship, with a hull made of rustic timber and a prominent, crenellated aftercastle: a galleon.

3

THE STORY OF DOÑA ISABEL DE OQUENDO

The City of the Golden Tower, Spring of 1639

On a galleon like that, I left Spain, the land of my ancestors. So many years later, I still remember a luminous city with a tower made of gold. A city with intricate little streets and dark corners, buildings with geraniums and roses in the windows, and galleons along a wide river with gentle waters crossed by fishermen's boats and larger ships. A city that smelled of fried food, garlic, and strong wine, with the constant hustle and bustle of merchants' carts, pealing church bells, and hawkers' cries.

My mother, a tall, beautiful woman, never let go of my hand for fear of losing me when we went walking. For a long time, maybe months, we were boarders in the modest house of a widow. All I remember of that is the blistering sun, my mother's anxiety, and a succession of boring days as we awaited our sailing permits from the Recruitment House.

Finally, the permits came through, and we set sail on one of the grand galleons. I remember the excitement I felt when I climbed the gangplank, its wobbly boards separating dock from deck. On board, a young officer greeted us with polite disinterest. My mother was only the young wife of a Crown soldier who was stationed at a fort on a

Caribbean island. We weren't headed for the viceroyalty of New Spain or the rich lands of Peru. But later, when the captain noticed my mother's last names, Oquendo y Lazcano, he bowed to her with respect. Don Martín de Arriola didn't think it right for the daughter of Admiral Don Antonio to travel in steerage, so he offered her a first-class cabin, near the aftercastle, as if my mother were nobility. The captain's deference would change our destiny.

We glided down the Guadalquivir River and along the coast of Cádiz toward the Canary Islands and the Sea of the Mares. On that beautiful spring day, the voyage was tranquil; a gentle breeze pushed us southward. From the bow, my mother and I watched the other ships in the enormous Windward Fleet: heavily armed galleons with cannons and *carracas*, merchant ships to carry the cargo. Our ship was in the convoy's rearguard, very near the flagship.

That first night, Don Martín de Arriola invited us and other notables to supper in his simple cabin. The table was just a long board, and the captain presided over it in an armchair tied to the floor. A long bench was attached to the wall on one side, and stools were lashed to the floor on the other. My mother sat on a corner of the bench, next to Don Martín, her back against the cabin wall. I perched next to her. I can still hear the captain speaking with admiration about Don Antonio de Oquendo, Admiral of the Armada and victor against the Dutch at the Battle of Albrolhos in Brazil. My grandfather, whom I had never met.

"Where is he now?" he asked.

"He was named governor of Menorca."

"Then the Mediterranean is safe. Your father is a great man." Don Martín went on, enumerating my grandfather's feats.

My mother listened in proud silence, her eyes full of tears. At one point, she sighed. "I've caused my father nothing but pain," she said softly.

Then Don Martín changed the subject. He talked to the others at the table, clergymen headed for America and public employees being posted to the viceroyalty of New Spain, about the English and Dutch pirates infesting the Caribbean and the entire route to the Indies.

One day when we woke up, there were clouds over the ocean, and a little while later, a hurricane wind came up from the west. The sailors rushed to lower the sails. Soon, lightning bolts crisscrossed the horizon, and the galleon began lurching in a foaming sea. We spent anguished hours shut inside our cabin. My mother put me in a hammock and started to sing. From her lips came that ancient Basque lullaby, the same song old Matt would sing to me in the pantry. But I couldn't sleep; I felt nauseated and dizzy.

Finally, the storm died down. When we went on deck, our ship was all alone. The wind had separated us from the convoy, carrying us to the north; I heard an officer say we weren't far from the Portuguese Algarve coast. I saw the worried expression on the captain's face as he set out in search of the other ships.

Some happy times followed. I remember my mother on the galleon's deck, the ocean breeze ruffling her shining chestnut hair. She told me about my father, Don Pedro de Montemayor, about the new life we would have with him, far away from gossip and dishonor. But she never saw him again.

One morning when the sun was making the sea glitter, the watchman shouted, "Ship ahoy!" I could feel the excitement on board. Could it be another straggler from our fleet? Then the ship hoisted its flag. As it fluttered atop the mast, there were cries of indignation and anger from our crew. It was a pirate ship for the Royal Navy, as the English fleet was known, hunting some lone galleon like ours.

There was a call to battle stations, and we were sent back to our cabin. Even today, my ears still ring with the cross-firing of shells, and I can still feel my mother's protective embrace. I could hear the sailors running back and forth up above, cannons exploding and muskets being fired, the cries of wounded and angry men. Finally, the combat ended. Some sailors appeared, speaking a language I didn't know. They ordered us to go up on deck. Then I saw the chopped-off mast and, for the first time, the color of death on a man's face. Sprawled there on the quarterdeck lay the captain, Don Martín de Arriola.

The pirates divided the passengers into two groups: the first for people with cabins in the aftercastle and the second for everyone else. Our ship was taking on water, listing dangerously. They transferred the merchandise to their ship, then the first group of passengers. The second group they left on the high seas. We watched them crowding into lifeboats as the galleon sank. If my mother and I had stayed in a lower room, we would have been among them. But since the pirates saw first-class passengers as hostages they could ransom, they led us to austere cabins on the English ship, and we set sail.

That's how my mother and I came to the English lands. My first impressions are of a river with rushing waters, a sky laden with clouds, green riverbanks crowded with trees, and a city with buildings of wood and stone, a fortress, and a bridge. In the background, blurred by memory, I can still see the slender spires of St. Paul's Cathedral, the windows of Westminster Abbey, and the king's palaces. They took us to a riverside mansion belonging to a nobleman who'd sponsored the pirate expedition.

At the house in Holborn, they treated us well at first while awaiting the ransom they had demanded. Now and then I would hear my mother sigh that only the Oquendos could help us. Later, I heard her complain that they had abandoned us, that it would be to their advantage if we were lost. She said her father was the only person who truly loved her, but he was too far away and might not even know what was happening.

When the ransom was not forthcoming, she was escorted to the Spanish embassy. I remember her holding my hand tightly as she strode through the muddy streets of London with resolute steps, determined to set us free.

Near the house in Holborn was a lovely church with tall steeples, St. Etheldreda's Church. Next to it sat a spacious, Tudor-style house: headquarters for diplomatic missions from the Spanish Crown.

Before we went in to the ambassador's residence, my mother stopped at the chapel to ask the Lord for help. I recall the great stained-glass window, sunlight filtering through its colorful images of saints. We left that magical place and entered the brick-and-stone mansion. They showed us to an anteroom, where many people were waiting. We looked at one other silently; perhaps, in those difficult times, we were all there seeking protection from the most powerful country in the world.

A servant arrived, leading an old woman whose face was furrowed by wrinkles. As she walked by, the woman brushed against a package under the arm of a gentleman with tall boots and a starched white collar. The man drew back a little, and as the cloth slipped partly off the package, my mother and I gazed, astonished, at a beautiful painting. It was of an amply proportioned nude woman with ivory skin, her blonde hair pulled back and a pearl necklace at her throat. She was lying down, petting a dog while listening to a gentleman play the lute. My mother gripped me tightly by the hand and led me away. I suppose she thought it inappropriate for an eight-year-old.

I could hear sobbing from the ambassador's office. Finally, the door opened, and the old woman came back out, looking distraught. She shuffled toward the door while they ushered the man with the painting inside. Suddenly, the woman staggered, and my mother ran to hold her up. The women sat down together, and I watched them curiously. I heard the lady pronounce some words in Latin with an English accent. She said something like *filius*, *preste*, and then *Tyburn* over and over again while she sobbed. Later, my mother explained that the lady's son had been sentenced to death; she had asked the Spanish ambassador to intervene, but the envoy of our powerful king said there was nothing he could do. Her son would be sent to the gallows the next day.

A footman came looking for the lady in black, and she walked out leaning on him. My mother accompanied her to the door. The other people waiting didn't seem to notice the woman's grief; they just stared straight ahead, each lost in their own sorrows.

We waited a long time, hearing snatches of male laughter. They were talking about the painting, saying something indecent about the nude lady. I asked my mother what the ambassador wanted with a picture of a woman without any clothes. She told me that the king of Spain liked the painting and that the English monarch needed money and was selling his collection. Finally, the man emerged without the painting, and they let us go in next.

The Spanish ambassador, Don Alonso de Cárdenas, listened attentively to my mother as she told him about being taken captive by the pirates and how indignant she was at having to be freed.

"At this time," he declared, "Spanish–British relations aren't especially cordial—"

"You can't allow a subject of King Philip to be unjustly detained!"

Don Alonso frowned and consulted some papers. "You have been captured by a pirate whose sponsor is someone very near the throne. The only solution is to pay what they are asking."

"Our imprisonment is totally illegal!"

"My information doesn't tally with your story. They deny that a ship flying a British flag attacked a Spanish galleon. They say they rescued you after a shipwreck and incurred significant expenses in the process. You can't return to lands belonging to the Spanish Crown until you repay them."

"But that's a wicked lie! We were attacked!"

"Possibly. But, at the moment, to recognize a pirate attack against subjects of the Spanish Crown might jeopardize diplomatic relations, and we aren't prepared to do that. We are fighting enough wars in Europe as it is."

The ambassador went on to say that he'd like to help, but the amount that the pirates asked was beyond his resources. My mother looked pointedly at the portrait leaning against the wall; he'd been willing to pay a pretty penny for that. In response to her wounded expression, Don Alonso de Cárdenas softened a little and inquired about her family. The Oquendos were wealthy; perhaps they could pay the sum?

"I have written to my father, but I have had no response—nor will there be one." My mother glanced at me and lowered her voice. "You don't understand. My mother died. I had a daughter of my own. They considered me dishonored." Her voice broke. "I got married later, but my husband had to leave for America, and they captured me when I was on my way to join him."

She started to cry, which made the ambassador squirm. Finally, my mother pulled herself together and went on in a voice muffled by sorrow. "When my daughter was born, my aunt Juana, who was head of the family during my father's prolonged absences, wrote to him, telling him an indecent story. The admiral, a proud man, flew into a rage and disowned me. My father," she said, her voice trembling, "might— *might*—have forgiven me, if I had just been able to speak with him."

"Then, Doña Isabel, it is your husband's duty to pay the ransom. According to our records, he is Don Pedro de Montemayor, an officer posted to the fort in Santo Domingo."

When she heard his name, my mother seemed to wake up from a dream.

"I've written to him, too, and he hasn't answered, either. As you know, letters take a long time to reach the other side of the ocean, and sometimes they never arrive. Anyway, what could a poor soldier like my husband do?"

The ambassador thought a moment. "Madame, Doña Isabel, you must keep trying with the Oquendos."

"There is no hope! They have made me pay dearly for my alleged sins. Señor Ambassador, my aunt Juana stands to benefit from my repudiation. She has a daughter, Teresa, who is married to my father's bastard son. If they remove me from the line of succession, they will inherit the admiral's wealth." She fell silent a moment, then added softly, "Don Alonso, sir, I'm paying an exorbitant price for marrying someone my family didn't approve of. I beg you—no, I beseech you!—to help me."

The ambassador put on a sincere face and responded, "I'll try to do what I can."

But Don Alonso de Cárdenas didn't do anything. Desperate, my mother wrote time and again to America, but perhaps her correspondence never reached Santo Domingo, or perhaps it arrived too late.

When my mother's captors realized that nothing would be paid for her, that no one acknowledged her, and that she was not a noblewoman, they decided she was an adventurer, off to America in search of fortune. Or maybe she was a prostitute. They knew the Spanish government didn't allow single women to travel to the Indies alone, and they began to think she was lying. The owners of the house deemed her a fallen woman, perhaps predestined for hell. That's why they sold her to a scoundrel who kept a beer hall on the outskirts of London. And so, we went to Moorfields.

Moorfields! I can't say the word without dread. It was a neighborhood riddled with taverns, bordellos, and gambling houses. That's where they left us, locking us in a dark hovel full of strange women in heavy makeup; their caresses frightened me. There were constant shouts and obscenities. I remember the smell of beer, boiled greens, and fried sausages. I felt like I was suffocating.

My mother's breathing became more and more asthmatic, and she would frequently cry, but no one sympathized with her. Since the women couldn't understand her language, they thought she wasn't very bright.

They had put us in a tiny attic room with a sloping ceiling. One night, not long after we arrived, we heard the hurried approach of a man, his studded boots clanging against the wooden floor. My mother made me climb into a chest and said not to let on that I was there, no matter what happened. She closed the lid and locked it. That night and many after, I heard them abusing her, heard her pleading and sobbing, but I could never do anything to help her. Her stifled groans are etched in the depths of my soul.

At the Moorfields tavern, they made the beer in-house. Martha, an older woman with a face scarred by smallpox, was in charge of brewing it. Through gestures, my mother offered to help and, little by little, won her over. Martha watched out for me and hid me in the kitchen of the bordello, keeping the depraved clients from noticing a girl of barely nine. It was with her that I learned to speak the language of England, which became my own.

The tavern was where news of, among other things, the constant rebellions in downtown London arrived regularly. We heard they were against excessive taxation and the papal intrigues involving the English king. My mother would marvel that being Catholic in England was almost as bad as being Jewish in Spain, and she would pray all the more, asking for a miracle to free her from that den of iniquity.

A few months after our arrival, my mother became very ill. I remember her labored breathing and her bluish lips. I will never forget her long white fingers with their violet-tinged nails. The clients rejected her, afraid they might catch something. Martha, realizing how sick she was, let her lie in a cot in the kitchen, where it was a bit warmer.

Lying there, getting steadily sicker, my mother would whisper prayers. And she would try to explain to me things about the past: how, for years, her aunt had shunned and belittled her in our house on Mount Ulia and how they had kept her from contacting my grandfather, who was always at sea. She would caress my blonde hair and tell me it was like my father's. Everything she told me in those days was disjointed; I only understood part of her words.

It tortured her to think that, if she died, I would be left alone in that house of horror. There seemed to be no hope for us at all.

She didn't want me to leave her for a moment, but I was still a little girl, full of vitality. I would sneak out to the yard behind the kitchen to play, a canopy shielding me from the perennial London rain. My only friend was a starving little dog who sometimes appeared; I would take him the crumbs left over from our meals.

One day the rain had stopped, and I'd rushed outside to tussle with the dog. Suddenly, I saw a man's boots next to me, covered in mud. I was frightened. If it was the owner of the bordello, he would surely punish me. If it was one of the clients, I didn't dare think what might happen.

But when I looked up, I saw a strong old man, his hair entirely white, smiling kindly at me. He knelt to pet the little dog, and in a low voice, speaking my mother's language, he asked my name and whether my mother was Isabel. I timidly replied in broken English that my name was Kathleen, which is what the people at the house in Holborn called me. I was afraid to tell him my mother's name. He reassured me that he wanted to help us. He took my hand, and we slipped into the kitchen.

My mother sat bolt upright in bed, then sank back down again; a fit of coughing prevented her from speaking. When she managed to breathe again, she called him Uncle Andrés. Then I remembered seeing him, when I was little, at the house on Mount Ulia. Here in England, Uncle Andrés was called Andrew Leigh. He was a tall man with gentle blue eyes, wearing a great cape, wide pants tucked into his boots, and a shirt with big white ruffles.

My mother told him, crying, that she was unworthy; she was stained. He gazed at her with immense tenderness and begged her forgiveness for not having found her sooner, as he had been asked to do.

"Asked by who?"

"Your father, Admiral Antonio Oquendo."

"My father!" She turned pale. "My father wants nothing to do with me . . . I have written him many times, but he never responded."

Uncle Andrew looked at her sadly. "One of your letters finally arrived. Haven't you had any news of him?"

"No, nothing."

He fell silent a moment. "Your father did combat with the Dutch squadron almost a year ago, in the English Channel," he finally said. "It was a great battle, lasting three days; then the Spanish squadron took refuge on the English coast to repair their boats."

"My father is here on this coast?"

"His ship docked on the south coast of England to buy provisions. From there, he managed to send a message to my family's house in Essex, asking my nephew to tell me your letter had reached him."

At that, my mother beamed with hope and happiness. "Then, my father has forgiven me?"

"I spoke with him. I explained everything, discrediting the gossip that had reached his ears. He understood that your daughter isn't a bastard. He was the one who begged me to come find you. Ever since then, I have been looking. I had no idea that they would take you to such a despicable place. I started at the house in Holborn. The owners denied all knowledge of you. It has taken a long time for me to trace you here, my dear."

This news made my mother sit up again. She choked out a few words: "Will you take me to my father?"

Uncle Andrew looked away. "A month after I saw him, your father returned to sea. The Dutch violated English neutrality and attacked Spanish ships. He was defeated in the Battle of the Downs and went to Spain."

"But is he nearby?"

4

The Beach

Oak Park, Spring of 1641

Oak Park . . . a beautiful place, surrounded by snowy woods in winter and songbirds in summer. To the northeast, gentle hills led to thick forests; to the east, they opened up to the sea. Beyond the hills, dark cliffs descended to golden beaches.

Piers and I felt irresistibly drawn to the coast. On our afternoon walks, we would pass fields of rye and alfalfa and green pastures sprinkled with woolly sheep. When we reached the edge of the cliff, we would stop and look out at the silver-gray ocean. We could spend hours there, despite whatever punishment might await us at home, watching the clouds and the seagulls and staring toward the horizon.

That spring afternoon, our ears rang with the echoes of waves breaking and the revelry of a thousand birds. Gulls, swallows, and cormorants darted back and forth, tracing swoops, arcs, somersaults, and handsprings in the cloudless sky. Some of them swooped up rapidly, majestically, then dropped precipitously down to the sea to catch fish. The sun's rays toasted our skin while the sea breeze ruffled our hair. For what felt like an eternity, our souls overflowed with the grandeur of the ocean stretching before us. The open sea, infinite and elusive.

Piers jumped up and stretched his arms wide, letting the spray drench his face. I watched him as if in a trance; the light of that brilliant day embraced and united us. Then he was suddenly himself again. He hopped along the edge of the cliff, and I trailed behind, though I was afraid the wind might throw me into the cove.

We made our way down a narrow, forking path. To the left, the path led to a cave carved into the rock. Out of it jutted a small wooden structure, like a wharf, and on the right was the beach. In the sand, we took off our shoes and pranced around through seaweed and mud or played tag with the waves.

On an earlier visit, after being kept at home by storms, we'd discovered debris from a shipwreck; there were boards, remnants of casks, shards of candles, and fishing tackle. We wondered who had sailed on that ship and why they had risked coming so close to those dangerous shoals.

Oak Park was located on the Naze, a peninsula, and every year, the waves would eat away at the rocks, making the coastline recede over the centuries. In the middle of the Naze was our little cove, and within it sat an island, a cluster of rocks only visible during low tide. From a distance, it resembled the horse from a chess game, so the cove was called Horsehead Cove. During low tide, that fierce, perpendicular cliff made it difficult for ships to approach. But when the horsehead was submerged, even large ships could drop anchor near the wharf in the cave.

"Look!" Piers cried as we sat down on the sand, tired of playing. "The tide's so high you can't see the horse at all."

"Why is it so high?"

"Because of the moon." He pointed to the horizon. "When the moon is this full, it makes the water flood the cove. The moon pulls the ocean water toward it."

"How do you know that?" I asked.

"Mr. Reynolds explained it to me. We sailors have to know these things," Piers boasted, "so we can reach faraway places. We orient ourselves by the sun and stars." The sea breeze tousled his chestnut hair.

I gazed at him admiringly; he seemed so wise. "Mr. Reynolds is teaching you all that?"

"And I read the books my father brought back from his trips; that's where I've seen the maps of the New World. The maps are Spanish, like you, Len. Your countrymen have discovered lands beyond the open sea—"

"I've been out there, you know. For days and days. The ship rises, falls, tilts this way and that." I illustrated my words with gestures, bringing my hands together and swinging them through the air. "It makes you seasick, and you feel like throwing up all the time. I don't like it."

"Well, I don't mind it a bit," he remarked, flashing me another look of superiority. "But when you return to land, it's hard to walk right." In response to my questioning look, he went on. "Last year I went with my father on one of his trips to the Basque coast, to the port of Pasajes. We took a cargo of fine textiles there."

"That's where my mother was from."

"I know."

"You do?"

"Yes. When we went there, you had just arrived at Oak Park, and my father told the Oquendos you were with us, but they didn't want to believe you were still alive."

What he said chilled me to the bone; I think he must have seen me turn pale.

"My father told me not to say anything to you about it."

"They don't want me to be alive?"

"It's better," said Piers. "This way, you get to live with us."

I told myself it didn't matter. I rarely thought about my family in Basque Country. Yes, I'd rather live with the Leighs, with Piers and two of his sisters and Thomas, who would come home whenever his studies at Oxford allowed. That's what I told Piers, but he wasn't paying much attention; his thoughts had returned to his future as a sailor.

"I'll join a ship from the Armada, cross the sea, become captain of a ship. And then, when my father is older, I'll take over his ships."

"What about Thomas? He's the heir."

"No, Thomas doesn't like the sea. He told me I can keep all the ships I want! Anyway, you know, his eyes are bad. You can't be a sailor if you don't have good eyesight. When Thomas finishes his studies at Oxford, he'll go to London and represent our father in Parliament. He'll be a member of the House of Lords; that's what Father has decided."

Whenever Piers mentioned Lord Leigh, it was with unbridled adulation. A reprimand from his father devastated him; a word of praise made him glow with pleasure. Fortunately for Piers, Lord Edward Leigh always behaved with decorum and moderation.

The sun was beginning to set on the horizon, and the breeze had turned chilly. We got up. Since it was Sunday, we didn't have classes. In the morning, we had gone to the village church. The pastor recited pious phrases in a slow, lugubrious way. I remember Piers getting impatient, crossing and uncrossing his legs, twisting his rebellious locks, until a glance from his father made him sit still. As usual, Lady Leigh followed the service with a solemn, absent expression. Every now and then, Margaret and Ann couldn't help sneaking a peek at the other girls' dresses. Mademoiselle Maynard always turned the pages of the prayer book with great devotion, while Mr. Reynolds, a large man, was put to sleep by the long sermons; sometimes he even snored.

After services, Lord and Lady Leigh would bid farewell to their children and me until suppertime; they would stay in town visiting their tenants. We children and our teachers returned to the estate, where a light lunch awaited us. After eating, Piers and I went for a walk and, inevitably, ended up at the beach.

We stayed too late; the sun was already setting over the sea. The steep, narrow path curved, so we took a shortcut over the wet stones. Piers helped me climb, going ahead of me and offering a hand. When we reached the top, the royal road, a horseman rode by; he seemed to be in a hurry, and we had to step aside to let him pass.

"Wonder who that was."

"Some messenger, probably bringing news from London. The other day, we got a letter from Thomas reporting on more protests and rebellions in the city."

"Against whom?"

"It seems the Commons refused to pay their taxes to the king, which he needs in order to put down a rebellion in Scotland."

"Why have the Scottish rebelled?"

"The king wants to make them Anglicans. But they're Presbyterians, and they think he's a papist."

"Is he?"

He looked at me, annoyed. "How the hell is the king of England going to be a papist? The English aren't papists! Mr. Reynolds explained it to me and Thomas. We English have risen above the Roman religion without the extremism of the Calvinists and Lutherans."

I followed Piers quietly, thinking about how my mother had been a papist. At Oak Park, religion was a forbidden topic. We were walking faster now, so we wouldn't be late for supper. The path was lined with early flowers. For the past few days, it had rained constantly, and rivulets ran down the gutters; we jumped over them, laughing contentedly. When we got closer to the house, we looked up at the moon again; it was still shining, but was higher in the sky.

Suddenly, Piers stopped and confessed in a mysterious tone, "Len, I think there really are ghosts at Oak Park. A few weeks ago, I was awakened by a lightning bolt. I couldn't get back to sleep, so I went down to the kitchen for something to eat. That's when I heard them, the strangest noises—from downstairs, from the dungeons."

That's what we called the cellars under the kitchens. I started to tremble, but tried to be brave.

"Even if there are ghosts, there's no need to be afraid. My mother always told me that you need to fear the living, not the dead."

"Well, these are dead people you do need to be afraid of," he said. "They're the spirits of the monks murdered in the dungeons in Queen Elizabeth's time."

"You're crazy!"

"No, I'm not!"

To shake off his fear, he started laughing and shoved me, pretending to be a ghost. I fell in the muddy ditch, getting mud all over my dress. Piers just ran off toward the house. I had to run to catch up. Before long, a gentle spring rain began to fall. Soon we were soaking wet.

I told Piers Mademoiselle Maynard was going to give me a good scolding.

"Maybe she won't be at dinner. Mademoiselle Maynard gets headaches on nights when the moon is full."

"She must be another one of your ghosts!" I mocked.

He burst out laughing and started to imitate Mademoiselle Maynard, running along like a ghost. He was moving so fast that he soon left me far behind. Every now and then, he would pause to make faces; when I had nearly caught up, he would take off running again.

On the front steps, Margaret was waiting for us impatiently. She shouted that we'd better hurry up because they were waiting for us. Piers got there first, then me; I was nervous about being so late. Sunday suppers were more solemn than other nights. The whole family, and often some visitors, would gather in the huge dining room. It was unacceptable to arrive late for any reason.

Margaret went in first, prattling away, excited and nervous about the news the messenger had brought from London. It had nothing to do with politics or rebellions against the king, as it turned out.

Margaret told me that, Elizabeth, the eldest of the Leigh children, was arriving the following week, and other ladies from the court might join her, including the Countess of Carlisle.

I asked who she was, and Margaret retorted, "Just one of the most curious, attractive, and enigmatic ladies I have met in my whole life!"

When we entered the dining room, everyone was already seated, including Piers, who had run ahead and adopted an angelic expression. Margaret took her place at the table, and I headed toward mine. All eyes were fixed on me, especially Mademoiselle Maynard's. She looked me up and down, and her frigid eyes stopped on my mud-stained dress. She stood up, grabbed me roughly by the hand, and dragged me out of the dining room. Margaret tried to speak up in my defense, but the governess ignored her. Once we reached the stairway, she scolded me furiously.

"This is indecent! You mortify me, Miss Kathleen! How could you possibly behave this way? You have upset the masters and everybody else. Shame on you! Soiling my reputation. Ruining a beautiful new dress."

"I slipped," I apologized tearfully.

Suddenly, I was overcome with anger. She was picking on me because I didn't belong in the house; they had taken me in as a stranger. I told her so, and it made things worse.

"You're grounded until tomorrow! No dinner for you. It's time you learn your manners."

That really stung. I loved the exquisite dishes they prepared on Sundays: roasts, stews, tarts, cakes. I especially liked the buns and honey candies. Ignoring my shouts of protest, she shut me in my bedroom.

As she was leaving, she spat out, "You are confined to your room so you can reflect on your wicked ways. Sin engendered you!"

It was like a slap. I hadn't been engendered by any sin, as far as I knew, but her cruel words made me remember Moorfields, where there was indeed sin, suffering, and crime. She was so angry that she slammed the door and forgot to lock it.

I flung myself, sobbing, onto the bed, and before too long, I fell asleep.

A few hours later, I was awakened by the growling of my empty stomach. I could hear a wolf howling in the distance. I shuddered, but my hunger was stronger than my fear. Going barefoot so I wouldn't make noise, I crept down the stairs from the third floor to the entryway, where I was startled by a silhouette in the shadows. I tried to keep calm, telling myself it was only the ancient suit of armor or the deer antlers looking ghostly in the moonlight.

To one side, an enormous closed door led to the great dining hall from which I had been so dishonorably expelled. I ventured inside to see if there was anything left of supper, but of course the table had been cleared and not a morsel remained. I headed toward the kitchens.

Very slowly, I descended the creaking wooden steps and slipped into the corridor leading to Matt's domain. From the jaws of the furnace came a reddish glow. To one side, under a napkin on the table, there were several meat tarts, still warm. I snatched one and started to devour it. As my appetite began to be sated, I began to feel calmer, even content. That's when I heard them: the muffled sounds of dragging footsteps, of canticles in Latin.

I flattened myself against the wall, trembling, and strained my ears. It was the souls of the monks Piers had told me about. For several long minutes, the canticles continued. Then everything went quiet. Next came a mournful voice, seeming to address the phantoms. I dropped to the floor, my head between my knees, as a ringing bell reverberated in my head. Then finally the silence returned, and I decided to make a run for it.

I left the bakery for the gloom of the corridor. Suddenly, I heard heavy footsteps and deep, panting breaths. Terrified, I ran like a demon.

I reached the entry hall and realized that the ghost was still following me, but more slowly now, cautiously.

I took the stairs three at a time and finally reached my bedroom. I shut the door without taking the time to throw the bolt. In a few short leaps, I reached my bed and dove under the covers, sobbing with fear. A minute later, I heard the door opening and felt a presence inside my room, watching me. I held my breath so long that I thought I might faint. Even when I heard the door close, I didn't know if the ghost was still in my room, so I lay still as a statue for a long time.

I fell asleep dreaming about ghosts. The next morning, the sound of a woman's voice awakened me. I peered out from under the blankets. Through the window streamed warm sunlight. There was no one there.

While I got dressed, all I could think about was running to tell Piers what happened. When I got to class, dear Ann noticed my haggard face and the dark rings under my eyes. She assumed I was upset about what had happened at supper.

"Don't worry; neither Mother nor Father is cross with you. But you must be more careful around Mademoiselle Maynard. It's her responsibility to teach us how to behave properly, and last night you didn't."

I smiled, and Ann squeezed my arm affectionately. Then the governess appeared and scolded me again.

After lunch, I was finally able to speak with Piers. It had started raining again, and they wouldn't let us go outside, so we settled into low benches in front of a big window, pretending to read. As soon as the teachers were distracted, I told tell him everything. He listened attentively, drinking in every word.

"I told you so, Len. I knew there were ghosts."

5

THE UNICORN

The memories stop. I'm still in my armchair, trying to not fall asleep, because when I do, my dreams turn into nightmares. But finally I nod off. For a few seconds, a unicorn appears, with a shining horn and golden mane.

Then I wake up. Josefina isn't here. I walk over to the window. Outside, on the river, the Caribbean mist is lifting. Floating on the fog, the image of the unicorn appears before me again.

My thoughts return to a day when we were up in the study, and noise and shouts of excitement came from outside. Ignoring Mademoiselle Maynard, we ran to the window. A great litter, an enclosed framework with two long poles, was advancing slowly, carried by a pair of mules, one situated in front of the box and the other behind. As it drew closer, Margaret and Ann exclaimed that it bore the insignia of the royal house. They pleaded with the governess to let us go downstairs.

When we got to the big stone patio, the litter had just stopped. On the doors swung a great insignia, the coat of arms of the House of Stuart: a shield with the English lion on one side and the Scottish unicorn with its golden mane on the other. I stared raptly at that mythological figure.

Through the curtained windows, I could make out embroidered damask with opulent bands of mother-of-pearl and gold. My school-mates shouted a name: "Elizabeth!"

A little crowd had formed: the Leigh children, doormen, assistants, gardeners, and many others. Just a child, I observed the young lady with admiration as I stood behind them all. I can still see her, grace-fully descending, refusing the doorman's arm. In one hand, she held the wide-brimmed hat that protected her delicate skin from the spring sun. Her vividly colored dress fluttered in the breeze. Some chestnut curls spilled out of her coiffure, giving her a worldly look. It seemed to me that a celestial being was emerging from a magic coach, perhaps a fairy from one of the storybooks Martha had once told me about. Elizabeth looked like Piers—the same dark hair and the same hazel eyes, but more delicate.

As Ann and Margaret embraced her, showering her with compli-ments, Piers stood back, a bit intimidated. She gave us a coquettish pout, but didn't smile with her eyes. I realized that in their unadorned dresses, the girls felt provincial next to her. They tried to introduce me, but Elizabeth ignored me. For her, I would always be a charity case with Spanish blood.

Piers walked up to Elizabeth then. She paused to smooth his hair and scolded him for not combing it. The young lady turned to greet Lord and Lady Leigh, and I saw with amusement that my friend was blowing aside a long lock that had fallen over his nose.

Elizabeth Leigh, the eldest child in the family, had a natural air of distinction. She was Lord Edward Leigh's daughter by a prior marriage to a lady from the Percy family, the Earls of Northumberland, and had been educated by her maternal grandmother. When she reached adult-hood, the Percys had sent her to court.

With her return, it was as if we children had suddenly grown up and become a part of adult life. We were allowed to share the midday meal with the adults in the great dining room and even join the evening soirées, which lasted longer than usual.

For the duration of Elizabeth's stay at Oak Park, my conversation was reduced to monosyllables. I wasn't accustomed to saying much when Lord and Lady Leigh were present anyway because they inspired a reverent fear in me. Nevertheless, when we children were alone, I had always spoken to my heart's content. But now, the eldest Leigh daughter shut me out. What I said simply held no interest, so she didn't listen. Her slightest opinion was always more important than what a little orphan girl might say. Once, I opened up to Piers, telling him that Elizabeth was contemptuous of me, but he trusted and admired his eldest sister too much to see it.

Despite my reservations, I couldn't deny that Elizabeth possessed a natural charm. Bubbly and animated, she brightened the house with her anecdotes and London gossip. She had a thousand stories to tell about Whitehall Palace and Queen Henrietta Maria. Despite Elizabeth's sarcasm about nearly everything, she admired the customs that the French queen had brought.

Through her, we learned about court fashion, a French style filled with ribbons, flowers, frills, and furbelows, a sharp contrast to the Puritans' black dresses and high white collars. Thanks to the queen, the wardrobe of courtesans, ladies of the court, and other dandies now tended toward baroque pomposity. Coming from the Parisian court fifteen years earlier, Charles I's wife had brought diamonds, pearls, rings, satin and velvet dresses, embroidered capes, skirts, hoods, chandeliers with a thousand lights, paintings, books, clothes, and bedding for both her and her ladies-in-waiting. What upset the English the most was the Catholic priests who accompanied her. In our staunchly anti-Catholic country, the queen's papism was begrudgingly tolerated and in the end would be one of the many reasons for the king's downfall.

Henrietta Maria squandered money right and left. She had acquired several court dwarfs and collected wild animals, dogs, monkeys, and birds. Elizabeth also described, in great detail, the performances: masques extolling the absolutist monarchy of the Stuarts. Uptight London was scandalized by this, as well as by the performances at Whitehall in which the queen herself would take part.

I remember Elizabeth's amusement when she told us that King Charles had squandered his annual income on marvelous paintings that he now had to sell at a loss to finance the war against the Scottish rebels. I was reminded of the beautiful painting I had seen changing hands in the Spanish embassy, when my mother was still alive.

At one of our luncheons, she described the Catholic chapel that the queen had built for herself: a temple with an altar, candelabras, and an altarpiece, the likes of which had not been seen since the Reformation. The plans had been drawn up by Inigo Jones.

"He had to in the end, of course," laughed Elizabeth. "The queen gets everything she wants."

"What's it like?" Margaret asked.

"On the outside it looks simple, but inside there are reliquaries of gold and silver, statues, and a magnificent altarpiece painted by a Dutchman named Rubens."

"An altarpiece? Reliquaries?"

"Yes, but what provoked the most anger was a monstrance wrought in gold."

"That's been prohibited since the Tudors!" Margaret exclaimed.

"It's scandalous," Elizabeth scoffed. "The Puritans are horrified; they don't believe the worship of God can involve any luxuries. But what can I say? Some of us like our luxuries."

"What's a monstrance?" asked Ann.

"I think it's used to display the host in Catholic Mass. It's a lovely golden vessel."

I could tell the adults were uncomfortable. The young woman's blithe comments were inappropriate at Oak Park, where we never spoke about religion, especially in front of the servants. All Lord and

Lady Leigh's caution was lost on shallow Elizabeth. Lady Leigh tried to put a stop to her indiscreet chatter.

"You speak too freely. In the gallows in Tyburn, they were hanging Catholics not so long ago."

Tyburn. I remembered hearing that name before, on the lips of the old woman with a furrowed face, in the anteroom of the Spanish ambassador. But I didn't dare speak.

"Oh please. That's all past. The queen has made Catholicism fashionable. She herself has gone to Tyburn to pray. She says that the people drawn and quartered there are martyrs to the faith."

"Enough!"

We all turned in surprise to Lord Leigh. "Elizabeth, you must stop making such unsubstantiated claims. The persecution hasn't let up. They're still arresting and executing Catholics, nearly as much as in the early days of the Reformation. I won't allow you to be so thoughtless and disrespectful in this house!"

Elizabeth lowered her eyes before her father's upbraiding, but her attitude was not conciliatory.

"You must remember," he continued, "that our family was accused, not so long ago, of participating in the Gunpowder Plot led by the Catholics. We succeeded in proving our innocence, but not before your grandfather was thrown into the Tower of London. Since then, we Leighs have been ostracized. They accuse us of being papists, and in this country, there is no worse accusation."

The evening ended solemnly, and Elizabeth never again spoke so freely in the presence of Lord and Lady Leigh, but she would sometimes make provocative remarks to us children.

"I enjoy the culture imposed by the queen, but I also like being adored by young Puritan men, who see me as the incarnation of evil—and I'm all the more entrancing for it."

Margaret gazed at her in admiration. "Will you take me with you to London?"

"Our father won't let you go. In fact, I owe my place at court to my grandmother Percy." She spoke as if she were the queen's senior chambermaid. "She's a woman of the world, nothing like these boring Leighs Londoners frown upon."

"Why?" I asked.

"Because—"

Thomas, who had come from Oxford to see his older sister, cut her off. "That's enough, Elizabeth."

She glared at him and turned to Margaret, her back to me.

"I'll do you one better, dear Meg," she said. "I'll ask Father to organize a ball here, at Oak Park, so I can present you and Ann to society. I'll make sure that the very best people from court attend."

Margaret clapped her hands happily, while Ann looked somewhat frightened.

It was after the ball that everything began to change.

6

THE BALL

On the day of the ball, a current of excitement ran through the Leigh mansion. The first guests had already arrived from London. In the afternoon, Elizabeth ordered Piers and me to change into our best clothes, but when the guests began to come down, they let us run off. Perhaps the Leigh sisters, nervous about receiving so many important people, didn't trust a pair of rambunctious children. By that time, I had turned ten, and Piers was thirteen.

In the rotunda, all types of carriages, litters, and handcarts pulled up. Piers and I watched from the window as elegant ladies and gentlemen from the county nobility descended. Once most had arrived, we retreated to the top of the first-floor stairs and were hidden behind the bannister. Through the bars, we could make out the silks, velvets, and jewels of the visitors filling the entry hall and the candlelit drawing rooms of Oak Park.

I was nervous, fidgeting with the silk and lace dress borrowed from Ann for the occasion. Piers had actually combed his hair, and it hung to his shoulders. For the first time, he struck me as handsome, with his silk jacket and impish face. We whispered, poking fun at the guests.

"Look how fat she is! Like she ate a cow."

"With a calf still inside it!"

Then we turned our attention to the Leigh sisters, who were standing at the entrance, greeting the guests.

"Don't Margaret and Ann look lovely?" I said.

Piers nodded proudly. If he had known what would become of his beloved sisters, it would have broken his heart, but he never would know. In that moment, I felt sorry for the two young women, though I'm not sure why. Perhaps because they looked frightened at so much commotion, self-conscious about being the center of attention. Also, I think they felt awkward since the party was ostensibly for them, but all eyes were on Elizabeth. The family's eldest was chatting with a buxom lady in a turquoise satin dress glittering with precious jewels. It was impossible not to notice her.

"That one," whispered Piers, pointing, "next to Elizabeth. She must be the Countess of Carlisle." We knew she had arrived late the previous night, when we were already in bed. "Her name is Lucy Hay. She's the wife of James Hay and is one of the most dangerous women at court. When she was single, her name was Lucy Percy, and she's Elizabeth's second cousin, but she's not related to us, the Leighs."

The lady leaned toward Elizabeth protectively.

"They say that she's a spy," Piers continued.

"Who does she spy on? For whom?"

"Sometimes she promotes the interests of the king, and other times she goes against him."

I looked closer. Around her, several ladies and gentlemen had congregated, seeming charmed.

Then a young redheaded man strode over to Piers's sister. He was dressed in an incongruously somber suit. With a formal bow, he asked her to dance. She smiled coquettishly, pretending to be flustered, but accepted.

"Who's that man in the dark suit?"

"A Scottish Presbyterian named William Ruthven. I think he arrived yesterday with Lady Carlisle."

"He's sure paying a lot of attention to Elizabeth."

Piers's face darkened. "Father doesn't like that fellow. But lately, you know, he'll put up with just about anything. He doesn't want to make any enemies."

We kept watching Lady Carlisle, who was laughing loudly and covering her mouth with a little white fan.

"She sure laughs a lot," I said.

"I don't know what she's got to be so happy about. Yesterday, Thomas told me that they just executed her lover, Lord Strafford."

"Lover?"

Piers looked at me like I was a fool and explained that a lover was someone who wasn't your husband but acted like he was. Feigning innocence, I asked him what the real husband thought about it. He burst into hysterical laughter. Several heads turned to look, prompting the housekeeper to rush up and expel us from our observation post. She marched us to our bedrooms, warning us not to come back for the rest of the party. We smiled and nodded, but as soon as she was gone, we escaped. I wanted to go back and watch the dancing, but Piers said no, they would catch us again. Instead, he said, we should go to the East Room. In our explorations, we had discovered a hidden passageway used by the servants that led to the rear of the office. The doorway was hidden from view by a tapestry—and two little people like us fit perfectly behind it.

We snuck over to the East Room, where several men, including Lord Leigh, had gathered to smoke, drink, and talk. That evening, there was only one topic of conversation: the execution, two weeks earlier, of Thomas Wentworth, Earl of Strafford, Lady Carlisle's lover.

"It was vile of the king to sign the execution order," someone said.

"He had no choice." That was the measured voice of Lord Leigh.

"Charles will pay dearly for it. Wentworth was utterly loyal to him. It's outrageous that the king gave in to Parliament's pressure."

Then we heard a heavy Scottish accent. "Let's give thanks to the Almighty for freeing us of Wentworth."

And an elegant English voice replied, "You members of Parliament in the ruling junta know perfectly well that there were only two options: either Wentworth was executed as a traitor, or you would have been."

"And just what do you mean by that, sir?"

"You've been negotiating with the Scots to invade England."

"Outrageous! I have no idea what you're talking about."

Piers clenched his fists and whispered, "What a hypocrite!"

We heard footsteps approaching our little hideout, so we fled. We scurried through several passageways, then ran up a service staircase. Finally, we paused on a wide landing on the main stairs. I remember how, on one side, music from the ball drifted in, and on the other, a large window looked out over the park, which was bright with moonlight.

We sat down—Piers on a lower step, so we were at the same height, with our heads close together. Here, we wouldn't have to whisper. Though he still looked like a boy, Piers was quite mature and would often discuss politics with Thomas. I loved it when he explained things to me, so I asked him who Wentworth was.

"He was Lord Deputy and the leader of the Irish army, and he was on his way to London to protect the king from traitorous members of Parliament. But they convinced Charles to accuse him of treason and condemn him to death."

"How is it possible for someone to be loyal to the king and also be a traitor?"

"I've asked myself the same question. There's a lot I don't understand, honestly. Like how the Protestant members of Parliament could deny they're plotting with the Scots but then accuse Strafford of treason. I don't understand how the king could sign the death sentence of his only defender, who was on his way to London to protect him."

Piers furrowed his brow, incensed by the injustice. Ever since he was little, he couldn't stand hypocrisy. I suppose, when you're a child, good and evil seem more clearly defined.

I tried to cheer him up. "Maybe when we're older, it'll make sense."

"I'm not so sure," he replied gloomily.

We looked out the big window. In the distance, we could make out the shadow of a stag with huge antlers strutting through the park. I felt so happy next to Piers, in spite of his brooding. I started wondering about that sophisticated spy.

"What do you think of Lady Carlisle? Don't you agree she's awfully elegant?"

"That woman has no principles. They say she was the Duke of Buckingham's lover, and he was the king's staunchest supporter, next to Strafford."

"In order to collect more taxes, King Charles had to convene Parliament, which he hadn't done in eleven years. When he did, the Puritans pounced on him. The king's only defender was Lord Strafford—the one they executed."

"The one you said was Lady Carlisle's lover."

"Right. And now, according to Thomas, she is with John Pym, leader of the faction of Parliament opposed to the king. She has shared her bed with a noble opposed to the queen, with a military officer loyal to the king, and with an enemy of them both!" Piers looked disgusted. "That lady will dance with the highest bidder."

The horrors of Moorfields crossed my mind again, and I shuddered.

The notes of a pavane wafted up to us, with its slow, processional airs. I stood up. "I'd like to dance."

He looked startled to see me bowing like the ladies of the court. Then he exclaimed with a smile, "But of course!"

He took my hand, and we climbed two steps to the landing and repeated the bow. Solemnly, we started swaying to the rhythm. We didn't speak, concentrating on our steps. After that song ended, we kept on dancing to the rhythm of the different melodies drifting up from below.

After a very long time, tired of spinning around, we sat down on the stairs again.

"I noticed," I told him, "that your sister Elizabeth danced several times with that redheaded gentleman, William Ru—I can't remember his name."

"Ruthven. Lord William Ruthven. The one my father doesn't like."

"Why not?"

"I suppose because the man's courting Elizabeth. And I imagine Father thinks him too, well, extreme for her."

"What do you mean?"

"From what I hear, he hates Catholics so much, he's personally persecuted several priests and sent them to the gallows in Tyburn, where they execute all the criminals."

"Are Catholics criminals?" I thought about my mother. This time I didn't dare touch the medallion.

"For William Ruthven, they are. And for most people."

"What about for you?"

"Father says you shouldn't condemn anyone for their beliefs. He says that makes you worse than the men you're condemning."

"Then," I reasoned, "if William Ruthven sends priests to the gallows, he must be evil."

"No, he's just convinced of his ideas. Anyway, Thomas says Ruthven's a man of contradictions: a fanatical Presbyterian on the one hand and a loyalist to the king on the other."

"Didn't you say the Presbyterians detest the king for imposing the Anglican prayer book and all that?"

"Yes. But I think in Scotland everything depends on clans, and if one clan hates the king, another might decide to support him, just to oppose their enemies. A real mess."

"And will he marry Elizabeth?"

"I don't know. I hope not. Elizabeth inherited a great fortune from her mother. And William is ambitious, so he probably wants to get his hands on the dowry."

"What about her?"

"Well, he is a count, and I'm certain Elizabeth would like to become a countess. Anyway, she'll probably marry him if Lady Carlisle tells her to. She's dazzled by that disgraceful woman. They say Lady Carlisle pretends to be friends with the Stuarts, but she amuses herself by passing information to the leaders of Parliament. The woman can't be trusted. Thomas says she's a harlot."

"I know some prostitutes," I whispered.

"Come on. How could you possibly?"

"I do. But they wear lots of makeup, and she doesn't."

"Oh, she may be a high-class whore, but she's still a whore!"

I had never heard him speak so hatefully about anyone.

"She's using my sister, no doubt. Maybe it's a favor to Ruthven since he's friends with her husband and is also a Scotsman."

"But would Elizabeth want to marry a Presbyterian?"

"My sister doesn't realize she's playing with fire. She just wants to triumph at court. She deserves someone better than that stuck-up, penniless zealot."

Overwhelmed about the enormity of all this, I rested my head on Piers's shoulder, and we held hands. We were so tired that we fell asleep right there on the stairs. Very early the next morning, I felt myself enveloped in the smells of sweat and bread. A strong pair of arms lifted me up and carried me to my room. Along the way, I could hear a lullaby in my mother's language. I think Piers followed drowsily to his own room. We slept deeply, perhaps dreaming about each other and about a more just and peaceful world.

7

Lord Leigh's Anger

The next morning, it felt impossible to tear myself out of bed. Piers and I both stumbled down to the great dining hall much later than usual and found we were nonetheless the first to arrive. Next were Margaret and Ann, who couldn't stop talking about the ball: whom they had danced with, the ladies' coiffures, the gentlemen's good looks . . .

Then Lord and Lady Leigh came in, followed by Elizabeth and the guests, though not all of them. Through a window overlooking the terrace, I caught a glimpse of William Ruthven and Lady Carlisle engaging in animated conversation. It must have been confidential because when one of the servants approached to offer pastries, they fell silent.

Later, they joined us in the dining hall. Lady Carlisle looked serene, but the Scotsman seemed nervous. Our meal proceeded without incident until it was nearly over, when the lady and William Ruthven asked if they could meet with the lord of the house alone. Elizabeth blushed.

Looking grim, Lord Leigh agreed to meet with them as soon as the other guests had left. He went on chatting with everyone, but a deep line had formed on his forehead. It was still there when he invited the two into the East Room. Lady Leigh had gone up to her chambers to lie down. The rest of us filed into the drawing room, where we could keep an eye on the closed office door. Elizabeth was uncharacteristically quiet. After a while, the door opened, and Lord Leigh came out with an ashen face.

He called for the head butler and announced, "This lady and gentleman will be leaving Oak Park immediately."

Elizabeth turned pale and was about to rush to her friends, but a frigid look from Lord Leigh stopped her in her tracks. Then he said he wanted to speak with her alone, and he headed back into the East Room, followed by his daughter. The rest of us stayed put in the drawing room, catching snatches of muffled voices.

But all at once, the door swung open, and Lord Leigh's angry words resounded like a thunderclap. "These Scottish Presbyterians aren't just Protestants, Elizabeth! They're Calvinists. Their leaders are fanatics who are blindly obeyed. They don't think rationally; their faith isn't subject to reason."

"What good is reason?" exclaimed Elizabeth. "All that matters is the heart. Sir William loves me, and he will do whatever I want."

"Daughter! That man and you are from different camps, and these are troubled times. If you marry him, you will betray your family."

"Nonsense! I simply must be like Queen Henrietta Maria; she rules over her Anglican husband just as I will rule my Presbyterian one."

"I beg you to not make a rash decision that will prove disastrous for you and for us all."

"Father," she retorted, "I'm already twenty-two! I won't let the Leighs make me an old maid! You have rejected other marriages, and I obeyed. But Lord Ruthven has an ancient title! He's the Count of Gowrie; it's a very good match. The Percys agree with me."

"But I am your father, and I must authorize this union."

"Well, the royal house authorizes it. You heard Lady Carlisle! The queen herself wants the marriage to take place. Will you oppose our queen?"

Through the open door, we could see Lord Leigh's face, red with frustration. Before him, proud Elizabeth stood her ground. She knew that her last argument was the coup de grace. If Henrietta Maria favored the wedding, the Lord of Oak Park couldn't oppose it. Not only because he was obliged to obey the Stuarts, but also because the family had been under suspicion since the Gunpowder Plot. Should they fall out of favor with those in power, they might be denounced as traitors, losing their patrimony and possibly their lives.

In the days that followed, Elizabeth refused to speak to her father. Then one day, the great carriage with the Stuart crest pulled up before the house. This time, the unicorn on the shield looked menacing. And when it pulled away, in it went Elizabeth Leigh, future Countess of Gowrie.

Not long afterward, at the Percy mansion, Elizabeth Leigh married William Ruthven. An event of great social significance, it brought together a multitude of court figures.

No one from the Leigh family was there, causing a great scandal, especially because the queen attended through her Lady of the Bedchamber, Lucy Hay, Countess of Carlisle. Piers told me that their failure to attend had brought even more ostracism. Elizabeth's sisters lost any prospects of making a good match, and Piers's chances of joining the navy were now remote.

8

ONE AUTUMN

Oak Park, Autumn of 1641

A few weeks after the wedding, a letter from Elizabeth arrived for Lord Leigh. We never found out what it said, but after that, the girls' correspondence with her resumed. In her missives, the new Countess of Gowrie boasted about her relations with the court and her mounting social success. The young ladies of Oak Park devoured her letters, but Lord Leigh looked deeply troubled when he heard us reading them aloud.

Once a prudent amount of time had passed, Elizabeth invited her sisters to the grand mansion where she and her husband lived, on the Strand, near the royal residence at Whitehall. It had gardens reaching down to the river and its own wharf.

She reported that her husband would be delighted to receive them, and she promised to introduce them to London society and the court.

For weeks, the only thing Margaret and Ann talked about was how to persuade their reluctant parents to let them go, especially because the political situation in London was unstable. At last, after much scheming and discussion, they secured permission. Now their talk turned to dresses, jewels, coiffures, and luggage. Piers and I avoided their company.

One autumn morning, we watched them leave on a hand-carried litter trailed by a great carriage. It was stuffed to the roof with trunks of clothing, their arsenal for the many parties they were to attend. From the rotunda of Oak Park, Lady and Lord Leigh watched them go with worry etched on their faces.

And so it was that Piers and I were left alone for the first time. Thomas, who had abandoned his legal studies, was also in London. Despite his youth and his incomplete studies, he was already representing his father in the House of Lords. The young heir to Oak Park was convinced that royal authority came from the Almighty, and he supported the absolute power of Charles I. He believed that God would protect the king and would free him, sooner or later, from his enemies.

However, his father couldn't support absolutism, much less the intolerant Protestantism of Parliament. Now, so many years later, I admire the Lord of Oak Park for seeing the times clearly. As a worldly businessman who traded with the continent, he recognized that the king's absolutism would lead to his disgrace and that Parliament's increasingly sectarian and insular attitudes would bring great troubles. The House of Commons, led by John Pym with his Puritan majority, was rabidly antipapist. They blamed Catholics for all evils in the kingdom and could not tolerate the changes the king had imposed on the Anglican Church, bringing it closer to Catholicism. The House of Lords was more moderate, but it also opposed the Stuarts' pompous Anglicism.

In November, the Chamber of Commons presented a list of grievances, the Grand Remonstrance, in which it listed objections to international politics, finances, and the king's religious position. At the end of the month, following a heated debate, Parliament approved the petition by a narrow margin. Thomas actively opposed it, along with many other nobles who thought the demands excessive.

When Thomas returned to Oak Park for the Christmas season, it meant that I lost Piers again; he followed his big brother around like a shadow. They would go riding together when the snow let up or talk for hours in the library. I was not invited.

As for Ann and Margaret, they showed no inclination to return from London. They had written to say they would soon be presented to society again. In their absence, Mademoiselle Maynard took greater pains with my education, trying to make a lady of me. But I didn't appreciate her efforts. I would have liked to be a boy, like Piers. The governess decided that the most important thing in my life would be sewing, but I was hopeless at it. Through the window, I would enviously watch the Leigh boys coming home, tired, hungry, and happy from shooting ducks on the frozen lake or wild boars in the snowy woods. I became evasive and disobedient, provoking Mademoiselle Maynard's anger. She would ground me to the house, make me write some foolishness a thousand times or take endless dictation in French.

Since I barely went outside, I didn't get much exercise and didn't sleep well. Perhaps that's why I began dreaming about ghosts and goblins. I would wake up with a start and run to take refuge with Lady Leigh. I remember her vividly: tall, with red hair beginning to turn gray, pearl-white skin, and gentle wrinkles at the corners of her eyes and mouth. Her gaze was open and friendly, though she could sometimes be harsh and demanding. Once I heard her singing in Gaelic, the ancient Irish language. She came from Limerick and was the daughter of an Irish rebel, Sir John Burke of Brittas. She had a noble air and was very close to her husband, whom she adored.

As much as I could, I would sit next to the Lady of Oak Park and sew my interminable sampler. And I would hear her sigh. She missed her daughters and was troubled by having them so far away. She was consumed with worry over the radicalization of the country. I remember her lifting and lowering the embroidery needle while barely speaking a word. The snow falling on the other side of the windows deepened the melancholy. I think Lady Leigh could foresee the destruction coming for her country, as well as her family.

9

CHRISTMAS

Oak Park, Christmas of 1641

It was my second Christmas at Oak Park, a place where the holiday truly seemed magical. I recall sitting down next to the big classroom window to work on my sampler. Snowflakes were falling softly outside, and I heard the Leigh boys' shouts. They were dragging a wild boar, leaving a trail of blood in the snow. Nearly the whole household ran outside. The animal would be skinned and gutted, then cooked for the party. I, grounded yet again by my hateful governess, had to watch it all from the window.

Then Lady Leigh opened the classroom door and declared that I was no longer being punished. Mademoiselle Maynard, she said, had suddenly asked for permission to spend the holiday with family. As I skipped downstairs, I wondered how Mademoiselle Maynard could celebrate at all, since she had been complaining that it was all paganism and moral danger. I spent the whole day with Lady Leigh. We decorated the house with holly, rosemary, and boughs of ivy and laurel and helped prepare for the great feast.

The next day, I woke up excited and ran downstairs. Piers and Thomas were in the entry hall. Thomas was opening a letter, and I heard him tell his brother, "The king, naturally, has rejected the list of complaints presented to him."

Then they left, without even acknowledging my presence. I felt terribly alone and missed Margaret and Ann even more than usual. I headed down to the busy kitchens and looked for Matt. When the baker saw my sad face, he proudly showed me all the delicacies they were preparing: veal roasts, goose and lamb, spicy meat pies, raisins, dried figs, and gooseberries. The cream and apple tarts were piling up, along with white bread and little marzipan cupcakes. Then Matt was called away, and while no one was looking, I snuck one of the beautiful tarts.

I climbed the stairs slowly and headed for the East Room. As I suspected, the boys were inside, discussing the letter with their father. From what I could hear through the partly open door, Lord Leigh disagreed with the king's position. Then someone shut the door, and I couldn't hear anything else. I went looking for Lady Leigh, but she was busy giving the housekeeper instructions. Everyone was ignoring me, so I went to my room to read. A few hours later, the bell rang, calling us all to dinner.

It was the first call. By the fourth, we should be in our places. A maid dressed me in a silk suit that Ann had handed down to me. Then I went down to the grand entry hall, where the enormous yule log was burning. There, the lord would break bread with the tenants, employees, and servants of Oak Park. Lord Leigh presided at the head of a long table; next to him sat his wife and children. They seated me with them, next to Piers. The delicacies Matt had shown me in the kitchen were piled on several tables in the center of the room. On wooden benches along the wall, or standing up, the guests crowded together, decked out in their finest clothes. Musicians played carols on the zither and violin while we all savored the food. For most of the guests, this was the only time of year they got to eat dishes like these. The lord and lady brimmed with contentment when they saw how people were enjoying themselves, but in Lady Leigh's blue eyes, I could make out a glimmer of longing for her absent daughters.

As we finished our meal, Lord and Lady Leigh made their way to the center of the great hall to inaugurate the dance. A man at the back of the room caught my attention; he was hidden in the shadows, smiling at me. My heart leapt. I was just about to shout, "Uncle Andrew!" when Thomas took my hand and asked me to dance. I saw Piers frown.

Swept away by the music and the thrill of Thomas being nice to me, I forgot all about Uncle Andrew for a moment. When the first movement brought us together, Thomas leaned down to me.

"Don't talk to Andrew," he whispered, his brow knit with worry.

"Why not?"

"Just don't. Not here, in public, in front of so many strangers."

When the dance ended, Piers asked gruffly, "What was it you and Thomas were whispering about?"

I decided not to answer, so he would feel more jealous. Instead, I smiled coquettishly. He repeated the question, but I pretended I hadn't heard. He said fine, that he didn't care about our dumb secrets. Then the musicians began playing the same pavane that we had danced to a few months ago. I forgot about everything, and as if in a dream, I spun around with Piers. He looked happy again, his jealousy forgotten. My cheeks glowed more and more, as one dance followed another.

The music finally stopped, and they were about to begin the best part of the Christmas celebration. Now was the time for stories: about Hereward, the outlaw who fought against the Norman invasion; about Robin Hood, who stole from the rich to give to the poor; about Tom Thumb. I was headed for the table to listen when I felt a hand on my shoulder. When I looked up, I saw Andrew Leigh smiling at me. He put a finger to his lips and led me into another room.

Once we were alone, he asked, "How are you, little one?"

"I'm well, Uncle Andrew. Where have you been? I haven't seen you since you brought me here."

"I've been very busy." He stroked my hair. "Are you happy here, with my family?"

"Yes!"

"Do you miss your mother?"

I almost said no. I had gotten so used to this house and its people that I didn't think about my mother very often. But now, the image of her beautiful, tortured face appeared in my mind. I didn't answer, but he could read my expression.

"Do you have the medallion I gave you when she died?"

"Yes."

I lifted it off my chest, and he kissed it.

"It will protect you; it belonged to the best man I've known in my whole life: your father."

"My mother said he was on the other side of the sea. Will I get to meet him someday?"

Uncle Andrew didn't answer, but his eyes filled with gratitude and longing that I didn't understand. Without another word, he kissed my head and left.

I went back to the dining room, where everyone was awaiting the climax: the cutting of the cake. Whoever got the piece with a bean hidden inside would be king of the party. My first Christmas in Oak Park, Matt had been the winner. He decreed that the tenants should go to the kitchens and help themselves to whatever they wanted. He gave all the children candy and called for more dancing. But this year, it was Roberts, a middle-aged coachman who always dressed in black. Because of his position, he had a great deal of influence over the other servants. I noticed that Lord Leigh looked uneasy when he won the prize.

Roberts raised his voice, tremulous from drink. "I'm the king now, so I can do whatever I want. You must obey the king. Now, repeat everything I say."

"We shall obey you, Your Highness," everyone responded.

Then Roberts shouted, "Long live Parliament!"

Everyone exclaimed, "Hurray!"

"Death to the traitors!"

They all repeated the phrase.

"Death to the papists!"

The room shouted it with him.

Lord Leigh left the room, and his wife waved over a maid and asked her to put me to bed at once. I wanted to resist, but I could never disobey Lady Leigh.

As I stepped on the stairs, I heard Roberts shout, "Down with Christmas!"

A tense silence ensued. Then a servant cried, "Roberts, you're drunk. How can you say such nonsense?" An argument broke out. One man yelled that Christmas was for the nobles to show off their power to the poor.

Another retorted, "What do you mean? The lords have always been good to us."

Then I heard someone say, in a low but audible voice, "Lady Leigh is a witch, an Irish witch."

I spun around, desperate to run to her defense, but I couldn't tell where the voice had come from. The servant took me firmly by the hand and dragged me away. Downstairs, there was still much shouting. When I reached my room, I could still hear their voices. I stayed awake a long time, my heart heavy with sadness.

Around midnight I woke up, feeling ill. I had eaten far too much and was terribly nauseated. I got up and drank some water from the basin. I heard strange noises from the woods and inside the house— some kind of creaking and slow footsteps. I tucked myself back under the blankets fearfully, and after some time, I fell asleep again.

The next morning, I couldn't wait to talk to Piers to find out how the party had ended and why Roberts had said those strange things. Also, I wanted to tell him about the noises. But all he would say was that there was a fight, and the coachman had been fired. As for the rest, he sighed and said Christmas was a time for ghosts.

10

WALTON-ON-THE-NAZE

Oak Park, Winter of 1642

January was exceptionally cold. The snow froze, and the servants struggled to clear the roads. When they finally succeeded, news reached us from London. After the king had rejected the Grand Remonstrance, there was rioting. On January 4, Charles attempted to arrest the leaders of the opposition, but the five men weren't present that day. It was rumored they had been tipped off by none other than Lady Carlisle. Thomas set off for the capital to defend the king and offer his services.

Mademoiselle Maynard returned, and she seemed very different. She was often distracted and would sometimes smile. If anything, she was even more religious than before, and often sat reading a little book of sermons and psalms, lost in thought. Only the arrival of the mail would shake her from her reverie. As soon as she heard the hooves of the messenger's horse, she would run downstairs. She would come back either euphoric, a letter in hand, or melancholic at the absence of news. In any case, she allowed me greater freedom.

When there was a full moon again, Piers and I thought we heard strange noises in the house and on the estate. But those days, we were more worried about political turmoil than ghosts haunting the basements. A letter finally arrived from Thomas, and Piers read it to me later. In it, he reported that the king had retreated to Hampton Court Palace, the former palace of Henry VIII, to protect his Catholic wife from the commoners' wrath. He also hoped to alleviate pressure from Parliament, which was getting out of control. Thomas had followed him to Hampton Court.

"Thomas says, and I agree, that by leaving London, the king has weakened his position," Piers explained. "Charles doesn't realize that he's leaving most of the army, the munitions, and especially the Tower, the greatest powder keg in the kingdom, in the hands of Parliament!"

"Piers, what are your sisters still doing in London?"

"They say they want to keep Elizabeth company, that she needs them there. I wish they'd hurry up and come home. It seems that ambitious Ruthven has switched sides and become a zealous defender of Parliament. There's been more rioting, apparently."

"I'm so worried. I just don't know what's going to come of all this."

"I don't know, either, and wish I did." Piers ran his fingers through his hair and thought a moment. "Well, I know how we can find out."

"How?"

"Your Mademoiselle Maynard is down with a migraine again, and Mr. Reynolds gave me the afternoon off. So, we could go to the village and find out what people are saying."

I was thrilled. I loved going places with Piers, and Walton was nearly an hour's walk. We bundled up against the cold and headed down the winding path that circled Oak Park, amid trees bare of leaves. The sky was covered with dark clouds that would part now and then, letting wan sunlight peek through. At the crossroads before Walton-on-the-Naze was a medieval stone cross with a simple image of Christ. When we got there, we saw that it had been knocked down and smashed. Piers let out a curse and knelt to examine the damage.

"What could have happened?"

"Can't you see? The Puritans think it's blasphemous and idolatrous to make an image of Christ." He rummaged through the jagged pieces of stone until he finally found Christ's head and stuffed it into his pocket. I realized Piers felt bad to see it rolling around on the ground, like the head of an executed man.

The Naze peninsula, where Oak Park stood, was separated from the village by a little river. We crossed the wooden bridge and were greeted by the ancient cemetery. Soon we reached the first houses, passed the church, and climbed a gentle hill to the center of town. Since it was market day, we wandered from stall to stall, poking around, and bought some sweets.

A boy walked by, shouting, "Last-minute news: Parliament prohibits all theater and parties!"

Piers pulled a coin out of his pocket and paid for the broadsheet. We noticed that some people were celebrating this news, while others shook their heads in disapproval. We overheard one say that a war was coming against the Antichrist, and it would eradicate popery from the kingdom. Someone argued it was a question of honor, and others called for moderating the excessive power of the king. No war had yet started, but even in that place so far from the court and Parliament, people were already taking sides. Suddenly, we heard a familiar voice rise above the rest.

"Let it be known to you fine gentlemen that Lady Leigh is a witch. There are strange goings-on in that house; yes, the devil has possessed her. And no one does a thing about it. I'm glad—yes, I say it with real conviction—I'm deeply glad that they fired me. Oak Park is cursed."

Someone recognized Piers and nudged Roberts. Undaunted, he went on. "Yes, boy, you, witch's son! Mark my words, one day that house will sail away on the winds. Yes, I tell you, when the moon is full, we heard strange noises. I've no doubt it's the witch convening her coven."

I tugged at Piers, who was clenching his fists, wanting to hit that man, but he was just a boy. The former coachman walked away, laughing. Then Piers shoved his hand in his pocket, pulled something out, and hurled it at him. It only grazed Roberts, but he spun around in fury.

"You're going to pay for this, you brat! I'll have my revenge on you and on your caste!" he shrieked.

A vacuum formed around us. Everyone pretended they were buying something, so they could turn their backs to us. No one said a word. Roberts stalked off, and Piers walked over to where the weapon had landed. Christ's head, even more broken than when we found it, gazed up at us from the middle of the busy lane. Just then, a carriage rattled by and crushed it to dust.

Piers let out a sharp cry and fell to his knees.

I took his arm and pulled him away from there. All the way home, Piers looked worried and tense. He didn't say a word.

11

The Expropriation of the Ships

Oak Park, Summer of 1642

The months went by, and Piers and I kept slipping away every now and then to Walton and especially the coast. Since the incident in town, he was eager to enlist on a warship. He spoke often about cannons and culverins, how to calculate a bullet's trajectory, and how to improve your shot. The winds of war were blowing, and he wanted to fight.

The thaw was followed by a rainy spring. Then summer finally came, though it hardly seemed like it. One afternoon in that cold, rainy season, we heard horse hooves ringing on the stones out front. Mademoiselle Maynard and I peered out the window and saw some men dismounting. The governess told me they were important guests representing Parliament, "which God protects." She warned me to behave myself and helped me put on more formal clothes. When we got downstairs, the new arrivals, who wore dark clothes with tall collars and wide-brimmed black hats, were chatting with Lady Leigh and were shown to the grand dining room.

I don't remember what was served at supper, only that there was endless talk of politics. The gentlemen from London were so eager to convince Lord Leigh of some position that they didn't seem to realize there were children present or that it was a family meal.

"As you surely know," one pronounced, "some months ago, Lord John Hotham didn't allow the king to enter the garrison at Hull."

"An unprecedented act of insubordination," replied Lord Leigh.

"Hotham was only following the orders of Parliament," said the other man, who had a sharp eye and a severe face. "Hull has an enormous arsenal, and Parliament didn't want the king to get control of the munitions."

The Lord of Oak Park respected authority, and I knew Lord Leigh must think it shameful for a military man, and a noble at that, to treat the king this way.

He asked, "Does that mean that it's now Parliament's job to control the supplies of gunpowder?"

"And not just that! Since July, the navy has been under the command of Robert Rich, Earl of Warwick."

"Warwick is opposed to the king," Piers whispered.

"I'm told they've dismissed all the Royalist captains in the navy," confirmed another visitor.

"That's very serious!" exclaimed Lord Leigh.

"The king was asking for it," was the man's response.

Piers's eyes narrowed with interest. Warships belonging to Parliament were unlikely to accept a sailor from a family that supported the king. Under the table, I patted his leg, but he shot me a furious look. Pity was for weak people, like girls, and he was going to be a valiant sailor.

As we were leaving the table, he whispered, "It doesn't matter; I'll just be captain of one of my father's merchant ships."

Before the gentlemen retired to smoke, one of them from London whispered something to Lord Leigh, who retorted, "That can't be! If they do that, they'll ruin commerce!"

By the time the visitors left, Lord Leigh looked like he had aged several years. The next day, he left for several weeks, and after that, he kept traveling back and forth to the capital. Piers finally explained to me that his business was in danger. Those gentlemen from London had come to inform Lord Leigh that they were requisitioning most of his merchant ships. Piers also told me that, for reasons he didn't understand, his sisters were being held in London by Ruthven.

Every time Lord Leigh returned, he looked more worried. He protested the requisition, verbally and in writing. But in London, they didn't trust him. Anyway, the Admiralty argued, they needed ships for the war that was clearly approaching. The chances of Piers becoming a sailor looked slimmer still.

One day he said, "Mr. Reynolds made me translate a Latin phrase that has me thinking. *Nihil difficile volenti.* It means something like, 'Nothing is difficult for he who wants.' He told me it's written at the top of a building in Rome. I want to be a sailor, and I know I will be, one way or another."

12

The Cell

At the end of that strange summer, things suddenly got hot because of not only the strong sun, but also the king flying his royal banner at Nottingham. That outdated, medieval symbol would usher in the first English Civil War that would change our lives forever.

While the world was going mad, Piers and I had the run of Oak Park. When I arrived, they'd taught me to ride. But unlike the Leighs, I wasn't skilled at it, since I didn't have a horse of my own. Now that Ann was in London, they loaned me hers, and I started to improve.

Piers would challenge me to race him, sometimes to the Norman Tower, the highest point on the estate. We would tie the horses to a bush in the meadow surrounding the ancient watchtower and then climb the narrow stone steps to the crenellated summit, the open sea stretching before us.

Other times, we would go to the cliffs and look down at the waves crashing against the rocks in Horsehead Cove. Some rowboats rocked there, tied to the wharf by the cave. Protected by the North Sea currents, the cove was a natural port for those who knew about it and had been used since the days of the Saxons. We had seen small-keel boats, perhaps belonging to smugglers, an occasional single-masted sloop, and even, from time to time, a two-masted brig. Piers had heard tales of a Spanish galleon, the largest ship of the time, once dropping anchor there.

As we rode, Piers would scan the horizon with an old spyglass he'd found. Then he would invariably start talking about the subject that most fascinated him in the world, the ancient art of navigation. Piers loved ships as much as I loved him. He had memorized the tonnage, armaments, and flags of the ships in the Royal Navy and of those belonging to both allied and enemy countries. He insisted that one day he would find a way to enlist on a ship in the Royal Navy and would become a captain. If I reminded him there was no Royal Navy now because all the ships belonged to Parliament, he would be furious. His father had promised him he could be a sailor, he would say, and Lord Leigh always kept his promises.

One radiant day, we rode to the edge of the cliffs and stopped, as usual. We were forbidden to descend to the cove on horseback since the path was dangerously steep. Up until then, we had obeyed.

At the count of three, we spurred our mounts to see who could get down the hill first. Piers had started the narrow descent first, and just before we reached the finish, the path widened just enough for me to pass. I urged the mare on fiercely and made her jump, but she took a wrong step, and we both tumbled to the ground. When I came to, everything was spinning, and Piers was calling my name, shaking me by the shoulders. I finally managed to stand up, and Piers began to shout. We stopped quarreling when we heard Ann's mare groaning. She had broken a leg.

We stared at each other in horror. We knew what that meant: the beautiful animal would have to be put down. We were going to be punished for real this time. And we were.

Lord Leigh decided that Piers would be whipped. He himself implemented it with his riding whip, and he made me watch. I was mortified to see his hand trembling as he landed the whip on his son's back.

Piers bit his lips to avoid screaming. Having let his father down pained him more than the blows.

My punishment was even worse. Lord Leigh wouldn't even look at me; he simply reminded Mademoiselle Maynard that she was in charge of my education, and she had turned me into a disobedient young woman, so she must do something about it.

I turned pale before the governess's hard look.

"The only thing that frightens this little rascal is closed-in places. You will spend a night in the cell!"

I screamed in terror.

"Please, Mademoiselle Maynard, I ask that you have compassion," a voice said.

It was Lady Leigh, who had just arrived.

Mademoiselle Maynard frowned. "The lord has told me to proceed accordingly, and I shall do so."

"But tonight—"

The governess looked intently at Lady Leigh, as if to ask what was happening that night. Then her eyes grew wide.

I went down to the cellars in tears. I would have given anything to share Piers's punishment instead. The governess gripped my hand, dragging me along. We left the kitchens behind and kept descending, then walked through a dim passageway. At the end, she opened a door and pushed me inside the dreaded cell. It was a narrow, frigid room, with a creaking bed and a little table. Above it hung a crucifix that was a foot tall with a skull at its base. It was a very small skull, no doubt ridiculous to the adult eye, but those empty eye sockets terrified me. I screamed for her not to do it, not to leave me there, but the stern governess was unaffected by my pleas. I could hear her shutting the door and locking both locks.

I covered up the crucifix with a pillow and took refuge in a corner of the room. High up on the wall, nearly at the ceiling, there was a tiny opening that let air in; through the crack, a weak ray of daylight still filtered in, growing dimmer as night fell.

I climbed under the sheets fully dressed. With my heart pounding, visions of my mother's ravaged face filled my head, and I burst into tears again. At some point, sleep overcame me, but in the middle of the night, I woke up. Through the vent, I could see the glow of the full moon, and I could hear noises. The ghosts, I thought. I heard footsteps in front of my door and a murmur of voices praying in Latin. Through the crack in the door seeped a soft glow.

I stifled my moans and sobs under the blankets; I didn't want them to hear me and come into the cell. It sounded like they were trying to open the door, and I buried myself deeper under the covers.

After a while, the whispers and footsteps trailed off into the distance. There was soft chanting and the sound of an organ. The gathering of ghosts fell silent, and all I could hear was a far-off male voice, speaking in an awful, guttural tone. I couldn't make out what he was saying. Suddenly, everything was silent, as if in expectation, and then I heard the ringing of a bell. It fell silent, then rang again. Finally, I could hear all the ghosts speaking in unison.

I lay rigid under the covers, wishing I could disappear. I tried to tell myself my mother might be among the ghosts, so I shouldn't be afraid, but I couldn't calm down. Some time passed, and then I again heard footsteps on the other side of the door—the ghosts were leaving. Again, it seemed like they were trying to force their way into the cell. I stifled a scream and sat up in bed. Under the door, I could make out a faint, eerie light.

Finally, everything was quiet again. It was only much later, when, exhausted from the strain, I fell asleep and had one terrifying nightmare after another.

The morning light coming in through the vent woke me. Noises came from the passageway. The door opened, and Lord and Lady Leigh appeared, looking at me anxiously. I flung myself into Lady Leigh's arms, sobbing and babbling incoherently about ghosts.

"There are no ghosts, dear," she whispered.

Her husband knelt so that his serious face was level with mine. He was crestfallen at seeing me so distraught.

"Len," he said, "we're living through difficult times. Beyond Oak Park, there's a war and many fanatics. I hope you've learned your lesson. If you're told not to do something, you must obey. Disobeying could lead to your death. Yours and that of many others."

13

THE SHADOWS IN THE NIGHT

After that, we were forbidden to leave the house. Under the supervision of Mr. Reynolds in the mornings and Mademoiselle Maynard in the afternoons, Piers and I spent all day shut in the classroom. I remember the hours of dictation, Latin translations, and additions and subtractions. They would slap our hands if the smallest drop of ink fell onto the paper. The sky clouded up, along with our state of mind.

Whenever our jailors left us alone for a moment, Piers would pull out the navigation book from its hiding place under the table. He confided that the best nautical navigation books were from the navigation school attached to the House of Trade in Seville and that this one had cost his father a fortune. We would read it together. I could make out the words in my mother's language, but not the meaning of the nautical terms. So, he would explain to me what it was to "lie to" or "lash down" and what *windward* and *leeward* meant.

As soon as I could, I told him about the ghosts of that terrible night: the glow that seeped under the door, the voices, the footsteps descending into the depths of Oak Park. He sat there silent a moment. Then he surprised me.

"I didn't want to tell you, but for the past few months, when I wake up in the middle of the night, I go down to the kitchens. Most times I don't hear anything, but sometimes I do. Do you want to go down there with me on the next full moon?"

I trembled at the thought, but I didn't want him to think me a coward. So, I swallowed my fear and promised to go.

Over the next few weeks, we planned it and decided that it would be best to explore the cellars a bit and then hide in the room with the skull. The ghosts would walk down that dark passageway, and we could spy on them from there.

Evening after evening, we would gaze up at the sky, waiting for the moon to be full. Piers had fun frightening me with stories about men turning into wolves and dead people rising.

Finally, the moon was full, though we couldn't see it, since the sky was covered in clouds. The wood in the main stairway creaked when we headed down to the cellars that night. Though Piers put on a brave face, he was as frightened as I was. Leaving the kitchens behind, we kept going until we reached the passageway that led to the cell.

There, another stairway began; it was excruciatingly narrow and steep, its stone steps worn and slippery. By the light of Piers's candle, we descended slowly, taking great pains not to slip. At the bottom, there was another long passageway. The candle's flame projected phantasmagoric shadows on the wall, and as we made our way nervously along, it faintly illuminated entrances to mysterious tunnels and strange hollows carved in the stone. Piers whispered that they must be the dungeons from the times of the Plantagenets. I remembered the stories, and a shiver ran down my spine. For a moment, I imagined I heard the rattle of chains and the lament of tortured prisoners.

At the end of the long passageway, we encountered a large oak door with an enormous lock that required an equally large key.

"I think this is where the ghosts meet," I whispered.

"Hmm. If there's a lock and key, they must not be ghosts. We should go back and watch from the cell to see what's going on here."

We retraced our steps and slipped inside the cell, leaving the door ajar so we could spy through it. Piers blew out his candle, and everything was dark. Behind me, I knew, was the crucifix with the skull. But with Piers by my side, I didn't feel so scared.

Time passed slowly. At first, our hearts pounded in terror. Then, after a while, we got used to being there and sat down on the floor to wait. We could hear scurrying rats. Through the vent came the hoot of an owl. Around midnight, we heard a horse stop in front of the main door, and someone dismounted, but they didn't come down to the cellars.

It must have been nearly dawn when Piers nudged me awake. Through the crack in the door, we could see a faint glow and hear heavy footsteps. Piers stood up.

"I'm going out there," he whispered.

I shook my head, but he opened the door and stepped out.

I heard a curse.

"What are you doing here?"

"Me? What about you?"

"I came down to get more flour."

When I realized it was Matt, I emerged from my hiding place.

"Little Catalina, too! What's wrong with the young masters of this house? Don't you ever sleep?"

Piers was confused, so I explained, "Last month, Mademoiselle Maynard locked me in this cell to punish me—and there were ghosts!"

Matt laughed with his toothless mouth. "Ah! You're looking for ghosts? That's not so bad."

Then Piers piped up. "For a while now, whenever there's a full moon, I hear noises down here. I'm sure you must have heard something."

"It's not my place to speak about the secrets of Oak Park."

"Then there are secrets?"

Matt started whistling. He backed up a few steps, and we followed. He opened another door in the passageway, which turned out to be a normal granary. He threw a large sack over his tired back and went up to the kitchens, where he started preparing the dough.

Piers finally broke the silence. "When did you arrive at Oak Park?"

"Many, many years ago."

"They say you were shipwrecked."

"Not exactly. My ship was anchored in Horsehead Cove."

"You're a Spaniard—"

"A Basque from Donostía."

"Same thing."

"No, it's not the same. We Basques, especially those of us from the coast of Guipúzcoa, are bound to the water. Our country isn't Spain, but the open sea. Many, many years ago, I enlisted in a great enterprise. We were going to get rich doing great things for God. But I suffered untold sorrows, and then our ships were scattered to the north. Mine was forced to take refuge by the cliffs. That's how I arrived here, and how my life changed forever."

Then he started to laugh and cry at the same time, like a madman, and said, "Children, if there's a ghost in those cellars, it's my Rosita. She's buried down there. Sometimes, when I go down to get flour, I think she's going to appear to me. But she doesn't. The only Basque I see anymore is dear Miss Catalina, with that determined little face that reminds me of her great-grandfather, the admiral. But her hair is blonde, like my Rosita's."

"Tell us about her."

"I'm not going to tell you anything, young master Piers. Now back to bed with both of you, and you just forget about ghosts that don't exist, you hear?"

His words were friendly, his tone scolding, but in his eyes, I could see a profound worry for us, which we couldn't yet understand.

14

THE TIDE

Oak Park, Autumn of 1642

The leaves were beginning to fall when Margaret and Ann returned. A whole year had gone by since they'd left Oak Park, yet no one said a word about their time in London or mentioned Elizabeth. One day when we were alone, I asked Ann. She smiled sadly and said her sister had committed a grave error in marrying Lord Ruthven, who didn't respect her. They hadn't been introduced to Ruthven's acquaintances because he was embarrassed by them. She didn't want to tell me why. Then I asked her why they hadn't come home sooner, if they were unhappy there. She told me they weren't so bad off and that Elizabeth needed them. She wouldn't explain any further.

Lord Leigh had accompanied them back. At that time, he was most worried about his elder son. Thomas had become a fervent Royalist— one of those gentlemen of high breeding and good family who committed their conscience and their honor to the king. Parliamentarians sarcastically called them Cavaliers because of the extravagant way they dressed. Lord Leigh thought them little better than idealistic fools.

Thomas had participated in the Battle of Edgehill under the command of Prince Rupert of the Rhine, dashing nephew of King Charles and commander of the royal cavalry. He had been slightly wounded, and in the letter he wrote his parents, he described the battle as follows: "We rode with great dignity, holding our swords high to receive the enemy's charge, without firing a pistol or a rifle." This gentlemanly but impractical tactic had meant that the Cavaliers took the brunt of the battle. Lady Leigh was relieved that her son had been spared serious injuries, but like her husband, she was afraid for him.

Ever since I had learned that Piers's sisters would return at last, I'd been consumed with worry about what to say to Ann when she learned about her mare. To my great surprise, she didn't complain. Shortly afterward, her father brought her a young, gentle horse from a fair. Now it was Margaret and Ann who would ride around the estate. I would have been left at home, but Piers let me sit behind him in the saddle. We would usually outpace them because Piers couldn't resist the pleasure of galloping at full speed. More than once, I was on the verge of falling off.

One afternoon we galloped to the bottom of the hill, where there was an apple orchard traversed by a pool. We stopped under the boughs to pick some apples, which we stuffed into our pockets. Piers's horse lowered its head and nibbled the fruit on the ground. Then we rode away, toward the meadow next to the water mill. We were very fond of that place, with its sounds of the current and the mill turning on its hinge. The horse went to the water to drink, and we lay on the grass, which was wet with dew.

"Piers, do you know what happened to Ann and Margaret? Why they took so long to come home? Why they won't talk about it?"

"I think I finally do," he replied. "I've been eavesdropping, trying to understand."

"Tell me."

"London is a hotbed of political intrigue."

"Your sisters aren't interested in politics," I interrupted.

"My sisters like dances and social life. But at the home of a Presbyterian Calvinist like Ruthven, no one dances."

"But Elizabeth—"

"It seems, at first, before the court was disbanded, Elizabeth came up with lots of excuses for not presenting them to society."

"How mean! Margaret was so excited. And Ann has always been so kind; she didn't even get mad about her mare."

Piers looked at me and smiled. "She must be worried about other things."

"Anyway, I don't understand why they didn't come home earlier if things were so bad in London."

"Ruthven kept them there. He's a swine."

"But why?"

Piers explained that, in that year of silence, William Ruthven had shown his true colors: his fanaticism, his ambition, his greed. He mistreated Elizabeth, and she was afraid of him. When they were first married, he used her to obtain information and get ahead at court. But when the king and queen left London, and the war between Royalists and Parliamentarians began, he switched sides and didn't need her any longer. He had used up all the money from Elizabeth's dowry buying that huge house on the Strand. In that house, they never had parties or celebrations of any sort. Ruthven also forced them to participate in Presbyterian rituals, and to Margaret's displeasure, he forbade them from wearing adornments or even bright colors.

Lord Leigh had tried repeatedly to take them home, but Elizabeth begged him tearfully to leave her sisters with her, so she wouldn't be so alone. She swore to Ann and Margaret that she would present them to society and once, when her husband was away, managed to organize a small gathering. The girls, embarrassed for their sister, pretended to their father they were happy there, in that enormous, silent mansion.

A few months earlier, the Count of Gowrie, now riddled with debts, had decided to demand a ransom for his sisters-in-law. In a clandestine visit to Lord Leigh, he had demanded a large sum of money. He said he wouldn't let Margaret and Ann go until he received it, and if he didn't, he would moreover accuse Lord Leigh of being a traitor before Parliament. The whole family would be thrown in prison.

"Ruthven is contemptible," Piers fumed. "Who knows what slander he used to extort money from my father. Also, he did it this summer, when Father had no money because his ships had been confiscated."

That explained Lord Leigh's constant trips back and forth to London. He was not only trying to save his business but also seeking funds to placate Elizabeth's wretched husband.

My mind reeled at this. I'd thought such terrible things like holding young girls hostage belonged to a part of my life long past. We lay there in silence, gazing up at the late-afternoon sky. A pale moon was beginning to rise. Clouds meandered around in capricious forms.

"A sheep!" I exclaimed.

"No, it's a snail!"

"Matt's cap!"

We laughed.

A large grayish cloud appeared and began to cover the moon.

"A ship!"

Piers sat up excitedly. "It's a galleon!" Then something seemed to dawn on him. He jumped up. "What if those weren't ghosts in the cellar?"

"What else could they have been?"

"You said you heard footsteps, voices, bells—all that seems very real. I've heard them, too. And, Len, when there's high tide, ships can enter the cove! Matt said that a Spanish galleon once came up to the coast."

"I don't understand."

"There's a full moon tonight. Let's go to Horsehead Cove! We need to clear up this mystery."

He ran over and jumped on the horse. I was hesitant, but he gave me a hand up, and in an instant, I was seated behind him. When we reached the cliff, the final glimmers of sunset played on the horizon. We dismounted at a spot where you could see the cave in the cove and the slope of the coast jutting out to sea. The cool ocean breeze ruffled my hair and Piers's cape. Shortly, the full moon shone brightly; the moonlight rippled on the water. The waves crashed against the cliff. Piers said he'd never seen such a high tide.

We tied the horse to a tree and sat down with our feet hanging over the abyss. Piers had pulled out his spyglass and was peering through it intently. Suddenly, he shouted and handed me the glass. In the distance, I could make out some lights beginning to get bigger as they approached.

"A ghost ship?" I asked.

"No, a real ship. I think it's a Portuguese *carraca* with square rigging," he said.

A little while later, we could make out the ship's lanterns and some men running back and forth on deck. The ship came closer to the coast, and they lowered a boat. They rowed to the wharf, where a man in a dark cape stepped out of the little boat. Someone was waiting for him in the cave, and I saw them embrace.

"I told you so," Piers exclaimed. "It isn't ghosts. There are secret meetings at Oak Park!"

"We have to tell your father!"

The men had mounted horses and were starting up the path. Piers lowered the spyglass and stared at me, astonishment etched on his face. "We'd better not."

"Why?"

"I think the man who came to greet the ship *is* my father."

"But that can't be!"

"Let's get home."

We galloped toward Oak Park, our path illuminated by the moon and stars. Thanks to Piers, I knew their names: Aldebaran in the Taurus constellation, Centaurus, and especially the North Star and the Great Bear and Little Bear constellations, which sailors used for navigation.

We returned home to find that, in the excitement of our discoveries, we had missed supper. Lord and Lady Leigh had already retired. Our tutors sent us to bed without supper and locked us in our rooms.

I slept a short while, but then woke with a start. Someone was knocking at the window and whispering my name. It didn't frighten me; I knew who it was. I crawled outside, where Piers was waiting on the roof, his face filled with excitement and his hair more tousled than ever.

"Come on," he urged, "before they get here."

We found a large window that had been left ajar and used it to get back inside. We descended to the cellars as fast as we could without making noise.

The cell with the skull seemed as macabre as ever, but I wasn't afraid now that Piers was with me. We sat down on the bed and fell asleep, clinging to each other. Sometime later, we woke up. We could hear footsteps and murmurs in Latin, and that same glow appeared under the door. We didn't dare go out there while not knowing if the people passing by were alive or dead.

Then someone paused at the door. We jumped up and hid under the bed. The doorknob moved. My hair stood on end as I heard the door begin to open, but then it shut. When the sounds were dying away, Piers told me that now we could go out and spy on them. I was frightened to death, but he threatened to leave me alone in the cell, so I reluctantly followed. We descended the slippery staircase in the dark, then felt our way down the long passageway once more. We could hear a man's deep voice, growing more and more distinct. Light filtered out from under the massive oak door and through the lock. We pushed on it tentatively, and this time it swung ever so slightly open.

We were greeted by the light of a thousand candles. In the back was a beautiful alabaster altarpiece: the Virgin, shaded by a canopy, held the Christ child in her arms. She seemed to be gazing at us with a gentle smile. In front of her was an altar, and surrounding it, there were neither dead people nor ghosts. A small multitude packed the room: men and women, many with their heads and faces covered, all kneeling and with their heads bowed. We recognized Lord and Lady Leigh, Margaret, and Ann. Also some of the servants and one or two neighbors from town. It was impossible to identify the rest, but from their clothing, I knew some were humble people, and others enjoyed higher social standing. Next to the door, Matt sat on a bench, as if standing guard. But he had fallen asleep.

What most astonished us was that, standing there before the altar, with his back to us, was a man in a flowing red chasuble. He lifted his hands toward the ceiling and chanted a prayer in Latin. Then he fell silent and knelt. After a moment of ceremonious silence, the man in the priestly vestments stood and turned around. In his hands, he held a small white object. I recognized him at once: it was Uncle Andrew. He looked up and saw us, a smile spreading across his face.

Before anyone else could see us, we slipped away.

15

THE MARTYRS

That's how we discovered the ghosts of Oak Park were the lords of the house, their servants, and their neighbors. They would slip secretly into the passageways to attend the sacred ceremony outlawed since Queen Elizabeth's time. The canticles in Latin, the ringing of bells . . . my mind flooded with snippets of the liturgical Mass from my childhood, from my mother's land, and then everything made sense to me. The previous Christmas, Uncle Andrew had visited, and at midnight, I'd heard noises in the woods and creaking in the house. And the night I'd been sent to bed without supper and went down to the kitchens, it must have been Matt following me. He was probably standing guard, making sure no one surprised the faithful Catholics.

The mystery solved, we went back to my bedroom, and I asked Piers not to leave me alone. We sat on the floor, our backs against the bed, holding hands, looking through the window at the stars. My friend had withdrawn into himself, as he often did when worried or nervous. After some silence, we began breathing in unison, and I asked him in a low voice if he had ever suspected. He admitted he had come to suspect there were secret meetings in the house, but he'd never imagined Masses. He was saddest, he said, that his parents hadn't trusted him with the secret.

Piers fell silent again. After a while, he squeezed my hand and left. I climbed into bed and fell into a deep, placid sleep.

The sound of heavy footsteps on the stairs awakened me. It was still very early, and weak light filtered into my room. All that had happened the night before returned to me. We had once again disobeyed, and if Uncle Andrew said something to Lord and Lady Leigh, I feared we would be in terrible trouble. The footsteps stopped in front of my room, and it was not Mademoiselle Maynard who opened the door, but Matt.

I was surprised to see him, especially at that hour. He told me that the masters wanted to speak with me and Piers and led me downstairs wordlessly. I was terrified that they might go so far as to expel me from the house. In the dining hall, I found Piers waiting with a grave but expectant expression. A few minutes later, Lord Leigh and his wife joined us, telling us to sit down. One of the servants I had seen the night before set out bowls of breakfast food and, at a sign from Lady Leigh, left.

Then Lord Leigh bolted the door. Lady Leigh smiled gently, came over to us, and placed her graceful hands on our shoulders, having us stand up. In a few strides, Piers's father crossed the room and lifted one of the tapestries; a little door was behind it. He opened it, revealing a dark stairway. Lord Leigh disappeared down it. We could hear him calling someone quietly. Then we heard footsteps returning and a familiar voice asking to be left alone with us. In the doorway appeared Uncle Andrew, followed by Lord Leigh.

Andrew Leigh's face was generous and friendly as always, but under his eyes there were dark circles and worry lines. It felt like he was the last person on earth who, in some way, belonged to me. Whenever I saw him, I was reminded of my mother. He said something like, "The spies must be hungry. We'll eat first."

We sat down again, and he joked with us over breakfast. When we finished, Lord and Lady Leigh left us alone. Uncle Andrew bolted the door again and returned to the table.

"Yesterday," he began, "you were present at the Mass I held in the ancient Saxon crypt. In times of Queen Elizabeth, they used that crypt for executing monks from the abbey that still sits in ruins next to the house. Now it is used as a chapel, and that must remain our secret. Not all the servants are loyal, and some have suspicions. You remember what happened with Roberts. If the happenings at Oak Park were to reach the wrong people's ears, if they knew that a Jesuit was staying here right now, then my life, your parents' lives, and even your own lives would be in danger. This is the only place for many, many miles around where the ancient rituals are still celebrated."

"Are you a Jesuit?" asked Piers.

"For more than forty years now."

We looked at him with different eyes. Mademoiselle Maynard had terrorized us with stories of Jesuits who ate children, who tried to murder the king, who wanted to burn down Parliament, yet there before us sat a Jesuit whose face shone with great goodness.

We were quiet for a moment. Then Piers asked, "Why did you become a Jesuit?"

Uncle Andrew propped his elbows on the table and leaned toward us. "There were many things that led me to follow that path."

"If they catch you, they'll execute you."

"I know. Others have died before me. I owe them a great deal."

"What do you owe them? Jesuits are dangerous—they're spies for England's enemies. What do those traitors have to do with our family?"

"Dear Piers, the Leighs have always been Catholics. It's the ancient religion of this country."

My friend seemed disconcerted but said no more.

"In times of Queen Mary Tudor," Andrew explained, "we enjoyed a certain amount of influence at court, which was held against us once Elizabeth took the throne. Politically ostracized, we devoted ourselves to commerce, making the family wealthy. For years, we have observed our religion clandestinely. These have been very difficult times for a

Catholic in this country, as you well know. The anti-Catholic persecution didn't let up with the Stuarts, but it was especially bloody under Elizabeth I. At that time, my father took me to observe the executions of Catholic martyrs at Tyburn. I attended the trial, and then the martyrdom on the gallows of three men, Edmund Campion and his two Jesuit companions. It was the most dreadful thing I have seen in my life."

He paused, beside himself with emotion, then went on. "I'll never be able to sufficiently thank my father—your great-grandfather, Piers—for allowing me to watch them die so bravely. Do you know Campion's story?"

We both shook our heads, and Uncle Andrew closed his eyes as if remembering a cruel, painful past.

"Like your brother, Thomas, Edmund Campion was educated at Oxford. Initially, he tried to accept the Anglican faith, but later fled to France, where he studied theology at the University of Douai, and was later ordained a Jesuit priest in Prague. Campion slipped into England disguised as a jewel merchant to offer support to the Catholics being persecuted. For more than a year, he preached in secret, celebrating the sacraments and the holy Mass. I met him here, in the Saxon chapel where we prayed yesterday. Many times since then, I have relived that holy ceremony in my mind. I remember his devotion, the absorption with which he celebrated rituals that he knew could cost him his life."

Overcome by affection for Uncle Andrew, I stood up and kissed his hand. "I won't ever forget last night's Mass, either. I was so happy to see you, Uncle Andrew! For me, you are the only link to my mother and my country."

"Len!" Piers said impatiently. "Stop interrupting. I want to know how Campion's story ends."

I blushed with embarrassment, but Uncle Andrew smiled at me and stroked my hair. Perhaps he wanted to give me strength, in light of what he was about to tell us.

"The priest hunters looked for him everywhere. Finally, they trapped him in Berkshire and took him to the Tower of London, tied up and wearing a placard that read, 'Campion, the Seditious Jesuit.' There, they tortured him for over two months. They said he apostatized, but he never did.

"Then the trial took place, the one my father took me to see. They judged him, along with two other Catholic missionaries. I remember how, after they read the death sentence, the priests sang a Te Deum. I heard Campion's words: 'By condemning us, you are condemning your own ancestors, all the ancient bishops and kings, everything that was once the glory of England, the island of saints, the most devout daughter of the Holy See of Peter.'

"Then they took the men to Tyburn. My father and I followed them. Edmund climbed up onto the cart they had installed under the gallows, and he placed the rope around his own neck. I remember him asking to exercise his legal right to last words and exclaiming loudly: 'I'm innocent of the acts of treason that they accuse me of. I am a Catholic and a priest in the company of Jesus. Within this faith I have lived, and in it I want to die.' They immediately ordered that the cart beneath his feet be withdrawn. They left him dangling there, starting to suffocate. They cut his chest open and, while he was still alive, tore out his intestines. They castrated him. It was"—Uncle Andrew was shaking—"a horrible slaughter. Some of his blood splattered onto my clothes. I have kept that piece of bloodstained cloth as a relic. I will never forget it."

There was a long pause as Uncle Andrew fought back tears. I covered my eyes with my hands. Piers was pallid.

"When I heard those words," he went on, "I decided to become like him. But I was still a child, younger than you are now. I lived here, at Oak Park, beset with doubts and eager to follow the martyrs' example. The years went by. Then the Spanish Armada came, and my father and I collaborated with King Philip's spies because for us English

Catholics, the king of Spain was our last hope of returning to the faith of our forefathers."

"Your father was a traitor to the queen?"

"My father, Piers, was faithful to England's ancient religion, the same one that the Tudors betrayed."

Piers frowned angrily. He loved his country and thought the defeat of the Spanish in the invasion nearly fifty years earlier was a glorious episode in its history. Anyone who had aided that invasion was a traitor.

"Let's continue with the story. This is where Len's family comes in."

I sat up in my seat, proud but surprised.

"My father, Lord Percival Leigh, and Don Miguel de Oquendo, your great-grandfather, had done business together for years," he said, setting his smiling eyes on me. "From the port of Dover, ships set out for Pasajes. The English merchandise was stored for a time at the house of Don Miguel on Mount Ulia before going on to the Indies. Then, in the years leading up to the attack on the Armada, trade between the two countries was prohibited. But our collaboration with the Oquendos still continued secretly through Horsehead Cove on nights when the moon was full. Along with the merchandise came books, and every now and then, Catholic priests. When the invasion was planned, your great-grandfather was named commander of the Spanish fleet. After its defeat, the storm dragged his ship toward the English coast, and he took refuge in our cove. He knew how to enter since he had visited many times before."

He paused, remembering the past.

"Dear Len, when your great-grandfather dropped anchor in the cove, I was eighteen, and the words of Edmund Campion still echoed in the depths of my conscience. I was the heir of this noble house. If I became a priest, I would have to abandon everything: my family, the option to marry, the chance to exert direct influence on the politics of this kingdom. Still, there was something inside that called me to become a Jesuit priest. My little one, your great-grandfather took me with him to Spain, and before he died, he wrote letters vouching for me as someone worthy of ecclesiastical studies. I am forever in his debt.

"That's how I, a young Englishman who barely spoke Spanish, arrived at the house on Mount Ulia. Andrew Leigh of England became Don Andrés Leal in Basque Country. From the coast of San Sebastián, I journeyed south and carried out my studies in Valladolid, at the Royal College of St. Alban. That school prepared priests to bring the English people back into communion with Rome."

Piers could take it no longer. "The head of the Church of England is the king. What you're telling us, Uncle Andrew, is high treason."

"I know. There's something you must understand, Piers. For me, obedience to my conscience takes precedence over loyalty to any king. In Spanish, they called me *Leal*, which means *faithful*. I left the primogeniture of this family to my younger brother, your father's father. He died soon after, and your father has always seen me as a second father. You and your brother and sisters are the people I love most in the world. I have always followed your family from the shadows, trying to ensure that it perseveres in our forbearers' faith. This house, which is mine by inheritance, is a brilliant point of light in the darkness of this country. That's why you must help me protect it."

My playmate didn't seem convinced, but I could see his eyes shining with admiration.

"Yesterday, you discovered the secret hidden in the depths of this ancient mansion. I beg you, don't say a word that could betray your birthright, your people. You must keep quiet."

We both nodded solemnly. Then I asked, "Can we attend, too?"

"I'll talk it over with Piers's father. In any case, Lord and Lady Leigh want you both to be acquainted with their religion."

"Is Thomas a Catholic, too?" asked Piers.

"Your brother knows our secret, but he is devoted to King Charles and the Church of England. Margaret and Ann only discovered the truth in London, where they were being held hostage because Elizabeth unintentionally revealed it to her husband. William Ruthven used the information to extort money from your father. Disgusted by his attitude, your sisters decided that, since they had been unjustly accused of being Catholics, they would become the real thing. Yesterday, they participated in Mass for the first time."

Piers looked at him pensively. Uncle Andrew returned his gaze, letting his nephew know that he would respect whatever he decided.

"Uncle Andrew," he said solemnly, "I don't know if I want to be a Catholic like you. For me, they have always been traitors. But I respect you for your bravery."

"Would you like to learn about the religion I have devoted my life to?"

"I think so, and once I know more about it, I will decide which path is correct for me."

"I would greatly enjoy teaching you."

So, Uncle Andrew decided to stay hidden in the cellars until the next full moon, when the ship would come back for him. During those weeks, classes were suspended at Oak Park. They sent Mr. Reynolds to keep Thomas company while he convalesced from the Battle of Edgehill. As for Mademoiselle Maynard, who was much more dangerous, they gave her a month's leave to visit her family. She looked surprised, but made no comment. She even seemed happy, and I wondered if it might have something to do with the mysterious letters she had been receiving.

I can still see us there, next to the great window in the study, watching the autumn leaves fall. Uncle Andrew was propped up in a huge chair, its arms carved out of oak. I was at his feet, seated on a little pillow. Ann and Margaret joined us, sitting attentively in two straight-backed chairs, while Piers sat on the nearby study table, his legs dangling. Andrew Leigh used the *Catechism of the Council of Trent* to explain his ancient doctrine, and he shared the Holy Scripture from the Catholic perspective, telling it to us like a story. At times, Piers seemed distracted and at others, confused. But when we were all quizzed after the lessons, he usually gave the right answers.

Even now, when so much time has passed, I remember those classes, and it seems I can see, within that image, a clear light, soft and comforting. He spoke to us of heaven, something to which we were all inclined in the depths of our souls. He told us tender stories about Jesus being born between an ox and a mule and even an occasional racy one like the tale of Judah and Tamar, which made Piers wink at me.

When the moon reached its zenith again, he celebrated his last Mass before leaving us. We now saw what had once seemed so dark and phantasmagoric in a new light. The faithful came from near and far, people who lived their faith in secret and kept their faces covered to avoid being identified in case of a betrayal.

Today, in this foreign country so far from the land of my childhood, Uncle Andrew's prayers and words return to console me. In light of all that has happened, I remember those secret meetings as something supernatural, outside of time or space.

16

HISPANIOLA

Santo Domingo, April 1655

The sea mist is scattered by a warm rain and a gentle breeze that's cooler now. It brings me back from my reverie. I cough; the climate here doesn't agree with me. It's like the humid air can't enter my lungs. Josefina has returned, and she smiles at me. She says I should get ready, that my uncle is waiting. From a trunk, she takes out a brocade dress and lays it on the bed, urging me to get up, which I do reluctantly. First, Josefina puts on my long-sleeved blouse trimmed with lace, and on top of it, the tight corset. Then she slides the petticoats over that. Next, she sits me down. She sings softly as she carefully untangles my hair with a fine mother-of-pearl comb. Finally, she shows me my image in a mirror. I can make out my face in the cloudy glass: dark rings under my eyes and my skin pale from so much time shut in. Josefina has skillfully pulled my hair back into a low chignon, leaving a few loose strands that she has curled with hot irons.

"You should be happy, Señorita Catalina," she says. "You're going to a party. Don't make that face, or you'll upset Don Juan Francisco. He worries about you a lot; he's a good man."

I fix my eyes on her as if in a daze. Yes, Don Juan Francisco de Montemayor is a good man, I think. I can still hear the Spanish ambassador who convinced them to free me from prison because an uncle had claimed me, a judge in the Court of Santo Domingo, a loyal subject of the Spanish Crown.

I remember our first encounter well. When I landed from the light patache, an unfamiliar gentleman tentatively spoke my name: "Catalina?" I scrutinized his face shyly; he was bald, very tall and slender, with a long face and a prominent aquiline nose. He was dressed in black, an outfit softened by a white ruff at the throat. He was a young man, but the gravity of his face made him look older, as did his faded, old-fashioned clothing.

The Spanish family with whom I had traveled led me to him. They had picked me up in the port of Seville and taken care of me throughout the journey because they felt bad for the young woman so mistreated by life. The mother whispered something into my uncle's ear; perhaps she told him I had lost my mind, that he should be careful with me.

I curtsied to him, gently bending my knee. He took me by the shoulders, pulled me up, and looked me in the eye. Then he greeted me by kissing my forehead and firmly embracing me.

Don Juan Francisco de Montemayor is a man of few words, but since I arrived on Hispaniola, he has looked after me with a nearly paternal concern. He wants me to speak, to behave with decorum toward his frequent guests. I don't wish to upset him, but there is too much horror in my past. For a long time now, I have lived shut inside myself.

Now, when I let a little moan escape, Josefina says, "Don't sigh, my lady. The governor's palace is the best house on the island. You're going to like it."

She affectionately pinches my cheeks to redden them, and I look at her with gratitude. Then she helps me put on the brocade dress and a pair of laced boots with high heels and a little platform; my feet shouldn't show under the skirt. I stand up with some effort; the dress is heavy, the corset is too tight, and I'm not used to walking on such high heels.

Just as we're finishing, Vicente Garcés knocks at the door—he is the servant who came with my uncle to the island and who serves as butler for the house. He says Don Juan Francisco awaits me downstairs. Josefina leads me out to the large balcony overlooking a patio with stone arches and a bubbling fountain. Some mulatto servants turn their heads in surprise. I smile timidly.

Holding Josefina's hand, I descend the travertine marble stairway. It's unpolished and worn. Don Juan Francisco is standing next to the fountain. He has donned a dark cape, lending him a dignified air, and he holds a wide-brimmed hat.

With some difficulty, because of the heels, I gently bend my knee and say softly, "Good morning, Uncle. May Your Excellency go with God."

When he hears my unexpected voice, he looks pleased. He kisses my forehead and exclaims, "How lovely you look today! I'm glad to see that your melancholy is leaving you. Let us be off. The fresh air will do you good, and the Alcázar de Colón is but a few blocks away."

Josefina helps me put on the hat, so the sun won't darken my skin.

We go out to the street and walk away from the stone façade of the judge's house. It is the former residence of Don Nicolás de Ovando, founder of the city. We pass by the Chapel of Our Lady of Remedies, where my uncle goes up to the door and crosses himself before the Virgin. I tense up. In England, worshipping an image had meant a death sentence. Don Juan Francisco sees my stricken face, but says nothing.

I lean on his arm, feeling as if I might faint at any moment in this heat. The petticoats, the corset, the dress—it all imprisons me. We walk as far as the wall that separates the city from the Ozama. The river is faster-flowing than the Guadalquivir, but not as great as the one that crossed London. The fortress wall is under construction. A foreman approaches Don Juan Francisco, who asks how their work is coming.

"There's still a lot to be done on the other side, but this part, on the river, is nearly finished."

"This is the most important part. How much longer will it take?"

"A few weeks."

"Sooner—it has to be sooner," my uncle presses him.

"We shall do what we can, whatever is in our power, my lord," responds the foreman in an unhurried island cadence.

In the distance, I see the part where the wall hasn't been built yet. There, only lemon trees and bushes border the colonial city. Santo Domingo is no larger than my mother's Basque village.

From Calle de las Damas, we go out to the great plaza where the Alcázar de Colón sits. Behind it is the Royal Audiencia, a huge stone building where my uncle works. In the distance, we can hear church bells playing the Angelus.

The new governor, recently arrived from Spain, is holding a reception for the most distinguished members of the colony.

In the doorway of the palace, under the arcades, some soldiers stand to attention before my uncle. Since the death of the previous governor, Don Andrés Pérez Franco, the island has been in the hands of the principal judge in the Audiencia: my uncle, Don Juan Francisco de Montemayor. I look at his tall figure, his beard with almost no gray, his long face with just a few wrinkles, and I remind myself that he isn't an old man. Perhaps he has been prematurely aged by the duties and problems to which life has led him.

A staircase leads to the second floor, and we traverse a long corridor with arches overlooking the plaza. The doors of the room where the governor receives guests, nearly a throne room, are open. Inside have gathered the Creoles, the bureaucrats who have arrived in America, the local high society. The ladies observe me curiously while my uncle leads me over to our neighbor, Doña Luisa Dávila.

"Don Juan Francisco, your niece looks quite lovely today. Who does she take after?" she asks.

My uncle ignores the impertinent question and says instead, "I beg you to accompany Catalina at every moment. As you know, since she arrived, she has scarcely left the house."

Doña Luisa introduces me to her daughters, three young women who seem to never stop chatting. One of them is at an advanced stage of pregnancy. Meanwhile, Don Juan Francisco heads for the center of the room, where a vacant seat of honor awaits the governor's arrival.

I hear fanfare, and the side doors open. A man enters the room, greeting all present. He is relatively young, about thirty, and belongs to the Spanish upper nobility. His protector is Don Luis Méndez de Haro, a favorite of King Philip IV. The heralds announce him: Don Bernardino de Meneses Bracamonte y Zapata, Count of Peñalba. The new governor.

Then my uncle reads the official appointment of the count, reciting all the man's titles and experience. In conclusion, he reminds those gathered that, given the danger of an imminent attack by the English, many trials will be postponed, and everyone must cooperate in the island's defense. Times of privation, he warns, draw near.

A worried murmur runs through the room. The oldest remember the looting of the city by the pirate Drake, seventy years ago, and many of those present have an ancestor who died during that invasion. In the houses and especially in the religious buildings, there are still signs of the attack.

However, the ladies at my side seem less worried about the arrival of the British than the suspension or postponement of the trials. Pregnant Doña Beatriz, the eldest of Doña Luisa's daughters, exclaims, "But then Don Rodrigo Pimentel won't ever be stopped!"

Seeing the confusion on my face, she explains, "My husband says Don Rodrigo is the worst scoundrel who has ever lived on this island."

Her sisters, Doña Berta and Doña Amalia, giggle.

"In Santo Domingo," says Doña Amalia, "the only law is Don Rodrigo Pimentel."

"Look at Inspector Bonilla," Doña Berta adds. "He's distraught. If the trials are suspended, Don Rodrigo will get away from him."

"Girls, be quiet!" Doña Luisa snaps.

"Mother! We aren't the ones saying it; it's on the wall of the Audiencia. Someone has written there what all of us are thinking."

Doña Beatriz turns to me with a sly look. "A few years ago, Don Rodrigo was elected alderman of the city. He has only committed outrages. He has violated all the laws one possibly can in this colony."

"The worst part is Inés de Ledesma," Doña Beatriz opines.

People are watching, but the ladies lower their voices only a little.

"Look, Pimentel is over there," Doña Beatriz says, pointing. "He's buttering up the new governor so he can keep getting away with his schemes."

I turn my gaze in that direction, where a strapping, rather heavy man with a sullen face is indeed acting obsequiously toward the governor.

"I'm sure he'll do the same thing with the Count of Peñalba that the previous governor, Don Andrés Pérez Franco, did with Don Juan de Bitrián y Viamonte. He gave him a bed with sumptuous hangings and silver cups filled with gold coins," Doña Beatriz explains to me. "In exchange, he was allowed to organize pirates who extort money on the coast."

"Don Juan Francisco de Montemayor has tried to prosecute him several times, but for the court to be suspended now, right when he was finally about to be put on trial . . . it's curious that the trials have been suspended because of an alleged attack." Doña Amalia laughed. "I wonder how much he gave the judge?"

"I do not believe," I say in a low but firm voice, "that my esteemed uncle can be bought."

They fall silent, glancing at each other with wide eyes. Since my arrival two years ago, the rumor has run through the colony that I am feeble-minded and mute, having gone mad in England. When she hears my voice, Doña Luisa Dávila fixes her eyes on me with some astonishment.

The presentation ceremony begins. Before the governor's seat of honor, the people parade past in a sort of royal audience. My uncle announces the different families: the Caballeros, the Dávilas, the house of Bastida. I notice his face darkens at Don Rodrigo Pimentel's turn.

Afterward, people scatter around the room in animated conversations. Doña Luisa's daughters set about questioning me. It's the first time I've left the stout walls of the judge's house. Perhaps they want to know if I'm as mad as they've heard. I feel distressed by so many strangers peering at me, but at least the young women's attitude is affectionate.

"Do you like music?" Doña Berta asks me.

"Yes."

"I play the *vihuela*, and Amalia has a lute. Perhaps you could visit us! You're our neighbor, after all."

"Yes," I repeat.

"We'll expect you at the house tomorrow, just before sunset."

"We'll tell Josefina to bring you over; Mother says she's the only one who has any influence."

I let myself be won over by their gaiety, these young women who haven't suffered, whose only concern is finding a good match. They remind me of the Leighs before the war. On the other hand, I—how can I go on living with everything harbored in my mind?

17

THE EAST ROOM

Santo Domingo, April 1655
Oak Park, Summer of 1643

When the reception ends, I leave with the Dávilas; my uncle has signaled for me to go ahead with them. Perhaps he has to discuss matters with the new governor. We slowly descend the marble staircase, but when we reach the entrance to the palace, a heavy tropical rain obscures the esplanade. We join the other guests waiting under the arcade for a covered vehicle to arrive.

My neighbors take advantage of the tumult to gossip about gentlemen. Perhaps they've seen one they like because they insist that their mother accompany me in the sedan chair; they'll stay behind until it returns. We advance slowly down Calle de las Damas, the lady submitting me to a torrent of warnings and advice. I am relieved when we arrive.

A footman steps out with an umbrella to protect me from the downpour. I thank him for his kindness, and he breaks into a smile, showing huge white teeth. I climb the staircase, leaning on the bannister; I can't wait to take off the painful shoes. Josefina isn't in my room, and I miss her. I feel so alone. I slowly remove the clothing weighing me down until I'm left with just a white petticoat. They bring me some dinner, and I peck at it.

Then, through the large window, I see the clouds have parted. The sun sinks into the sea, and the full moon shines over the city. I am lost in thought, and hours go by before I hear my uncle's voice downstairs. I know he will come up to tell me good night. But I don't want to speak with him. I don't want him to ask me if I had a good time at the reception or ask how I am feeling, so I climb into the canopy bed and shut the mosquito net. Moments later, I hear the door open and flickering candlelight penetrates the room. I close my eyes and pretend I am asleep. Don Juan Francisco walks over to my bed. He stands there, looking at me for a long time; a tired sigh escapes his lips. Then he leaves.

Sadness keeps me awake. Far away, in the cathedral, the bells toll once and again; I count twelve peals. I finally get up.

I walk out onto the porticoed gallery. The whole house is asleep. I go downstairs, walk around the animals' drinking trough, and sit on the rear wall of the house, which looks out on the Ozama River. I can make out an anchored galleon. Candlelight glows on its deck, but everything is silent.

In Oak Park, it was like this, too. At night, everything seemed to be dead, but it wasn't. Every full moon brought, if not Uncle Andrew, then other priests. We two children had begun to join the celebrations. While the ceremonies moved me, I noticed Piers was frequently distracted, and sometimes I even caught a disapproving look on his face. But that wasn't his greatest worry at the time.

It was summer again. Nearly a year had passed since we'd discovered the secret of Oak Park. I was still practically a child, but Piers was now an adolescent—and thought himself an adult. He made this clear by talking politics as if he were a member of Parliament and about the war as if he were a seasoned soldier. By way of the servants, he got his hands on all sorts of tabloids and newspapers. Through Mr. Reynolds, he secretly received the *Mercurius Aulicus*, published in Oxford with a Royalist bias, and thanks to Jack, the new coachman, he read the *Mercurius Britannicus*, published in London and therefore supportive of Parliament. My friend avidly followed everything that was happening outside our little world, especially news of the navy.

Mr. Reynolds would frequently leave to meet with Thomas, and free of his preceptor, Piers would drag me down to the coast. He thus forced me to defy Mademoiselle Maynard, who was ever more convinced that I was incorrigible and truly destined for hell. With his spyglass, my friend would scan the horizon, watching ships of different tonnage and rigging pass by. He was itching with impatience and wanted at any cost to fulfill his dream of becoming a mariner. He had spoken repeatedly to his father about it, but since Lord Leigh's ships were still requisitioned and he himself was regarded with suspicion, he could not help his son. All my restless friend could do was follow the war via the papers and go down to the bay to navigate from one side to the other in a little boat. I'd watch him from a peaceful perch at the top of the cliff.

One source of entertainment was provided by Lord Leigh's covert meetings in the East Room. When he sensed a meeting might take place, Piers would come get me, and we'd listen in.

I remember when Thomas secretly returned from Oxford, where the Royalist headquarters was located. He was accompanied by two other gentlemen. Their horses' hooves resounded on the great patio after nightfall, and shortly after, Piers knocked on my door. I jumped out of bed and threw on a light robe, then ventured out into the dark corridor, where he awaited me, smiling happily. Through the windows in the back of the hallway, starlight streamed in, along with the cool August breeze. We snuck down the stairs barefoot and followed the back passageways to our hiding place in the East Room, the hollow covered by the tapestry. Through the knots in the cloth, the strong odor of tobacco reached me, and I nearly coughed.

"And we need your help in the king's cause. We know you maintain good relations with the Spaniards and that you know King Philip's ambassador," one of the arrivals was saying.

"Maintained. My ships were requisitioned, and I have been unable to negotiate with them."

Lord Leigh's voice was commanding, gruff from tobacco. I took Piers's hand, and he squeezed mine to give me confidence. We both revered the Lord of Oak Park; the thought that he might catch us hiding there terrified us.

The other Royalist noble exclaimed, "A wicked act, requisitioning the ships! They had no right. Those Parliamentary rebels!"

"You must help us if you wish to carry on with your commerce."

"I cannot do battle with Parliament. My lands are in eastern England, so they are controlled by the government of London, which is now Parliament. Today, Thomas," Lord Leigh said, "you and these gentlemen have taken a great risk. I hate to think what would have happened if you had been spotted."

"But we weren't, Father. Don't worry. The Parliamentarians—"

"I tell you again, I cannot rise up against them. Gentlemen, when the war is over, whichever side wins, the ships will be returned to me. Meanwhile, I prefer not to take sides. We should all look for a peaceful solution."

"I understand. You don't want to get involved." It was the first voice again. "But the moment comes when commitment is inevitable."

"We Leighs are only interested in trade, not in wars that destroy countries and ruin kingdoms. I have often thought that King Charles could have arrived at a compromise. The path he has taken will lead nowhere."

His interlocutor rudely replied, "The Parliamentarians are nothing but miserable traitors. Puritan Calvinists, as dangerous as the papists."

"My most esteemed Sir John Mennes!" Lord Leigh replied. "You don't care for the papists, and yet, you have come to ask me to intercede before His Catholic Majesty."

"It's John Mennes!" Piers hissed. "He's a famous captain. Two years ago, he managed to cross the Parliamentarian naval blockade and carry Queen Henrietta Maria to Holland."

I put a finger to my lips, and we listened to Mennes's response.

"The king is in need of all possible alliances. We know that you still maintain good relations with Alonso de Cárdenas, the current Spanish ambassador. Don't try to deny it. We need Spain to stand firm in its support of Charles."

"I don't know if he'll do it. Cárdenas is intelligent, a man who defends the interests of his empire."

"You're not saying that Catholic Spain," the other gentleman asked, "is going to support the Puritan troops of Parliament over King Charles, who is married to a Catholic?"

Piers's father once again sounded tranquil. "I think that, for some time now, the diplomats of the Spanish Crown have set aside religious concerns in order to guarantee the territorial integrity of an empire in decline. I'll speak to you in confidence"—he paused emphatically—"Ambassador Cárdenas is not at all sure that the king's cause will prevail. Last year, Charles lost the navy, and a monarch who doesn't own ships can't possibly be king of England. I must tell you that, in fact, I don't have confidence in him, either, much less in his collaborators."

Silence filled the room, and then we heard one of the Royalists leap to his feet.

"Sooner or later, your family must take one side or the other!"

Next, we heard Thomas's rather nervous voice. "Father, you can't support that Puritan riffraff! We must defend the king as men of honor, as gentlemen."

"I see these Royalists have put ideas into your head, son. Our family isn't on the side of either the king or Parliament. Since the times of Queen Elizabeth, the Leighs take care to not be exterminated."

"Then is what they say true?" demanded one of the men. "Are you Catholics?"

"At present," answered Lord Leigh carefully, "no one may belong to any religion other than the one in power."

"So, you're papists! Well, if the Protestants win, you'll suffer more at their hands than you would at the king's."

"I don't believe the king can protect us indefinitely. Even if his wife is Catholic, Charles isn't. He's a religious man, fond of the pomp and splendor of the Catholic Church, but under Anglicanism, the king is answerable to no one, and he likes that even more. Whereas I don't like tyranny."

"So, you side with your daughter and her traitorous fanatic of a husband!"

"No, her marriage is no reflection of my own beliefs."

"No? Wasn't she also educated by the Percys, who are devout Protestants and side with the rebels? Perhaps you, too, are under Lord Ruthven's influence, and that is why you turn your back on our king!"

Piers and I exchanged pained looks, thinking about poor Elizabeth. Since Ann and Margaret's return, we'd had no news of her.

"How dare you! I am under the influence of no one." Lord Leigh's voice had turned glacial. "We cut off relations with my daughter and her husband months ago. All I know is that I want to remain neutral and that I'd better watch my back in case Parliament should triumph one day."

"I can't believe you are sympathetic to the Parliamentary cause!"

"I'm not," Lord Leigh shot back. "But remember that I am a member of the House of Lords."

"Though you haven't participated in recent years because you are under suspicion of being a papist. Just last year around this time, the houses of several Catholic nobles were looted by Protestant hordes."

"I know." Lord Leigh's voice trembled slightly and grew low. Piers leaned closer to the tapestry. "Fortunately, Oak Park has a strategic position. To the east, it's defended by cliffs, and on the north, by thick forests. The only access to the estate is through a narrow road to the west, which leads to the village and is relatively easy to defend."

"That was the case centuries ago. Now, any battalion armed with culverins and muskets could place you in danger."

"Yes, these are troubled times. Any day now, someone could accuse us of being papists."

"Then are you loyal to the king or not?"

"Up to a point," said Lord Leigh. "Though I've tried to stay on the margins, you know my son Thomas is a fervent monarchist. He has represented us well, and his loyalty has never given rise to doubts. Nevertheless, I'm concerned that he may be wasting his time on an adventure that won't lead anywhere and that he has abandoned the traditions of his family."

"Father! That isn't true! I stand by the traditions of my family."

Lord Leigh continued. "It's not your fault, Thomas—you're a child of the times. What I mean is that all you care about are these old-fashioned ideas of noble gentlemen fighting for their king instead of getting involved in the family business, which now weighs heavily on my shoulders."

A tense silence followed. Piers clenched his fists, and I could see how he yearned to go to his father.

On the other side of the tapestry, Lord Leigh went on. "We Leighs have been mariners for centuries. I've always wanted one of my sons to be a sailor. My elder son doesn't care for the sea, nor does it suit him. Piers, my younger son, longs to be a sailor, but with all that has happened, his hopes have been dashed."

"I don't believe they have." It was the voice of Sir John Mennes. "The war has taken a new turn. Just a few weeks ago, we recovered Bristol, the second most important city in the kingdom. And along with the city, we have recovered eight ships, among them the *Fellowship* and the *Hart*. This could mean the beginning of a new Royal Navy. Command of the little fleet has been given to Sir John Penington."

"Good news for the Royalist cause!" Thomas rejoiced.

Sir John Mennes continued. "I know John Burley well; Penington has given him command of the *Fellowship*. A good vessel. Yes, twenty-eight cannons."

Piers squeezed my arm, hurting me. "The *Fellowship*. I know which one it is! Fourth class."

I gestured for him to be quiet. He kept making excited gestures, but silently now.

"Any man would be lucky to serve on a ship like that," concluded Sir John Mennes. He paused a moment and then said, "If . . . if you could speak about our cause to Don Alonso de Cárdenas—"

"Don Alonso," Lord Leigh interrupted him, "is not convinced that the king is going to win the war, and he doesn't want to fall out with Parliament, but I'll try to do what I can for you."

"In that case, your younger son can join the *Fellowship*."

In the darkness, I imagined I could see Piers's hazel eyes shining with anticipation.

"Yes," Sir John continued, "the *Fellowship* could use a new cadet."

Behind the curtain, Piers jumped up and raised his arms in a gesture of victory, accidentally bumping the tapestry.

There was silence in the room, and we could hear Lord Leigh's loud steps. With one brusque swipe of his hand, he lifted the tapestry and revealed us. He placed his strong hand on Piers's shoulder, but a smile escaped the corners of his lips. Thomas stifled a belly laugh as we were ushered into the room.

The two Royalist nobles looked astonished as Lord Leigh said, "My son and Miss Len are little devils who run around the house to their hearts' content. Piers, in particular, is very interested in politics, and from what I see, they participate in meetings to which they have not been invited. But since we were speaking about him, perhaps it is appropriate for him to tell us what he thinks."

Piers's voice was trembling, but decisive. "I want to be a sailor, Father."

"Although some ships are now in the king's possession, I'm not sure he'll control them for very long," Lord Leigh said.

Sir John Mennes protested, but Lord Leigh ignored him and continued. "If that ship were to fall into Parliament's hands, you might find yourself in the command of someone who would like to assassinate your family or take us to prison."

"I want to be a sailor," Piers repeated. "But I'll never be on the opposite side of the Leighs. I'll always defend you."

Lord Leigh nodded pensively. "Good, good. That's how it shall be. My son Thomas joined Prince Rupert's Cavaliers, and now Piers, barely fifteen, will be on a ship. I'll have one son in the army and the other in the navy. The king will be saved, thanks to my sons."

His words made light of the situation, but beneath them throbbed the pain of having to part with his beloved children.

Then he turned to Piers. Though there were others in the room, he spoke to him as if they were alone. "Swear to me, son, that no matter what happens, you will not make war on the faith of your ancestors."

"Father, I swear it."

"Swear to me that you will always, no matter what happens, behave like a man of honor."

"Father, I swear it."

"Swear to me that you will never use violence to get rich."

"I swear it."

Despite his habitual impassivity and serenity, Lord Leigh was visibly moved by his son's childish voice. To conceal it, he ordered, "It's time you returned to your chambers."

I gave a little curtsy. Piers bowed his head and clicked his heels together in a military salute to Sir John Mennes. Then we left the East Room. He was skipping; I was crestfallen.

"I'm going off to the navy. I'm going off to sea!"

I said nothing.

"Aren't you glad for me? I'll return, you know."

"Maybe I'll disguise myself as a man and go with you."

"Are you crazy? You can't do that!"

He took me by the shoulders and kissed me on the forehead. "I promise you, when I'm captain, we'll embark on the same ship one day, and we'll sail around the world."

"My grandfather was a sailor," I said.

"And what difference does that make? A woman can't be in the navy."

He escorted me to my room and assured me again that we'd be reunited. But I felt weighed down by a great anguish. I didn't want Piers to go away; he was my best friend, my brother, my playmate, and my soul mate. Together, we had discovered the secret of Oak Park on nights when the moon was full. Anyway, I, too, loved that sea below the cliffs.

18

INVINCIBLE

I remember tossing and turning in bed the entire night. I longed with all my might to go away with Piers, to that open sea that lured him so. Finally, I got up. Leaning on the window jamb, I looked through the frosted glass windows. When the morning star appeared on the horizon, lights went on in the kitchens. I thought that Matt must be working; maybe I could go down and ask him for a freshly baked bun. I often went to sit next to him while he made short-crust pastry or painted the biscuits with egg. He always listened when I felt sad or worried about something, and he laughed when I told him about the little things that made me happy.

I got dressed, crept down the three floors, and then crossed the hallway leading to the ovens. I followed Matt's voice, listening to him softly singing in Basque. I paused next to the entrance and observed him: the firelight lit up the sailor's weather-beaten face as he loaded more firewood into the oven. He looked older; soon he would need an assistant. On the worktable, there were mounds of dough under their respective cloths and just one sheet of unbaked buns. But it wasn't only hunger that led me there; during the night, it had occurred to me that perhaps he could tell me more about my great-grandfather, the sailor. I needed to find out something about this Admiral Oquendo that would impress Piers.

When he saw me, Matt smiled affectionately, unsurprised. Then I asked him about my great-grandfather. At first, he didn't answer and just sat there, gazing at the glow coming from the oven's metal door. I sat down next to him on a bench. Some time went by. Then he stood, took out a pan of buns, and gave me one with a wink. I tossed the burning bun from one hand to the other. He inserted the other pan, and while they were baking, sat down again and started talking about the past.

"My father met Don Miguel Oquendo, your great-grandfather, on Zurriola Beach, at the base of Mount Ulia. At the time, they were just kids and used to play together like you and young master Piers. At fourteen, they set sail from Pasajes on a ship bound for Seville. Without lineage or fortune, their only hope was the sea. Miguel was the son of a humble man who wove hemp into cords, cables, and rope. They nicknamed him Antón Traxaka. His family lived in a house in the foothills, near Zurriola Beach."

The same house where I lived until I was seven, until my mother and I undertook the long journey south to set sail in the galleon that was supposed to carry us to America.

"Matt, I used to live there, but I can barely remember it. Was it a large, square, stone house with a big shield on the front?"

"Yes. I also visited as a child, and I remember it well. We were hungry in those days, and your family sometimes gave the poor people in the neighborhood hot bread; maybe that's why I became a baker."

"I bet their bread wasn't half as good as yours," I told him.

Matt smiled and ruffled my hair. "From Seville, your great-grandfather Don Miguel and my father set sail for the Indies as cabin boys. Together they crossed the ocean several times on a slave ship that went down the coast of Africa. They were well paid, but were sickened by that cruel business, so they left and enrolled as marine caulkers on a galleon in Spain's Armada."

"I'm glad."

He smiled, happy to be telling me all this, being reminded of his family, of the past.

"Not everything my father and your great-grandfather did was admirable. They got rich selling contraband merchandise and silver. They were denounced to the judges, and my father went to prison. Your great-grandfather, who was savvier, managed to avoid sentencing and invested all the money he'd earned in shipbuilding and exportation. English merchants would come to the port of Pasajes to negotiate with him. He obtained materials manufactured in the British Isles and transported them to the Spanish colonies in the Caribbean, which the English merchants couldn't access. That was around the time his relationship with Oak Park began. One of Don Miguel's business partners was Lord Percival Leigh, Lord Leigh's grandfather. In New Spain and the Caribbean, the colonists would buy everything they were offered at ten or twenty times the going rate, so the fortunes of both Don Miguel and Lord Percival kept growing. Your great-grandfather soon owned several ships that made the Atlantic crossing to the Indies—"

"What's wrong?"

"Nothing, dear. It's simply hard to believe I'm telling this story to—to the great-granddaughter of Don Miguel himself. Life is full of surprises!"

"Yes, Matt. Isn't it curious that both of us, born in Donostía, live here? In the Leighs' house?"

Matt laughed, I think at my ingenuity, but his eyes shone.

"Please do go on with the story of my great-grandfather. Tomorrow I'll tell Piers. Maybe then he'll show me some respect! How did he become an admiral?"

"Don Miguel managed to acquire many ships, a large squadron, and King Philip needed those ships. So, he expropriated them."

"Like the Parliamentarians did to Lord Leigh?"

"Not exactly. Lord Leigh hasn't been paid for his ships, and they look upon him with suspicion. But your great-grandfather, in return for the ships' confiscation, was given an important favor from the king: they named him captain general of the Guipúzcoa Squadron. He became a marine and fought as captain of his own ships."

I couldn't wait to tell Piers. I wasn't just some orphan. I was great-granddaughter of a captain general!

Suddenly Matt sniffed, jumped up, and opened the oven door. He took out the next batch of buns and threw it on the table. "Lucky break they didn't burn," I heard him mutter. "You're getting old, Mateo." He pulled away the cloths covering the mounds of rising dough. He made some cuts on the surface, put two of them on a pole, and lifted them into the oven. Then he came back and sat next to me.

"Where was I? Oh yes. While Don Miguel was thriving, my father died from an illness he caught in prison. My family, ruined, lived in misery and had nothing to eat. To help us, your great-grandfather got me a job as cabin boy on one of his ships, so I could pass money on to my family. I was just a little kid. I'll always be grateful to him for it. Since then, my life was bound to Don Miguel. At the time I set out to sea, his ships had been levied for the Great Armada, which was beginning preparations to attack England."

Matt's life, like Uncle Andrew's, had changed with the Armada. His voice filled with melancholy now. He told me that in Lisbon, as the Armada was about to set out for England, it was hit by an epidemic of typhus. Many people died.

"I remember," Matt told me, "how Don Miguel stayed with the sailors when they were ill. He was a great man! The worst part is that Don Álvaro de Bazán, a seasoned mariner and head of the whole expedition, died. To replace him, Philip II designated the Duque de Medina-Sidonia, who had no sailing experience. To make up for the nobleman's ignorance, your great-grandfather, together with Juan Martínez de Recalde, was named lieutenant."

"My great-grandfather was the second-in-command of the whole Armada?"

"Child! What is this yearning for grandeur?"

My cheeks burned. I was acting like Elizabeth Leigh, who constantly boasted of knowing important people and of belonging to a noble family.

"Matt, it's just that I know so little about the past. My mother died. She never told me of her family and spoke very little about my father."

"Yes, Catalina, I know your mother died."

"And my father is far away, in the Indies. He set sail when I was little."

He put his head down and was silent a moment. Then he said, "The sailors say there are three kinds of human beings: the living, the dead, and those who go to sea. Your father went to sea."

"Will I see him again someday?"

"I don't know." He sighed. "I don't know anything about your father anymore."

Something strange was happening to him. He lifted a hand to his eyes, fell silent for a long time, and got up to check the mounds of dough. He took them out, put some more in the oven, and came back, bringing me another little bun.

I thanked him and asked, "My great-grandfather, did he defeat the English?"

"No. Fortune eluded us from the first, but without Don Miguel, it would have been even worse. He was a natural leader and a good sailor."

Matt paused. Tears shone in his eyes as he remembered so many men who had died, friends he would never see again. Perhaps he was also pained by his permanent exile from the land of his birth.

But he went on. "We left Lisbon far behind schedule and with few provisions. A huge storm scattered the formation and took us to the coasts of Galicia. There we awaited more provisions; a long time passed. There was a moment when it seemed like everything would be suspended and the fleet would return, but direct orders from King Philip forced us to resume the mission. The sailors' morale was low. To raise it, they let us go ashore, not on the Galician coast, where no doubt many would have deserted, but to the island of San Antón, in the bay of La Coruña. There we confessed and received communion. They also gave us a medal. I kept it for many years, and when my son went to sea, I gave it to him for protection."

A son? I looked at Matt with wide eyes.

"I'd rather not think about all we suffered on the journey to England. The English didn't dare attack us directly. I remember how, as we entered the English Channel, I took my turn as lookout on the mainmast of the *Santa Ana*. From up high, I contemplated the more than one hundred twenty ships of the Most Fortunate and Great Armada, as we called it."

He smiled as if he could still see it.

"It was a marvelous vision: a great half-moon several nautical miles in diameter, made up of all sorts of vessels stretched out in perfect formation. The English, intimidated, kept watch from a distance, only attacking the rearguard. It was a hunt, where the bird's feathers were plucked without attacking the bird directly.

"But the Armada advanced very slowly, which led to a great short-age of provisions. The water was unsafe to drink. When we reached Plymouth, where the British fleet had taken refuge, some of the com-manders, among them Don Miguel, wanted to do battle. But we were ordered to continue creeping north in that strange way. We lowly sea-men didn't understand why a fleet as powerful as ours didn't attack once and for all or why we weren't sailing faster. We didn't know at the time that the Armada's objective was not to invade England, but to reach the coast of Flanders to pick up the Tercios or Flemish shock troops and form a bridgehead between the Netherlands and England."

He shook his head. I didn't dare interrupt and just waited for him to go on.

"That was the real plan: to lead the best army in Europe, the undefeated Tercios of Flanders, to Great Britain and thus conquer the country and topple its queen. Throughout the Catholic world, Queen Elizabeth I was considered a beast, a viper for executing her cousin Mary, Queen of Scotland, and for relentlessly persecuting British and Irish Catholics. The plan of the Armada was to destroy Elizabeth I and crown a new king allied with the Hapsburgs and Catholicism. If we had succeeded, everything would have been different in these lands, but nothing was achieved, partly due to the inexperience of Medina-Sidonia and partly due to the bad weather. Or perhaps it was God's will!" He shrugged. "Stalked by the English, we tried to drop anchor at the Isle of Wight, but a coast squadron began shelling us, so we were ordered to continue through the canal, toward Calais. We were told that the Duke of Parma, captain of the Tercios, awaited us.

"But when we reached the coast of Flanders, the duke hadn't managed to assemble his soldiers yet. The situation became untenable. On the one hand, the English were attacking us. On the other hand, the sandy shoals of Flanders could shipwreck the heavy galleons. The Tercios never appeared.

"Morale was very low. We were starving and ill. The beginning of the end came one night when the heavens lit up: the English had launched against us the ships they had emptied of men but filled with fuel and set on fire. The inexperienced Medina-Sidonia gave the order to cut the cables to the anchors and scatter to avoid colliding with the burning ships. How wrong he was! When we tried to regroup later, we had lost the powerful half-moon formation that was our protection.

"Then the battle began, a ferocious and very confusing confrontation. The English did all they could to force our ships against the

Flemish shoals. The wind and the weather got worse, and the English retreated to their ports. Medina-Sidonia made the worst sailing error imaginable: commanding the fleet to enter the tempestuous waters of the North Sea during a storm. It was catastrophic. But I was no longer on the ship."

Then he told me how the *Santa Ana* had been split open by cannon fire and had no choice but to head for the British coast.

"The admiral knew what he was doing when he anchored his galleon in a cove surrounded by dark cliffs. A noble lived there who wouldn't betray us: the great-grandfather of young master Piers. Child, the relationship between Don Miguel and Lord Percival had been more than commercial; they both wanted England to return to the Roman Catholic religion. That's why he helped us."

Matt sighed and exclaimed, "Miss Catalina, I'll always be grateful to your great-grandfather. But now I'm telling you more about my life than your family."

I assured him I wanted to know all about his life and how he had arrived at Oak Park.

"When we dropped anchor in Horsehead Cove, I was badly wounded. One of the enemy's projectiles had hit the foremast, and the wood that flew out embedded itself in my leg; that's why I'm lame. Your great-grandfather took me ashore with him for care. When the galleon had been somewhat repaired, Don Miguel de Oquendo left these coasts and somehow managed to return to Donostía. With him went young master Andrew, the eldest of the Leighs. I stayed here."

He paused a moment, and I saw again how painful it was for him to relive all this.

"Yes, the Leighs took me in. At Oak Park, I was bedridden for many months with a high fever; I was terrified they might have to cut off my leg. I was cared for by my poor Rose, a young kitchen servant who later became my wife."

When he mentioned his now-deceased wife, Matt's eyes filled with tears. With a tenderness surprising in such a large, grim man, he cried, "I loved her so much—and our son was a dear boy! Oh Miss Catalina, you should have met him. But that wasn't to be. It happened right at the entrance to the bay. The northwest wind blew all night. I could hear it from my bed, how it howled! I detest the sound of that wind, up to this day.

"In the morning, we learned that Mr. Leigh's ship, coming on its regular journey from Donostía, with Andrew, the priest, and my son as captain, had crashed on the rocks around Horsehead Cove and sunk. My boy, Jon, managed to save his crew, but there weren't enough lifeboats. The priest told me he had begged Jon to take his place in the boat, but my boy refused; he insisted he would swim to shore. The priest was saved—perhaps God was protecting him—but my son died and left me alone. I wish I had been the one to die!"

Thick tears were now falling down the sailor's face. I heard a noise, and Ethan, one of the kitchen boys, came in to pick up the hot bread for breakfast. Matt spun around and stuck the iron paddle into the oven so Ethan wouldn't see him crying.

I stayed with him a long time, in silence. I felt that my company did him good and his did me good, too. Matt bustled about from place to place, attending to his work, and only when he was more serene did I ask him if he knew anything more about my great-grandfather. He sat down next to me again.

"I learned that the admiral reached Spain in a state of deep despondency; he was incubating the illness that would lead to his death. Typhus again. Don Miguel left a widow and five children, one of them your mother's father, who would go on to become Admiral Don Antonio de Oquendo."

I recalled how proud my mother had been of being his daughter and how hurt by not receiving his blessing for her marriage.

"From here, from the Leighs' house, I have followed as best I can everything that has happened to your family. The Oquendos are now proud people—they would rather not remember that they come from a modest rope maker. That's why they wouldn't forgive your mother for marrying a man with no fortune."

He fell silent, lost in his thoughts. I realized he didn't feel like talking anymore.

When I stood to leave, he looked up and spoke some mysterious words. "Your family, Miss Catalina, are people of the sea. Many years ago, Don Miguel's mother made her living collecting seashells on Zurriola Beach. All her descendants have been sailors. You, too, will be carried far away by the sea."

His eyes shone. I kissed his cheek, and he smiled and withdrew into his thoughts again.

Many years have gone by, and Matt's prophecy has been fulfilled. I've crossed the sea, and here, on these Caribbean coasts, I let my gaze wander over the horizon. Nearby, on the wharf, a galleon rocks on the waters of the Ozama, and far in the distance, the first light of dawn sets the sky and the river aflame.

19

The Meeting with Governor Meneses

Santo Domingo, April 1655

The immense, ever-changing ocean always captivates me. It calms the anguish of a thought, painful and tenacious, forever pounding in the depths of my being: that he, Piers, sank forever to the bottom of this ocean now before me. I'm dirty, stained by sin. Perhaps it's a good thing he's dead and will never know what happened to me on that fateful day. And somehow, I feel the sea that unites us washes away my filth.

I hear Josefina's voice encouraging me to get dressed. The governor has invited my uncle and some high-ranking officials, along with their wives, to dinner. I must accompany them, though I'd rather be alone.

When we arrive at the palace of Diego Columbus, we are led to a dining room with a row of balconies and a long table adorned with tropical fruits and flowers. I sit silently next to Don Juan Francisco. They serve us a typical dish, *sancocho*—beef, pork, and chicken stew—but I'm incapable of swallowing the meat and, with a spoon, drink some of the broth. Every now and then, I catch snippets of conversation. Farther off, coming from the esplanade in front of the palace, I can hear shouts, music, and dances. The city is celebrating the arrival of the Indies fleet. There is a market on the plaza, filled with goods from the ships.

After dinner, the ladies sit down in low chairs that let them spread their ample skirts. They fan themselves and talk about the fashions in the Madrid court and the news from overseas. The friendly Dávila sisters haven't come, and it frightens me to speak with strangers. I hang back, observing. They think I can't hear or understand their comments: "The niece of Don Juan Francisco de Montemayor, she's mad or possessed."

I cross the room to where my uncle sits, placing my chair discreetly next to the wall. I know it's not proper—ladies should respect the men's after-dinner conversation. He observes me out of the corner of his eye and goes on telling the governor about the conquest of Tortuga, which was recuperated for the Crown a little over a year ago. Don Bernardino listens attentively as he swirls his glass of imported wine. When my uncle finishes, the governor congratulates him for expelling buccaneers and pirates from the little island.

"None too soon. Though a great danger hangs over Hispaniola. That's the reason His Majesty King Philip has sent me with reinforcements."

"News about that has reached me, yes, but fortunately England hasn't declared war."

"We must be prepared. The English will attack soon, with or without a declaration."

"To attack without a declaration of war is a despicable act!"

"This war won't be a question of honor, but of pecuniary interests. The English desire commerce with the Indies and to curb the great fortune that reaches Spain on the galleons."

My uncle responds thoughtfully. "I did not expect England to recuperate so swiftly from its civil war." He pauses and looks over to where I am sitting. "My niece came from there."

Meneses looks at me with pity. He may have already heard the story of Montemayor's young relative, a poor, mad girl who came from the British Isles, where she was tortured. Then, he goes on talking about the approaching enemy.

"Fortune is on the side of the English. They have not only recovered from the revolution that executed the king but also have emerged stronger. Now they possess a disciplined army and a powerful navy. Moreover, the country is led by a strong man, Oliver Cromwell, who rejected the crown but was named Lord Protector of the Commonwealth."

When he says the name *Cromwell*, I jump, and my face shows my anguish. My uncle notices, but pretends not to.

"What is this Cromwell like?"

"He feels called by the Almighty to force Protestantism on the whole planet. Now that his war has ended, Cromwell wishes to keep fighting, so he is going up against the kingdoms of his Holy Catholic Majesty, King Philip IV. He will try to stop the flow of gold from America—and lay his hands on that gold if he can. They will start here." Governor Meneses takes a sip of his wine.

My uncle nods. "By way of my niece, I received letters from the ambassador in London, Don Alonso de Cárdenas, warning of a possible English attack—that's why we took Tortuga. The English are wrong if they think they can conquer Hispaniola without a rearguard on Tortuga."

"But how long will we be able to keep our forces on the island?"

"I don't know."

"If the English attack," the governor insists, "we would do well to concentrate our forces in the capital and not disperse."

"Do you know how many ships Cromwell has sent?" Don Juan Francisco asks.

"Don Juan de Morfa knows a spy who has informed him that, on the islands of Barbados, nearly sixty ships, carrying about eighty thousand men, have dropped anchor. The ships are captained by Sir William Penn."

Somehow that name, William Penn, sounds familiar. I suddenly remember that Piers had talked about him.

My uncle turns pale and exclaims, "A great navy!"

"That's why we need to concentrate our forces in Santo Domingo and leave Tortuga to its fate for the moment."

"You aren't familiar yet with the Caribbean and its pirates," my uncle says bitterly. "They are waiting for us to leave some point unprotected in order to occupy it. If we abandon Tortuga, it will become a pirates' nest again. You can't imagine how hard it was to conquer!"

"What is coming now cannot be compared to a few pirates who go about looting stray ships," the governor insists. "The largest fleet ever seen in these waters will soon be arriving. Cromwell wants our island for his base of operations. As I've told you, this information reached us through Morfa—a trusted spy, an Irishman. Perhaps we should authorize him to act as a privateer for the Spanish Crown."

My uncle tries to contain himself, out of respect for his superior, but finally he explodes. "It is an error to cast our lot with privateers! As you know, Don Juan de Bitrián y Viamonte, your predecessor, authorized Don Rodrigo Pimentel, and that corrupt man took control of everything arriving in Hispaniola. The privateers claim to be acting on behalf of one nation or the other during times of war, but in fact they protect nothing except their own interests, just like any other pirates."

"They're not all like that. You yourself authorized Don Juan de Morfa to intervene in the conquest of Tortuga. We need these men who know the sea. It is being done in New Spain and also in the New Kingdom of Granada."

My uncle shakes his head with disgust. "I don't like Morfa," he replies, "nor do I think it honorable to deal with a pirate. I had no choice but to allow him to help with the conquest of Tortuga, but now he is no longer necessary. Neither Morfa nor those of his ilk."

The judge doesn't like having to talk about the pirates. He thinks it is contrary to the laws of God and those of war to support maritime thieves who have done so much damage in the Caribbean.

"My dear count," he insists, "you should place more faith in your servant; I have worked hard to achieve security on the island. The English and French pirates have devastated our coasts. Those cruel assassins don't respect any treaties." He tilts his head in my direction. "When she was a little girl, a pirate ship attacked the galleon that was bringing her here with her mother. She doesn't talk about it, and Ambassador Cárdenas only wrote that she suffered many humiliations in the English lands. The poor creature has nearly lost her mind. No, we must have no dealings with privateers or pirates. We should defend Tortuga with the means at our disposal: the Creoles, the slaves, and the *vaqueros* or cattle hunters, who make their living selling meat to the non-Spanish settlers. All these people are honorable. I will have nothing to do with pirates, whether they are called that or privateers!"

"You should trust the man I've spoken to you about," Governor Meneses says, remaining composed. "He is a nobleman who hates Cromwell. Apparently, they killed his family, and he took refuge in Barbados. There, he acts as a double agent."

My uncle is growing more furious. "A man without honor—"

"He may be a privateer, but his interests are contrary to the English lord protector."

"What has he revealed to you?"

"The English squadron in Barbados has joined with the pirates expelled from Tortuga. Thanks to Morfa, we know that Penn and Venables, the two men in command, are constantly quarreling. That disunity could favor us. What protection do we have from Barbados?"

"None. On the leeward islands, there is no Spanish garrison. It's impossible to control all the islands in the Caribbean," my uncle laments. "There, the English and French repair their ships and refill their holds with water. If what you tell me is true, we'll have them here in a couple of weeks at the most."

"Then we are in great danger."

"Damned Englishmen!" exclaims my uncle. "Will they ever leave us in peace?"

He observes me with an indecipherable expression, and I look down again. Over on the far side of the room, one of the ladies is playing a sweet melody on the clavichord.

"Why are you so against the pirates?" Don Bernardino de Meneses asks him.

"British and Dutch pirates have destroyed the peace of the Caribbean. They are mercenaries, thieves. We Spaniards have always rejected them as a matter of honor. And for me, honor is everything. With pirates, we won't know where we stand."

"Your reputation as an honest man precedes you; when I received this posting, they spoke of your great virtue. They even told me that you haven't married so that no one can pressure you—"

"That's what everyone should do, what the ordinances decree! Anyway, my duty is to the daughter of my brother Pedro."

Don Bernardino observes me carefully. Then he leans close to Don Juan Francisco, trying to keep me from hearing his words. "She's very beautiful. What are the details of what happened to her?"

"I'll tell you her story, and you will understand why I have such disgust for privateers and pirates." My uncle doesn't whisper or lower his voice; he wants me to hear the story he is about to tell. "But I'll have to go back many years.

"My father married twice. My brother Pedro, who was fourteen years older than me, is the child of his first wife, who soon passed. Years later, he married my mother, and I was born, and then, my brother Ambrosio. When our father died, Pedro looked after us the best he could. He dedicated himself to a military career and, with his meager salary, paid for me to study law at the University of Zaragoza. He was tall, dark, and strong. Affectionate, quick to laugh, and courageous.

"He hardly spoke about his life, until the day he came to say goodbye to me. Sometime before, without our knowledge, he had requested a posting in the Indies, and it had finally been granted, at the garrison of Santo Domingo. But that wasn't the only surprise. He was leaving behind a wife and a little girl, who would join him as soon as they could. Then he told me how he had met Doña Isabel de Oquendo."

My uncle glances at me anxiously. I'm hanging on his every word.

"Pedro's first posting," he goes on, "was at the garrison on Mount Urgull, in San Sebastián. He was just sixteen, and the man who would later become Admiral Don Antonio de Oquendo was imprisoned in the monastery of San Telmo, very nearby, for challenging royal authority. Don Antonio was allowed to make periodic visits home and to review his ships. Pedro was one of the soldiers assigned to escort him there and back.

"My brother fell madly in love with Don Antonio's beautiful daughter, and he thought she loved him, too. But he didn't dare confess his love, let alone ask for her hand. Both were too young, Pedro a soldier without fortune and Isabel the eldest daughter of the very wealthy Oquendo. Another military posting separated them shortly afterward. But as the years went by, he couldn't forget her. So, during a leave, he returned to San Sebastián. He declared his love, but she said she could not marry him.

"Wounded and desperate, he requested a posting in the Indies, where he might prosper and, if fortune smiled on him, acquire enough wealth to win Isabel's hand. The months went by, a year, two—you know what bureaucracy is like—before they granted him the posting. Before leaving, Pedro went to say farewell to the woman he loved. Isabel, older now, had worked up the courage to defy her family, and they married.

"After the day he told me all this, I lost touch with my older brother. I finished my legal studies, carried out various missions in different places, and finally managed to secure a post in Santo Domingo as a judge. When I arrived, Pedro had contracted malaria and was very ill. He told me he had arrived on the island full of hope, seeking a better future for his family. It took years, but the moment he had earned enough money for their crossing, he had sent for his Isabel and Catalina. The two set sail from Seville, but the fleet arrived without their galleon. Finally, rumors reached him that English pirates had placed the passengers from that galleon in lifeboats, and they had sunk into the sea. He thought he had lost them forever. But later, my brother received a letter from London. Isabel and the girl were being held hostage. It took him a long time to collect the enormous ransom their captors were asking, and he sent it, but heard nothing further.

"On his deathbed, he made me solemnly swear to find out what had happened and take care of them both if they were alive. I always wondered what Isabel must be like for Pedro to love her so much.

"After his death, I worked ceaselessly to fulfill my promise. Thanks to the Dávilas' contacts, I was able to reach Ambassador Alonso de Cárdenas. He informed me that after Isabel died, Catalina was raised by another family. Later, when she was in a women's prison, I sent sufficient funds to rescue my niece and pay for her passage, first to Spain and then here. Finally, about two years ago, she arrived in Santo Domingo." My uncle pauses and takes a sip of water.

Governor Meneses is about to say something, but my uncle stops him by raising his hand. "My niece, though she now seems to be recovering, has spent all this time undone by melancholy. She has suffered so much that she barely speaks. Though I don't know exactly what happened to her, it must have been very painful.

"The origin of her ills is those privateers who took her prisoner. Without that wicked act, perhaps Isabel would still be alive, and my brother wouldn't have suffered a profound grief that hastened his death. Now do you understand? Pirates and privateers are traffickers in human lives, men without conscience or honor. I hope someday Catalina will get better and be able to tell me everything that happened. In the meantime, I am devoted to her and to my profession as a jurist."

When Don Juan Francisco finishes talking at last, I realize that Don Bernardino de Meneses is at a loss. He doesn't want to get involved in such an accumulation of calamities, nor is he capable of offering any consolation to my uncle or to me. The governor is simply a politician who wants to get ahead, a man with a concrete mission: to defend Hispaniola against the British. His career as a bureaucrat will depend on the successful outcome of that mission. He doesn't share my uncle's prejudices about privateers; he just wants to do a good job for the court in Madrid.

And so, showing off his diplomatic arts, he praises my uncle. "You truly are a man of honor, and your niece is a fortunate young woman to have you by her side. I hope that one day her health will improve."

After chatting awhile longer, he gets up and embraces my uncle emphatically. Then he walks over to other men, converses briefly, and finally leaves the room. I stay with Don Juan Francisco, observing him silently. In his expression, I detect uneasiness and the affection he has come to have for me over the past two years. He is an honest man, bound by his obligations and by the oath he made to my father. Though initially he didn't know how to behave with a sick young woman, he now treats me with increasing tenderness.

My uncle doesn't move or say anything to me. He doesn't know where to begin. Remembering my parents' story has moved him, though I sense there is something more that he doesn't want to tell. In me, the painful story has unleashed a hurricane of memories: of the father I never knew, of the mother I adored, of those times at Mount Ulia that I barely remember, and of our departure from Seville. But my uncle knows nothing about what happened afterward: Moorfields and my mother's suffering there. He knows nothing about the terrible night in the Norman Tower or about what really happened in Bridewell. And he'll never know why I feel guilty about the past.

20

THE MEDALLION

When the reception is over, we walk home. Once again, I am lost, tortured by confusion and remorse.

I hear Don Juan Francisco murmuring, "Catalina, I've told this story to get some reaction from you, but it's as if you don't hear."

I don't answer, but I've heard everything.

Josefina is waiting for me in the doorway. Together we cross the patio, and she helps me up to my bedroom. I sit down on the bed, and perceptive Josefina, seeing how upset I am, is moved to embrace me.

She helps me undress and lays me down, gently pulling the covers over me. Then she sits down beside me and sings a lilting song from her homeland. Tears flow softly down my cheeks for a long time. It seems like something is beginning to break open inside me. I feel responsible for everything that has happened: the fire that ravaged the Leigh home, the deaths. Josefina stops singing in her language. Her words are clear and firm.

"Señorita Catalina, you haven't done anything wrong. Others have made you suffer, and you have lost what you loved. Forgive yourself. Forgive those who did you such harm. Forgive and you may find peace."

Then I think that, rather than a healer, she must be a witch who has divined what torments me. To forgive would be liberation from the horror of the past and from the anguish that stalks me at night. But I'm incapable of forgiving, especially myself. I can't forgive my cowardice, the cowardice that led to the death of someone I loved and to whom I owed my life.

I rise at dawn, distressed. The house is nearly silent; only a servant is sweeping the patio with a long broom made of twigs, making a monotonous and persistent noise. The fresh morning breeze clears my head somewhat. Crossing the patio, I reach the back of the house, the wall, and from there I can see a fine red line extending along the horizon. The line expands for a long time, until an intense red sun appears. Day breaks. I sit down on the wall with my legs hanging over it and lean my hands on the parapet.

I look down at the water and think if I jump, I'll stop suffering. I can't survive such guilt. Through my negligence, Andrew Leigh died in the most horrible way imaginable. I can't go on. One second, just a second, and I'll jump into the infinite blackness. Everything will end, the remorse and my torture.

I stand up to jump into the river, but then I spot small sailboats entering the estuary. The galleon that brought the governor a few days ago is rocking in the current. The sun's light fills everything. The stunning vision subdues me, and for an instant, I stop thinking of anything at all. Time goes by, I can't say how long, while I gaze at the sea's iridescence; it looks like a diamond made of light.

I hear a drumbeat sounding an alarm coming from the west side of the coast, perhaps the fort. I nervously scan the horizon and make out some points on the surface of the sea that grow larger until they are huge sails, a multitude of ships, most of them deep-water vessels.

Before long, Josefina comes running to find me.

"Doña Catalina! You must come with me. It is the English, come to invade like in the times of the pirate Drake!"

She tries to drag me away, but I resist. In front of me, near the horizon, are men who share a language with me, who perhaps fought alongside Piers, who perhaps attacked Oak Park.

I don't know why, but instead of distressing me, that vision of war gives me new strength. I can't go on this way, constantly feeling sorry for myself. An idea helps me: Piers wouldn't want to see me like this. One day, long ago, he told me that everything is possible for he who wants. I want—what do I want? I don't know, but an attack is imminent, and I must help. Somehow, I must defend the people of this island, as I was unable to defend Oak Park.

Finally, Josefina pulls me back to the house. She prepares a gourd of hot chocolate for me, saying it will cheer me up. She points to a rocking chair, where she has left some old cotton sheets. She says we must turn them into bandages, that there will soon be wounded men. I sit down and start ripping the cloth into strips. Soon, a servant comes to say Josefina is needed at the Hospital of San Nicolás de Bari.

She leaves me making strips of cloth. The task absorbs me for hours, but by midafternoon, having not slept the night before, I'm overtaken by drowsiness.

When I wake up, it's almost night, and Josefina has returned. She smiles. She slides into my hands a dark-colored package with my name written on it—Catalina de Montemayor y Oquendo—in letters so worn they are difficult to read, yet very familiar.

I rip it open and let out a scream as the contents fall into my palm. A tin medallion with the Virgin and Christ. I turn it over and over. Then I lift my head and look into Josefina's sparkling eyes.

"One of the sick men in the Hospital of San Nicolás. He arrived about two days ago, burning with fever, very weak. When they removed his clothes, they found this package for you."

"I want to see him!"

"There's a curfew. They won't let anyone go out."

"I don't care. I have to see him!"

There is a knock at the door. Startled, I close my fist. An unexpected shame fills me. I don't want anyone to know about my past, and this medallion is the link to that past. I rush over to the small dresser. I find a leather cord and string it through the medallion. I kiss it, tie the cord, and hang it around my neck. Then I drop it into my neckline.

When I turn around, Josefina has left, and someone else is entering the room.

21

THE ENEMY

It's Vicente Garcés; he's come to say my uncle wants to see me. Now that the medallion is hanging once more over my heart, life seems to return to my being. I want to speak with Josefina, but she has left. The good butler assures me she will return tomorrow.

He takes me to the small office crammed with scrolls and sheaves of paper, where my dear uncle writes the court reports he must send periodically to the Council of the Indies.

His face looks extremely thin; his cheekbones are visible under his skin; the aquiline nose is more pronounced than ever. I see that tension and fatigue have taken a toll on him.

"Catalina," he begins, "you're all I have left of my brother, who I owe so much. And since you arrived on the island, I've grown very fond of you. As you may know, the English, those heretics who tortured you, are now attacking. If you wish, I can send you far away from here. To Higüey or some inland town, far from the invasion. I shouldn't do it because tomorrow"—he mutters almost to himself—"I'll ask that women not leave the city. I shouldn't be unjust, yet—"

I can feel my mother's medallion on my chest. Someone is sending me a sign, someone I love more than anything in the world. Someone who might be nearby. I cannot leave Santo Domingo now.

"No, dear uncle," I tell him bravely. "I want to be with you. I beg you to let me stay here in the capital."

He is shocked by my words, my vehemence. Up to that moment, I had been a passive creature, a shadow.

"All right, Catalina. I'm so pleased to hear you speaking."

"And I—I can help. Another time—another time, I did!"

I see that he is even more astonished to hear me speak of the past.

"Well, the enemy won't go ashore for a few days yet. But if I later see that it would be best for you to leave the city, you can be sure that I will get you out."

Then he starts pacing, as if wondering what to do, how to prevent the coming war from harming a mind finally beginning to heal.

He stops and meets my gaze. "Catalina, for me you are like a daughter I didn't see growing up. Since you arrived, I haven't spent enough time with you. I haven't known how to care for you as I should, and someday I'll have to answer for it to God. I swore to my brother Pedro that I would take care of what he loved most in the world. But my hours are scarce, I'm overwhelmed with work, and there are enemies who seek my ruin."

I don't know how to answer, but I don't think he expects a response. He simply needs to unburden himself.

"For many years now, I have served as judge here. My profession is the law. The laws of the Indies were made to protect all His Majesty's vassals from injustice. Sometimes they are obeyed and sometimes they aren't; it all depends on the honesty of the judges. I'd like to be just because I'll answer to the Almighty for my actions. I have never circumvented the laws of God or man!"

In his eyes I see the zealous servant of very lofty ideals.

Suddenly, he seems to remember where he is.

"You must be tired, dear. It's been a long day. I have to return to the court—there's much to do. But you rest now. I'll be home later."

He walks over and kisses my forehead. Then he dons his cape and hat and leaves. I'm left alone in the office full of files. I dance up the stairs, euphoric; I could fly. For tomorrow, tomorrow I'll go to the Hospital of San Nicolás, with or without Josefina.

22

THE HOSPITAL OF SAN NICOLÁS

The next morning, Josefina arrives. I'm still wearing my nightgown, so she helps me to get dressed. I try to get her to tell me who had the medallion, but she doesn't respond. I tell her I want to see him, that I must see him. This time she agrees, but asks me not to mention anything to Don Juan Francisco. She explains that we have to go cautiously. Due to the anticipated English attack, women not only are prohibited from leaving the city but also cannot go out into the streets.

We make our way through the orchards along the Ozama, near the wall, up to the place where the houses end. There we go down a small, little-used road. There is no one around; the men have all gone to the forts along the coast. We proceed a ways down Calle de las Damas, then turn right onto Calle del Conde, and reach Plaza Colón.

In the plaza, the stray dogs don't bark. They wander around, hungry, from shop to shop, hoping to find some scraps. On one of the corners, a blind man with a wounded leg is begging. The remains of the fruit stands exhale an acrid smell. The market has packed up, and the plaza is empty. After one more block, we find the street that leads to a stone-and-brick building: the Hospital of San Nicolás de Bari.

A mulatto friar dressed in a Franciscan habit sweeps the patio deliberately.

"Is Brother Alonso in?" Josefina asks.

The friar looks up. When he sees the healer accompanied by a young lady, he says, "I'll go get him."

He drops the broom and runs inside. Another, older friar, with a round, smiling face, emerges and greets Josefina cheerfully. I can tell they know each other well, and he's happy to see her.

"Good morning!" he booms. "I am Brother Alonso. And you're Don Juan Francisco de Montemayor's niece, who arrived here two years ago and never goes outside. My daughter, how are you?"

I answer timidly, "Fine." We go through the main doorway, and I observe the interior with apprehension; the ceiling is very dark, marked by smoke.

"The building was looted and burned during the invasion by the pirate Drake," the friar explains. "He destroyed the hospital archives and stole many jewels and goods from the adjacent church."

Josefina speaks to him in a whisper I can't hear. He nods.

"Come in, my lady. Perhaps your suffering will be eased when you contemplate that of others."

We follow him through the cloister until we reach a large, dim room with a long row of beds. I stop short in the doorway; the smell is nauseating.

While I remain in the doorway, covering my nose with the back of my hand, they both go inside, and I see them stopping before a rickety bed where a man lies, moaning. The friar tells Josefina he doesn't know what to do for the young man.

As Josefina leans over the sick man, Brother Alonso moves down the line. He stoops down to inquire about one sick person after another. He cleans their wounds. He caresses them. His dark clothes disappear into the darkness at the back of the room.

Josefina stands up. She waves me over. I take a few steps, as if hypnotized. Perhaps, amid all those sick people, I might find Piers. Maybe he hasn't died! But to find him only to lose him again—the pain is beyond contemplation.

The slave healer caresses that young man, then helps him drink a dark liquid. Once I've made my way over, she turns, and in a soft voice tells me that he has *fiebres tercianas*, malaria.

"It's called *fiebres tercianas* because the fever comes every three days. He has been delirious for two days. It's possible that tomorrow he will return to his senses and be able to speak rationally again."

I kneel down beside him. He's a young man with clever, olive-green eyes; his face shines red with fever. It isn't Piers. I feel disillusioned and at the same time relieved that he isn't before me, dying.

"Yesterday, Brother Alonso took off this man's clothing to wash it and found the little packet with your name on it."

I gently take his hand and sit down on the mattress. Josefina comes back with fresh water and a cloth. She indicates to me that I should cool his forehead. Then she goes off to attend to a sick man who is complaining, shouting curses and filthy words.

Suddenly, the man I am looking after fixes his eyes on me. "Inés?"

I look behind me, but there is no one there. He repeats that name again, and I realize he has taken me for someone else.

Then he smiles and says, "I've come back."

He falls unconscious again, agitated and murmuring. Every now and then, he calls, "Inés! Inés!" At one point, he sits up on the mattress and exclaims, "No! Don't you touch her. Don't hurt my Inés!"

Josefina is by my side. I look up and ask her, "Who is he talking about?"

"Doña Inés de Ledesma."

I look at her inquisitively.

"This is Captain Rojas, who led the mission to Tortuga. We thought he had died, that Don Rodrigo Pimentel had murdered him. Listen, my girl," she says conspiratorially, "this has to be a secret between you and me."

"Shouldn't we tell my uncle?"

"No, not until the captain can explain himself. In this city, there are many ways to kill: a pillow in the night, a dagger, and"—she lowers her voice—"there's voodoo."

I shudder.

"It's not a good idea to let it be known that a man with so many enemies is alive and defenseless. Do you understand?"

I look at the sick man, scrutinizing his straight nose and honest face.

"We'll see that he recuperates, and then, when he's able to speak, we'll bring your uncle. For now, we should go to Las Claras, to see Doña Inés de Ledesma and explain to her that Don Gabriel de Rojas is alive."

I gesture toward our grim surroundings. "Will he be all right here? Couldn't we move him somewhere else?"

"I don't think anyone would recognize the elegant Captain Rojas in this state. But I'll ask them to move him to one of the monks' cells, where he will be safer and more comfortable and where no one can hear the words he is pronouncing in his delirium."

"Will he get better?"

"I don't know, but when this bout of fever has passed, he'll recuperate his reason and speak."

I long for him to get better so I can find out how the medallion from my mother that I gave to Piers has arrived on Hispaniola.

23

OAK PARK WITHOUT PIERS

Santo Domingo, April 1655
Oak Park, Summer of 1643

On our way back from the Hospital of San Nicolás, we pass in front of the doors to the Audiencia. Josefina asks for my uncle, to find out if he is coming home for lunch, but he doesn't come out. He sends us a message that he will eat there because he is very busy. On our way home, an official stops us and insists we can't walk down the street because women must be kept at home in light of the coming attack. Josefina tells him that I am the principal judge's niece, and I'm looking for my uncle. He shrugs and leaves us be.

When we get home, Josefina insists that I eat lunch. She sits by my side, on a low stool, and observes me with her arms crossed over her ample chest. She is nervous, continually shaking one foot.

"What will the friars do with the patients," she frets, "now that the foreigners are attacking us?"

Josefina's question brings to mind the suffering we have seen. The man carrying the packet might die before I can find out how he came to possess it. This tin medallion has changed everything, and a delirious hope fills my heart. If Piers is alive, then not everything in my past is gone. And if my past hasn't died, then I am alive, and, above all things, I want to live.

I want to do something—return to San Nicolás, go to Las Claras, or even see the Dávilas. But Josefina insists that I rest during the siesta. She shuts the bedroom windows partway and leaves me lying on the bed. Now more than ever, I remember Piers. The medallion has brought him back to me.

A few days after the conversation in the East Room, Piers boarded a small ship headed for Bristol, where the king's incipient navy was being assembled. From there, he would set sail on the *Fellowship*, the vessel commanded by the Royalist captain, Burley. We all accompanied him as far as the cliffs, then waited there until the tide had risen.

At one point, Lord Leigh and his son stepped away from the rest of us. I couldn't hear his words, but he spoke very seriously to Piers, as if imparting advice that was vital for Piers and the whole family. I felt a weight in my chest.

Finally, the horsehead rock was submerged, and from the wharf, a sailor shouted that everything was ready. Piers embraced his mother and his sisters. It seemed as if Lady Leigh wasn't going to let go of her younger son, but after a few long minutes, he pulled away from her, knelt, and kissed her hand. Then he kissed his sisters on the cheek. When he reached me, his eyes were shining, and mine were filled with tears. He caressed my wet cheek and said, "Don't cry. Soon you'll be grown, and you'll sail away with me." I smiled through my tears, and he left. I watched him skip down the path, alongside Captain Mennes.

From the cliff, we watched Piers setting sail at Mennes's orders, just like any other sailor, and the little tender headed toward the open sea. When it disappeared into the horizon, I started sobbing inconsolably. For me, Piers Leigh was everything. Lady Leigh hugged me against her, and I rested my head on her chest. Then I looked up into her lovely face; her eyes were damp from watching her younger son go away. He was fifteen years old, but still a child to her.

Over the following weeks, we had no news of him. I imagined he was blissfully learning the ancient art of navigation, that he would feel comfortable in that atmosphere he had always longed for. I thought he wouldn't think of me as often as I did him. In each of these suppositions, I was partly wrong and party right.

Two months later, by way of the *Mercurius Britannicus*, we learned that the *Fellowship* had fallen into the hands of Parliament. Lord Leigh's predictions had come true: Piers was now on the opposite side of the Leigh family.

Meanwhile, a new era had begun for me: the era of Oak Park without Piers. I grew closer to Margaret and Ann. I grew up alongside them while the civil war was playing out far away. The Leigh girls were now young ladies who kept their mother company and had few responsibilities, but also few distractions, apart from horseback riding, playing music, reading, and embroidering. They only shared with me an occasional drawing or music class. I continued with Mademoiselle Maynard, who demanded I apply myself to the study of languages, mathematics, and history.

Even so, the governess was less rigid than before, seemingly because of the mysterious letters she kept receiving. She softened if the mail brought her a letter, but when they were delayed, she took out her frustrations on me. Just like when I first arrived at Oak Park, she would accuse me of being a stranger, a papist foreigner, taken in out of charity by the Leighs and destined for the fires of hell. Her words wounded and frightened me, and now I didn't have Piers to reassure me that they didn't matter.

His absence made everything seem grayer and colder. Also, that fall, the snow came earlier than ever. When Christmas approached, the Parliamentary government railed against it, saying gaiety was heinous, an excuse for sinning and straying from the pure faith.

And so, we didn't celebrate at Oak Park. In the days leading up to Christmas, there was no commotion in the kitchen, no gifts or decorations, no laughter or cries of pleasure. All of that was now dangerous, all the more so for a family suspected of papism.

We attended services at Walton-on-the-Naze out of obligation. I remember the pastor repeating the then-popular claim that worse acts of evil were committed at Christmastime than the rest of the year. The licentiousness of Christmas incited robbery, fornication, and murder. The celebrations led to God's dishonor and the impoverishment of the state; they were nothing but the remnants of ancient pagan feasts.

Hearing him, Ann, Margaret, and I exchanged discreet glances. We smiled mockingly, and Margaret muttered, "So many sins!"

Mademoiselle Maynard looked offended by the comment. Ann gently nudged her sister to be quiet. The parishioners observed us warily.

When we left, the temperature had risen a bit, so we asked Lady Leigh to let us walk home while she and the governess returned in the carriage. Lady Leigh asked us not to take too long. Rumor had it that, in London, Royalist-leaning young apprentices would attack stores that Parliament had ordered to stay open during the holiday. Christmas had always been a day off, and many of those young artisans took issue with rigid Puritan ideas.

As we crossed the streets of Walton, we verified that the stores were indeed still open. There were no revolts there, but when we went into a bakery, the clerks addressed us rudely.

We hurried back to Oak Park and ate supper in near silence. Every male member of the family was far away: the boys were at war, and Lord Leigh was trying to keep his business afloat. As Parliament had confiscated the ships with the largest tonnage, he was attempting to carry out his trade with sloops and tenders and even fishing boats. It was dangerous, both because of the Parliamentary blockade and because those little vessels were unsafe for this kind of work. Some of them sank, and their cargo was lost. Since the beginning of autumn, he was almost always at sea.

The next morning, Ann and I rode our horses up the cliff, galloping through fields and woods tinged white, along a muddy road with patches of dirty snow. A winter sun peered out with difficulty amid thick clouds.

We scanned the horizon, and Ann bemoaned the fact that, somewhere on those waters, her brother Piers and her father might be right then risking their lives. As for Thomas, we hadn't seen him since that covert visit the previous summer. Ann felt abandoned without the protection of the men in her family. I shyly asked if she had received any news of Piers, and she said that, according to a naval gazette from London, the *Fellowship* had a new captain, a Parliamentarian named William Penn. Her brother must be sailing under the command of that man.

24

YEARS OF SCARCITY

Oak Park, Winter of 1644–Winter of 1646

Over the next two years, my body developed, and my moods were unpredictable and strange. I was constantly clashing with Mademoiselle Maynard. At the time, I was more concerned about her treating me like a child than about her accusing me of being a papist.

The house emptied out. Many of the servants left, signing up on one side or the other of the war. Mr. Reynolds was now fighting in the Royalist army, together with Thomas, his former ward. Several kitchen boys, to Matt's great disgust, joined the Parliamentarians. In Oak Park, the only ones left were the women and the old. Some of those who went away held firm political or religious convictions, but most left in hopes of getting rich in the turbulent river of war.

Thomas, who held an important position in the king's Cavaliers, would show up from time to time. I remember him, galloping with his long hair in the wind, his cape flying at his back, and a dog running between the horse's hooves: an authentic Cavalier in Prince Rupert's cavalry. In the course of war, he and his comrades, who at first were seen as elegant dandies, had made themselves feared by their enemies. Thomas always spoke with the security that came from believing that divine grace was on his side. He considered his adversaries unscrupulous rebels and misguided yokels.

His parents, on the other hand, still hadn't taken sides. They may have sympathized with the convictions of their elder son, but Lord Leigh still didn't trust the Royalists and always doubted that they could win the war. He was a level-headed and pragmatic man, cultured and well informed. Above all, he wanted to guard the family patrimony and preserve his faith.

On Sundays, we would invariably attend religious services in Walton. Lady Leigh had a rather absent air, and I imagine she thought it a betrayal of her true faith, but she had to feign devotion for her own safety. Her husband had been firm on this point: we were in Parliamentary territory and had to behave as loyal subjects, obeying their laws. It was imperative that the Leighs not raise suspicions so that we could keep celebrating the sacred liturgy in the Saxon chapel. Oak Park was the only place in the whole county where the ancient rites were still celebrated. During the war, capital punishment was a greater threat than ever.

With the Parliamentary blockade, access to Horsehead Cove was more difficult. We didn't know which full moon would bring Uncle Andrew or another Jesuit priest defying the danger. When they managed to come, the call of a bird in the forest signaled that there would be a meeting. Hours later, through the fields and groves, the faithful would come from near and far, making their way through tunnels leading to the chapel. I remember the magical atmosphere of those meetings, which were even more fervently anticipated because they were now so rare. The priest's whisper, the altar, the Latin words spoken at the culminating moment, receiving communion in tense silence: every Mass was a surprise and a gift. I've never experienced anything like it.

Now, in the very Catholic city of Santo Domingo, where so many people attend Mass out of habit, where I see the noblewomen showing off their figures on their way to the cathedral, I remember when a death sentence hung over our heads and how much more those same rites meant to us.

If the visiting priest was Uncle Andrew, we all thanked the Lord that he hadn't been arrested yet. He was getting old and gaunt; he walked with a limp, and his movements were clumsy. It was very difficult for him to climb down to the ancient chapel, and I frequently had to guide him. He told me I was his angel.

Meanwhile, the country was becoming more fanatically Puritan and Protestant. The following Christmas was another sad occasion. Lord Leigh had left a month earlier for the continent, food was scarce, and with no strong men in the house, we couldn't gather the enormous tree trunks that usually crackled in the fireplaces. Lady Leigh, the girls, and I took care of all the domestic duties since most of the servants were gone. Mademoiselle Maynard did nothing but protest, considering such tasks beneath a person of her position. Aware of the woman's own religious fervor, Lady Leigh said nothing.

During those days, neither side had a decisive advantage, and it seemed as if the war would never end. But early in the new year, we got word that Parliament had created a new army. It was made up of men of God sworn to defeat those who didn't submit to divine laws, which were dictated, of course, by Parliament. Since it was a professional army, officials were appointed according to military merit and not noble lineage. The New Model Army was commanded by Sir Thomas Fairfax, who had just been designated lord general, with Oliver Cromwell as second-in-command. The Royalists called them Roundheads because they wore their hair short to distinguish themselves from the Cavaliers. Six months later, that well-trained, highly disciplined army defeated the Royalists in the Battle of Naseby, turning the tide for the first time. One thousand Royalist soldiers died and five thousand were taken prisoner. Most alarmingly, some documents belonging to the king fell into the hands of the Parliamentarians. They proved he had forged alliances with the country's enemies in order to hold on to power, and this would later be used to try him as a traitor.

Still, our day-to-day lives at Oak Park continued. A moody adolescent now, I would laugh or cry at the least provocation. That summer, I often went horseback riding, especially with Ann. I remember one day when we were out riding and she told me that, in London, Elizabeth had once introduced her to a young man. As soon as Ruthven found out, he denied the young man admission to the Strand mansion since he didn't think his social connections valuable enough. Ann never saw him again, and in that closed world where we were living, she idealized him. Her romanticism was contagious, and I constantly thought of Piers, seeing him differently than when I was a child.

Margaret laughed at us when she discovered that, if she played certain pieces on the clavichord, Ann and I would sigh longingly.

When I got tired of Ann's melancholy and Margaret's teasing, I would go down to the kitchens and sit near Matt. He had been left in charge of all the kitchens, together with two servants who helped him. I felt safe with the sullen sailor. He represented the past, the link with my homeland, with my great-grandfather the courageous admiral, with my mother's world. He would tell me seafaring stories. Sometimes he would sing and translate the words for me. He would gaze affectionately at me with his dark eyes that sometimes filled with tears.

One day he told me, "As the years go by, you see that stories that began in your youth end in your old age." Caressing my hair, he went on. "It's beautiful and fills you with gratitude."

Then he gave me a freshly baked bun made of dark wheat because of the lack of provisions. I ate it there by his side, in silence, while he kept on with his work. The only sounds were Matt's paddle feeding firewood to the oven and a low conversation taking place by the back door. One of the servants was talking to a man from the village who had brought a few apples that we could use to make preserves.

"Rich, elegant dandies, but they don't know how to fight. I'm telling you, Jane."

"Are you referring to young master Thomas?"

"Yes. Him and others like him. They want to impose their Frenchified tyranny on us, but deep down, they are nothing but papists in disguise."

"I don't know what to tell you, Samuel."

"And that Thomas takes after his mother, who puts on an act at the Sunday services in Walton, but she's an Irish papist! A papist and a witch, as Roberts warned us."

"Lower your voice. They'll hear you! If the master found out—"

"The old man isn't here, and everyone in Walton knows it. He must be off negotiating with the enemies of Parliament and England. Another one who can't be trusted. No doubt that his witch wife has brainwashed him."

Matt turned pale and dropped his paddle. I followed him out, worried about what he was going to do.

"Shut up, you swine, and get out of this house! Never come back!"

The villager sized him up. "Protecting the papist witch because you're one, too, eh?"

Matt didn't respond. He raised his arm and knocked the man to the floor.

When the villager managed to get back to his feet, he said, "I don't want to fight you now, old man, but I swear, someday I'll get even." He left, muttering.

When I was alone again with Matt, I asked, "How can they talk like that about Lady Leigh? She is always so kind, so concerned about everyone."

"People don't care about kindness when they're drunk on zealotry. If they found out what goes on here, they would kill us without a second thought. There are many fanatics in the village, and Roberts spewed his venom to whoever would listen." He shook his head sadly. "The last I heard, he had enlisted in the Roundheads."

"The people of Walton would kill us themselves? They really hate Catholics that much?"

"The country is filled with stories of machinations and plots by the papists. We've been at war for three years now. People are tired and hungry, and the leaders in London need a scapegoat. They even spread lies of a Catholic plot to hoard all the food. There have been lootings in Walton."

"So I've heard."

"The people are desperate. They're secretly hunting deer and wild boars on our lands and stealing firewood. They're becoming bolder and bolder. One of these days, they will attack Oak Park!"

"Won't anyone stop them?"

"We're defenseless. I'm just an old man, and so is Jack, the coachman."

"But Lord Leigh—"

"Who can he hire that he can trust? When he's here, it's different, but he can't neglect his business. And Lady Leigh has never been respected in the village. Danger is stalking the estate: those who now steal game and wood will one day attack the house," he repeated.

25

AFTER THE STUARTS

Oak Park, Spring of 1646

It was still cold and rainy, but green buds had begun to appear when the king abandoned Oxford and headed for exile in Scotland. The war was in its death throes.

That year of the Parliamentarian victory was my year of freedom. We finally found out that Mademoiselle Maynard's mysterious correspondent was a Calvinist pastor. Under the Anglican king, he had been denied a lucrative appointment. But now, his loyalty to Parliament was repaid with a wealthy parish. The pastor needed a wife for his ministry, and he proposed to my detested governess.

The torments of my childhood ended when she left Oak Park, radiant with happiness, in a cart pulled by two old mules. Lady Leigh gave her a trousseau, a cookbook, and equipment for her new home, and her former students finally were left in peace.

On the other hand, hunger began to make itself felt, even at Oak Park. The harvests were poor. There weren't enough hands to pick the scarce produce, and what was picked was confiscated for the New Model Army. Matt was appalled that the great ovens no longer burned, but there wasn't enough fuel or grain to bake bread. The scarcity was even more pronounced because the mysterious cellars of Oak Park now harbored refugee Royalists, many of them wounded. There, they awaited a ship to arrive in Horsehead Cove during the full moon so they could set out for a new life on the continent. They had to be fed and cared for while they were waiting.

It was Lady Leigh who would tend to the wounded, and I would help her. At that time, she was everywhere at once, holding the entire house together. I remember her as a remarkable, courageous, cheerful woman with an incredible strength of character. She came from an Irish family that had suffered great persecution. She was the youngest of nine children, and her father had been executed for being Catholic. The family's possessions had been confiscated and turned over to the very person who denounced them. Lady Leigh's family was poor when Lord Leigh met her, but she retained the elegance of her noble lineage. Where so many ladies would have been helpless, she knew well how to cook porridge to fill our stomachs, waiting for better times.

The months went by, and when the new year began, Charles was turned over to Parliament by the Scottish. An unstable peace was restored. The Presbyterians who now dominated both houses of Parliament proposed to discharge most of the army. This led to rebellions among the soldiers; they wanted to send them home with no more pay than a few dubious bonds.

That's when Piers returned. The boy who had gone off to sea filled with childish dreams was now a tall and muscular man about to turn nineteen. His broad shoulders had filled out, and on his cheeks were the beginnings of a beard. His white skin had been tanned, and his curls had turned to steel wool, bleached by sea salt and the sun and cut short in the shape of a helmet. He dressed in black like the Puritans, with a big white collar, long coat, and wide-brimmed hat. He smelled of the sea.

We stared at each other like strangers. He looked me up and down, then asked his mother, "Len?"

Lady Leigh nodded her head, amused. Then he walked over, put his hands around my waist, and lifted me up like a feather.

"Let me go!" I shouted, laughing.

"Didn't you want to sail?" he joked. "Now you're going to sail very high."

After holding me up in the air a few instants, gazing at me admiringly, he set me softly on the floor. His sisters laughed happily.

Piers was saddened to find Oak Park in such deplorable shape. Still, it was his home, where he felt loved. Also, there was yet some food, and anything was welcomed by the starving young sailor, who devoured whatever was set before him. The sailors in the Royal Navy had undergone many hardships.

"While it might seem that Parliament has emerged victorious," he confessed, "I'm convinced the conflict isn't really over. In the navy, there has been too much hunger. It's been months since the sailors have been paid. Many look to Charles, imprisoned by the Parliamentarians. They think that, while life under the king wasn't so good, under Parliament it's even worse. Anything could spark a revolt and make the navy change sides."

"And you, what will you do if there are revolts?" Ann asked.

"I don't know," Piers answered. "I can't stand the Puritans."

"Then," I said hopefully, "you'll stay here with us?"

"No. I've requested a new posting. It won't take long, I hope. I can't live without the sea, and in a couple of years, I could be a lieutenant!"

We were all happy to have him home. He was a huge help around the house, chopping firewood and carrying out the hardest tasks in the stables and even the blacksmith shop. As always, I followed him like a shadow.

"How did Lord Leigh take it, that you were fighting on the side of the Parliamentarians?"

"I only ran into him once, in Plymouth. He told me the same thing as always, to be faithful to my conscience."

"That's the same thing Uncle Andrew would tell you."

"Have you seen him?"

"Yes."

"On nights with a full moon?"

I laughed. "Yes. On nights with ghosts. Now I'm one of them."

Then it was his turn to laugh.

We resumed many of our customs, taking long walks and reading together. Still, everything was different. He was trying to reclaim his comrade, but I wasn't the same Len as when he left. Sometimes he would joke like in the old days, but other times, he would act bashful and treat me like a lady. I didn't care; I was just happy to be by his side.

We would once again gallop through the meadows. Those days, we took to competing in long races where he would unleash all the fury he carried inside. But after several years at sea, he was no longer the better rider. I beat him much of the time, but it didn't bother him as it once had. He seemed pleased by my progress.

I remember one summer day when the sun beat down, and after a long gallop, we jumped half-dressed into the little lake near the house to cool off. When we climbed out, my wet clothing clung to my body. Piers stood there with his eyes wide, then pulled a cloth out of his saddle and wrapped it around me. He confessed that, for sailors, there were only two kinds of women: tramps and ladies. I blushed when he covered me with the cloth and noticed that when he placed it on me, his hands felt anything but fraternal. Then he suddenly walked away, as if frightened.

A few days later, he proposed that we explore the tunnels below the house. He still wasn't convinced that the war was over. Although the king was still in prison, Piers knew—here his voice sounded mysterious—that many weren't in favor of the religious and political changes the Parliamentarians had imposed. Soon they would rise up again and there would be another war. That house with its tunnels could be the salvation of many.

So, one afternoon when the house's few inhabitants were resting after lunch, we began our descent. We passed the kitchens, then the cell that had so frightened me as a child, and went down the worn stone stairway. By the light of the candle Piers held, we could make out the hollows in the wall and the ancient dungeons with straw on the floor. I had learned my way around helping Lady Leigh care for the hidden Royalists during the final months of the war. It all smelled of rot and dampness.

We headed for the door to the ancient chapel, which Piers opened with a large iron key. In recent months, no priests had gone ashore on nights with a full moon, nor had we celebrated Mass. It was the first time Piers had come down here since he arrived. On the altar stood the Virgin. In front of her were the benches that filled up with hooded worshippers, and in the central aisle, there was a great tombstone with letters in Latin marking the place where the monks from the nearby abbey had been buried when our chapel was their crypt. With the candle, we illuminated the walls containing the niches where several generations of the Leigh family and their servants had been buried. One of them was Rose, Matt's Rosita. Observing a respectful silence, we locked the chapel door again and went back up the passageway. There we found openings to three slender tunnels that, over the following days, we set about exploring. With Piers's hand in mine, I wasn't afraid during those long walks in the dark.

The first tunnel ran north and ended in the woods, its entrance hidden amid tree branches and bushes. We were tired from the long journey underground, and especially the steep ascent, so we sat down with our backs against an oak tree and gazed up at the sky. The light of sunset filtered through the branches. We looked at each other, smiling, and Piers ran a finger gently over my face. When it reached my mouth, I tried to bite it. He laughed and caressed my neck. I got up, embarrassed, and started to run, and he followed me, roaring with laughter.

The second tunnel was much longer. This time, at the exit, we could see the thick walls of the Norman Tower a few hundred yards away. From there, there was easy access to the cliff and the wharf inside the cave. We walked toward the coast. The sun was slowly setting on the horizon, extracting white glitter from the ocean. Piers put his arm around my waist, and we stood there, watching the sun set over the ocean of our childhood and now our youth.

We walked back slowly, his arm still around my waist, making my heart race. We arrived home covered with dust, but Mademoiselle Maynard and Mr. Reynolds were no longer there to scold us. Lady Leigh, who knew what we were up to, just nodded and asked us to change before supper. Piers had suggested to her that familiarity with the tunnels might someday save our lives.

We left the tunnel leading west for last. The first time we had tried to explore it, we had realized it was very long, a true labyrinth. The passageway wound around and divided into other small passageways with different lateral exits, many of them blind. Halfway through, there was a cell with some ventilation. It had been recently occupied—on the little table next to the austere cot sat two books. Later, they told us that it was where Uncle Andrew and the other priests hid. The tunnel finally ended very near town and was surely how the secret Catholics from the region reached our chapel.

Once we had inspected the tunnels, we resumed our lengthy gallops, sometimes beyond Oak Park but also, once again, up to the Norman Tower, the windmill, and the forest. Still, our most frequent destination was the coast. Every day that went by, Piers longed more and more to be sailing. He found respite only in gazing at the horizon, toward the open sea, but in his eyes, there was something bitter, memories that hurt him.

"War brings out the worst in all of us," he told me once as we sat on the cliffs. "At times I even enjoyed firing a gun, forgetting that there were human lives on the other end, people with families who were waiting for them."

"At war, you obey orders." I paused and added doubtfully, "And hopefully, you defend your ideas—"

"Do you?" he asked. "I'm not even sure what my ideas are. I'm not a Royalist like Thomas, but I can't stand the Puritans in Parliament, either. I could have run away when the *Fellowship* was captured, but I didn't. I swore loyalty to Parliament, in which I don't believe and which I don't respect."

"That's how war is, cruel." I stated the obvious, not knowing how to calm his anxiety. "Perhaps if you had run, they would have killed you."

"I know."

My friend looked deeply distressed. For three years, he had fought for people who would happily attack his own family.

"There's something more, isn't there?"

He gazed at the ocean, which was shining silver. "I haven't said anything to Mother so she won't worry, nor to my sisters. But Len, I have to tell you."

I looked at him wide-eyed, hoping he would unburden himself.

"The truth is, they expelled me from the navy. I joined a group of young officers, and we tried to arrange for the king's return from Scotland. After they expelled me, I spent some time thinking things over at a friend's house and finally decided to come here. My life is the sea; I want to go back. But I can only return to the navy if that clandestine movement grows."

"Do you think it will?"

"The rebels are planning to replace the current vice admiral with one who sides with the Royalists. If that happens, I will return."

"You miss the sea that much?"

"You can't imagine how this sedentary life drives me crazy. If it weren't for you—" He smiled.

We listened to the gentle sound of the surf.

"Aren't you glad to be at peace?"

It took him a while to answer. When he did, his face revealed his pain. "The war ended on paper, but I'm not at peace. In this tranquil place, dark memories return to my mind."

"What memories?"

"Dear Len, I hate to tell you. The looting of some cities was dreadful. The officers couldn't control the men. I did what I could."

"I'm sure you did!" I touched his arm.

He suddenly turned and gave me a furtive kiss on the cheek. I blushed with pleasure, but moved away, overwhelmed. Piers made me feel safe and gave my soul comfort. My heart was bursting with happiness to finally have him next to me.

"We missed you so much, all those years." I fell silent a moment. "And we were afraid, especially toward the end, before you returned. The people from Walton—Matt was afraid they would attack us."

He looked at me and said hoarsely, "Never! I'll protect you! Though"—here his voice broke—"now I know that isn't always possible."

"What do you mean?"

"The fanatics are the worst thing about wars. They're people who use religion or politics as an excuse to look on others as creatures unworthy of living."

I realized he was talking about something real, something specific and terrible. "What happened?"

It took him a few minutes to answer. He gazed out to sea, as if awaiting my words of pardon. But what did I have to forgive?

"A fellow called Swanley. We left Gales headed for the Dunas, and we captured a pirate ship operating on behalf of the king. In that flat-bottomed boat, there were 150 Royalist soldiers. Seventy of them were Irishmen. Captain Swanley ordered us to tie them up, back to back, and throw them into the sea. He said they'd be happy to 'wash away the Protestant blood that stained them.' I can still hear the screams."

"Was there nothing you could do?"

"He would have thrown me in, too. I still remember one of them staring at me, a man about my age. I thought of my Irish Catholic mother and how we would have tortured and murdered her just the same. While no one was looking, I pulled a knife from my belt and cut the cords tying him to his companion. I could see the fear in his eyes change to profound gratitude. I hope to God he survived!"

"I'm sure he did."

On the horizon, we could see sails approaching Horsehead Cove. Piers took out his old spyglass and focused it on the ship. He let out an exclamation of happy surprise.

"What? What's happening?"

"My father!"

We ran down the path to the pier. A tender was passing the horse's head that was nearly submerged by the waves. The boat dropped anchor, and Lord Leigh landed. Father and son were fused in an embrace. Then the Lord of Oak Park greeted me affectionately as well.

With his arm draped over his son's shoulders, Lord Leigh climbed the hill. I walked behind them. I heard snatches of conversation that seemed to be a continuation of what Piers and I had been discussing.

"My son, you're a soldier; you were carrying out your duty."

I didn't hear Piers's response, but I did hear Lord Leigh's answer. "Those on the other side are no better, I can attest."

"That's why you remain neutral," I heard Piers say.

"Not entirely. We help those being persecuted by Parliament, though I try to make Oak Park look neutral."

"I didn't want to take sides. My only dream was to be a sailor."

We had reached the top of the hill, where the horses awaited. Piers ceded his horse to his father, mounted mine, and pulled me up as well.

I rode sidesaddle, and we set out at a gentle gallop. He placed his arm around my waist, and I leaned my back against him.

He whispered happily in my ear, "My father doesn't blame me for anything."

"Have you told him you're out of the navy?"

He hesitated and his voice grew sad. "I'll tell him later."

He kissed me behind the ear, and I felt an unexpected pleasure as he whispered, "I only confide in you."

We looked at each other surreptitiously, not saying anything, filled with one another, while our horse slackened his pace. Lord Leigh had gone on ahead. In a few minutes, we reached the house. We saw Lady Leigh peering out a window, waving her hands in welcome. Then she ran out to greet her husband, and Ann and Margaret followed.

We all sat down in the drawing room, and Lord Leigh told us that, during those first months of peace, he had managed to recuperate much of his business. Though his situation was still precarious, he would no longer have to spend all his time away. At last, all of us were together.

"All of us? Thomas is missing," exclaimed Lady Leigh.

"He'll be back."

"We've had no news of him for over two years," she continued, her voice trembling. "What if he's dead?"

"He may be in hiding. Don't worry, Madam, our son will return."

They hired a few new servants, and one of Lord Leigh's sailors also stayed on with him. The house began to fill up again and recover some of its dignity. The fireplaces once again crackled. Lord Leigh would shut himself up in the East Room, writing letters. There was peace in the house. All that was missing was for the heir to Oak Park to return.

26

NASEBY

Oak Park, Autumn of 1647

Not long after Lord Leigh's return, Mr. Reynolds reappeared at Oak Park. Nothing remained of the sleepy, potbellied professor. He was dressed in the manner of Royalist gentlemen, and his figure had become slimmer due to the privations.

Piers happily went out to the patio to greet him, but his former tutor's grave face left him mute. Reynolds said he wanted to talk to everyone, and we gathered in the great room. Piers helped him over to a chair near the fireplace. He gave us the terrible news: Thomas had fallen nearly two years earlier in the Battle of Naseby.

"Our battalion was stationed in the Midlands. The state of His Majesty's army was chaotic. Men deserted out of hunger, and among those who remained, the lack of discipline was striking. Both the soldiers and the deserters looted nearby towns. The lack of provisions was aggravated by despair. News had reached us of the New Model Army. We officers tried to discredit it and even gave it a nickname: 'the New Noodle Army.' Thomas didn't appreciate the jokes. He argued that our greatest danger wasn't the enemy but our own lack of discipline. He told us that our job as officers was to maintain authority, and despite the difficulties, we managed to regroup the troops. However, then we learned that the new Parliamentary army had thirteen thousand men, in addition to the cavalry Cromwell led. In light of our disadvantage, the command ordered us to retreat, but they pursued us. A council of war was called, and several officials argued that we couldn't flee out of honor. Thomas was one of them."

"He was very brave," Margaret said and lifted the corner of her handkerchief to dry a tear.

I looked at Lord Leigh. I remembered everything he had told his son and the Royalist nobles several years earlier in the East Room. He had warned Thomas that fighting for a king who didn't deserve them would end badly. Having seen his son's future so clearly and not being able to stop him was what hurt him most, I think.

The former teacher sighed. His face looked even more anguished than before.

"We stopped near Northampton, on the plains of Naseby, and rested for the night. The next morning, there was a very thick fog. We knew the enemy was behind it, but we couldn't see them. Around ten, the advance of the Royalist cavalry, including Thomas and me, began. When I looked at our elegant army, clad in velvet and taffeta, and compared it to the poor devils wearing coarse reddish sacks making up the enemy ranks, I had no doubt that victory would be ours. A huge mistake! The adversary was well led, and they obeyed their commanders. Our troops were undisciplined."

Piers's knuckles were white. "You should have whipped them."

"Mr. Piers, the army isn't like the navy."

"Go on, I beg you," said Lady Leigh tearfully. "I want to know what happened to my dear son."

The tutor continued, "From behind a hedge, a battalion of dragoons fired on us, causing many casualties among our ranks. We spurred our horses and charged. I was riding immediately behind Thomas, and I saw how he dug his spurs into his horse's back so it would jump the hedge. A Roundhead dug a pike into Thomas's groin, and he fell to the ground. Badly injured, bleeding profusely, he withdrew from the heat of battle. The other horsemen in our company dispersed. As soon as the battle had shifted, I dismounted and ran over to Thomas, who was beginning to show the pallor of death."

The whole Leigh family sobbed, except Piers—a curse came from his lips. Mr. Reynolds turned and went on, addressing the younger Leigh brother.

"A few steps beyond where Thomas was, our infantry went into battle, fighting with such valor that it seemed victory might tip in our favor. But then Cromwell's cavalry arrived. As so often happened, our horsemen had already dispersed, bragging about having defeated the dragoons. By the time their commander, Prince Rupert, managed to reunite them, it was too late. It was also too late for Thomas. Piers, your brother acted with enormous discipline; he kept shouting orders to his troops from the ground. He fulfilled his duty up to the end."

"He was a man of honor," Piers averred.

"Did he suf-suffer much?" Lady Leigh's voice trembled.

"His death wasn't painful, Madam. It was impossible to stop the blood, and he slowly faded away. Before he died, he gave me this letter of farewell to those he loved most in the world, his family."

"I beg you to read it to us aloud," Lord Leigh said in a hoarse voice. "I don't think I could do it."

Then Mr. Reynolds read the last thing that Thomas had written:

> *Today we will surely go into combat. I don't know what the results will be, but I have a bad feeling. Behind that fog, the redcoats of the New Model Army want to change the world and alter the order that I have always defended. If I die, it is for my God and for my king, for the traditions of my ancestors, for the Church of England. I want this letter to reach my father and my only brother.*

Dear Piers, we saw each other in Bristol. You swore to always be loyal to the king. You haven't kept your promise; you're serving Parliament. I trust that, if I die, my death will convince you to renew your loyalty to the just cause, that of the king. We are fighting for him and for the true religion of this country against the savagery and rebellion of the Puritan troops. Dear Mother, pray for me to the Almighty, so that, should I die in combat, I will achieve everlasting glory. To my father, I ask your blessing and your forgiveness. To my dear sisters, who have always been in my heart, I give all my affection. Yours, forever,
   Thomas Leigh

We sat there in terrible silence. It was the ending that his mother—and, really, all of us—had feared for some time now.

"The worst part wasn't the battle," Reynolds went on. "The worst came afterward. The New Model Army treated the women who followed the Royalists brutally. They abused them, you understand, and then killed them in the most savage ways. My Lord," he said, directing himself to Lord Leigh, "I'm sorry to bring you such tragic news. Take good care of your family. I must take my leave. After what they did to those poor women, I . . . I don't want to go on living in this country."

"What will you do?" Lord Leigh asked.

"I'll join the Royalists in Holland."

Lord Leigh was pallid. I understood that he had not only lost his elder son, but he had also lost confidence that a policy of compromise and tolerance could protect his family.

"For a long time now, I've feared this would be my son's fate, but I can't believe we shall never have him with us again. Despite everything, he was courageous to the end and died for his ideas. That does him credit. Whereas what you have told me shows how low those Parliamentarian beasts will go."

Piers's face burned with rage. All his muscles were tense, and his eyes filled with tears. A new burden had fallen upon him: he was the heir to Oak Park.

In the months that followed this crushing news, Piers and his father began meeting often in the East Room. All over the country, there were uprisings in favor of the king. Another war was about to begin, this one even worse than the first.

27

COLERIDGE

Oak Park, Spring of 1648

One morning, a horse stopped on the great stone patio of Oak Park, and a young man wearing a sailor's waxed cloak dismounted. He was a young redhead, with slightly slanted eyes the color of chestnuts and a friendly smile. When Piers came out, they clapped each other on the back gaily. I felt displaced.

Piers introduced him to the family as his subordinate, a cadet a bit younger and from a good family. His name was Richard Coleridge, and he hadn't come for a social visit. He asked to speak in private with Lord Leigh. The three men shut themselves in the East Room for hours. No one dared interrupt them. At noon, Coleridge ate with us. He was very attentive toward Piers's sisters and especially toward me. In the afternoon, he departed.

After dinner, when night fell, I heard a pebble against my bedroom window. Outside, Piers was waiting for me, and I went out onto the same terrace we'd used for our childhood escapes. He shared his companion's news: a few days earlier, the navy had split in two. Some sailors had gone over to the king while others had remained loyal to Parliament.

Coleridge was among the former, and he had traveled to Oak Park to propose that Piers return to sea with him on the *Thomas*, under the command of an old acquaintance of Piers, Captain John Burley from the *Fellowship*.

"Must you really go away?" I asked him nervously.

"Dear Len, you know me. The sea has called to me since I was a boy. I'll carry you in my heart, and soon I will return."

"No, you'll abandon me for years again! When you're away, my life seems dark and gray. I think that, without you, I would lose my mind!"

"Calm down. We won't be so far apart. And I'll have to visit Oak Park frequently." Then he explained that Coleridge had also brought a request. The Royalist ships, completely without provisions, were not far from there, off the coast of Essex. Coleridge had come to ask Lord Leigh to secure supplies for them.

"Then your father has changed his position?" I inquired. "Years ago, when Thomas asked him to arm the Royalist troops, he refused."

"The situation has changed. And honestly, I think he had taken sides even before Thomas died. Now he has agreed to take charge of supplying the ships in the Royal Navy. They're going to drop anchor in the cove, when the tide is high again."

"So, you'll be going away on the night of ghosts?"

The moon hovered on the horizon, now in the first quarter. I managed to control my anguish and, somehow, spoke words of encouragement, but tears threatened to spill from my eyes. Piers noticed and hugged me. Then we sat there silently. In the semidarkness, we could make out the thick woods and the meadows, and we could sense the omnipresent sea beyond them.

He turned toward me, caressed my face, and I felt the roughness of his incipient beard when he kissed me, first softly, then more boldly.

"On my nights on board ship, I've often dreamed about a woman. I never would have guessed that woman was you."

When I felt the passion in his lips, my soul filled with happiness. I was overwhelmed with pleasure at knowing he was, in some sense, mine.

"I can't bear to think that you're leaving again," I finally said. "I dreamed about you, too. You're the only thing that matters in my life."

Then I gently separated his face from mine and wound my fingers into his hair, and we stayed that way a few seconds, looking into each other's eyes. It was like being in paradise. I didn't need anything else in the world, just to stay like that, embracing him, being reflected in his hazel eyes. Piers was more than a friend or a brother; he was my other self, the man I had always loved, the one I love now and will love forever.

We heard the hooting of an owl. A gentle breeze, smelling of the forest in springtime, enveloped us. We stayed there together until just before dawn, sometimes in silence, other times whispering words of love. Everything had changed.

In the days that followed, Ethan, a sailor who had come with Lord Leigh, and a loyal servant set about transporting bundles from the cellars to the cove under the direction of Lord Leigh and Piers, while Lady Leigh, Margaret, Ann, and I mended the boys' outgrown suits and old blankets, which could be useful on board the ships. We knew we were supporting the Royalists, and the work seemed to us like an homage to the ideals Thomas had upheld during his life. In the cave with the wharf, boxes and baskets of food and clothing piled up, as well as bottles, barrels of rum, and other drinks. The few servants left in the house and villagers from Walton were told that the comings and goings were simply due to a new business of Lord Leigh's.

Amid so much confusion, I didn't see Piers as much as I would have liked, but I felt him near. When he would pass by, he would smile at me, stop to ask what I was doing, or affectionately make fun of my poor sewing. A thousand ants would run up my skin as we beamed at one another.

Later, on those clear, soft spring nights, we would meet secretly on the terrace. Sometimes Piers would lend me his sailor's coat to protect me from the night dew. I gazed at the moon in the sky, dreading the moment when he would have to go away. We kissed again many times, and as our love grew even more intense, we found strength and consolation for those times that boded ill for us. Yes, we loved each other deeply, but in our passion, there was still the camaraderie that had united us since childhood. We would talk about the past and the present or discuss the country's political situation. Since we had received the news of Thomas's death, Piers had become entirely committed to the cause of the king. He argued that all of Parliament's excesses would be corrected with the return of the monarchy. Furthermore, he thought that Charles, having learned his lesson from the bloody war, would be more tolerant of religious differences.

I don't know how, but I knew even then that Piers's hopes were in vain. But I hoped that he was right, that we would return to times of peace and wouldn't have to fight anymore. In reality, I longed to return to that happy childhood that I had shared with him. But time doesn't run backward. You can never return to the past.

When high tide finally arrived, we bid Piers farewell. We watched again from the top of the cliff as he made several trips in a little sloop, carrying everything we had left in the cave out to the *Thomas*, the twenty-four-cannon ship under the command of John Burley. Piers wasn't just another sailor in the little sloop; he took the lead. I admired him, but I also felt a great weight on my chest as the person I loved most in the world headed out once again to the open sea.

28

COLCHESTER

Shortly after Piers returned to the navy, most of Essex County and practically all of Kent rose up in favor of the king. Then Cornwall and the regions that were traditionally monarchical joined them, and Scotland seemed to be forming an army to attack England. The people had grown tired of Parliament's tyranny, and war broke out again, the second English Civil War. Eastern England, which had been free of battles until then, caught fire in the terrible revolution that would shatter our lives forever.

The East Room became a nest of intrigue. Sir Charles Lucas and George Goring, first Earl of Norwich, and other Royalist leaders came to meet with Lord Leigh. Word that he had secured provisions for the ships loyal to Charles had spread, and they seized the opportunity to draw him deeper into their cause.

Margaret, Ann, Lady Leigh, and I weren't allowed to attend the gatherings, which were held in strict secrecy—and I had grown too large to hide behind the tapestry. There was no way for us to find out what was going on.

I remember how we would spend our days sewing silently in the great room, now ramshackle, the paintings and most of the furniture having been sold to finance the war. We would look at each other with concern, afraid to speak, afraid that events might hurl us into the abyss.

Finally, Lord Leigh called us together to announce that he had decided to join the Earl of Norwich and the Royalist uprising. Soon he would leave Oak Park, possibly for a long time. His words of farewell are engraved in my mind:

"A moment comes in a man's life"—he paused an instant, as if thinking of what to say next—"when you can't go on being indifferent to what is happening in your own country. They have forbidden the faith of our ancestors. They have killed my son. They have committed unimaginable atrocities and countless sacrileges and horrors. Most seriously of all, now Cromwell and Fairfax lead an army of fanatics that intends to give them unchecked power, more power even than the king had before. It's my duty to confront those vultures, those savage beasts."

Lady Leigh stood to oppose him. "This war will be even harsher than the previous one. The defeated Royalists gave their word not to fight against Parliament," she said. "Anyone who takes up arms again will be considered a traitor. There will be no clemency."

"You are right, but I can't sit idly by, my eyes closed to the barbarism. I'm especially afraid for you, my darling, and this is the only way I know to protect you. Piers told me how the men on his ship were commanded to slaughter a group of Irishmen, just for being Irish. Mr. Reynolds told us what happened at Naseby, in the same battle where our son died, how they raped and murdered the women. These Parliamentarians aren't gentlemen; they're wild animals. My dear wife, it is my duty to fight for you."

Lady Leigh begged her husband not to throw his life away like Thomas had before him. But Lord Leigh, desolate and furious, had lost the equanimity that had always characterized him. Now that he was convinced there was nothing else to be done, he let out all the anger stored up in his heart.

The next day, he led some two hundred men: sailors from the Leighs' merchant ships, tenants, and a few servants from Oak Park. They joined the army of Sir Charles Lucas, which was advancing toward London. We were left alone again, accompanied by Matt and a few servants. The robberies on the estate and in the granaries began; at night, we would hear strange sounds in the park. It rained and rained, and the final days of a spring without light were followed by the first days of a summer without light.

We soon learned that, on their ride to the capital, some of the Royalist troops had deserted when they received word that Fairfax had taken Maidstone, one of the staunchest Royalist enclaves. Despite the defections, the rest of the army had continued. They thought the city would be weary of the abuses of the Parliamentarians and would surrender gladly. But that wasn't the case. The gates of London were closed, and Londoners put up great resistance. The Royalist troops finally had to retreat, pursued by the Roundheads.

They fled to the nearby city of Colchester, not far from Oak Park. At its gates, a fierce battle took place, with no clear victor. The remnants of the troops supporting Charles I, among them Lord Leigh, Sir Charles Lucas, and Lord Goring, took refuge inside the city. During the first civil war, the town had sided with Parliament. Now it was occupied by the Royalists and was being attacked by soldiers from its own side.

The siege of Colchester was brutal. They resisted for two and a half months that horribly cold and wet summer. There were soon terrible food shortages. People ate dogs and horses. What few provisions there were, were rationed. Then a moment arrived when there was nothing left.

In Oak Park, we were also under siege in our own way, not daring to venture out of the house alone. We anxiously followed the pamphlets on the siege published by the Parliamentarians. We knew that

Lord Leigh was fighting behind Colchester's walls. Weeks went by, and the battle didn't tip one way or the other.

One dark afternoon, a man arrived, one of the sailors who had accompanied Lord Leigh. I remember his name was Ethan, and before he was a sailor, he was a kitchen boy working under Matt. Now he was fleeing and badly wounded.

"The siege has become merciless," he said as we ushered him into the kitchens. "Sir Charles Lucas believes that the Scottish are going to liberate them. He won't surrender because he knows it would mean capital punishment for him as a traitor. But the citizens are starving. Before I escaped, they had even eaten the rats. The townsmen mounted revolts against the Royalists and were cruelly crushed. Finally, some hungry women begged Sir Charles Lucas to let them go out and demand food for their children. We watched them leave with desperation painted on their faces. When they reached the Parliamentary camp, the soldiers started shooting the air around them, took them prisoner, and later sent them back to the city naked. Lucas's men refused to let them back in. The women stood there, in front of the walls, shaking, with no one to help them. I can still see Lord Leigh's face, up on the city's fortifications, contemplating with disgust the inhuman conduct of both armies."

Lady Leigh sobbed. "He went out to help them, I know he did."

"Yes, my lady. Lord Leigh shouted, asking if there were any brave men left, anyone capable of acting like a gentleman. Several of us joined him, especially those of us from Oak Park. It wasn't purely courage. We were so hungry that we would rather die in combat than stay any longer in that rathole, where the only thing awaiting us was a slow death." Ethan fell silent a moment.

Lady Leigh, her eyes filled with tears, urged him to continue.

"When we went out to rescue them, the Roundheads flung themselves on us like hyenas. Many died, and the rest were wounded and taken prisoner. When they captured him, Lord Leigh was wounded.

They took him to the enemy camp. There, they searched him, and in his clothing, they found a crucifix. When they saw it, they shot him point-blank, then cut off his head and put it on a stake in front of the walls of Colchester as an example. I managed to escape, but they're pursuing me. I need your help, my lady."

Lady Leigh's lovely face had turned waxen, and her eyes went blank, as if she was in a trance, incapable of accepting that the man she so loved was gone.

We hid Ethan in the cellars of Oak Park, which would never be the same after the death of Lord Leigh. And so, in a savage, cruel manner, the man who took me into his home and treated me almost like a daughter was murdered. I'll never stop mourning him.

That was the beginning of the end.

29

THE FAREWELL IN FRONT OF THE SEA

Oak Park, Summer of 1648

A few days after Ethan's arrival, before Colchester had surrendered, Piers landed in the cove below the cliffs. Only those closest to him knew; the walls had ears.

He had grown into a strong and determined navy lieutenant. The navy was now led by the Prince of Wales and his cousins, nephews of the king, Prince Rupert of the Rhine and Prince Maurice of the Palatinate. Piers was sailing on the *Antelope*, a ship that patrolled the nearby coasts of Essex. The navy needed to stay in contact with the remaining Royalist holdouts, and they also needed provisions. Piers, the second-in-command, proposed to the captain that they drop anchor in the cove at Oak Park.

He immediately guessed the news of his father's death from Lady Leigh's pained and absent expression. He spoke with Ethan, who told him what had happened and asked him to take him on the *Antelope*, as he was being pursued. Piers agreed.

He displayed no emotion before his mother and sisters and the servants, remaining grim and quiet. But when he and I were alone, in the woods behind the house, he let out all his anguish and pain. There was no melancholy, only an attack of anger like I had never imagined. Like a wounded animal, he stabbed the trunk of a tree over and over and over as if it were one of those Roundheads who had murdered his father. I went to him, but he pushed me away. I fell to the ground on my knees, sobbing, begging him to calm down. When he saw me like that, he put the dagger back into his belt. He pulled himself together and ran his hands through my hair as if asking me to forgive him. Then he ran away into the woods.

I didn't go after him. I knew he needed space to regain his composure and master his rage. I walked slowly under the tree branches, which were dripping water. Nature was crying, as was my heart.

Over the next few days, Piers's very countenance changed. He looked much more mature, containing his suffering with an iron will. He was all activity and decision, serenity and firmness, as if Lord Leigh's equanimity and enterprising spirit had been passed on to him. He organized provisions for the ship and strategized the defense of the house. He gave us instructions in case he didn't return. That idea upset me so much that I felt paralyzed. He knew I couldn't live without him. In all these activities, we helped him however we could.

Right before he left me forever, Piers and I once more rode the narrow path down the cliffs we had visited so often as children, and we reached the cave.

We tied the horses to the rusted iron rings and faced a stormy sea on that afternoon without sun. The waves thundering against the rocks made it hard for us to hear each other. The *Antelope* was rocking in the distance. After a while, I felt Piers's cold hand softly take mine. I turned toward him, and he looked deeply moved. He brought his lips close to my ear.

"It's a third-class ship, with thirty-six cannons. I've never fought on one like it. It's beautiful."

"It isn't beautiful to me. It's going to take you far away."

Then he said something I couldn't hear over the noise of the sea.

"What?" I asked.

"I love you," he repeated.

I couldn't speak; there was a knot in my throat. My heart seemed to stop beating from sorrow. When he saw me like that, he took me in his arms and kissed me hard. I tasted salt and a certain bitterness in my mouth. In that furious embrace beat his love for me and his fury toward everything keeping us apart. Then he stepped away, shouting something into the wind that I couldn't hear. We went into the cave, taking shelter from the storm raging outside. There, in the darkness, he ran his hands over my body; I let him do it. I felt overcome with desire. We stood like that, united by an ecstasy that felt like madness, until the icy wind penetrated the cave and somehow returned us to reality. I was seized with a nervous modesty and pulled gently away from Piers. I wish I hadn't! I wish I had become his at that moment. Now I will never belong to anyone.

Surprised by my reluctance, he drew me back toward him, hugging me again in a trembling embrace. Then I realized he was crying. I had never seen him sob like that. Thick tears ran down his cheeks.

"My love, don't cry!"

With his strong hands he wiped away the tears, embarrassed, and told me, "I'm crying because I think I'm going to lose you. I'm crying because this war is absurd, because I'm leaving all this, because of my father—he was my role model, the most honorable man, the most reliable. Do you understand, Len?"

"Yes."

"Oh Lord!" he cried, looking toward the raging sea, toward that sky filled with clouds. "Why did you let him die?"

"My dear Piers, my darling, for your father, there was never any other cause but you, his children. After your brother's death, he had no choice but to fight, even if he knew the cause was lost."

"Yes." Piers sniffed. "That is who he was."

He was shivering from the cold and also from sorrow. Piers's lips had turned bluish. I kissed them anxiously. Finally, I took refuge against his chest, and he said to me, "My father has died." His voice shook again when he pronounced these words. "Now I'm the Lord of Oak Park. I don't know whether I'll return, but if I someday do, I want you to be my wife, to be the Lady of Oak Park. For me, Oak Park is you by my side."

I bit my lip and nodded.

"I can't conceive of life without you. Since we were children . . . that's how it's always been and will always be."

Then I parted with the only thing in the world that was truly mine: the tin medallion my father had given my mother. I hung it around Piers's neck and told him it would protect him.

And now the medallion has returned to me, in this faraway place, in Santo Domingo. I look at it time and again, kissing it. I don't know how it got here, but with it I feel strength returning to my body and sanity to my wounded mind. Somehow, I sense that Piers is alive. I wake up trembling and think that, if not all the Leighs died, I don't have to feel quite so guilty.

Then the doubt sets in. The last news I had of Piers was through Ambassador Cárdenas. After he freed me, Don Alonso told me that Piers Leigh had gone to Holborn, to the Spanish legation, and begged for my ransom. When I asked him where that sailor was now, he shook his head.

"I received his letter from Ireland, written on board the *Defiance*. Then, a while ago, I read in the tabloids that the ship, under the command of Prince Maurice of the Palatinate, sank in a terrible storm. Surely there were no survivors."

That's when my muteness and wandering mind began. I had suffered so much, and I survived it, but that sentence—"Surely there were no survivors"—began echoing inside me in such a way that I could think about nothing else. The worst was that, deep down, I was almost relieved. If Piers had drowned, I would never have to face him, wouldn't have to tell him about the end of Oak Park, the end of his family, what had been done to me.

But now, when I see this medallion, Don Alonso de Cárdenas's words take on a different meaning. The *Defiance* may have sunk, but the fact that a ship has sunk doesn't "surely" mean all on board have died. The galleon on which my mother and I sailed had sunk, yet here I was. Like a ray of light, sanity penetrates my mind, and a blind hope fills my heart. Piers, my Piers, was strong and determined. He's alive and will return.

At other times, I think that the medallion probably appeared on a corpse and some kind friend of Piers brought it here to me. But that can't be. He told me that our love would last forever.

30

THE HOUSE OF THE DÁVILAS

Santo Domingo, April 1655

"Forever."

Josefina wakes me up, but Piers's words linger in my ears.

"It's cooler now. This is when the Dávilas usually receive guests. I could take you over to see them."

I jump up, and for the first time in ages, my mouth curves into a timid smile, which pleases Josefina. I'm anxious to find out more about the sick man in the Hospital of San Nicolás; perhaps the Dávilas will help me. Josefina dresses me, and we cautiously proceed to the house next door.

The Dávilas are feeling expansive. There are coffee and sweets laid out. We sit down on soft cushions on the floor.

At first, I don't know what to say because I've been shut up inside the house so long, and I don't know the custom of paying visits, which Josefina has told me is so common in this city. The noble ladies spend all morning at their devotions and taking rides. They eat quickly, take a siesta, and in the afternoon, they hold elaborate gatherings where they laugh and gossip.

I clear my throat, my desire for information giving me courage. "At the governor's palace, you spoke of Don Rodrigo Pimentel—"

"A scoundrel," declares Doña Beatriz, the married, pregnant sister, who has also come to her mother's house to visit.

Beatriz is the most beautiful of the three Dávilas. She has a long face, with big black eyes, thick red lips, and long hair gathered up at the sides, giving her an exotic air. Through her veins runs Indian blood, the beautiful result of intermarriage by the Spaniards since arriving on this island.

Her sisters, Doña Berta and Doña Amalia, have more European features, but they are less lovely than Beatriz, though she may not be proud of her mestizo appearance.

"Around here, there is no law and no king but Don Rodrigo Pimentel," Doña Amalia says.

"He plays around with prices however he likes," Doña Beatriz goes on. "He buys up the products arriving from overseas and then speculates with them."

"But hasn't he repaired a convent for the Clare Sisters?"

They laugh.

"Only because the good nuns have taken in Doña Inés," Doña Amalia says slyly.

"He has tarnished her honor," Doña Beatriz informs me.

"What do you mean?"

"Inés de Ledesma is a niece of his, heiress to a great fortune," Doña Berta explains. "She's a friend of ours. Don Rodrigo was her guardian, and it seems that he tried to abuse her."

"She went to the fort's captain, Don Gabriel de Rojas, who fell madly in love with her," Doña Amalia goes on. "I don't know if she loved him as much, but let's just say Inés let herself be courted and protected. Don Gabriel threatened Pimentel, and the scoundrel left poor Inés alone. Don Gabriel asked for her hand, but before they were engaged, he disappeared from the city."

"Don Rodrigo seized the opportunity and tried to force her to marry him," Doña Beatriz continues.

"Even though," Doña Amalia interrupts, "he is practically an old man, and she is a beautiful young woman. We helped Inés escape from Pimentel and took her to Las Claras, where she has taken vows as a novice. Don Rodrigo is very pious and is related to the clerics of the city, so he had no choice but to accept that his niece had gotten away from him. Still, if he ever got his hands on her, I doubt Inés could manage to escape again."

"Has anything further been heard about the captain?" I ask innocently.

"Alas, no! If only Don Gabriel would return, maybe he could help her. It's a shame that Inés de Ledesma is becoming a nun just to escape Pimentel."

"Captain Rojas is a true gentleman," Doña Beatriz says. "My husband knows him well."

"Your husband is in the military?" I ask.

"At sea. He's a . . . sailor."

Her sisters look at her.

"A privateer," Doña Berta adds with a sneer.

"My sister's husband is a brave man," Doña Amalia says apologetically. "Last year, he was named field marshal."

"My mother doesn't care much for Don Juan de Morfa," Doña Berta explains, "because he's a foreigner and devotes himself to privateering. Still, she tolerates him because he is rich."

The atmosphere has become strained, and to break the tension, I ask Doña Beatriz, looking at her protruding abdomen, "When are you due?"

"Perhaps toward the end of the month, though Josefina says it could come early."

The young ladies serve me a sweet made of egg yolk and sugar. I eat it with pleasure.

"It's from the Convent of Las Claras," Doña Berta says.

"I'd like to go there," I say offhandedly.

"That would be difficult since we're not supposed to go out."

"Aren't you afraid to remain in the city?" Doña Amalia asks me kindly.

"My uncle has prohibited leaving."

"Don Rodrigo Pimentel, on the other hand, wants to evacuate women."

"Will you go?" I ask with some concern. I wouldn't like these cheerful women to leave just when I've begun to get to know them.

"My sisters will do as they wish," Doña Beatriz declares, "but I will wait at home for my husband."

Her two sisters have started to chat with each other quietly, and Doña Beatriz asks me curiously, "Why do you want to go to the Convent of Las Claras?"

"I'd be interested in meeting Doña Inés."

"I could go with you, though I don't know how we'd avoid the patrols in the streets. I used to go there frequently to visit her. My husband asked me to take care of her. To be honest, I don't understand why you're interested in meeting her."

I don't answer. I'm not really that interested in seeing Doña Inés, the woman Captain Rojas confused me with. What I really need is to talk to him again.

31

GABRIEL DE ROJAS

Josefina and I leave the Dávilas' through the back orchards, near the wall. A sea breeze wraps around us. Palm trees and white buildings line the banks of the Ozama. I protect myself from the burning Caribbean sun with a wide-brimmed hat. Next to me, Josefina holds up a white parasol.

We don't stop at my uncle's residence. Walking between orchards and by low walls, we head for the Hospital of San Nicolás. Brother Alonso greets us, saying the sick man's fever has gone down a little; he is no longer delirious. He accompanies us to the cell where they have moved him. I sit at the sleeping captain's side, drying his forehead pearled with perspiration. His bed is soaked from the fever. He half opens his large, dark eyes and observes.

"Who are you?" I ask him to make sure it's really him.

"I'd rather not tell you my name," he responds in a hoarse voice.

Then Josefina speaks. "Your Grace is safe here. Don't worry; we won't say anything."

"In your dreams, you mentioned a woman named Doña Inés de Ledesma," I continue.

He sits up when he hears that name. "How is she?" he asks, excited.

"Be quiet, Don Gabriel," the slave urges him as she helps him lie down again and cools his lips with a little water. "Don't give yourself away. Only the young lady, Brother Alonso, and I know your identity. Everyone is looking for you. You have been away from the city for a long time. They said you were dead. What happened?"

"When I was on my way back to Santo Domingo, my ship sank to the north of the island." He stops to gather strength. "I was badly injured. Some buccaneers rescued and cured me, but then held me captive for months. When I managed to escape, I embarked on the path here. I'll save you the list of hardships I endured. I don't know how I managed to get here." He pauses a moment, remembering the load that weighs on his heart. "How is Doña Inés?"

"She took refuge with the Clare Sisters," Josefina says.

"Thank God!"

"She has taken vows as a postulant nun."

At this, Gabriel de Rojas gets angry. "That wretch!" he cries. "He's not going to force her to become a nun. I must see her!"

This time, with great effort, he gets out of bed before we can stop him. But he is so weak that he falls right back down.

"The fever is killing me," he laments. "I have so little strength that I couldn't defend myself. I'm not safe in this city."

"You have nothing to fear from us," Josefina says. "And with quinine, you will get better."

"I should have taken it a long time ago; it won't help much now."

I observe him with pity. He is terribly weak, but he is the only one who can help me find the man I love. "Where did you get this?"

I show him the tin medallion.

"I don't know what it is."

"It was in a packet with my name on it."

"Yes! Len, he called you."

Speechless, I nod.

"Last year, when we attacked Tortuga, a foreign sailor helped us. Thanks to him, our victory was possible." He speaks slowly, trying to remember. "After the attack, we separated. I had to return to Santo Domingo to liberate Doña Inés. When we said good-bye, he gave me this packet. He said I should ask for a lady. For you."

Gabriel de Rojas's face looks haggard; his fever is rising again. I dry his forehead to soothe him.

"That man, the foreigner who gave you the packet, did he say anything else?"

"That he would look for the lady."

"Where is he?"

"At sea. He was captain of the ship that assaulted the vessel where Don Rodrigo Pimentel locked me up."

"What is his name?"

"Pedro. Don Pedro Leal."

The name fills me with hope. *Leal* was the last name Uncle Andrew used in Spain. And Piers's name in Spanish would be *Pedro*. I see Gabriel de Rojas looking me up and down, confused.

A light goes on in my head. "Is he a pirate?"

"Not anymore."

"Was he one?"

He doesn't answer, but that silence is an accusation. Piers, my Piers, what has happened to you, breaking all your promises?

"I must see him," I say.

32

THE SECRET

Santo Domingo, April 1655
Oak Park, Summer of 1648

See him? But how could I confess the horror to him?

When I first received the medallion, I was overcome with joy, an exalted joy. My mind opened; I could do anything. Now the fear and anguish have returned and I'm sick again, this time with horror at the idea of him finding out what happened. With dear Josefina, I walk home from the hospital amid exuberant tropical vegetation. Yesterday, the flowers would have seemed beautiful to me, but not today.

Josefina looks at me, worried, when she sees my face contorted as before. I don't want her to worry. I twist my head, looking at the rocky beaches, the river in the distance. A warm rain begins to fall. Nature is crying along with my soul, distraught over all I have lost, for having done evil, for being stained, impure . . . I can barely walk, and I lean on the healer. I torture myself with questions. How would I ever explain it to him? How could I tell him what happened that terrible night?

Back alone in my room, I go over to the window. Night is falling. Above the sea, a full, shining moon hangs, as full as the one that terrifying night. My last at Oak Park.

Several days earlier, I had gone with Matt to cut wood, and we had dis-covered a man spying on the house. We recognized him: Roberts, the vindictive former coachman. He was dressed like a Roundhead. I had never seen Matt so angry. In his cracked voice, he shouted at Roberts to leave, that he had no business on those lands, and even pointed an old blunderbuss at him.

Roberts just laughed. "Well, if it isn't Matt the saint, who sings in that unintelligible language. You're the only man in the house now, isn't that right?"

"No. Lord Leigh's sailors are here."

Roberts smirked at Matt's obvious lie, then walked away with a grimace of contempt.

We had seen men canvasing the estate before. Many were poachers looking for game, but I sensed something else: that they were watching us, stalking us.

Back at the house, we didn't say anything to the Leigh women. But from that moment on, I was jumpy. I knew that something horrible was going to happen. I couldn't unburden myself with Lady Leigh, who, since Lord Leigh's death, moved around Oak Park like a specter, inconsolable. The house became sadder, darker, filled with ghosts, both living and dead, and all I could do was hope that Piers would come home soon.

When the desperation and fear became intolerable, when a raw terror began to take hold of us, Uncle Andrew arrived in a wagon with the remains of his nephew, Lord Leigh. We never found out how he had secured them. As he and Matt unloaded the little box, I heard him mutter, "Children shouldn't die before their parents. You were like a son to me."

Only he was capable of easing Lady Leigh's sorrow. He spoke with her for many hours and then proposed that they say a proper farewell to Lord Leigh that night. They would bury him in the Saxon chapel and hold a requiem Mass in his memory. Many full moons had passed since the ancient rites were last carried out in our cellars. As usual, Matt would be in charge of alerting the faithful by imitating the call of a bird. Yes, Matt was the one who convoked the Mass and stood watch over it.

Just before midnight, Ann knocked on my door, and we went to fetch Margaret and Lady Leigh. Margaret was trembling with fear, but the lady looked surprisingly serene. We were all dressed in black.

As we descended to the ancient dungeons, I heard the cry of a strange bird. The moonlight was streaming through the large window, the same one under which Piers and I, as children, had danced a pavane.

Then I heard the bird's cry again.

I hadn't been so terrified since that day I had been locked into the cell with the skull and had heard the ghosts passing. Those specters didn't exist, but the danger did, and it was steadily growing. We descended the slippery stone staircase. Ann and I leaned on one another, and Lady Leigh hung on Margaret's arm.

We entered the chapel. Matt, helped by someone I didn't know, had lifted away the stone slab covering one of the niches in the floor. They buried Lord Leigh's remains there right away because they stank. Then they covered the tomb. Lady Leigh stooped down and kissed the slab. Uncle Andrew, now dressed as a priest, sprinkled holy water on her, saying a blessing for the dead. Then he stayed there awhile, praying over his nephew's tomb.

The silence and contemplation were only interrupted by the gradual arrival of the local faithful. Several hooded people, not many. Perhaps fear had kept the rest away. While Matt lit the torches on the sides of the altar, they gathered together on the benches, their faces hidden by veils or wide-brimmed hats. All were dressed in black. In that terrible war, everyone had lost someone.

Uncle Andrew walked up the central aisle from Lord Leigh's tomb to the altar, and we all stood up. He stood with his back to us, and when he raised his arms to begin, there came a distant commotion over our heads.

"It's all right, children! Nothing's wrong!" Lady Leigh whispered.

But something was wrong. Something horrific was going to happen, and no one could stop it. The sacred liturgy continued, though people were now abandoning the chapel for the tunnels. Ann squeezed my hand. Margaret's shaking had grown worse.

Then we heard an enormous thundering sound, muffled by the walls of the house but cutting through the silence of the night. We looked at each other.

Uncle Andrew turned around, exclaiming, "They've torn down the front door; they're attacking Oak Park. Run!"

The few faithful who had remained ran for the tunnels.

Uncle Andrew stood there quietly for a moment. Then he whispered that he should finish, that the sacred supper couldn't be left incomplete.

Lady Leigh told us in a firm voice, "We're staying. It's the only thing we can do now for Lord Leigh."

Tears began running down her cheeks. None of us dared to move.

Finally, the ceremony ended. We left immediately, following Matt. When he reached one of the tunnels, he stopped. Uncle Andrew had fallen behind.

"Help him, Catalina," said the old sailor.

I helped Andrew catch up. Matt addressed Lady Leigh: "My lady, this passageway comes to the surface far from Oak Park, near the Norman Tower. From there, it is easy to reach the coast. We can flee in one of the boats."

"What about Andrew?"

"We'll hide him where it's impossible for them to find him. Miss Catalina knows the tunnels well." He looked at me. "Will you accompany the father?"

I nodded.

"Take him to the cell where he usually stays, in the passageway leading to town. Lock the door with the key, and afterward, Miss Catalina, run to the Norman Tower as fast as you can. We'll come back for him when the threat has passed."

"That will put Len in danger!" Uncle Andrew objected.

"It's the only way."

Matt left with the two Leigh sisters and Lady Leigh, while I stayed behind with Uncle Andrew. He leaned on my shoulder, and we advanced very slowly through the cold tunnel. As we walked, Uncle Andrew whispered strange words; even today, I don't know what they mean.

"Fate again, you saving my life. There's something hidden in your past. One day you'll find out. It's linked to your mother's tin medallion. You do still have it?"

"I gave it to Piers."

"Then it's safe."

We had reached the cell. On the door, which only opened from the outside, hung a heavy iron key. Uncle Andrew asked me to lock it, as Matt had instructed. That would make it difficult for any Roundhead to get inside. Then the old Jesuit I had known since I was a child, the man who had saved me from the horrors of Moorfields, who had led me to the faith, who was like a father to me, told me to go, hugged me, and said good-bye. Forever.

In the distance, we could hear boots crashing against stone—they were coming. With one quick movement, I locked the door and stuck the key in the pocket of my skirt.

Then I fled. Next, I heard discharges of gunpowder. The ceiling trembled, and a beam fell, raising a huge cloud of dust. My heart leapt from my chest, but I kept running. A voice in my head kept repeating that Uncle Andrew was trapped, that he would never be able to get out of that place. But I did as I was told and kept running, though I felt overwhelmed with remorse, like I was abandoning him.

Behind me, I heard footsteps; perhaps they had heard me and were chasing me. I knew what I had to do. I went out to the passageway and entered the tunnel leading to the tower and the sea.

When I finally reached the mouth of that endless tunnel, I took great gulps of the night air. Very near, I could make out the Norman Tower, where the others would be waiting for me. Suddenly, the night lit up. They had set fire to Oak Park, and the flames climbed up to the sky.

When I got to the tower, I threw myself into the arms of Lady Leigh and started to wail with fear and horror, in an attack of anguish like I'd never experienced before. They covered my mouth so I wouldn't be heard. Finally, Matt smacked me on the cheek. It took my breath away, and I fell silent.

We collapsed onto the floor and lay back against the wall. Matt told us that we would stay there until the attack had ended, until the Roundheads—for it was they—had gone away. The hours went by, and finally, overcome with exhaustion, I fell asleep. Matt stood guard at the door.

Before daybreak, we woke up and peered outside. From the tower, we could make out the great house, which was still burning.

"We can't return. They may come back."

"Where can we go?" asked Lady Leigh.

"To the wharf. There's a sloop anchored in the cove that I know how to steer."

Then a thought passed through my mind. "We can't leave Uncle Andrew in the cell. He's locked in! He'll die!"

"The Lord will help him," replied Matt serenely. "There's nothing we can do now."

"No," I said. "I'm going to go get him."

"Miss Catalina, don't do that."

"Don't go, Len!" Lady Leigh begged.

But I disobeyed. And I shall be haunted by that for the rest of my days.

I started running. I heard another shout from Lady Leigh for me to come back. But all I could think about was Uncle Andrew, so I ran all the way back to the house.

I slipped back inside Oak Park, using a secret door hidden by ivy. The furniture in the great hall was burning, but the fire didn't seem to have reached the kitchens. I passed by the ovens, where I had talked with Matt so often. Everything reeked of smoke.

I ran down the staircase again, until I reached the passageway with the tunnels. I saw that the door to the ancient Saxon chapel had been broken. Everything there was destroyed; the beautiful Virgin was decapitated, the tabernacle opened and dismantled. Panicked, I spun around to take the tunnel toward Uncle Andrew. Then I heard a noise behind me and rough hands grabbed me. I screamed my head off. It was Roberts, along with some others.

"Excellent. Here's the thread that will unravel the ball of yarn. If you're alive, Mrs. Leigh and the girls are, too. Take us to the Irishwoman. We must burn the papist witch!"

I fought as hard as I could.

"Where did they go?"

I didn't say anything.

He grabbed my hand and started to tear out a fingernail. My screams seemed to come from outside my body.

"I know where they are," he suddenly said. "They must have gone to the cove. Why didn't I think of it before?"

"No! No—not there."

In a flash, I realized my vehement denial had given them away.

Roberts led his men on horseback down to the cove. He took me with him.

They trapped the Leigh women as they were descending the path down the cliff. I saw them kill Matt. It is seared into my mind how they drove a pike into his abdomen, a spout of blood flowing out. The old servant who sang me lullabies in Basque, who gave me buns to eat, who told me the tale of my great-grandfather, who—sometimes grumbling and sometimes bad-tempered—showed me his affection countless times. He who was always in the shadows, watching over me and taking care of me. He died defending us.

Then they took the four of us back up to the Norman Tower. Their eyes were filled with lust. There was something animalistic in those rioting men. They tied up Lady Leigh so she would be forced to witness everything.

First, Roberts went up to Margaret. "So pretty! I always used to dream about you. At last I have you in my power."

Margaret began to scream.

"I want this one for myself!" Roberts roared. "The others are yours!" He turned back to Margaret. "You knew I liked you, didn't you? You were always taunting me. I could tell. Now you won't do it anymore. I'm the one in charge here."

Roberts flung her to the floor, and she started kicking him. Then the former coachman banged her head against the stone pavement. Margaret kept resisting, but her aggressor hit her harder and harder. We wanted so badly to help her, but the other men held us tight. Suddenly, after a brutal slap, we heard Margaret's skull crack. Her eyes looked straight ahead, her whole body went into a spasm, and . . . she was gone.

Meanwhile, the other lunatics worked hard on Ann. Two held her and the third—oh! I don't want to remember. One after another, they raped her, in front of her mother, laughing about it. Roberts joined them, half-drunk. He seemed indifferent to having murdered a woman just moments before.

And me—they treated me the same way. Many nights, the thought of what they did comes back to me, and I pray for the release of death.

They would have killed all three of us, but my screams caught the attention of the officers who were searching the property.

Someone outside the tower fired a single shot and exclaimed, "Sons of damnation!"

That voice sounded familiar. I had heard it before, a long time ago. I heard Ann murmur, "Ruthven." So, William Ruthven was captain of the squadron that had carried out the attack. I thought he would save us, that he would punish those beasts for committing such barbarous acts against his wife's sisters.

"Sons of damnation!" he repeated when he saw us. "Is this how you follow orders?"

"We caught them celebrating papist rituals!" Roberts said defensively.

Ruthven spotted Margaret's corpse.

"What have you done? We should have executed them all publicly! As a lesson to the papists."

"They're just strumpets," Roberts insisted. "We've treated them as they deserve. And she—" Here he looked at Lady Leigh.

"She is the Irish witch," finished Ruthven triumphantly. "She'll be publicly burned. Their property will be expropriated—"

Then Roberts said, "And it'll go to a loyal servant of Parliament like yourself. Isn't that true, Lord Ruthven?"

"I'm the rightful owner of these lands! My wife and I have denounced the iniquities carried out in this house of perdition."

Then I understood everything. The greedy swine had spied on us for months. When he was sure there would be a Catholic Mass, he denounced us and took command of the squadron that assaulted the house. He burned it down because he thought it impure. I shouted in his face what I thought of him, and he beat me for it.

First, they took us to a military prison in Walton. From there, Lord Ruthven saw to it that we were sent to London, where they locked us up in a women's prison in Bridewell.

Gentle Ann couldn't take it, and she died in prison of the wounds from her savage rape. Lady Leigh was condemned, as a witch, to be burned alive. We wrote to Elizabeth begging for assistance, but she was powerless over Ruthven.

After Lady Leigh's execution, I was left alone in prison, like a living dead person. It is a time that has been erased from my memory, a time of scorn, privation, and scathing sadness. The days seemed like eternities, and only one thought comforted me, kept me from losing my mind: that Piers was alive and one day I would find him.

Eventually, the Spanish ambassador freed me from prison, but I could find no consolation. The people I loved most—the family that raised me—had died. Also, I knew that the cellars of Oak Park held a terrible secret: a great man buried alive. But still I held on. My mind was filled with sadness, but it hadn't shattered. Only when Don Alonso de Cárdenas told me that the love of my life had sunk to the bottom of the sea could my mind finally endure no more.

I remember hardly anything about the long voyage to Hispaniola. From London, we went to Pasajes and then to Seville, where we stayed for several months, like when my mother was alive. Finally, we embarked for Hispaniola. I just stood there, gazing at the ever-changing water of the open sea, thinking over and over again that beneath it lay my lord, my lover, my darling Piers.

Part 2
PIERS

33

THE DESERT ISLAND

Caribbean Sea, September 1653

Exhausted from the sleepless night, I lean on the bow, gazing toward an island where palm trees shade the beach and the sand glistens under a scorching sun. A cool breeze blows. In the middle of the cove, my sloop rocks, listing slightly and brushing against the sandy bottom. A storm carried us here, shredding a sail that hangs in strips impossible to tie to the masts. We have reached one of the multiple atolls of the Caribbean Sea, a devilish labyrinth of islands where I have been captain of a pirate ship for . . . how long? About a year already?

I move away from the bow and examine the deck, discouraged; from stem to stern, there is a chaos of junk and bundles. The cannons have slid out of their gun carriage, and the foremast is rocking, about to fall. Several sick men lie about listlessly, looking haggard and hungry. I turn toward Rodrigo de Alcalá, the curmudgeonly ship surgeon, who is leaning over the damaged mast. He doesn't hear the shouts of the carpenter, Esteban Centeno, and his assistants. He is concentrating on tending a nasty-looking wound on the head of Portuguese sailor Antonio da Silva.

While he applies the bandage, Alcalá grumbles, "May the devil take you, damned Englishman!"

His reproaches make me livid. For much less, I have had a man whipped until he was bathed in blood, until he lost consciousness from the pain. The men fear me; I wouldn't have it any other way. A ship without discipline becomes ungovernable and dangerous. My reputation as an angry, violent man precedes me, but I'm not unjust, so they respect me. Everyone but Rodrigo de Alcalá, who knows that I need him. On a ship, it's essential that someone care for the wounded, and he does it well. Still, he's just a tooth jockey we saved from the gallows in Bermuda. What little he knows, he learned from barbers in the many ports where life has led him. But he can recognize illness, lance and amputate, and give potions and infusions. And the crew likes him, despite his foul temper.

"What's that, you wretch?" I growl at him.

"When can we land? Look at this. If we don't go ashore soon—" He shows me a terrible gash in the man's head. "And they're all hungry. I can't believe you left our ship to that swine Kennedy and set out hunting in this . . . this eggshell! I've told you a thousand times that we have to go ashore. Nefarious humors build up inside the body when you don't breathe the air on land. May the devil take me for ever having gotten on board with you!"

Anger rises to my head. A few days ago, one of my top men ran off with my brigantine and the plunder in its holds. I could strangle the physician for throwing it in my face. But it's not worth it, so I just curse him right back.

"Goddamn you! If you hadn't come with me, you would be in hell now! Besides, where do you propose we land? On Hispaniola, by the Alcázar de Colón?"

De Alcalá simply points to the vegetation on the island in front of us.

"It doesn't look propitious," I tell him, because I don't want to admit he's right. "We don't know if there are water sources."

"I'm telling you again, there is no alternative, if you don't want to lose half the crew."

He may be right. We not only have to let the wounded men rest and replenish our provisions, we also have to repair the ship. But I'm irritated by his insolence.

The physician, who knows me well, puts on a more conciliatory tone. "One of the prisoners tells me he has been there. He says that, inland, there is a stream of clear water where we can fill our barrels."

"Who is he?"

"Gabriel de Rojas, the one we found tied up in the holds when we seized this sloop."

"Is he trustworthy?"

Rodrigo de Alcalá pauses. There is a price on our heads, and anyone could lead us into an ambush or to the gallows.

"I believe so," he finally responds. "He should be grateful to us. We freed him from the people holding him prisoner, and I've spent several days treating his wounds. I don't think he's misleading us."

"He'll go ashore with you, and you will answer for him," I warn him.

De Alcalá shrugs.

I call my second-in-command, my old friend Coleridge, who has been overseeing the carpenter and his assistants as they use a hatchet to trim the half-fallen foremast.

He agrees we should go ashore, and at a nod from me, he shouts, "Lower away!"

We hear curses and blasphemies among the sailors, who quickly take their positions next to the boats.

"It's about time!" the physician mutters. "This much delay isn't good!"

The boats are slowly lowered toward the water licking the ship. Then they advance toward the beach. From the lead vessel, I watch the beach drawing near.

Beside me, Coleridge asks, "Do you think we can trust this Gabriel de Rojas?"

"Can't be sure. The physician says we can."

"He has tried to escape several times. There are rumors among the men that he was thrown out of Hispaniola."

I examine the face of this so-called Rojas, who is in the boat next to ours: he's a man with a straight nose and a dark beard. There is something tough yet sincere about him. I'm amused to see that Rodrigo de Alcalá isn't taking his eyes off Rojas; he's more worried about my threats than he let on.

The boat hits the sand. When we step onto firm ground, I feel the unnerving sensation that comes after being on the high seas for so many days. It seems strange that the floor doesn't move under my feet.

The vegetation surrounding the beach is thick and dark, but near the shore, a large palm bends its trunk, letting coconuts fall, and we gather them in a sack. Following Gabriel de Rojas, we make our way onto the small island. As we climb, I realize it's nothing more than a volcanic formation sticking out of the sea; there is a tall cliff on its north coast and the sandy beaches where we have landed.

The men are panting as we climb up the steep rock. Luckily, Rojas leads us into the shade of an exuberant tropical forest, and the heat is somewhat relieved. We move forward with machetes until we reach a spring formed by the constant tropical rains. We follow its course and discover a waterfall cascading down a cliff into the sea. From above, I shout down to my men, and they begin to haul up barrels to fill.

I stand to the side, with Gabriel de Rojas, as the men collect water. We are both gazing at the immense sea that is interrupted by occasional rocks and islands.

"How did you find out about this island?" I ask the Spaniard.

"I know all of the Caribbean."

"That's impossible."

"Well, almost all of it." He smiles, brushing back his dark hair hesitantly. "I've been on these coasts since I was a lad." Then he, in turn, asks me, "How is it that an Englishman can express himself so well in my language?"

"I had a painstaking education. My family did business with the Spanish Indies, through Basques and Castilians. Learning the language made our business much easier."

"Still, your fluency is remarkable."

"I had practice as a child."

In a flash, the past returns: it seems like I can see Oak Park still standing. Blonde hair, a soft smile, and the light of those blue eyes appear before me. "Do-nna Catalina," I called her, and she corrected my poor Spanish. I feel suddenly chilled in the golden tropical light, and I say nothing more.

Once the barrels are full, we return with them to the beach. There, Rodrigo de Alcalá scrutinizes the dense vegetation along the coast.

"We need to hunt for monkeys," he declares. "The men already ate all the rats on ship."

I force a resigned smile; I doubt that we could find any such animals in this place.

We hear cries behind us and turn around. We see some of the men firing at something in the sea. We run down there. They have found a tortoise, a much greater delicacy than monkey.

In response to the noise and shouts, the animal has withdrawn into its shell, but the men surround it and move it onto the beach. There, the cook takes charge amid exclamations of joy. Domingo Rincón is a fat, blasphemous, womanizing yokel who knows his craft well. I know from experience that he will cut off the head, put the tortoise on the fire, and, only after some time has passed, separate the meat from the shell with a boning knife. Then he'll take out pepper and other spices from his grimy sack, and after it simmers for a few hours, a delicious aroma will begin to rise from the stew.

Some sailors have left the beach in a rowboat to fish. Two of them have jumped into the water, trying to capture fish with a harpoon. I squint and recognize them: George Kerrigan, a good gunner, and the cabin boy, Valentín de Torres, nearly a child. I enjoy seeing them like this, playing in the sea, in a cove with gentle waters. Suddenly, I hear a cry and see a red stain on the water.

I hear the sailors shout in unison: "A barracuda!"

The sailors in the boat throw a rope, and they manage to hoist Valentín, but Kerrigan is still in the water, grappling with the barracuda. His head disappears, then reappears, again and again. Finally, he manages to grasp the rope. The men pull on it and begin to lift him into the boat, but the barracuda wounds him again, and Kerrigan slides below the surface. The sailors watch, horrified, from the boat.

I dive headfirst into the water with my large, curved knife between my teeth. In a few instants, I reach where the gunner sank and dive down. I see an enormous fish several feet long that has sunk its sharp teeth into the sailor's thigh and isn't letting go. I grab it by the tail and stab its slippery skin again and again, until the monster liberates its prey and flees. I dive to the seabed, where Kerrigan is drowning. I put one arm around him and try to pull him up to the surface, but, frightened, he thrashes, and his weight drags me down, too. Then there is someone at my side. He seizes Kerrigan, freeing me, and carries him up to the surface. When we emerge gasping, I see that it is Gabriel de Rojas.

The sailors hoist the gunner into the rowboat and carry him to the beach. Rojas and I swim back and I stumble out, spitting the water I swallowed. I take a few steps over to Kerrigan, who lies bleeding on the sand. Rodrigo de Alcalá hurries over and examines the deep wounds in the man's leg and his abdomen.

"Oh God, what pestilence! What the hell did I come here for without my instruments? Captain, we must move him to the ship!"

Richard Coleridge says to me in English, "He will have to remain here. We have to shore up the sloop so we can caulk it."

It does need to be cleaned. We've been sailing for a long time; in the ship's timbers, mollusks have gathered, along with other debris that weighs us down and damages the hull.

Rodrigo hasn't understood Coleridge's words, but it's obvious to him that they're not what he wants to hear.

"Damned Englishman! I can't operate on a beach!"

Meanwhile, poor Kerrigan is bleeding out on the sand. What a disaster. A gunner who knows how to shoot cannons is indispensable on a pirate ship, and we have only two. I've known Kerrigan since the time of the Armada. He's a good fellow who has fallen on hard times, like the rest of us.

I say in English, "Come, Coleridge, there's time for everything. Before we careen the ship, we can repair the foremast. That'll give the bonesetter a little time."

I turn toward Alcalá and tell him in Spanish, "Move the wounded man to the ship, and be quick about it. You can operate on him, and when you're finished, Mr. Coleridge can careen the ship. We'll stay on the island tonight."

Coleridge isn't too pleased by the decision. We should head out as soon as possible toward a port to secure the wood we need to replace the foremast and the tar and oakum for caulking. But I'm also thinking about the crew. The sailors would like to spend at least one night on solid ground, in a place that seems safe. We'll fix things provisionally and then look for a port where we can carry out the real repairs.

Suddenly, I turn around and see Rojas sitting on the sand. He's cleaning out a surface wound of his own, and it occurs to me that he just risked his life to save mine. Who is this man?

34

UNDER THE STARS

That night, we light a campfire under a full moon. In a large pot, the tortoise soup bubbles. The men eat until they're stuffed and chase it down with copious rum. Richard Coleridge is terribly drunk; his drinking worries me. He wasn't always like this, but he can't stand the tropics and the heat. Moreover, he is tormented by the past, a once-elegant fellow who can't live with the Royalist defeat. Rum alleviates both his thirst and the pain of having lost his whole world.

The Rojas fellow isn't getting drunk like the others. He has gone off by himself and is sitting at the shore, sending flat stones skipping across the calm water. I don't care for the atmosphere of revelry around the fire. I never get drunk, preferring that my men always see me sober. I join the Spaniard, also picking up a flat stone and making it skip. Gabriel de Rojas watches, amused. He stands up, and we start to compete. Finally, we drop onto the sand, looking up at the sky. In the distance, we hear the men's shouts.

"I'm grateful for what you did this morning. Kerrigan nearly took me down with him."

"He should be grateful to you for the rest of his life for killing that barracuda."

I change the subject and ask, "Don't you drink?"

"Not like that. It seems improper for a gentleman."

"Are you one?" I ask with interest.

"Yes, I am."

"There aren't many gentlemen on my ship. Only Juan de Beltrán, Coleridge, and I are of noble descent."

"What good is distinguished lineage if there's no fortune to go along with it, right? In Castile, I was Don Gabriel de Rojas del Valle y Figueroa, a noble on all four sides. But my aristocratic family went broke. The usurers made off with our patrimony. After that, my father got sick and died. Since my rancid last name didn't allow me to make an honest living, as a very young man I had to embark for America. I've made the rounds of these islands. Finally, I was named captain of the fort on Hispaniola."

"And what was the captain of a fort doing being held prisoner on the flat-bottomed boat I seized?"

Gabriel de Rojas's face registers deep bitterness. "One of the city's aldermen, Don Rodrigo Pimentel, plotted to have me kidnapped from the island."

"Do you hate him?"

"You don't know how much."

"What happened?"

"A complicated story. I've got a grievance with him. That's why—just so you know—I intend to escape."

"And, just so you know, I will have you whipped if you do."

"I don't care. I just want to reach the city of Santo Domingo, and I'll succeed."

"We're not going to Hispaniola. Our destination is Bermuda."

"Are you sure you want to go there?" His expression is friendly.

"What's wrong with it?" I ask, surprised.

"There are rumors among the men that you left England to get away from Cromwell since your family was a follower of King Charles. Well, the governor of Bermuda has fallen, and now it's controlled by men loyal to the lord protector. You could end up on the gallows, as a pirate and a traitor. Officially, they would sentence you for the former, but in reality, the English don't care about pirates. What they don't like in the least are Royalists prowling about the Caribbean. They had enough of that with Prince Rupert!"

"I came to the Caribbean with him," I say with some pride. "I was a lieutenant in His Majesty's navy. And what if I can't go to Bermuda?"

"Go to Tortuga. The buccaneers will welcome you. The island is nearly independent. There's a French governor, Fontenay, who is only interested in gold and who lets the buccaneers and pirates govern themselves."

"I doubt that, in such a pirates' nest, there are enough supplies to repair our ship, much less wood for a new foremast."

"You're wrong! Tortuga is as good a place as anywhere else in the Caribbean. There is commerce, provisions, no one asks any questions . . ."

I realize why he's so keen on Tortuga.

"Damn you, Rojas! And it's much closer to Santo Domingo, where you want to go at any cost."

Looking straight ahead at the waves, he tells me, "True, but if you go to Tortuga, I can help you out. I know the buccaneers well. When I was captain of the fort on Hispaniola, I reached an agreement with them, and they stopped attacking our ships for a while." Rojas speaks with startling serenity and self-control; he seems very sure of what he wants to do. "Afterward, I beg you to let me return to the city of Santo Domingo. I have a debt of honor pending."

I feel a stab of envy. Perhaps this gentleman is too honorable to stain his hands robbing and pillaging; he wouldn't be a thief and murderer like me. The angular features and direct gaze of Gabriel de Rojas inspire confidence. Perhaps he is telling the truth.

When we last reached port in Bermuda, the island was still Royalist, but that was over a year ago. It's very possible that Cromwell's government has taken charge, making a spearhead for the English in the Caribbean, whereas Tortuga and the eastern part of Hispaniola are practically beyond the control of the European nations. Now that I'm a man without a country, pursued by everyone, I need a place like that.

"I thought the buccaneers and the Spaniards were natural enemies, but I see you know them well."

"As you're well aware, the government of His Majesty King Philip considers the Caribbean a closed sea, property of the empire. He doesn't allow foreign commerce on these coasts."

"The sea should be open, without roads or frontiers! That's why I became a sailor many years ago. The captain of a ship dominates not only his ship but also thousands of marine miles. On that, I am in agreement with the buccaneers."

"The buccaneers," he says calmly, "in some sense admire me. Though almost all of them seem to me contemptible. They consider themselves free, independent of any government, but they're no more than criminals, only worthy of hanging from the gallows."

And that, of course, is the punishment awaiting me, whether I eventually fall into Spanish or English hands. It doesn't frighten me—a few minutes in the air, and I'll stop suffering. For a long time now, death hasn't worried me because I'm a man doomed to live.

I marvel that Rojas would speak so candidly, risking my wrath, but I do not rebuke him. Our silence is only broken by the soft sound of the waves lapping on the beach.

"Why did they throw you out of Santo Domingo?"

He gives a weary sigh. "Don Rodrigo Pimentel. A contempt-ible man, he bought the job of city alderman. A swine who buys up merchandise arriving on the Indies fleet so he can sell it at an abusive price. Also, he forces foreign ships to land so he can take possession of their goods, and he exercises illegal control over commerce on the island. Years ago, he used bribes to win the favor of Governor Bitrián y Viamonte, and the latter authorized him to arm privateers. Don Rodrigo controls a fleet and does with it whatever he likes."

"I didn't know there were pirates in the Spanish Armada."

"Yes, there are, though officially they aren't allowed since their smuggling displeases the Crown. Still, many governors, in various parts of the Caribbean and even on the mainland, have authorized them because it's an effective way to fend off attacks by the English, French, and Dutch. In any case, the ones who follow Don Rodrigo are the vilest criminals. The interim governor of Hispaniola, an upright judge, ordered the arrest of some of them. He's against privateers, thinking them no better than pirates. I agree with him completely."

I was a privateer; now I'm a pirate. Rojas has contempt for both groups. After sailing with outlaws for so long, I'm reminded of the world where I used to live, where decency and honor existed.

"One night," Rojas continues, "some men in hoods surrounded me and beat me savagely, then took me captive on the sloop where you found me. I overheard them plotting to throw me overboard so there would be no trace of the crime."

"Now you want revenge."

"It isn't only that. You see, Don Rodrigo was responsible for his niece, Doña Inés de Ledesma, a beautiful, wealthy, educated woman. One day she came to me and asked for my protection because Pimentel was, shall we say, pursuing her and forcing her to sign documents placing her inheritance in his hands. I fell in love with her. I went to see Pimentel and threatened him, saying that if he didn't leave her alone, I would have him thrown in jail. He pretended to repent from his evil deeds and even let me court her. Finally, I persuaded Doña Inés to accept my hand." Don Gabriel's voice wavers, but he presses on. "Now that I'm not there, anything could happen. She could even be forced to marry that scoundrel."

He pauses, as if embarrassed, and tells me, "She's what I love most in this world."

Upon hearing that, my head spins. I also loved once, but she died. I put her memory out of my mind, so it won't make me suffer.

Rojas goes on. "Don Rodrigo let me court Inés, but he was just playing with me. The sanctimonious hypocrite! As soon as he could, he got me out of the way. Just before he kidnapped me, the Court of Santo Domingo had offered me a mission that could have given me sufficient funds to marry her. Then, that . . . that wretch nearly had me killed and took away what I love most."

Rojas's words remind me that there is something other than wars and ships and savagery. Decency, honor, a woman to love—all that still exists.

"I also lost everything," I confess. "The house I grew up in, my fortune, my family, the love of my life, and even my own dignity."

Captain Rojas knits his brow. "The English war?"

"Yes, the war, treachery, and a dark fate leading me to damnation."

"No one is damned if they don't want to be," he insists. "Just today you saved Kerrigan from that barracuda!"

I turn away. "I just didn't want to lose a good gunner."

"Nonsense. No normal captain would have risked his life for a sailor. You were lucky it was alone; when they swim near shore, they usually do it in a school."

"I know. Not much scares me anymore."

"I believe you. I saw the sailors' alarm when you dove into the sea. When you returned, they looked so proud. Your men trust and admire you. And they matter more to you than you let on."

"Yes," I tell him hesitantly, "they do matter to me. They're all I have left."

Saying these words, I realize it's true. Although I shout at them, curse them, and if they deserve it, punish them harshly, I feel responsible for their fate.

"They matter to me because we're traveling on the same ship. We have a common destination." I pause, then say in a low voice, "The gallows and eternal damnation."

"You're wrong. That's what heretics think. No one is damned if they don't want to be."

"Then perhaps I've chosen it. When I enlisted, my father made me swear I would always be a man of honor." I feel a deep sorrow in my heart. "I haven't kept any of the vows I made to him."

Rojas observes me with pity. "And yet, you still care about everything your father taught you. Perhaps there is still hope."

"I've lost all hope of salvation. I live as if in a nightmare."

"Captain, some time ago, I heard a little play by a Castilian author. It said that life is a dream and dreams are only that. Maybe you should forget about the past, like a dream that is no more."

"No," I reply angrily. "The past is not a dream. It's ever present. It tortures me every day."

I can be silent no more. On this starry Caribbean night, the dam breaks and everything pours out of my soul. Sometimes I speak softly; other times I think I might be shouting. I don't know how or why, but I tell Gabriel de Rojas stories that I haven't even shared with Coleridge. The Spanish captain's profound dignity reminds me how blind fate has led me here, largely against my will. So, in the dark hours of the night, I tell him my life story, making no excuses, confessing all that has happened since my whole world was destroyed.

35

THE PAST

Caribbean Sea, September of 1653

"Mr. Rojas," I begin, "I come from a noble family, one which always had dealings with your country, as it shared our ancient faith."

I tell him about Oak Park, my parents and siblings, and my step-sister. I describe the happy days of our childhood and how war changed everything. The news of Thomas's death and then of my father's. Permeating everything, she comes to life again in my mind. Len is the only woman I have truly loved in my life.

"I needed her, I still need her, but she died." I pause. "I don't know why I'm telling you all this."

Gabriel de Rojas has let me speak for a very long time without interruptions. His dark silhouette is outlined by the moon, and some-how I feel he understands what happened in those times, maybe even better than I do.

He speaks at last. "Ships are careened so they will lose weight. You carry a very heavy weight, that of all you have lost. The time has come to free yourself from it."

I bow my head in grief, and the medallion I always wear falls onto the sand.

"All I have left of Len is this little tin medallion. I think it's the only thing that ties me to sanity when I have so often been on the verge of losing my mind. I remember the day she gave it to me. The sea was roaring. In the cove, my ship, the *Antelope*, was waiting. That's when I asked her to become my wife and the Lady of Oak Park. But I left and never saw her again."

Don Gabriel observes me compassionately, silently urging me to keep sloughing off the oppressive weight.

"After saying good-bye to Len, I boarded the *Antelope*. There, I found an unexpected situation; there was a difference of opinion about the course our Armada should take. Some wanted to head for Holland to secure supplies; others wanted to steer His Majesty's ships to Scotland. Coleridge told me that he and many of the other sailors thought it would be best to blockade the Thames River and attack the Parliamentarians' navy. I agreed. And that's what we finally did.

"We might have emerged victorious if it hadn't been for the fleet commander's indecisiveness and if the wind weren't against us. We remained for a long time—hours that seemed eternal—at the mouth of the river. From the bow, we could see the enemy's sails. A cool breeze was blowing, billowing our sails in the right direction, but we were anchored to the bottom of the estuary. The clouds streamed by overhead in the direction of London, where we should be going . . . but we weren't.

"'What the hell are we waiting for?' I shouted to Coleridge.

"'I don't know, damn it! It's absurd! If we attack those bastards now, we could have a shot at defeating Parliament. If we delay, that swine Cromwell will never relinquish power. Oh Piers, how I hate him and all the Puritan trash surrounding him! They think themselves the chosen ones, but they're nothing but cruel murderers.'

"'Our men aren't much better,' I replied. 'Nothing but blockheads, dandies, ballroom fops.'

"'At least they're nobles!' he protested. 'But right now, they do seem like a pack of cowards.'

"'Don't they realize that we need a quick victory? Our provisions are running low; morale is flagging.'

"Coleridge then said out loud the very thing I was thinking, the thing we couldn't say in front of the other officers. 'Our commanders have no backbone. Vice Admiral Batten is an incompetent coward who doesn't dare attack the men who used to be under his command.'

"'It's rumored that a Parliamentary squadron has left Portsmouth and is now in the canal. It could be here before long. Richard, if we don't attack soon, we'll be trapped in the crossfire.'

"As we were speaking, we noticed the wind suddenly turning, pushing us toward the open sea, away from the enemy. The commanders did nothing. Coleridge and I watched the sun setting, illuminating the river we should have sailed up. Deepest night fell. In the distance, we saw the lights of ships, and at first, we thought they were merchant marines. We sent a small vessel, a ketch, to find out what sort of ships we were confronting. But fog set in, and the ketch couldn't find the lights.

"Hours went by, and Coleridge and I stayed on the bridge, trying to see something in all that mist. Suddenly the fog lifted, and we discovered that our fleet sat square in the middle of the enemy squadron from Portsmouth. There was a moment of hesitation. I thought we should attack, but morning had not yet broken. In the dark of night, we ran the risk of firing on our own ships. We decided not to endanger the Prince of Wales, who was sailing with us, and we fled. The fate of the war was decided there, in a cowardly retreat by some sailors who didn't dare to fight.

"The Royalist squadron split up. Some of the ships returned to Holland, where the Prince of Wales, Vice Admiral Batten, and most of the sailors abandoned the navy. On the other hand, Prince Rupert of the Rhine, his brother Maurice, and a few others stayed on board and became pirates on the canal.

"The *Antelope* didn't take either of these routes. When they were ordered to head for the Dutch coasts, following the Prince of Wales, the crew mutinied. I don't blame them, though I remained loyal to the order given by my superiors, and I resisted the mutiny. The rebels took over the ship and headed toward the nearby coast of England, where they planned to join the Parliamentarian navy. As for those of us who refused, they forced us into the lifeboats and left us on the high seas, not far from the coast of Essex.

"I took command of my lifeboat. I realized we weren't too far from Oak Park, where we could get help. I never imagined what I was really going to find there."

I fall silent.

Gabriel has followed my tale with great interest. Now, in suspense, he asks, "What happened?"

36

THE ASHES OF OAK PARK

Oak Park, Summer of 1648

The sea was choppy, a wind was blowing from the east, pushing us where I wanted to go, but the lifeboat had no sails, and we were having to row forward. Thankfully, Ethan was on board—he was a strong young man who knew the coast well, having lived in my family's home as a servant.

In the rosy light of dawn, Coleridge's lifeboat was separated from mine. I could make out his tall figure directing the rowers, as if he were still on the bridge of the *Antelope*. They disappeared amid the waves of that choppy sea, and I thought I would never see him again. Fortunately, that didn't prove to be the case.

I think about Richard Coleridge. At present, he is the only link to my past as a sailor in His Majesty's navy. He is a courageous and generous man, but we aren't in the habit of unburdening ourselves with each other.

We spent all day on the high seas. Finally, in the distance, I could make out the cliffs of the Essex shore, the peninsula of Naze, the place of my childhood.

The sun was setting when, in the distance, I spotted the entrance to the cove. But the sea was still so choppy, and our lifeboat so poor that we would be dashed on the rocks if we dared enter, so we needed to drop anchor and wait.

Time went by. Suddenly, in the midst of the blackness, a bright light appeared just where Oak Park should have been. A fire. I tried to row the boat to land, but the sea was still too wild. I screamed at the sailors to approach the coast, but they could not obey.

We spent the night doing battle with the waves. I was horrified by the massive blaze. Then, just before daybreak, in the place where the Norman Tower stands, some crows flew off, and I thought I saw torches. I suspected that something terrible was transpiring. At that moment, the wind changed, and our little lifeboat was swept away from the anchorage. Finally, we managed to land on a beach far north of Oak Park, near Harwich.

I ordered the men to scatter in different directions so as not to draw attention and told them which towns were closest. We embraced, clapping one another on the back. They were loyal and honest men, able and disciplined sailors. As they were leaving, they told me they would like to serve under me again someday.

Ethan and I set out toward Oak Park. I calculated that we must have been about ten miles to the northeast. After walking for hours, we approached the Naze peninsula, and smoke filled our nostrils. I didn't say anything to Ethan, who watched me with a worried expression. I've never been able to forget that gray, sorrowful day. I've never spoken about it to anyone.

At last, we climbed a hill, and there before us was the house, still smoking, the granaries and stables already devastated. Throwing caution to the wind, I took off, running, followed by Ethan. I couldn't find anyone. I thought my mother, Len, and my sisters might have hidden in the cellars, so I went down to the ancient Catholic chapel, now destroyed by Puritan hordes feverish with hatred. The open tabernacle had been profaned, the figures of the saints mutilated, the benches broken. I kicked my way through all that debris, looking for some trace of my loved ones. I found nothing. We left that place.

We went on inspecting the ruins of what, for hundreds of years, had been my family's estate: the pond of now-darkened water, the dovecote, the patio with the well. There was no one anywhere. All we heard was the wailing of the wind. A drizzle was falling, so light that it didn't soak us. I told Ethan to search the house and the kitchen again, as best he could, and I headed for the Norman Tower.

The crows seemed to be calling me, drawing me toward the ancient watchtower. I knew I was going to find something terrible there. The tower stood impassively; it didn't seem to have sustained any damage. The old door creaked when I pushed on it.

A faint light from the doorway revealed the form of a woman. I took a few hesitant steps and knelt. Then I discovered the lifeless body of my sister Margaret. Her beautiful dark hair was stained by a river of dried blood, her skull shattered by a brutal blow. I knelt there for a long time, howling over her. Oh Lord! What could have happened? Margaret was pure joy, carefree trust. How could they have done this to her? I caressed her hair. At last, I kissed her face and gently lifted her up.

With my sister's body in my arms, I left the tower. It was sundown and fog was rolling in again. It was hard to carry the now-rigid body, and I stumbled along under the weight, my eyes on the ground as I tried not to think of anything at all. I walked through the mist toward the small hill with the grand oak on top. I set poor Margaret's cold body under the tree and sat a moment to catch my breath. Then I heard something swaying above me, creaking like the pendulum of an old clock.

I lifted my head and screamed. From the old oak tree where Len and I used to play as children swung the body of my great-uncle Andrew, an elderly Jesuit priest.

Ethan heard me and came running. He could only stammer, "My God! My God! So much evil!"

With the knife in my belt, I cut the rope, and we took the body down. I can still see his bruised face, his black tongue hanging out. We set him gently on the ground next to Margaret.

Ethan left to find some shovels. When he returned, he found me kneeling over the corpses of my loved ones, doubled over, my face in my hands. He touched me on the shoulder, and it seemed as if I was waking from a dream. We buried my sister and my uncle there, under the oak tree. I struck at the earth repeatedly for hours, trying to vent my fury. I was held together by the hope that my mother, Ann, and Len were still alive. I had to find what was left of my family and try to save it at all costs.

Since Ethan wasn't well known in Walton, I sent him to find out what had happened and sat to wait by the back of the house. Suddenly, I heard hooves. I hid, thinking the assassins had returned. But it was some of our horses. They had managed to escape and, frightened by the fire, galloped nervously around the estate. Now that everything was quiet, two were returning to the stable—the very ones that Len and I had ridden years earlier. I whistled to them, and they approached. I know they'd be useful later.

When Ethan returned, he told me that, in the village tavern, the only topic of conversation was the events at Oak Park. "Who would have guessed!" people murmured. "Who would have suspected that behind the Leighs' elegant walls lurked a horrible papist plot?"

All sorts of lies about the family spread around Walton. But what really interested me was the news that my brother-in-law, William Ruthven, had been in town. Perhaps he could tell me the whereabouts of my mother, my sister, and Len. If he had been there, I thought, perhaps they had been saved.

37

LADY ELIZABETH RUTHVEN

London, Summer of 1648

Around sunset on that foggy day, we set out for London. We rode well around Walton-on-the-Naze to avoid anyone recognizing me. We had to keep to the woods anyway, as our appearance was suspect: two men dressed as sailors, riding horses bareback. We didn't have any money or the safe conduct pass we needed to travel in those times of conflict.

Along the way, I mulled over who could intercede on behalf of my family. My father's Royalist friends had all been executed or were in exile. And who would defend some Catholic women? But perhaps my sister Elizabeth could help us. She and especially her husband had friends in Parliament. That's where I fixed my hopes. How wrong I was!

We reached London two days later and tried to reach Aldgate, but night had fallen, so the gate was closed. We circled around the eastern part of the wall and passed by the ancient abbey of Santa Clara until we reached Tower Hill. From there, we could make out London's streets, which were illuminated by the misty glow of the windows and street lanterns. Everything seemed closed to us.

We would only be able to enter the city by way of the Thames River. Cautiously, we rode toward the pier next to where St. Katharine's by the Tower once stood. We left the horses shut in an empty warehouse and went on foot down to the dock. It was deserted at that late hour, but full of vessels. We untied a small boat and ventured into the dark waters, rowing countercurrent with all our strength. The fog was as thick as I've ever seen it. We passed the London Bridge, the Cathedral of Saint Paul, and the western wall.

A bit before Westminster, the river lapped at the gardens of several beautiful palaces. I managed to spot my stepsister's pier, and we climbed to the Ruthven mansion. On the ground floor, some lights burned. We slipped through a wrought iron gate and headed to the back door, where we hid behind a cart. I knew it would be safest to speak with my sister alone, so I asked Ethan to knock and find out if the owners were at home and whether they had any guests. He took one step, but I stopped him, saying, "No, it's better to wait until someone comes out."

Half an hour later, the door opened, and a servant stepped out to throw away some dirty water. She jumped, frightened, when Ethan approached, and tried to run back inside.

The sailor stuck his foot in the threshold. "Don't scream. I won't hurt you. Do you have something to eat?"

"Why should I give it to you?"

"I've fought alongside your master, against the Royalists. I'm sure he would help someone like me."

"My master isn't here."

"Then let me speak with your mistress."

But I had already stepped out of the shadows.

"Master Piers!" she exclaimed. "We know what they have done to your mother and your family. My mistress is distraught."

It was Mary O'Neal, a young Irishwoman who had been my sisters' maidservant.

"Will Lord Ruthven be home soon?"

"I expect so. He doesn't usually stay away for long."

"I must see my sister."

"Hurry, come in!"

Ethan stayed behind, while Mary, who talked on and on, horrified by what had happened at Oak Park, led me to my sister's room.

Elizabeth was writing by candlelight. She didn't seem as beautiful as when we were children. Much of my sister's charm had been her gaiety; now nothing of that remained. Her mouth and eyes oozed bitterness. When she saw me, she yelped in surprise, then broke into tears.

Apparently, Ruthven had returned two days prior, bragging about uncovering a horrible papist plot. He'd told her that our family got what they deserved.

"When I got married," she confessed, "I told my husband that Father and Lady Leigh were papists, that the Leighs had always been. I know, Piers, don't look at me like that. I was furious with Father because he didn't approve of my marriage. And Ruthven didn't seem bothered by it. At that time, I didn't know him well and thought I was in love. Then I discovered that he is cold, calculating, greedy. And he has always hated the papists. He waited to use that information when it suited him best: when he needed money and when Margaret and Ann were staying here at the house."

"Yes, I remember. It hurt Len and me so much when Uncle Andrew told us about it."

"My husband is so ambitious, Piers. He used me to climb in the court. Now he only wants to score points with Fairfax and Cromwell's henchmen. A few months ago, he needed more money, and he planned to blackmail Father again, but he was already in Colchester and then he died. I thought he would end up extorting it from Lady Leigh. I never imagined that he would go this far."

I clenched my fists when she mentioned my mother, but said nothing.

Elizabeth continued. "Some time ago, a new pastor arrived in the church we attend on Sundays. To my surprise, his wife was Mademoiselle

Maynard, Margaret and Ann's old governess. Ruthven invited them to dinner repeatedly, and he always got her to talk about the Leighs. One day, she mentioned the ghost stories about the cellars. She said it was just foolishness, but my husband started to connect the dots."

She took a breath and bitterly went on. "He had people spy on Oak Park and bribed former servants. Finally, he learned about the clandestine Masses. As soon as he found out they were going to celebrate a Mass, he left right away. He had everything prepared. Ruthven knew full well that, if he demonstrated that the Leighs were holding papist ceremonies under their roof, their goods would be expropriated and that patrimony, the lands and house, would increase my fortune—which is to say, his. He himself led the Roundheads to Oak Park."

I was blind with anger, but still said nothing. I wanted Elizabeth to go on with the story, to tell me where my mother, Ann, and Len were.

"He told me," she said in a weaker voice, "that Margaret died, but I don't know how and don't want to know. He said your mother, Ann, and the little Spanish girl have been taken to a prison in Bridewell. He threatened me and said if I don't obey his every whim, I'll end up the same as them. He's proud of what he's done, Piers. His friends all congratulated him."

Elizabeth was trembling, stricken with grief and guilt. I almost felt sorry for her, but then she said, "Honestly, Piers, I don't much care what happens to the Irish witch, but I beg you, if you can, do something for Ann."

I could have strangled her, but it wasn't worth it. Elizabeth was nothing more than a vain, selfish woman who had played her cards wrong. How could I have admired her so? How could I have trusted that she would help me? At that moment, I thought of Len, who my sister had always underestimated and who, for her part, had her own reservations about Elizabeth.

Outside, we heard the wheels of a carriage. Elizabeth peered out the large window and turned pale.

"Ruthven! You must go."

She ran over to her desk, and out of a hidden drawer, took a purse with a few coins. She gave them to me, saying it was all she could do. Then she opened a little door leading to the servants' stairs.

I followed them down to the kitchen, where Ethan was talking with Mary. The servant gave us some food and accompanied us to the pier. Downriver, we passed right in front of Bridewell. I stopped the boat, but it was impossible to infiltrate a place like that.

In the warehouse, the horses neighed softly when they saw us. We ate what Mary had given us and lay down on some old fishing nets. But I didn't sleep. Len, Ann, and my mother were just a few miles upriver. I had to save them.

At dawn, we heard the stevedores coming to load the ships. We grabbed the horses' reins, and they tamely followed. We followed the wall and ended up on Tower Hill. From there, we could see the inside of the Tower of London: soldiers on watch, cooking fires . . . At a sad-dlemaker's shop outside the city walls, we bought harnesses and saddles for the horses, and at a used clothing stand, cloaks and dry clothing.

Ethan suggested we head for the port, find a boat, and get out of there before we were caught, but I told him I couldn't leave my family. I debated where to go. Suddenly, I remembered the Spanish ambassador. He'd had friendly relations with my father; perhaps he could help us. I said good-bye to Ethan at the entrance to Ely Place, and we agreed he would wait for me with the horses on St. Katharine Docks.

The ambassador was very cautious, which wasn't surprising. Cromwell had triumphed, and Don Alonso de Cárdenas was the am-bassador of King Philip IV, a firm champion of the pope. Still, I called for his help stubbornly, almost impertinently.

Don Alonso listened to me respectfully, but insisted he couldn't do anything. Then he begged me to go because I put him in a compromis-ing position. Before I left, I asked that he at least do something for Len, who was a Spanish subject. Wide-eyed, he repeated her name: Catalina de Montemayor y Oquendo. He told me about the captivity of Isabel de Oquendo and her daughter, of the large ransom demanded for their freedom. Len's current imprisonment posed an even greater challenge. He would try to help, but couldn't promise anything. I left the embassy deeply discouraged.

I paid a boatman to take me to Ethan. From the boat, I once again passed in front of the prison. In the light of that grim, cloudy day, I stared at the rough walls enclosing everything I had left in life. Little by little, slowly, they were left behind. The boatman, a somber and cross man, rowed unhurriedly down the Thames. I landed at St. Katharine Docks, but as I walked toward where I was to meet Ethan, I felt myself being watched. Two masked men were following me. I picked up my pace. In the distance, I could see Ethan: I signaled to him, and at that moment, they attacked. I struggled with the men, and during the fight, one of them fell to the ground. His cape came open, and I recognized the shield of the house of Gowrie, Ruthven's livery. Taking advantage of my surprise, the other man slugged me, and I lost consciousness.

When I came to, I felt the rocking of a ship and heard the sound of the sea. Ethan had managed to free me from the attackers and had located a boat headed for Ireland. He had traded the horses to pay for the passage. He told me later that the captain hadn't wanted to run the risk of taking on two men, one of them wounded. He suspected we were Royalists escaping from the city.

The trip to Ireland was eventful. The waves were so high that I thought we would shipwreck, but that storm was overpowered by my shame at leaving behind my mother, Ann, and my darling Len. I felt I had failed them.

We reached Dublin, controlled at the time by Governor Jones, a man loyal to Parliament. Without funds, food, or anyplace to go, I needed several days to recover from the beating that Ruthven's men had given me. I longed to return, but the naval blockade prevented it. With no other options, I got a job as a stevedore in the port.

38

A Sailor Again

Ireland, Winter of 1649

That winter in Dublin was soaking wet and ice-cold. Often, we couldn't get work because there were few ships to unload. We slept in one stable or another until we were discovered and kicked out. Other times, we slept in the doorway of some church devastated by English persecution. Most of the time, we slept on the streets. When we scratched together some money, we would always head for the taverns in the port. Afraid that the governor's men might interrogate us, we tried to slip by, unnoticed. In those dives, you heard all kinds of rumors. Once in a while, someone would arrive from London, and I would try to glean news of my family, but I had no luck.

One day, I found a newspaper left on a table. There, in the *Mercurius Britannicus*, I read that the Leighs' land had been confiscated and turned over to the Countess of Gowrie following the deaths of her last family members. The *Mercurius* went on to praise God for freeing his chosen people from three papist demons. That's how I knew that my mother, Len, and my sister Ann had been executed.

After that, my desperation was infinite. I became an extremely violent and aggressive man. Through physical work, I developed great strength, and everyone in the port began to fear me. Kindly Ethan was afraid they might arrest me in a brawl and recognize me as a Royalist.

"My lord," he told me, "you must calm down; you're killing yourself."

"And what the hell do you want me to do? I'm a navy officer, not a goddamn dockworker. Give me a ship, and I'll kill all of Cromwell's thugs! I won't leave a single Roundhead alive!"

Despite my sorry state, Ethan never abandoned me. He managed to find out that Prince Rupert, along with what was left of the Royalist navy, had dropped anchor on the southwest coast of Ireland, where the blockade was. Begging, we made our way to the port of Kinsale, looking for our former comrades. The trip across Ireland revealed to us the horror Cromwell's troops had inflicted: devastated villages, profaned churches, ancient monasteries toppled to the ground, lost harvests, hunger, suffering everywhere.

In Kinsale, I met with the remains of His Majesty's navy. Oliver Cromwell was now in charge, since Charles II's father had been decapitated—like mine. I recuperated some of my lost dignity when they gave me a posting on the *Defiance*, the ship of Prince Maurice, brother of Rupert of the Rhine. There, I reunited with Richard Coleridge. We were delighted to see each other again, each having thought the other dead. When he asked about my family and Oak Park, I couldn't bring myself to answer.

For several months, we remained blockaded in the port by the ships of Admiral Robert Blake. Meanwhile, Cromwell's forces defeated Ireland's Catholic federation, and his cruelty toward the population was unimaginable. He is a brutal fanatic, and someday, history will judge him as such. Fortunately, toward the middle of October, storms forced Blake's ships to retreat, and in the middle of hurricane winds, we were able to escape the port and set a course for the open sea.

39

THEN A PRIVATEER

Caribbean Sea, May 1652

After acting as privateers for three years in the Mediterranean, pursued by the ships loyal to Parliament, we were forced to abandon the European coast, and we ended up in the Azores and Mauritania. Following many hardships, we crossed the Atlantic.

We reached the Caribbean and landed on Saint Lucia. We secured provisions and water, repaired the sails, and then set out for Bermuda, the first colony to recognize Charles I. The Royalists had expelled the governor and elected a local fellow named John Trimingham in his place. Trimingham received the troops led by Princes Rupert and Maurice effusively, providing weapons and provisions as well as a privateer patent that allowed us to attack Parliamentary ships and required us to pay tribute to the Crown. Coleridge and I, together with others from the *Defiance* (they didn't let my faithful Ethan accompany us), had transferred to a recently captured brigantine, the *Charles*. Buoyed by the strength of the ship, Captain Robert Allen accepted men from different nationalities and interests to complete the crew.

Bermuda was also where Rodrigo de Alcalá joined us. Richard Coleridge's face was swollen from a terrible toothache. In a tavern by the port, a barber pulled the tooth after getting Richard drunk to dull the pain. The next day, we went to pay him, but found the governor's men trying to arrest the man as a spy for the Spaniards. Richard was grateful to him, so we intervened and took Rodrigo aboard.

After we left Bermuda, there was a truly terrible storm. The hurricane winds whipped up waves higher than the towers of Westminster Abbey, lifting ships to the sky and then plunging them into the abyss. Captain Robert Allen, a despot fond of rum and lashings, was drunk, so it was up to me, his twenty-two-year-old officer, to save the *Charles*. We sailed behind the *Defiance*, my former ship, and saw it lifted on the crest of a gigantic wave . . . and then disappear. That wasn't the only ship we lost.

That storm led me to break my final ties to the Royalist cause. Up to that moment, I had still felt like a man of honor. I was the first lieutenant of a brigantine in the Royal Navy. We would attack ships, yes, but in the service of the Crown. Now it seems absurd, but at the time, we considered ourselves honorable privateers. Captain Allen changed my view of things. He was incompetent and cruel, one of the many wealthy dandies who had fought in the war. On the Royalist side, it wasn't the best trained who were promoted, but the ones with claim to the highest nobility.

After some terrible hours, when we all thought we were going to die, the wind and rain ceased, and the waves subsided. The sun shone once again over the ocean, and the remnants of the squadron regrouped. When we confirmed that the *Defiance* was gone and that Maurice was surely dead, brave Prince Rupert decided we should return to Europe to support his cousin, Charles II.

Allen wanted to follow Rupert, but our ship was too damaged to make the crossing, and anyway, I was done fighting for kings. Richard was conflicted, but always a loyal friend, he supported me. Most of the crew did, too. Allen accused me of insubordination and threatened me with a council of war, but I was the true captain of that ship.

And I didn't want to return to England, where my loved ones had been murdered. Anyway, I had never been a true Royalist, just a young man desperate to sail, and later, to avenge the death of my brother and the wicked execution of my father.

Now I see that perhaps Allen was right, and we should have followed Prince Rupert. When Richard and I deserted the Royalist squadron, we had no idea that decision would lead us to a hell of excess, crime, and horror. Thus began the worst period of our lives.

40

FINALLY, A PIRATE

Caribbean Sea, October 1652

I set course back to Bermuda, while Sir Robert Allen took refuge in his cabin, drinking and cursing me. The winds took us toward the nearby coast of Maracaibo, where we were attacked by a pirate ship. They couldn't let such appetizing prey escape. Though it was damaged, the *Charles* was a beautiful, twin-masted brigantine with square sails and eighteen cannons. In the course of the rapid attack, most of our men were killed, including Sir Allen.

When the pirates took over our ship, they made the survivors choose between death and joining their crew. We chose the latter.

In the beginning, Richard and I were repulsed by the pirates. All we thought about was escaping. Accustomed to the discipline and order of the Royal Navy, we found the anarchy, filth, cruelty, and impiety of those men repugnant. An incredibly brutal life began, with atrocities and barbarity I would rather not relate, and over time, I began to enjoy it. We would board ships, destroying everything, then dock in small ports and lose ourselves in the godforsaken taverns and in the arms of women whose faces we couldn't remember afterward.

That was when Coleridge began to drink more and more. I, on the other hand, discovered something I'd had a taste of in Dublin: that violence freed me from the painful weight of the past; it produced in me a release similar to what rum produced in Richard. I began to get a reputation as harder than anybody, but sharp-witted and an expert sailor. After another harrowing storm, the old pirate ship sank, and our brigantine was all that remained. Then the survivors elected me as the new captain.

We went on being a pirate ship, but I imposed an iron discipline and wouldn't tolerate the least insubordination. I organized the chain of command with the strict severity of the Royal Navy. George Kennedy, one of the old pirates, became my chief mate. Coleridge was second mate. Juan de Beltrán, an expert in nautical charts who was educated at the University of Seafarers in Seville, became my pilot. Hernando de Montoro, a Dominican Creole, was named third mate. Montoro had no sailing experience, but he was a strong leader with an explosive but loyal temperament. I felt a kinship with the man, knowing that in the depths of his soul, he was a farmer who wanted nothing more than to return to an honorable life with his family.

As for the rest of the crew, it was made up of people from every class and circumstance, each with his own history. There were Englishmen who, like me, were forced to join the pirates; pirates of every race, nationality, and religion; runaway slaves; some men who'd joined voluntarily, mostly Spanish and Portuguese; and a few Irishmen exiled to the Caribbean by the Parliamentary government.

When I agreed to be captain just over a year ago, I demanded blind obedience from them. As you know, ships are closed worlds where relationships play a decisive role. He who governs them must achieve cohesion in the interests of a common destiny.

And I achieved it. Even the old pirates, unaccustomed to any authority, respected me because they saw the effectiveness of my methods. Before long, we had taken a large number of prisoners. We would board

English and Spanish ships, Dutch ships loaded with salt, Portuguese ships filled with spices, and ships flying the French fleur-de-lis. The fame of the pirate Leigh spread all over the Caribbean, and all the powers operating here have put a price on my head.

After I tell Rojas this, I fall silent. I grab a handful of fine sand and let it slip slowly through my fingers. The songs and shouts of my men can no longer be heard; they are sleeping like logs some distance from where we sit.

Gabriel de Rojas shakes his head and says, "I still marvel that a noble gentleman with an exquisite education could turn into a notorious pirate."

"Nothing comes suddenly," I respond. "After a horrific war, after the death of my loved ones, after the loss of the woman that I loved, something shattered inside me. Which is worse, a brutal war or the organized crime of piracy? Where is there more wickedness: in the corrupt Royalist army or in this wandering life of maritime thieves?

"As you know, in honest naval service, food is often insufficient, inept officers abuse their inferiors, and salaries are low or never paid. Here, the sea belongs to sailors. We are authentically free. The most capable is the one in command.

"I'll confess to you, though, that deep down, the three vows that I made to my father still resonate: that I wouldn't use violence to get rich, that I would behave as a man of honor, and that I would remain faithful to the traditions of my ancestors."

I lift my head and let my gaze wander over the black horizon that is broken by the silvery trail of the moon.

"I know that, because of my crimes, I'm condemned to hell, but sometimes a little light opens up, and memories emerge of the faces of the past. The golden hair of my sister Ann as she bends over a book. The soft voice of Margaret, singing a ballad. My honorable father, my warm mother. My uncle Andrew, who died a martyr. Above all, the adorable face of my Len, my Len! She was innocence and joy itself.

No one was spared from the brutality and fanaticism of Cromwell's Puritans, but she wasn't even from our country.

"When I gaze at the ever-changing, unfathomable sea, I feel that there is someone beyond myself, a merciful being who perhaps one day will take pity on me and carry my ship to a good port."

There is once again silence between the two of us. Gabriel de Rojas finally breaks it.

"You can't take the blame for everything," he says. "What happened to your family is not your fault. There was nothing you could do for them."

"Talking with you, Mr. Rojas, has brought back the years of my childhood, the joys of an honorable life, the days of peace with my family at Oak Park. Why have I survived instead of them, who were infinitely better than me? Perhaps that's why I feel that I'm damned. My only duty is to my crew, though I can't entirely trust them."

"Captain, my journey has also been complicated, and the path fate has led me on is twisted. Perhaps Providence brought us together. When you captured the sloop on which I was held prisoner, you saved my life. But how did you lose the *Charles*?"

41

KENNEDY'S BETRAYAL

Caribbean Sea, October 1653

"After a few idle weeks in the waters of Pernambuco, we made out a convoy of ships of great tonnage. Pereira, one of the old pirate crew, thought they might be ships from Brazil and were carrying riches. We hid the cannons, and I had most of the men go below deck so we could pass as a merchant ship. When one of the Portuguese ships fell behind, we attacked. In its holds, we found sugar; skins; tobacco; and, most importantly, forty thousand gold doubloons, chains, and jewels of considerable value. We transferred the load to the *Charles* and fled when the rest of the convoy came back and began firing on us.

"Shortly afterward, not far from Hispaniola, I overtook the sloop where you were chained. While I was searching its hold, a watchman spied yet another boat on the horizon. Encouraged by our string of good luck, I decided to head after it in the sloop, while Kennedy, damn him, remained in command of the *Charles*.

"It was madness, but I had gone mad. To jump from one attack to another, to wield the sword, to fire the musket, to beat, lance, kill . . . I had become drunk on the need to do battle, and I left without verifying that your sloop had enough provisions and without imagining that

I couldn't trust Kennedy. When night fell, we lost the boat we were chasing, and the next morning, the storm began. Kennedy took advantage and fled with the Portuguese treasure—and the *Charles*. Let him be hanged! Someday he'll get what he deserves. These past two weeks, fighting against adverse winds, have been exhausting."

I take a breath and say, "My dear Mr. Rojas, you told me that life is a dream. For me, life isn't a dream but a nightmare in which I don't know if I'm dead or alive. I can still see Len in the cave the day she gave me this medallion. It's the only thing that relieves my anguish. It reminds me that Len existed and that there was a time when I was a man of honor."

My voice dies out, and I sit, looking at the heavens. The stars have turned slightly in the sky. Don Gabriel de Rojas watches me; his expression reveals compassion, not disdain. Why have I made this confession to him tonight? I don't know. Something about him inspires trust.

He suddenly speaks, firmly and gently. "Captain, someday I'll help you. I swear I will. You have saved me from certain death, and despite where life has led you, I know you are a good man."

I am shocked by his words, and by the sincerity in his voice.

"All right," I tell him. "We'll go to Tortuga, and if you help me, you'll be free to go wherever you like."

"That's not what I meant! I swear that, one day, I shall help you escape the hell where you find yourself."

Gabriel de Rojas rests his head on his knees, and after a long time, I can hear his slow, rhythmic breathing. He has fallen asleep. I fall backward on the sand and stare at the thousand stars of the night. Something in their tranquility comforts me and gives me hope.

42

THE BOARDING

Caribbean Sea, October 1653

We're once again on the open sea, and an immense horizon without laws or prohibitions, apart from my own, spreads before us. When I woke up from that night with the Spaniard, my men were still sleeping off their drink. I kicked them awake, shouting curses, and they soon got to work. They careened the ship, repaired the damage as best they could, and loaded the water, meat, and fruit we had found on the island, while I discussed our new course with Coleridge.

"It seems that Bermuda is now controlled by Cromwell's men," I explained. "Rojas has proposed that we head for Tortuga instead."

"Do you think the Spaniard is trustworthy?"

"He strikes me as a gentleman. We have nothing to lose and perhaps something to gain."

"All right. But if he's trying to trick us . . ." Richard passed a finger over his neck as if it were a knife.

I watch the captured sloop rapidly approaching us. It's shining with a name that seemed a sign of luck: *Indomitable.* The foremast has lost its original height, but it's upright again. Esteban Centeno, the carpenter, and his assistants have done a miraculous job. A soft, warm wind puffs up the mended sails and pushes us toward our destination. A flock of gulls follows off starboard. Above the noise of the waves, I can hear the intermittent sound of the rigging, a joyful music. There is something luminous and happy in this warm morning.

Coleridge and I exchange glances. I signal to him, and we begin racing up the foremast. The sailors have already seen us do it a thousand times, and they follow our contest with interest. Today, I reach the crow's nest first. From the top, I point at the horizon, and Richard shouts, "Onward toward Tortuga!" We laugh. The world is at our feet, like when we were cadets. Ten years have passed since then. Suddenly, all remorse vanishes from my mind. I think that our way of living might be just like any other, always moving ahead through the ocean.

From the crow's nest, I can survey the orderly ship from stem to stern. The deck gleams; it almost looks like a navy vessel. We stay there for a while and then descend, sliding down from the tallest rod in the mainmast, sweating.

"I'll be damned! Richard, I've beat you again."

We realize that some of the sailors are standing around, watching us.

Coleridge shouts, "Cosme, what are you doing? I don't want to see anyone slacking."

Once they've all gone about their business, I smile and tell Richard, "If it weren't for the huge quantity of gold he made off with, I'd almost be happy that rascal Kennedy has left."

Coleridge's slightly slanted eyes crinkle at the corners when he smiles; he understands me perfectly. The wind ruffles the little hair he has left.

"Yes, he ended up with the worst of the crew. Luckily, when we boarded the *Indomitable*, we did it with our best."

From my crew on the *Charles*, in addition to Hernando de Montoro, Rodrigo de Alcalá, George Kerrigan, and Cosme de Azúa, we've got helmsman Blas de Alcolea and pilot Juan de Beltrán, a strange fellow. The rest of the crew are those who survived when we boarded the *Indomitable*. These new sailors aren't crafty, nor have they committed the atrocities I have witnessed and ordered in recent times. Little by little, I'm getting to know them, like I got to know Valentín de Torres and Esteban Centeno. They have accepted their fate and seem to trust in me as their captain.

After we have sailed for a while with a constant following wind, the watchman gives a shout of alert: "Sail ho!" I hurry toward the forecastle, and once I'm on the bowsprit, Juan de Beltrán passes me the spyglass.

"Which way is it sailing?" I ask. "Windward or leeward? Situate it for me on the compass!"

"It's headed windward!"

The sails on the horizon are becoming more visible.

"Bow windward!" I order.

For a few instants, I observe the potential prey, the same flat-bottomed boat that we lost sight of a few days earlier. We speed up, but I'm not as happy as on previous occasions. Perhaps, after the conversation with Rojas, something trembles inside me: the remains of my decency? Another assault; there will be death, pain. Once again, I feel condemned to hell. After this one, there will be more. I will keep on destroying, killing, and looting.

Suddenly, an excuse crosses my mind, and I shout so everyone can hear. "Mr. Coleridge! Do you think we can catch up with it? Is our ship up to the task?"

"Don't worry, Captain," he answers from the aftercastle. "It isn't totally rigged yet, but our *Indomitable* is sailing well and will give it chase."

I feel the men's eyes on me. They want to attack; perhaps on that approaching ship lies the fortune that slipped out of our hands with Kennedy's escape. I can't let them down.

I look through the spyglass again. I can distinguish the X-shaped cross of the white flags on the patache or flat-bottomed boat, indicating that it belongs to the Spanish Empire. I order that Rojas be taken below deck; I don't trust that he will remain neutral. He protests, but I am sure my decision is correct. Coleridge agrees.

During the hours that follow, a strong wind propels us over the sparkling waters. When we are about three hundred breaststrokes from the prey, we hoist the pirate flag, two black cutlasses against a red background, and we hear the crew's shouts. I turn around and see that Kerrigan is awaiting my orders.

"Aim with the culverins in the bow. We're going to give a warning shot!"

The wounded gunner limps over; his eyes are shining. He and other sailors support the pins, point the culverins in the direction of the patache, and adjust the angle.

"Ready, Captain!"

"Hold on!" I tell him.

At that moment, the wind dies almost completely. The two ships are rocking on the water, with both crews closely watching the sails, waiting for the gust that will fill them up again and give one of us an advantage. We are the fortunate ones. When we have it within range, I think it's now or never, and I shout: "Fire!"

I hear the thunder of the first cannonball; the deck fills with smoke. The gaff near their mast flies off, shattered. The patache slows its speed and sails straight into the barrel.

"Fire with the starboard cannons!"

We hit the mizzenmast, on the deck, in the hull. We must have taken many lives.

"They've surrendered, Captain! They're lowering the flag!"

It's the sharp voice of Valentín de Torres, who is perched almost at the end of the bowsprit. The cabin boy's chestnut hair flutters in the wind.

"Cosme, prepare the boats for boarding," I order the petty officer. As he obeys, I say loudly enough so everyone can hear, "Coleridge, you stay here, in command of the sloop."

Richard nods. What happened with Kennedy and the *Charles* isn't going to happen again.

I grasp the edge of a lifeboat and jump into it. Instead of sitting down on the aft bench, I head for the bow, turning my back to the oars. I want to get a good look at the patache as we approach, and I don't want my men to see my reluctance about the final attack.

I hear Coleridge's voice from the forecastle. "Lower the lifeboats!"

The two boats are hoisted and descend gently down the starboard timber. I turn and see that the oarsmen, from the original crew of the *Indomitable*, look hesitant.

"Row like mad! A good booty awaits!"

At the mention of a possible reward, they start rowing vigorously. As we approach the patache, we are greeted by musket fire. I hear a shout behind me; a bullet must have hit one of the oarsmen.

"Bastards! Didn't they surrender?"

I aim at a man near the stockade; he falls into the sea, plummeting from the port bow just a few yards away. I hear the thunder of a cannonball. In our sloop, they have realized what has happened and are firing on the Spanish ship.

When I jump onto the stockade, wielding my cutlass, I encounter several Spaniards. With one blow, I wound the first one deeply in the neck. Another one pierces my coat. A few steps away, Esteban Centeno shoots his musket. A man falls dead on the deck. The carpenter kisses the medallion of the Virgin hanging around his neck, shouting a blasphemy.

The rattle of musketry gives way to the clash of steel amid grunts and curses. My pirates are acting courageously now that they see the prey at hand. Those from the merchant ship also defend themselves well, but they're obviously sailors, not soldiers. Finally, the Spaniards surrender. Many of them have died; the deck is stained with their blood. I abhor these deaths, which happened because their fool captain didn't honor the surrender. And yet, what right do I have to kill some sailors who are just defending their cargo?

I snap to and start shouting orders to my men. We have also taken a beating; several of my men are wounded, and a few have ended their careers as pirates. I ask Blas to check the rudder. It is often targeted during attacks, rendering it useless, but the helmsman quickly informs me that hasn't happened this time.

"And the cargo isn't bad, Captain," he adds with a smile. "Mahogany, brocades, and other fabrics and Talavera china headed for Veracruz. We can get something for it in Tortuga."

A surviving Spanish sailor speaks up. "Don't count your chickens before they're hatched. Our ship can't have been far from the fleet; they'll come to our defense."

"Nonsense," says Blas. "A fellow down below says his captain was in a hurry to reach land for some reason. He says this patache arrived a couple of months ago from Seville. It made a stop in Santo Domingo, where most of the passengers got off, and they took on more passengers headed for New Spain. The mahogany was intended for construction work there."

I'm glad to hear we aren't about to be confronted by a powerful Spanish fleet. I have enough to worry about already. There's appalling disorder; we have caused much damage with our cannons. The men are shouting. Water is pouring into the lower deck, and we hurry down a hatch to see. While they staunch the flow and plug the hole, I examine the holds.

That's where the few passengers are packed in: families looking like farmworkers, coming to the New World in search of fortune but nearly encountering death. They look at me with fear, but also with contempt. I decide I don't care. I've taken a good quarry, and that's what counts. Then I head toward the cabin of the captain, who died in the fray. Normally, Spanish captains carry with them contraband gold and silver, nautical charts, and copies of the general electoral rolls of the University of Seafarers in Seville. The latter are essential instruments in these latitudes. Over my head, the deck is vibrating with the sound of running footsteps, but here, there is some order and calm for my troubled mind. Light streams in through the large stern windows, and digging around, I find the passenger list. None of those I saw in the hold looked like nobility, but if any are, we might be able to ask for a ransom. I sit down in a chair, prop my elbows on the desk, and carefully study the list of those who set sail. The meticulous record lists the names, circumstances, and destinations of all those who left Seville. I see no noble titles or church authorities. Then suddenly a name jumps out and stabs me through the heart.

43

IN THE CABIN OF THE SPANISH CAPTAIN

Señorita de Montemayor y Oquendo, Catalina. An orphan, she is going to meet her uncle, one of the judges of Santo Domingo.

God exists! Time and again, I reread the name. It's impossible. She's dead. It can't be her! I hesitate. That long-ago day at the lake in Oak Park returns to my mind: "I know my full name: Catalina de Montemayor y Oquendo." How I had laughed at Len's lengthy name, which I thought pompous. It was the first time I had heard it; Uncle Andrew had brought her to us recently, and she had barely spoken about her past, as if wishing she could erase it. Montemayor y Oquendo! It has to be her.

All these years I thought she was dead. I pictured her in heaven and condemned myself to hell. But if this list tells the truth, then Len is on this earth, not even far away from me. I open the door and stumble up the staircase, repeating to myself a thousand times, "Len! Len! Len!"

Outside, there is blood, dead and wounded men, and packages that have shifted around. A pole from the mizzen trembles in the air, about to fall onto the deck. *Len! Len! Len!* My thoughts split in two. Her image dominates my mind, and yet I must focus on what's happening on board. I shout orders here and there and have the sails run up the masts. Coleridge is doing the same thing, and our two ships are sitting parallel to each other. *Len! Len! Len!*

I tell Richard to send Rodrigo over; there will be work for him. With Centeno, I examine the mizzenmast. *Len! Len! Len!* Fortunately, the damage isn't serious; the shot has hit the rigging more than the mast. With planks from the hull, the carpenter and some sailors set about reinforcing it. *Len!* I'm in shock, moving as if through an unreal world.

Rodrigo de Alcalá arrives and sets about examining the wounded. I go to him. As usual, he is grumbling while he treats a wounded man.

"Drat my luck!"

"How is he?"

"Can't you see? Are you blind? His guts are nearly hanging out. Musket wounds are the worst. We've captured very little for the quantity of gunpowder we used. Now, Rodrigo de Alcalá must fix it, as usual. And Rodrigo de Alcalá is fed up, very fed up."

The sailor, leaning on the mainmast, is tottering from the pain. The open wound in his abdomen looks horrific.

"Don't worry; it's superficial," I tell the man in a croaking voice.

Then I, too, stumble, and not because of the grotesque wound. I lean on the physician, who shakes his head in annoyance. Then he turns to look at me. Despite his ill temper, he is an experienced man; he knows human nature. And he respects me, no matter how much he complains.

"Ahoy there! What's wrong with you, Captain?" he asks, worried. "Are you wounded? You look pale."

"No. Nothing's wrong with me."

"You look terrible."

"No, nothing's wrong."

Then I can't hold back from asking him, "Have you been on Hispaniola?"

"Yes, many times."

"Do you know the judges of Santo Domingo?"

"I wish I didn't!" he says with a snort.

"Do you know if one of them is named Montemayor?"

"Certainly. He's well known."

"Does he have a family?"

"I don't know. He used to live alone. He always dresses in black, but you know, we Spaniards like black. Judges in the Indies are supposed to remain single. I don't know much more than that. Perhaps Gabriel de Rojas can tell you more, considering he was captain of the fort."

I go on organizing the chaos of the captured ship, but my mind whirls. When the tasks are all distributed and the revelry has ceased, I row across the narrow stretch of sea separating the two ships. I take refuge in my cabin and pull out the list of passengers again, reading and rereading her name. Like a wild beast, I pace from one side of the cabin to the other. After a few minutes, I open the door and call for Gabriel de Rojas to be brought to my cabin.

I'm lost in thought, going over this life I lead. When I kill, as I did today, it seems to free me from my burden of hatred and guilt. When someone dies at my sword, I avenge myself, yes, but what good does that do me? I have murdered a man for defending what belonged to him. That death and so many others, what have they brought me? Nearly constant remorse, self-hatred, and a malaise that gnaws at my soul.

You wish it hadn't happened, that you hadn't brandished your sword, fired the musket, and destroyed your honor and the chance at an honest life. Dreadful dreams torment you at night. You think that being in constant action will help you find balance, peace, but that isn't the case. With this violence, with this life of a pirate, the one you're hurting most is yourself.

Oh Len! Len, come back to me! Return with me to that long-lost time of purity and innocence!

44

CHANGE OF COURSE

I think about this life that I lead, and it takes me a while to realize that someone is knocking on the door.

"Come in."

Gabriel de Rojas looks confused, but he just says, "You called me, sir?"

"Do you know a judge in Santo Domingo with the last name of Montemayor?"

"Of course, I know Don Juan Francisco de Montemayor well. He's my boss." I gesture for him to continue. "He has been serving as the interim governor of Hispaniola. I mentioned him several days ago; he was the one who had me arrest some of the pirates Pimentel is protecting. He is a man of honor."

"The sort who would hang me if he caught me!" I say.

He doesn't answer, but from the look in his eyes, I'm right.

"Is his niece living with him?"

"I remember he was expecting a niece, who was arriving on the Indies fleet."

"Did you ever meet her?"

"No. Thanks to Pimentel, I, uh, took my leave before the fleet came in."

"Thank you, Rojas. You may go."

Rojas bows his head and leaves. I'm left on my own, and my thoughts once again torment me. If it is Len, what do I have to offer the niece of Santo Domingo's principal judge? I, a pirate, a man who would be hanged in any port where he dropped anchor. How could I explain what has happened to me over the past few years? Could a being so pure love a thief, a murderer? Would I even be able to look her in the eye? Wouldn't it be better for me to forget her? To let her make a new life in these lands, with a new family, perhaps a new love? I'll keep heading out to sea, toward an unknown destination with no hope of return, following blind fate to perdition and the gallows.

Pulling out the tin medallion hanging on my chest, I kiss it. For in the depth of my soul, I feel that Len is nearby and that something supernatural is protecting us.

Through the aft window, I watch the sun sinking into a brilliant sunset. Time goes by, lights are lit on board the ship, and there are noises on deck: shouts, then a roar.

Before long, they call the captain.

There's a fight. By the light of the stars and a few candles, I see two sailors facing off with knives while the others gather around. I give a shout, and the brawl stops.

Hernando de Montoro hurries to explain. "They stole a barrel of sherry from the Spanish ship. They're dead drunk and fighting over a neckerchief."

I raise my voice. "You all know the rules. No fights on my ship, and if you steal booty before it's divided, we'll abandon you to your fate."

Coleridge grabs my arm.

"Piers," he whispers in English, "one of them is Duckey. He has sailed with us since Kinsale. And the other is Lope de Villarreal, a first-class sailor from the *Indomitable*."

Two worthy men, but I can't turn back if I want to maintain discipline, though perhaps it would be enough to have them whipped. I tell them how many lashes they should be given at noon the next day: sufficient, but not an exorbitant number. Then I turn to the guilty men. "You should give thanks that we're short on crew!"

The fighters are taken to the hold; no one says a word. Everyone knows that there are laws on my ship and that the captain is always obeyed.

I order that the booty they were fighting over be divided up. From a smoking pot comes a pleasant aroma; for once, dinner is substantial, since the hold of the Spanish ship was well stocked.

Coleridge, Hernando de Montoro, Juan de Beltrán, and I go down to supper in the officers' cabin, on the second deck. For the first time, I invite Gabriel de Rojas to join us. I know that Montoro and Coleridge don't entirely trust the Spaniard, so in between glasses of rum, I'll let them tease out his reasons for taking us to Tortuga.

While waiting for supper, we uncork the first bottle. Everyone drinks except me. I'm in a somber mood, and they can tell. I don't like having men whipped, least of all Duckey, who has been sailing with me for so many years. Juan de Beltrán begins to needle me.

"Corporal punishment goes against the laws of God."

Beltrán is a self-righteous fool, a sloppy man with rough features and long gray hair falling in greasy clumps. He's a good pilot, who once gave it up to become a friar. He had to hang up his habit when the Holy Inquisition began persecuting him, because his ideas verged on heresy.

"Would you rather that I hang them?"

"No, my captain, but if the men behave according to God's laws—"

"No more talk about God!" I roar. "We are in hell, goddamn it!"

"The captain just saved these men's lives. According to the laws of the sea, they should be thrown overboard," says Coleridge calmly.

Hernando de Montoro also rushes to my aid. "Ahoy there, Beltrán, always so fussy! We aren't in a whorehouse! There's order here! The captain is right!"

I like Montoro, a muscular, irascible fellow, smart and efficient though sometimes hard to get along with.

I compare my table companions: Montoro, his face red with anger; Beltrán, with his pretense of enlightenment; Gabriel de Rojas, mute and impassive. Richard is unflappable, as usual. Unlike the others, drinking makes him serene. He has already put away several glasses of rum. And though his Spanish accent is terrible, he understands everything.

I pause to look at him. Aside from his growing baldness and the incipient wrinkles around his eyes, Richard's face is the same as two years ago: classical features; dark, slanted eyes; very white skin. He intervenes again.

"After they whip him, Duckey will stop stealing. I doubt that Villarreal will, though, seeing as he's a Spaniard."

Rojas just arches his eyebrows, but Hernando de Montoro's hand moves to the handle of his weapon.

"What do you mean?" he shouts. "Shall I take the measure of Creoles and Spaniards with my sword?"

Coleridge ignores the threat. "Over these years, I've gotten to know the Spaniards: somber, strong, defiant, hot-tempered people. Individualistic, but not very disciplined. They can't take corporal punishment. Villarreal will do what he likes, whether he's punished or not."

"That's just my point, Captain. Corporal punishment won't correct our men and . . ."

Juan de Beltrán uses Coleridge's words to support his position, which is a ridiculous one on a pirate ship. For a long time now, I've realized that the pilot respects Coleridge and will accept whatever he says.

Montoro interrupts him, offended, and they get into a shouting match. Here in the officers' cabin, I let them speak, but up on deck, I wouldn't allow anyone to question me.

But now I'm fed up, so I put a stop to it. "Enough of this, damn it!"

Everyone falls silent; they're afraid of me when I'm angry. For a moment, a tense silence hangs in the air. Then Coleridge turns to Rojas and asks him what we all want to know.

"I understand you know Tortuga well. Tell us, please. I know nothing about the island."

"After Osorio's devastation—" the Spanish captain begins.

"A wicked act!" Hernando de Montoro jumps in again, furious. "My family rebelled against it."

They explain that, many years earlier, Governor Osorio had wanted to stop smuggling on Tortuga, so he made residents of western Hispaniola move to the other side of the island, near Santo Domingo. The Montoro family had been among those affected; the government expropriated their lands, which they had owned since the Conquest.

"Yes, there were a series of rebellions and uprisings," Rojas goes on. "The order was unjust, but the authorities thought it was the best way to prevent piracy. Unfortunately, many of those whose lands were expropriated joined the *bucaneros*."

"What are *bucaneros*?" Coleridge asks in his British accent.

"Buccaneers are outlaws who, for the most part, earn their living trafficking in cattle hides and smoked meat called *bucán* or jerky, which they sell to the pirates, privateers, and lowlifes. Though I should add that there are buccaneers who have no dealings with pirates; we call them *vaqueros*. There aren't many of them, but they have a good relationship with the Audiencia."

Rojas observes Montoro, who looks sad. At times, I think the Creole is also tired of being a pirate.

Rojas continues. "For a while, the government of Santo Domingo tried to wipe out the pirates on Tortuga, but they forged a common front: the Brethren of the Coast."

Montoro interrupts him. "They're nothing but a gang of criminals, demons. They forced me to work with them and threatened to murder my family! So, I committed robberies, and the government of Santo

Domingo put a price on my head. I had to abandon my land, along with my wife and children, and enlist on a pirate ship, which is where we met, my captain." He shakes his head. "They're despicable; their laws are wicked, their government perverse." Then he falls silent, beside himself. He drains his glass of rum, and Coleridge serves him another, then refills his own.

"An autocratic, idiosyncratic group," Rojas continues. "Their laws aren't written down. Everyone submits to it to protect himself. They are united by their sense of fraternity. They have neither judges nor juries, just an assembly made up of the oldest Brethren. They have curious customs, like *malotaje* or bad luck, where a Brother with no family members names someone unrelated to be his heir. They divide up all booty equally and even set aside some for the wounded."

"A common government, concern for justice, care for the wounded . . . as you describe it, it sounds pretty reasonable," I declare.

Montoro shoots me a furious glance, but Rojas just goes on. He explains Tortuga is still controlled by the Brethren, but it has a French governor, Timoleón Hotman de Fontenay. He has had to submit to the Brethren, but he has persuaded them to side with France. It does seem that island is our best destination at the moment. I'm also thinking about how close it is to Santo Domingo. It's as if Providence were guiding me toward Len. How I long to see her! But how will I reach Hispaniola without ending up on the gallows?

"Captain Rojas," I say, "one last question. France and Spain are at war. How is it possible that you, captain of the fort on Hispaniola, have had dealings with pirates loyal to France?"

"I've been on these islands for a long time. It was thanks to my good offices that some of the Brethren didn't end up on the gallows, so they have worked as spies for me. It's good to have friends, even in hell, and that's what Tortuga is. Nevertheless, I must tell you that my relations with the governor, Monsieur de Fontenay, are not good.

Captain, I will risk my life by going to Tortuga. I will do it with one sole purpose: that you let me return to my loved ones. If you allow me to return to Hispaniola, I give you my word as a gentleman that I will never betray you, and I will forever be in your debt."

"We shall see. It all depends on your services. Remember that here, you pay for disloyalty with your life. But now, let's eat."

Domingo Rincón, the cook, and another sailor came in a minute ago and are serving us a dish. Apparently, there was a cage full of chickens in the hold of the Spanish ship, and on our plates we have the result. It smells delicious.

As Domingo pours me another finger of rum in the glass I haven't touched, he whispers in a clearly audible voice, "Captain, are there ladies on that island?"

We all break out laughing. He has a reputation as a womanizer; life on the high seas has taken its toll on him.

Gabriel de Rojas, who doesn't know him as well as we do, answers, "Well, white women are forbidden there."

The cook's face registers disappointment.

"The Brethren consider white women a source of conflict because there are fights over them, but"—Rojas observes the cook, amused— "there are mulattas! And black women."

We all roar with laughter. Off-color talk begins; each man tells us about his battles and talents in love. I don't join in the conversation. Since reading that list of passengers, I've forgotten all the times I've lost myself in a woman's arms, seeking animal pleasures and forgetting. All I can see now is one sweet face, and I keep hearing a voice whispering in my ear: *Len.*

45

TORTUGA

Tortuga, November 1653

The sun is at its zenith when the sloop and the patache line up with the island, which is a modest mound over the sea and resembles the hunched back of a gigantic tortoise. At the north end, a large cliff blocks access; at the south, a cove serves as a port. My two ships head toward that anchorage after several days of sailing. From the bow, I contemplate the scene with mixed feelings: to starboard is the coast of the island where Len lives; on the port side, the hell, where, according to Montoro, all demons have their meeting place.

The sloop gently pushes its bow into the cove, which offers good anchorage in its sandy floor. The masts of all sorts of ships rock on the water: large canoes, tenders, and small sloops; a Portuguese *urca* or cargo vessel; two *pinazas* or pinnaces; one *filibote* or flyboat, possibly Dutch; and a few *jabeques* or xebecs. I order the men to drop anchor and hoist a boat; Gabriel de Rojas, the helmsman Blas de Alcolea, Domingo Rincón, Hernando de Montoro, and I climb into it. We slowly approach land. Another boat follows us; launched from the patache, it carries Richard, Cosme de Azúa, Esteban Centeno, and Juan de Beltrán.

The beak of land dominating the jetty draws closer. Up above, on a steep rock wall some thirty feet high, stands a fort with a powder magazine and a battery of two cannons.

"La Aguilera. It was built by Levasseur, a brutal, paranoid man who was killed a year ago by two of his henchmen, Martin and Thibault. They were fighting over a woman. Now it's the 'palace' of the current governor, Fontenay," Rojas says wryly. Then he becomes serious, as he studies it more closely. "It looks different than when I saw it last—they have widened it and built a wall around it."

The wooden pier leads us to some houses making up a small square, open to the sea. From there, a road climbs toward the hill. Along its sides, I see more scattered houses. In the shacks surrounding the pier are crowded people of the most curious description: men dressed like Spaniards, as Frenchmen, or seminaked. Some of them wear women's necklaces or clothes. There are even some dressed in priests' robes adorned with feathers and pendants.

Two come up to us as if they are guards of the port. One wears a shirt that was once white; it is open and reveals a mop of chest hair. Over it is a French-cut coat with no sleeves. The other is wearing pants made of coarse cloth and a shirt so blackened that it looks tarred. It is held closed by a rawhide belt. From his belt dangle four or five large knives and a bag for gunpowder and lead.

"A buccaneer," Montoro whispers in my ear.

"Who are you?" the first one asks.

"Gilbert, don't you recognize me?" Rojas exclaims.

The one in the coat smiles, revealing sparse, blackened teeth.

"Such decency on this island!"

"Who are these two fellows?" the buccaneer asks him.

"Honorable men," Rojas responds.

"Honorable? Here, there are no honorable men." Gilbert laughs.

"Listen, these friends have come to buy provisions and repair their ships. This is Piers Leigh." He pronounces it "Pirs Ley." "They call him 'the Englishman.'"

The buccaneer eyes me admiringly, scrutinizing me with a ferocious, penetrating look.

"The Englishman here, on Tortuga!" He whistles. "We've heard talk of you. Quite the pirate! But someone came through here who played a dirty trick on you."

"Kennedy is here?"

"I've got bad news for you," he jokes. "Your friend Kennedy was arrested by the Spaniards, and they hanged him as a pirate. You would have hanged him as a traitor."

It crosses my mind that he didn't have much time to enjoy his treason. And that the same fate may await me.

Rojas has stepped aside to speak with Gilbert. We can't hear what they're saying, but he must be asking about the situation on the island. The buccaneer joins them while I assign tasks to my men. Juan de Beltrán, with the petty officer Cosme de Azúa and carpenter Esteban Centeno, will find wood to repair the damage to the ships. Montoro, who knows the island, together with the cook, will find a store to buy oil, vinegar, dried vegetables, and salted codfish. Blas will stand watch over the ships.

On our way to Tortuga, I had proposed that Richard take over as captain of the patache and that we keep on sailing together. He accepted. Now he's going to try to complete his crew—where better than this?—and see if he can find a secondhand cannon since the patache is a merchant ship, not a warship. Now, he goes off to one of the taverns.

When Rojas finishes speaking with Gilbert, he signals me, and we head up the hill leading to the fort. A French merchant lives up there; we have been told by Rojas that we should negotiate the sale of the cargo with him. Halfway there, we stop and observe the enclave down below us. The settlement is arranged around the cove in groups of houses too small to be called neighborhoods. Near the coast stand the taverns, bordellos, and gambling dens. Set back from the tumultuous activity of the coast are the warehouses and little stores.

We resume our climb, panting from the heat. Every now and then, I see dirty, half-naked children playing in the mud left by the latest rains. The older ones fight with sticks, pretending to be pirates. Finally, we reach the merchant's house, a thatched hut a bit larger than the rest. We are welcomed by a stocky man with a large moustache and a dirty coat who introduces himself as Monsieur François Emmanuel Renard. After many rounds of negotiation, he finally agrees to pay us a fair sum for the contents of our catch. Also, he mentions the possibility of financing Coleridge's cannon in exchange for a percentage of our future catches. He accompanies us back to the cove, where the ships await. It's hot, and all three of us are thirsty. On the side of the road stands a little tavern, and we don't think twice.

Renard and I walk inside first, while Rojas goes off to relieve himself nearby. The contrast between the intense light on the outside and the darkness within prevents us from seeing anything, but we can hear conversations.

"A conceited fellow, that's what this Fontenay is, having people call him 'royal governor of Tortuga and of the coast of Santo Domingo.' He respects the laws of the Brotherhood, I'll give him that, but I don't know if he's any better than Martin and Thibault."

"And he's a papist pig who says he is *catholique*. Bah! A fool with religious delusions, now and then. Sometimes he's filled with mystical fervor, beating his chest and shouting that he's a sinner. Other times he's a fanatical sadist and—"

The French merchant interrupts them. "Monsieur de Fontenay protects commerce. He's not as mad as he seems. He's a blessing to this island."

They laugh at him.

Another voice speaks up. "Actually, for Fontenay, silver is the true God."

We're used to the darkness now, and I can make out the person who said it, a redhead. His accent sounds familiar.

"Are you English?" I ask.

We sit down at the nearest table. Renard raises his hand to ask a waiter for rum.

"God forbid! An Irishman from Galway."

"What's your name?"

"John Murphy."

Gabriel de Rojas, who is just then entering, shouts, "Don Juan de Morfa!"

"That's what they call me in Santo Domingo." Morfa stands up laughing and embraces the Spanish captain. "Gabriel, the last thing I heard, you were going to lead the mission to Tortuga. I hoped to see you here and was surprised when I didn't. I feared you had died."

"And I was hoping to meet someone who could help me return to Santo Domingo, and I'm delighted that it's you! You were right to worry, but it's not so easy to get rid of me."

"What happened?"

"Someone—you can imagine who—had me beaten up and put me in a sloop. But the assassins didn't finish the job; they put me to sea in a sloop. This gentleman"—he gestures to me—"you might say rescued me. Morfa, allow me to introduce you to Mr. Pirs Ley, a former officer in the navy of His Majesty, Charles I."

"Piers Leigh . . . that name sounds familiar."

Murphy fixes his eyes on me, looking me up and down. He suddenly turns pale. "Did you serve under Captain Swanley?"

"Yes."

The Irishman is astonished. "You saved my life." His face reveals the deepest gratitude I have ever seen.

"I did?"

"During the war. My ship was captured by that criminal, that heretical Puritan, Swanley. He tied up all the Irishmen, back to back, and threw us into the sea. All my comrades drowned, except for me and the man I was tied to, because an English officer cut our ropes. Thanks to him, I'm still alive."

I haven't forgotten that episode, which one day, I recounted to Len. It was that inhuman act that made me start to lose faith in the Parliamentarian cause.

"Why did you do it?" asks Morfa, moved.

"My mother was Irish Catholic. What they did to you was a felony, an act of barbarism with no justification in the laws of war. I'm glad to have found you again. But tell me, how did you end up here?"

He sits down at our table. They've brought us rum now, and I fill the glasses.

Morfa drinks his, wipes his mouth with the back of his hand, and says, "When you saved me from that horrible death ten years ago, I made it to the coast of my country. I participated in the Irish rebellion and was finally captured again by the English. Many of us were sent to Barbados as indentured servants. Along with a group of my countrymen, I managed to escape. We assaulted one of the ships in port and sailed as far as the New Kingdom of Granada. There, they accepted our ship into the Windward Fleet, supporting the Spanish Armada. After many military actions, I was promoted several times, and though some of the judges on Santo Domingo still look at me with suspicion, I've become a field marshal."

"And what brought you to this island?"

"I'm preparing"—he pauses—"I'm preparing a . . . matter for which I will need the services of this old comrade, Captain Rojas. How providential to find him here!" He turns to him. "I have a lot of news—"

Don Gabriel cuts him off. "How did you get here?"

"In a tender, anchored in the cove."

"I must return to Santo Domingo at once. It's imperative!" exclaims the Spanish captain, fixing his eyes on me.

He has kept his word, so I tell him, "I return your freedom. In exchange, I ask that you take the prisoners on the patache back to Santo Domingo."

Rojas looks at Juan de Morfa, who doesn't understand what we're talking about.

"That won't be a problem," he responds.

While we've been chatting, Renard has been squirming in his seat. Now he tells me that it is late, and we should go to the port and speak with the men from the Dutch *filibote*; he plans to resell them the cargo from our catch.

I leave Gabriel de Rojas chatting with Morfa and go with the merchant. When we reach the port, I find Coleridge drunk but still standing. He has recruited some new crew. I tell him what we are planning to do with the passengers on the patache, and I feel a stab of envy. They are returning to Hispaniola; I can't go anywhere near there. And yet, that is what I long for, more than anything in this world.

There has to be a way.

46

THE PROPOSAL

"I'm like them—despicable, a criminal."

When he hears my bitter words, Gabriel de Rojas's warm eyes show compassion.

We have been on Tortuga four days, repairing the boats and se-curing rations. We have witnessed continual drunken sprees, orgies, cruelty, sadism, and obscenities of every sort. Fontenay had some men hanged for a triviality, and several pirates have died in knife fights and drunken brawls. But what shocked me the most was the blasphemous Mass. That's why I'm with Rojas, talking over a glass of cane alcohol that I down in one shot.

Shortly after we got here, a pirate ship arrived that had captured a Portuguese *carraca*. They divided up the booty and, before long, had drunk it down. Then the fighting began, and several of them died. So, Fontenay came down from La Aguilera, emboldened by alcohol and intent on imposing order. He spoke to the pirates like a priest—admonishing them to convert and mixing blasphemies with religious curses.

But a real priest was among the hostages on the seized *carraca*. After Fontenay's sermon, the pirate captain drunkenly dragged the priest to the port and began carrying on hysterically. He wailed, confessing he was a sinner, a man condemned to hell. After that, he got down on his knees before the priest, begging for forgiveness.

Other drunks followed suit. The terrified priest tried to get away, but they stopped him.

The captain loudly demanded bread and wine. Then they held a sort of procession toward the ancient, semiruined chapel, forcing the priest to lead. He pleaded with them to leave him alone, calling what they were doing blasphemous, but one of the pirates pointed a musket at his head and covered him with a purloined chasuble. Trembling, he took a little prayer book out of the pocket of his faded robe, and the liturgy began. At the high point of the Mass, his voice became tremulous. The pirate captain ordered everyone down on their knees. One sailor muttered a blasphemy and remained standing; the captain fired a bullet into his forehead. The priest turned around and stopped the ceremony, but the captain ordered him to carry on.

I had followed them. At that moment, despite all my years of horror, I felt so disgusted that I wanted to vomit. I remembered Uncle Andrew's bruised face when I freed him from the noose and all he had taught me about the Roman liturgy, respect for the sacred, and honesty.

Beside me was Gabriel Rojas. His face also revealed his revulsion. We exchanged glances, and I slipped out discreetly. I went down to the dock, where I leaned on a wooden balustrade and looked out to sea.

That's what piracy was: a world of disturbed, dissolute, blasphemous drunkards. And I had become one of them.

My love, my Len, was so close, and I felt totally unworthy of her.

I stayed there, gazing at the dirty water beating against the pier until Rojas arrived. We began talking there, then moved to this tavern, where we've spent hours over a bottle of cane alcohol with an indecipherable taste.

"I'm a wretched criminal," I moan.

"No, you aren't. You saved my life; you're a gentleman, a captain of men. Juan de Morfa agrees with me. Amid the barbarism of the war, you saved him from a horrific death."

"I was an officer in the Royal Navy; now I'm a pirate, a murderer, a thief. My father was a nobleman, perhaps a martyr. I have betrayed all the principles he taught me."

"You're not really a pirate."

"Yes, I am; I talk like them, I curse like them, I've robbed, I've killed—"

"Yes, but the difference is that you have a conscience. Listen"—he lowered his voice, which wasn't necessary, since the people around us were too drunk to hear—"Morfa and I are preparing an imminent attack on Tortuga. The Audiencia of Santo Domingo can't tolerate this refuge for delinquents so near its coasts, blocking the passage to Cuba. Every year, the pirates from this island capture hundreds of ships. If you help us, I can make you a coast guard for the Spanish Crown."

"It's too late."

"No, it isn't! I really can help you," he insists. "When I was taken prisoner by Don Rodrigo Pimentel's men, we were preparing an assault. I was going to direct the expedition on land; Morfa would command the ships. Don Juan has confirmed that the plans are still in place. A fleet will leave Santo Domingo, but we need more ships—pirate ships, to the displeasure of Principal Judge Montemayor. I can authorize them. You can join us, along with your whole crew. You will go from hunted men to valiant subjects of the Spanish Crown. All the ports in the Spanish Indies will welcome you."

"Even if I wanted to, my men won't agree."

"Your crew respects you. Those men will follow you to the death."

Don Gabriel's offer is tempting, but I pause, considering all the obstacles we would have to overcome.

"Very well, Mr. Rojas," I tell him. "You know my past. I'm counting on your friendship and gratitude, which honors me. Still, do you believe . . . ? Can you honestly imagine that the interim governor of Hispaniola might agree to recruit a pirate?"

"I assure you that I will vouch for you to the judge. I know you are a man of honor."

I hold my silence, not feeling like a man of honor in any sense. But I'm sick of being a man without a country, without honor or creed. And the hope of reuniting with Len draws me forward. Rojas's proposal can be my salvation. The moment has arrived, I realize, and I can't let it pass. I think about my men. How can I tell them that I plan to leave this life? How many of them will follow me?

I shake hands with Rojas. We look each other in the eye; a pact of loyalty binds us. Now I need to face my crew.

47

THE PREPARATIONS FOR THE MARCH

Down the muddy road, I return to the waterfront. There I meet Coleridge, who is sober and uncharacteristically agitated.

"Where have you been?"

"Talking to Rojas."

"Do you know that Fontenay nearly pulled a dirty trick on us? The cunning bastard tried to make off with almost all our cargo!"

"When?"

"Last night. Some boats approached the patache. Fortunately, the man on guard duty sounded the alert, and they were able to drive them away."

"How do you know it was Fontenay?"

"Who else could it be? Anyway, the rooster crowed."

"The rooster?"

"Yes, Juan de Beltrán knows how to make men spill the beans."

"Isn't he opposed to corporal punishment?"

"Apparently, torture is just fine by him," Coleridge jokes. "Come on, let's go to the tavern, and you can tell me what you've been up to."

"Richard, we should speak."

He has already taken a step, and he stops, looking at me in surprise. "And we can't do it over a drink?"

"No, here."

I look to the right and left; we're alone on the wooden pier. Richard first looks amused, then realizes from my expression that I'm serious.

I tell him about my conversation with Rojas. As he listens, he turns red. Finally, his natural equanimity prevails.

He explains calmly, "Piers, I'm an Englishman, loyal to the English Crown. I don't like Spain. I don't understand their customs, much less their character, which is so excessive. Anyway, I want to make my fortune at sea. I don't consider myself a pirate—I'm a Royalist official."

"Are you sure, Richard? Since we arrived in the Caribbean, and especially since the pirate ship took us prisoner, you've been drinking heavily. Tell me, why do you drink? Aren't you trying to silence your conscience?"

"No." For once in his life, he comes clean. "I drink because the Parliamentarian pigs robbed me of my career in the Armada. I drink because they confiscated all my belongings, and I lost my family. Parliament is the winner now, but perhaps one day England will get fed up with that hypocritical Puritan, Cromwell, that black beast who assassinated the legitimate king to put himself in his place."

"You're waiting for the monarchy to be restored? Right now, that seems impossible."

"Not so. In Europe, strings are being pulled. There are men loyal to the new king. One day, I will fight with them."

I shake my head and say, "And aristocratic Charles II, you think he'll accept a pirate?"

"He'll accept a good sailor."

We look each other in the eye. I smile at him. I realize that I'm going to miss him terribly after so many years of sailing together. "It seems we'll have to split up."

"What do you propose?"

"Those who choose to continue will go with you in the patache; I'll chart another course in the sloop."

"That Rojas must be very convincing."

"Remember my father?" He nods, but I don't give him time to answer. "His shadow somehow pursues me."

My breath catches in my throat, and I can say no more, but Richard understands. "What are you going to do, Lord Leigh?" he asks genteelly.

"I'll speak with the crew."

"They could betray you!"

"No, I trust them. I'll offer them an honorable exit and a reward."

Hours later, we gather the men on the beach. In the distance, in the cove, the patache and the sloop are rocking.

"Some of you have been with me for a long time, others less. We have sailed together, making excellent catches. Now a good opportunity has arisen for us all." There is an expectant silence. Their eyes are fixed on me. I look at them, one by one, and I think I know before speaking what each will decide.

"They've offered me . . . they've offered me the protection of the Spanish Crown. With it, we could carry out our work without ending up on the gallows. We will participate in an enterprise that will give us a nice reward. We will no longer be free, but agents of the Spaniards. In exchange, they've promised to forget any crimes we've committed."

I hear grumblings of disagreement, but see looks of interest.

"We will divide up the crew," I tell them. "There will be two ships and two captains. Whoever wants to follow me will sail on a ship belonging to the Spanish Crown and will act as a Spanish subject. Those who don't want that can sail with Captain Richard Coleridge and carry on with this ancient profession of piracy. On the one hand, you have the life you know and enjoy. On the other, a chance to be honorable again and to escape the gallows."

The sailors exchange glances.

Coleridge steps up to the front and exclaims, "Those who want to continue on the high seas, on an ocean free of restraints and barriers, let them come stand with me."

"And those who want to return to an honorable life," I say, "who are finished with robbery and murder, let them stand with me."

Slowly, the men begin dividing themselves up.

Hernando de Montoro, the Creole from western Hispaniola, takes a step forward and tells me, "I want to return to an honorable life!"

Rodrigo de Alcalá exclaims, "Captain, how could I leave you? You'd be lost without me!"

Cosme de Azúa, the helmsman Blas de Alcolea, and many other Spaniards join my side, but it surprises me that many Englishmen loyal to old Charles also do so. They include Kerrigan, the gunner I saved from the barracuda, and my friend Duckey, whom I had whipped for robbing and brawling. However, the sailor he was fighting with, Lope de Villarreal, stands with Coleridge. Juan de Beltrán doesn't want to return to an honorable life, either, or perhaps he just knows that the Inquisition won't be likely to pardon his many heresies.

It is a painful separation. We know we are divided by something more profound than loyalty to the Crown. And the act of deciding is itself frightening because you feel the pain of abandonment more keenly than the happiness of what you choose.

There is silence on the beach, interrupted only by the sound of the sea. With a warm embrace, clapping each other on the back, Coleridge and I say good-bye. Then the rest of the men also say their farewells. The Englishmen who have decided to follow Richard crowd around me. One tries to talk me out of it, arguing that the Spaniards aren't trustworthy and that I can't join the dirty papists. Coleridge, who knows my past, turns and smiles sadly. I'm leaving behind a brother.

We climb into the boats and return to our ships. When the tide rises, the patache leaves the cove, headed for the open sea. Their sails get smaller in the distance, and I watch them until they are lost on the horizon.

48

A New Course

Tortuga, December 1653

The *Indomitable* leaves the port of Tortuga pushed along by a soft breeze. It has taken us a few days to finish repairing the sloop and look for more crew members. Once we are on the high seas, Rojas and I meet in my cabin, where he reveals to me the plans and the destination, which I rapidly transmit to the new pilot, a Basque from Vizcaya named Íñigo Zudaire. Rojas and I also plunge into a conversation about the future. He suggests I change my name—to jettison it with the years I spent pillaging and robbing, as if they had never existed. No one must know that I am the Englishman, that feared pirate. Not only should I change my name, but also my nationality. A new name, a new life. In honor of Uncle Andrew, I adopt the last name Leal.

From that moment on, I am Don Pedro Leal, an Irish sailor, captain of a merchant ship licensed to the Spanish Crown. In times of peace, I will be a coast guard, safeguarding the empire. In times of war, a privateer. Gabriel de Rojas, captain of the fort on Hispaniola, has enough jurisdiction to make me his ally. He draws up a document spelling out the terms of the contract.

My dual identity won't be known by anyone but Coleridge, Morfa, and Rojas—and, of course, my crew.

When we finish, we go up on deck. Rojas admires the order and discipline that prevail on the ship. The men are content; the bunting shines. The sails are taut with wind. On the perch of the mainmast is little Valentín de Torres; no one knows where he got a spyglass. Possibly from the officers' cabin. I smile to myself, but order him, in what sounds like an angry voice, to get down at once and return what isn't his.

We are sailing along the coast of Hispaniola. Splendid scenery stretches out in front of us, under a sun at its zenith: white-sand beaches surrounded by palm trees. The sun shimmers on the intensely blue sea. We leave behind us, to the north, some uninhabited islands and keep along the coast, passing Puerto Plata, Monte Cristi, Bayajá, and La Yaguana. We can make out the ruins of towns abandoned after Osorio's ravages.

Montoro looks furious as he points to a spot beyond Monte Cristi. "My family's lands were there."

I squeeze his shoulder.

"Señor Leal, my family arrived on this island with the first voyages of Columbus. One of my ancestors married a daughter of Guarionex, the Taíno cacique, and colonized all these lands you see. I am Dominican to the core. In my family, we spoke *ciguayo*, the language of the northern Taínos. The Spaniards played a very dirty trick on us when they destroyed our lands."

"Don't you feel yourself to be a subject of King Philip? Part of the empire?"

"Part of me is and part of me isn't. Maybe it's the cacique's blood."

"Why didn't you go off with Coleridge, if you feel so alienated from Spain?"

"I trust you, Captain. Also, I'm getting old. I can't always be on the run. From time to time, I have managed to go ashore on the island, near the family plantation, and I've seen my wife. She has managed to give our children a good education, but she always asks me to leave the pirate life and come home. It was impossible, but now you and Don Gabriel have given me a chance. I want to rehabilitate myself and return to a decent life. I don't want my grandchildren talking about a grandfather who was a killer and criminal, but about a man who, after an unlucky past, became honorable again."

I understand him. I could reach Len so easily from here, but not yet; I'm rehabilitating myself. When I have her in front of me at last, I'll look her in the eye, and she will know she is before a man who has at long last regained his honor.

Montoro and I fall silent. Before us is the Dominican coast, lined with marshes and thick vegetation. We sail along a large peninsula and enter Samaná Bay. There, Juan de Morfa awaits us in his tender. He left Tortuga a few days ago to return the captured passengers from the patache to Santo Domingo. Our two ships align in a small cove, hidden from sight by thick tropical forest.

In the cove, there are also five massive Spanish warships crowded with soldiers wearing metal helmets. When we approach, Don Gabriel greets them from the deck, waving his arms. When they recognize their captain, the soldiers break into cries of joy.

Rojas is beside himself with happiness. "Those men have been under my command for many years. I owe you so much, Señor Leal!"

"I owe you even more," I say sincerely.

From the tender, Morfa signals us to go to the largest ship in the fleet. We drop anchor and head there in a tender. Shortly afterward, others arrive from the different ships, the captains and some of their trusted men, to hold a council of war. They embrace Rojas like a lost comrade they never expected to see again. But in the officers' lounge of the ship, the atmosphere becomes tense. One of the captains hollers at Morfa that they have been waiting for him for a long time and are running out of provisions. He proposes they return to Santo Domingo to stock up. Another supports him, saying that soon the stormy season will begin and that it would be wise to postpone the assault on Tortuga.

But Gabriel de Rojas responds that the attack should take place as soon as possible. Gilbert, one of his spies on the island, informed him that Fontenay still hasn't been accepted and that there are divisions and riots among the pirates. The other captains repeat that there aren't enough supplies.

Montoro proposes that we all go ashore in Samaná; not far from there is the sugar mill where his family lives. They could provide us with bacon, water, and fruit. It's a good solution. Gabriel de Rojas accepts, and Morfa tells Montoro that they will repay him for the food with the spoils of war.

The four of us, along with several sailors, walk down to the immense beach surrounded by forests of palm trees and begin hacking our way through the thick vegetation. Montoro's lands are a few miles to the south. We are greeted by his wife, a heavy woman with mulatto features who must have been beautiful when she was young. She makes quite a fuss over her beloved husband. He, in turn, looks conflicted and sheepish about this display of affection in front of his superiors.

We rest several nights on their plantation while securing provisions for the ships. While this task is proceeding, the sky clouds over, and a hurricane wind picks up. We return to find that one of the ships from Santo Domingo has run aground and another is badly damaged. Thanks to my men's expertise, our sloop has remained intact. Rojas orders that part of the supplies from the damaged ships be transferred to my *Indomitable*. And when the weather improves, three of the ships from Santo Domingo, along with my sloop, set a course for Tortuga.

49

ASSAULT ON TORTUGA

Tortuga, January 1654

The attack was planned before leaving Samaná, and the *Indomitable*, until recently a pirate ship and well known on Tortuga, was to play a central role. As soon as we passed the eastern tip of Hispaniola, foot soldiers would board the sloop under Rojas's command. They would land at the cliff that closes off Tortuga from behind in order to climb the steep wall to the highest point on the island. From there, they would attack La Aguilera, Levasseur's ancient fort, where Fontenay lived. I would go with them. Meanwhile, the *Indomitable* and the other ships would have to situate themselves in front of Tortuga's cove and shoot cannons over the sea and into the pirates' nest. The idea was to catch them in the crossfire. Surprise was crucial.

It was a struggle to scale the massive wall, which was covered with undergrowth. We were guided only by the dying light of the moon. What's more, we were carrying a catapult on our backs, and when we reached the top, we silently set it up. Hours went by while we waited, hidden in the bushes in silence, for Morfa's ships to reach the cove.

Everything happened as we had foreseen. As soon as we heard the cannons on Morfa's ships and the fort's battery in response, we attacked

La Aguilera from behind, hurling rocks and projectiles. Their walls began to collapse, and we succeeded in silencing the battery. Finally, Juan de Morfa's men landed in the anchorage while we chased the pirates, who had fled in the direction of the cove.

The heaviest combat took place in the houses around the wharf. There, Morfa was surrounded. His big pistol wouldn't fire; perhaps he had run out of bullets or the powder had gotten wet. Several pirate cutlasses surrounded him, one against five, and I ran to his assistance. I took a blow to my arm that still hurts me. The fight was fierce: hand-to-hand, house-to-house. Finally, they surrendered.

Timoleón Hotman de Fontenay negotiated the terms of surrender with Rojas, who was as much of a gentleman as ever. He spared the governor's life, and the man agreed to abandon the island. Since Montemayor's orders were to empty out the pirates' nest, the few civilians who lived there—women, merchants, and children—were also brought on board. In La Aguilera, we had captured provisions that would last a month, plus weapons, gunpowder, bullets, cord, and other supplies, along with forty-six artillery pieces, eleven small boats, and three vessels in the port. Two of them were turned over to the Frenchmen, so they could be transported to their colonial possessions in the Caribbean.

Renard, the French merchant, bought the spoils of war, and the money was then divided among the participants in the campaign, after reserving one-fifth for the Crown. Scribes from the Royal Court of Santo Domingo oversaw the distribution; I was surprised by their order, diligence, and efficiency. Rojas explained that it was all due to Don Juan Francisco de Montemayor, always a meticulous and upright man, especially in matters involving the economy. A message was sent to the Dominican capital, giving an account of the victory.

I was happy when the booty was divided among the sailors and foot soldiers. For my men, that money, which wasn't the fruit of horrors and robbery but of fierce combat, was even a greater reward. They were beside themselves with pleasure, but I noticed that, this time, they didn't squander it on whores or drunken sprees. Life was opening up before them, and they would need this money to set a new course.

Several weeks have gone by. Rojas, Morfa, and I must separate. Juan de Morfa is headed for the Bahamas, with the three ships from the Spanish Armada, to protect the Indies fleet. They're awaiting the arrival of the new governor, who will replace Montemayor, the interim governor.

I've been ordered to spend the coming months in Barbados, spying on the movements of the English ships there. A while ago, rumors began to spread around Tortuga and Santo Domingo of a possible attack by the English fleet on Hispaniola. My mission is to find out how many English ships are coming and what their plans are. The captains of the other three ships will remain on Tortuga to prevent it falling once more to outlaws.

Gabriel de Rojas will return to Santo Domingo with the men wounded in combat and some prisoners from Tortuga he must turn over to the judges of the Royal Audiencia since they are considered traitors. Among them is Monsieur Renard. Also, the Spanish captain yearns to confront Don Rodrigo Pimentel and free Doña Inés de Ledesma from his tyranny.

In the port at Tortuga, I tell him good-bye. Over the months we have spent together, we have forged a strong friendship. We have in common our advanced educations, our painful pasts, and the hope of recuperating the women fate snatched from us. We embrace, and he thanks me for saving his life, but I think the life that has truly been saved from a terrible fate is mine.

Before we leave, in a little package, I give him the tin medallion that I have worn near my heart for so long. The woman it is for is the only person in this world who ties me to sanity and goodness. I tell Don Gabriel her name, Doña Catalina de Montemayor y Oquendo, and I write it on the envelope.

Then it's out to sea once more, toward Barbados, the waters of the Atlantic opening up forcefully before the *Indomitable*. My men are content; they have been paid for their first military action since we allied ourselves with the Spanish Crown. Soon, a huge storm begins, yet another interminable Caribbean hurricane. After three days of struggle, the storm abates; I trust that Rojas and Morfa have managed to overcome it, too. But my sloop is seriously damaged, forcing us to stop on the coast of the New Kingdom of Granada, and my mission is delayed. Until I complete it, I can't even think of setting foot on Hispaniola or seeing Len. I can only hope Gabriel de Rojas has spoken to her and that she is waiting for me.

50

OPEN SEA

Caribbean Sea, March 1655

Out here, there are no seagulls. Far from any coast, the sea is all mine. Before me, the horizon curves in an immense orb, impossible to take in. Since I left Tortuga just over a year ago, I have carried out a long mission in Barbados, spying on the enormous navy Oliver Cromwell sent to usurp Spain's empire in the West Indies as part of his Western Design. Cromwell has set out to appropriate Spain's great wealth and at the same time advance the cause of Protestantism against Catholicism. Finally, I can take news of the fleet to Santo Domingo.

The wind is blowing harder and harder, filling up the sails and leading me to Len. At night, I imagine the woman that she has become; I dream about her. My impatience dazes me a little; it seems as if the ship can't sail fast enough.

The crew goes about their morning duties, the daily maintenance and management of the ship. Life on board, though disciplined, has become less strict since we are no longer pirates. A new fraternity has emerged among us, those who chose an honorable life fighting alongside the Spaniards.

I go down to the pilot's cabin, and we review the course.

"When will we arrive?"

Íñigo Zudaire, a curt but friendly man, responds, "In two days, at most. Good wind, good course."

"Are you familiar with Santo Domingo?"

"I was raised there, Don Pedro. A beautiful city, strongly fortified. The English will have a hard time conquering it."

"They already did," I object. "Sir Francis Drake demolished it."

"But now the forts are there. Also, at the mouth of the port, there is an enormous chain that can be lowered to block entrance."

"I see. Indeed, it won't be as easy for them as it was in Drake's time. The island is much better protected, and moreover, we are taking the Dominicans some valuable information."

Montoro, who has been listening, interrupts excitedly: "We owe it to Mr. Coleridge!"

I nod. It's true that we owe what we found out to Richard. I was delighted to encounter him a few weeks ago in Bridgetown, capital of Barbados.

The rumor of a possible British attack had spread from port to port, from atoll to atoll; then we learned of more than thirty ships arriving in Bridgetown. In Barbados's lovely Carlisle Bay, pataches, *filibotes*, galleons, and all kinds of ships were rocking, awaiting the order to unfurl their sails so they could be pushed by the wind toward booty and glory. Many adventurers had joined the English army since the fleet sent by Cromwell needed local support for the attack on the Spanish possessions. Any man able to wield a weapon was accepted.

That's why, after roaming around, looking for prey for a while, Coleridge had decided to seize the opportunity to return to his natural milieu, the British army. If the commanders had reservations about his past as a pirate, they preferred to overlook them; the English are practical. Amid so many runaway slaves, indigenous men, and Spaniards gone over to the enemy, Richard, an Englishman with refined manners, seemed sufficiently trustworthy to them. If they were suspicious about his Royalist past, the urgent need for arms and ships made them overlook it.

Still, after his first few days back in the navy, Richard felt distant from the officers, many of them fanatic Presbyterians or Puritans, over-ripe fruit of the English Civil War who wanted to debilitate the papist enemy and, in the process, achieve fortune and glory. My old friend rejected all that in his heart of hearts. When we ran into each other in Bridgetown and I asked him to help me as a spy for the Spaniards, he was pleased to accept.

"Ahoy! May the lord protector be damned!" he exclaimed, while his eyes shone with a mixture of amusement and malice. "Let's punch them in the nose! Since we didn't do it that time on the estuary of the Thames, we'll defeat them here. The colonists of Hispaniola will give the Parliamentarians a good beating and knock them down a peg." He displayed that euphoric happiness given by rum; in his eyes, there was a touch of jaundice, and his breath smelled of alcohol.

"Given the huge quantity of ships and men," I said, trying to bring him back to crude reality, "I doubt that the Spaniards really can defeat them."

But Richard had a clear head when it came to military strategy and the naval situation.

"Bah! More than a lot of men, what we have here are many mouths to feed. The ships with provisions were detained by a storm in Ireland; it will take them weeks to arrive. They didn't have any brandy! You know what that means for a sailor. All they had to drink along the way was putrid water, and many of them got sick. Also, the troops of our beloved and esteemed lord protector are short on arms and munitions."

"Who is in command?"

"Old William Penn. Remember him?"

Yes, perfectly. He was my captain on the *Fellowship*, in the fleet commanded by that Richard Swanley, who nearly killed John Murphy.

He was an experienced official and had participated in various naval battles. "He wasn't a bad sailor."

"He's traveling with his wife! Where the hell have you ever seen a sailor set sail on a mission of war with his wife?"

"Who else is there?"

"A fellow called Robert Venables, in command of the foot soldiers."

"That name sounds familiar."

"He participated in the war. I think he was a committed Parliamentarian."

Then I remembered. Venables had been involved in Cromwell's cruel military invasion of Ireland. When I worked as a stevedore in Dublin, I heard many things about him, none of them good. I sat there, thinking: two commanders with opposite personalities in one military campaign, since a land army and a sea army are nothing alike. That didn't bode well.

"How are they behaving here?"

"They don't know what they're going to do yet. But there's something interesting I can tell you because I know it firsthand: those directly below them are disunited and ineffective. I'll introduce you to Butler! A clear example of what an officer shouldn't be."

Coleridge, with his impassivity and British humor, had won over one of the most important officials in the navy, Commissioned Officer Gregory Butler, an insecure, pious man, guided more by the Bible than by the laws of navigation, who trusted Coleridge implicitly.

"He pisses Bible verses!" Richard scoffed. "Good Lord! For Butler, everything is Divine Providence. I don't know why, but he has taken me for a messenger of the Almighty to guide him through the sinister waters of the Caribbean!" He laughed. "And I haven't done anything to deserve such an honor."

Butler's fanatical Puritanism amused and at the same time repulsed Richard. He presented me to the commissioner as a distant relative of Lord Ruthven. The story was that, pursued for my "Calvinist convictions," I had arrived in the Caribbean years ago. I lied and told him I knew Hispaniola well. Butler was delighted, seeing me as a martyr for the Protestant faith. Also, he needed someone who knew the island firsthand so he could set himself apart from the other commanders.

As for me, I lived up to his expectations. I explained that I had lived on Tortuga, one of the Brethren of the Coast, and that Spanish renegades like Montoro and Zudaire were on my ship, and they were good guides for the English assault on Santo Domingo. He asked me about the Spanish capture of Tortuga; it interested him as a possible beachhead for the conquest of Hispaniola. I described the Brethren's defeat as if I had fought on their side; I told him tales about my need for revenge against those who had turned the sea into something closed, a monopoly of the Spanish Empire. I also let it slip that there was a Spanish garrison so the island wouldn't be easy to attack. Butler, more and more interested, introduced me to Admiral William Penn and to Venables, the land general.

Sir William didn't recognize me—no one could blame him. What resemblance could he find between the leathery man of the sea that I had become and the clean-shaven cadet who had served under him in the first civil war? But something about me aroused his suspicion, and he tried to warn Venables. The two men were so embroiled in squabbles and suspicions arising from their shared command that anything that seemed fine to one, the other would reject. Venables made me his right-hand man.

Finally, thanks to Coleridge's skill, we were both called to an important council of war, where we would discuss the attack plan on Hispaniola and, crucially, the place where we would land. Penn and Venables were there, assisted by three commissioned officers: Sir Edward Winslow, a man in poor health made worse by the Caribbean climate and who never opened his mouth; Sir Daniel Searle, the governor of Barbados, who wouldn't accompany us on the expedition; and the fanatical fool, Gregory Butler. Only Searle had any experience in the Indies.

"The wise hand of the good Lord has saved us, preserving us from storms and bringing us to this coast," Venables began.

"Praised be the Lord!" Butler interrupted. Then, gesturing to Richard and me, he said, "He has sent us two envoys of heaven who will guide us on the path to victory."

Venables nodded tolerantly, but he was anxious to point out what seemed to him our biggest challenge.

"His Almighty wants to destroy the enemy, but there are devils among those who should be supplying the troops." Pronouncing these words in a threatening tone, Venables pointed at Governor Searle. "Your promises of men, weapons, and provisions are nothing but that: promises."

"We don't have as much food as you need," Sir Daniel said defensively. "Anyway, the planters don't want to scrimp on their slaves' rations; it's sugar cane harvest season, and the blacks need to eat, or they can't work. I can't force the planters. Gentlemen, I don't have any provisions beyond the ones I have given you. It seems to me that keeping so many men here for so long will only make things worse. The navy should leave for Hispaniola."

"Before the ships with supplies have arrived?"

"Hispaniola is rich in cattle and plantations. There, you can secure the provisions that you need."

"Once we've conquered it!" shouted Penn. "It isn't so easy! There is hunger on my ships—"

"You have lingered too long here," Searle insisted. "The troops are misbehaving in the port, and I've had complaints from the colonists."

Penn and Venables, for once, were in agreement and accused the governor of undermining the lord protector's plans. Indignant, the governor accused them of cowardice. The argument was becoming heated.

Butler intervened in his mellifluous voice. "Gentlemen, please, let's stop arguing. We must prepare the plan of attack. As I've told you, I've secured the assistance of these two gentlemen. They can tell us how things are on Hispaniola."

"It's an island where, my informants tell me," said Penn, "many places have been appropriated for the landing."

"The fleet should come as close as possible to the city of Santo Domingo," Venables countered. "That would spare us human losses and the exhaustion of a long journey through hostile terrain."

"Are you mad?" exclaimed Penn. "You want to put my whole fleet within firing distance of the Spaniards?"

The two top commanders began swearing and shouting. I took the admiral's side.

"My pilot and my second-in-command are of Spanish origins; they have confided in me that Santo Domingo is strongly defended."

I unfolded a map on the table. I had studied it previously with Zudaire and Montoro. On it, you could see the city on the mouth of the Ozama River and the forts that protected it.

"To the west, on the coast, is the San Jerónimo Fort. We've received word that it has recently been repaired and is well supplied with munitions. Closer to the city is the San Gil Fort, whose cannons cover the entrance to the river. And even farther along, the Ozama Fort, directly on the mouth of the Ozama River." I pointed with my finger to each of these sites. "All these forts prevent us from landing directly in the capital of the island. Also, we've been told that the port has a chain that can be lowered to block access. The best thing to do would be to land farther to the west, at the opening to the Haina River, where Drake landed. Although"—here I knitted my brow—"it's possible that there might now be a garrison in this location."

I proposed that I go ahead and explore the terrain and decide on the best point for beginning the invasion; then I would return to explain the situation to them. Penn was reluctant to leave the important decision to a nearly unknown man. But Butler and Venables not only trusted me, they urged me to leave as soon as possible.

That's why I'm sailing now toward Santo Domingo. Still, instead of thinking about the mission, I can't get Len out of my mind. I need to see her, receive her forgiveness, remember the past with her, perhaps plan a future. I don't know if she received the medallion; I haven't had any further news from Rojas. How have I survived this long year knowing she is so close by? I want to see her eyes, kiss her lips, listen to her laughter, hold her in my arms. It won't be long now, but it seems like an eternity.

51

Arrival in Santo Domingo

Santo Domingo, April 1655

The mouth of the Ozama River opens in front of us and, along with the estuary, the port. The Spanish flag, with red crosspieces against a white background, waves above the fort. Rumors of an English attack against Spanish possessions have made people take extra precautions. As soon as we dropped anchor, the port guard climbed onto my sloop. Now they are inspecting it.

The troops are led by a fierce-looking corporal, diminutive and despotic. He is suspicious of this ship with a Spanish flag, sailors from different places, and a captain who claims to be Irish. I tell him I am under the command of Gabriel de Rojas, and he looks at me as if I were a ghost. He sputters something, and I gather that they haven't heard anything about Rojas since the attack on Tortuga. I show him the guarantee that he gave me, but the corporal doesn't even glance at it. I doubt this man knows how to read.

The news of Rojas's disappearance troubles me. And Hernando de Montoro is about to lose his temper. Finally, after an exhausting discussion with the awful corporal, a name saves us. I have asked to speak with Don Juan de Morfa. After a moment's hesitation, the officer sends for him, but he still won't let us land, and his soldiers keep their muskets pointed at us.

After a while, I see a figure covered in a dark cape and a wide-brimmed hat coming down the pier. Under the hat, some straw-colored hair sticks out. When he approaches, I recognize the Irishman's features. He vouches for us with the corporal, and thanks to his explanations, the port guard, who doesn't trust the newly arrived foreigner but must obey a field marshal, allows us to go ashore.

Morfa himself leads me to the governor's palace, along with my second-in-command, Montoro, who is cursing his own compatriots under his breath. Since I know him well, I know this anger means he is frightened; he has no confidence that, after years of a wandering life, they are going to respect him. But despite his curses, I sense that he is happy to return to his people; he is strutting like a peacock, showing with his attitude that the beautiful island is his homeland.

We walk around the lively city of Santo Domingo, with its cobbled streets, low houses plastered white, and black grills and flowers in the windows. We walk by some imposing stone gates that have shields of nobility. Between the houses, in the distance, I can make out the Caribbean Sea.

I ask Morfa, "What happened to Rojas?"

"No one knows. It seems we were the last to see him, and that was over a year ago."

Montoro and I exchange uneasy glances. Without the testimony of the commander of the fort, the judges and aldermen of the city might investigate our past, which would mean our perdition.

Finally, we reach a large plaza preceding the Alcázar de Colón. Under the entrance arcade, the soldiers on guard stand to attention before Don Juan de Morfa. We are led up a wide stone staircase to a room with a deep window that, despite its thickness, doesn't succeed in keeping out the noonday sun.

Morfa leaves to announce our arrival to the governor. Hernando and I wait nervously; he can't stop pacing and finally blows his top.

"Fine fellow, that Rojas. Nice words, but now he leaves us in the lurch. If he betrays us, he will pay dearly!"

"That's enough!" I bark at Montoro.

We stand there in tense silence until Morfa reappears.

"The governor looks forward to meeting you. I've told him that you are bringing very important news from Barbados. Be careful—he may interrogate you. You shouldn't speak of the past; only say that you are a Royalist noble, an Irishman, and that the English trust you, but in fact you only serve our Lord and his Most Holy Mother. This will open more doors for you than anything else."

He leads us to a low-ceilinged room with dark beams; everything smells damp, like rotten wood and ancient files. The man awaiting us there is about thirty years old, dressed in silk pantaloons and an elegant ruff. He is introduced to us as Don Bernardino de Meneses Bracamonte y Zapata, Count of Peñalba, a knight of Santiago, president of the Royal Court, governor and captain general of the island, a nobleman of honored ancestry. Beside him is a man with a military air and a large moustache. Don Álvaro de Aguilar is the captain of San Jerónimo Fort and the fortifications of the island since Don Gabriel de Rojas has been missing.

After exchanging appropriate greetings, they sound me out briefly about my origins and occupation over the past few years. They shorten my interrogation because they are anxious to know the status of the attackers and because they trust Don Juan de Morfa.

The light coming through the windows illuminates a large map spread on an oak table with curved wrought iron legs. I point to the western part of the island of Barbados, where the invading troops are quartered. I tell them there are five regiments from the British Isles, together with a sixth recruited in the Caribbean. They ask me how many men there are exactly. When I respond that there are about eight thousand, and that they have mortars and cannons, Don Bernardino turns pale.

He turns nervously to Don Juan de Morfa. "Do you know that we only have six thousand men capable of bearing arms on the whole island?"

"That's not many. Are you sure there aren't any more?"

"That's the number we could count on if everyone showed up. Montemayor has ordered them to review the census and has sent teams to the north."

I stiffen when I hear that name.

"Those men, are they well-armed?" I ask.

"They have lances, some muskets, and their farm implements." Governor Meneses hesitates and then adds, "But they aren't battle-hardened."

"Men from the north coast are feared throughout the Caribbean. They are vaqueros who know how to handle the lance since they use it to control cows and runaway slaves. Also," Montoro declares with poorly disguised patriotism, "our men defend their people. That gives us courage and strength against an attack."

Aguilar responds, "The vaqueros won't arrive for a few days yet."

"I could bring people from my lands," says Montoro. "Some of them have been buccaneers, but if you promise to pardon them, they would be willing to fight on the side of the Spaniards."

"You can count on it," Governor Meneses assures him. "We'll also grant freedom to any slaves who fight with us."

"Let's hope the enemy's landing is delayed so we have time to train them," murmurs Captain Aguilar, shaking his head.

"We have to organize the defense!" Morfa exclaims. "The best safeguard of the city is its forts."

"As you're well aware, Montemayor has been in charge in recent years," Governor Meneses points out. "The forts are well equipped with gunpowder and munitions." He looks at me and asks, "How many ships did you see in Barbados?"

It takes me a few seconds to respond; every time I hear the name *Montemayor*, a knot forms in my stomach.

"The fleet that will reach your coasts is composed of fifty-six vessels, some of them large," I inform him when I come to.

He gapes at me. During the conversation, I have noticed his overwhelming anxiety about the attack. Morfa has told me that Meneses just arrived on the island. This is one of his first state missions; he needs to demonstrate his leadership ability to secure future promotions. The assault by the English could be his chance to excel or could sink his political career.

"Do you know where they are going to land?"

"They're still debating. General Venables would like to land directly in Santo Domingo."

"That's crazy," Aguilar says. "We would shell from the forts on the coast; they would lose ships. But if they managed to land, we would be completely lost."

I agree but add, "Fortunately, the admiral of the fleet, Sir William Penn, has refused."

"I'm glad," Morfa says with a sigh. "It would be very dangerous for us."

"They're looking for a safer place to land. They have sent me to find it."

"Try to lead them far away from the city," Aguilar hastens to say. "That way, we could ambush them. We know the terrain, which could give us some advantage."

"They mentioned Bajos de Haina," I say, "where Drake landed."

"For them, it would be a good place; it's just over two leagues from the capital," Aguilar says, stroking his moustache. "But for us, it would be the worst because it's too close. And the northern part of the city is almost without defenses. Then again, this time of year, the rising of the Haina River would make it difficult for them to land there, and the currents will push them toward Nizao."

Aguilar runs his shining eyes over everyone present and finally fixes them on me.

"Yes. Try to get them to land on the beaches of Nizao; that would be very helpful to us. In the Bajos de Haina, there is water, but none in Nizao."

I remember something Coleridge said. "Also, they don't have any canteens."

"All the better for us!" Aguilar slaps his hand on the table. "And it's very important that all the English troops land in the same place, so we can concentrate our defenses in the south and abandon the north. That way, we would have reinforcements from the region of Puerto Plata, Monte Cristi, and Santiago de los Caballeros."

"Do you agree that we should leave the north defenseless?" the governor asks me.

"Yes. Venables doesn't plan to divide his forces. And I'll advise him not to. The attack will target the south. Your worships should rest easy. I'll convince my . . ." I stop, thinking about my former compatriots. "I'll let the English think they're trying to land at La Haina, and when the currents make it hard, I'll guide them to the beaches of Nizao."

"Good, then it's decided! You should return as soon as possible, before they begin the attack and take us by surprise. It's paramount that you not delay. Leave with the first tide."

I look at Aguilar with a hint of desperation. I've waited so long to reach Santo Domingo, and now I have to leave without seeing Len or even knowing how she is?

They notice my silence.

The commander of the fort asks brusquely, "Is something wrong?"

"No," I respond immediately. "You're right. I'll be off with the tide."

I leave the conference room with my shoulders slouched, my head low. Morfa accompanies us to the port. The streets of Santo Domingo are colorful and exuberant. As I walk along, I look for a woman's face, but don't find it. I try to shake it off and focus on the important mission at hand. After the victory, the time will come to be with her.

52

IN BARBADOS AGAIN

Barbados, April 1655

As soon as we reach the boat, I order the crew to weigh anchor immediately; the tide is already rising. They greet us happily; they'd been afraid the Spaniards might take us prisoner. In our absence, they had secured water and provisions. We sail off to rejoin the attackers, Cromwell's men. If my double game is detected, I will end up on the gallows. I give thanks that my crew is absolutely loyal, especially as they know that the success of this mission means the possibility of a dignified life, of no longer being on the run, and for many of them, of recuperating their families. A constant breeze fills the sails, and we arrive in Barbados in just a few days.

As the sloop slowly enters the port at Bridgetown, I see from the port bow that the English squadron is loading provisions and tightening the rigging. Some ships have moved on toward the mouth of the bay, but most haven't set sail yet.

As soon as we anchor, I head for Coleridge's patache, which is still moored in the same place. Walking up the stairs, I run into Juan de Beltrán, who greets me coldly. His face looks as unpleasant as ever. I'm so glad that when we divided up the crews, he stayed with Richard.

On the other hand, when I see my old friend, we greet each other effusively with a warm embrace. Beltrán makes a nearly imperceptible grimace of displeasure, which helps me understand the pilot's antipathy. It's the gesture of someone who is resentful, jealous of our long-standing friendship. Richard doesn't notice; I decide not to pay Beltrán any mind.

With a generous glass of rum in hand, Richard tells me what has happened in my absence. Both in the port and on the ships, there has been a succession of fights between sailors and ground soldiers, reflecting the tension between the general and the admiral.

Apparently, it had all started when Robert Venables once again urged Sir William Penn to land right in the city of Santo Domingo, but the latter kept refusing, unwilling to put the ships within cannon range. The general protested that his troops would have to march a long way to reach the capital. With a twisted smile, the admiral called him spineless for not wanting to attack the enemy head-on. According to witnesses, Venables then accused Penn of hiding behind his wife's skirts. The admiral, red-faced with fury, rebutted him, pointing out that the mission involved not just conquest but also colonization. Also, he argued that the lord protector had not only wanted his wife to accompany him, but had urged many other sailors to bring theirs as well; they could be optimal nurses in times of war. Venables bitterly objected that he also had a wife and had left her in England because a soldier in a campaign could not be distracted by a lady and even less by his own wife. The admiral's attitude, he said, could only mean that he was a coward.

Richard finishes his rum and serves himself another.

"Sir William was so offended that he ejected Venables from his cabin. Since then, they have barely spoken a word." Coleridge roars with laughter at both of them; he has been imitating their voices. Then he adds, "Spaniards speak by shouting, but they understand each other. These distinguished compatriots of ours pretend to pay close attention to each other, but neither of them knows what the other has said. There is no communication between them. Worst of all, the argument has extended to the sailors and the ground soldiers. The sailors have sided with Penn, of course, while the ground soldiers, who don't want to carry out a long march through an unknown country, have supported their general.

"They act like two fighting cocks, cackling but never making up their minds to attack. Meanwhile, we go on consuming provisions and losing precious time that Hispaniola is taking advantage of to prepare its defense. You can't imagine how low troop morale is."

"I should see them," I tell him.

"I'll speak with Butler. I'll let him know you've arrived and have some valuable information."

Thanks to Richard, not only does Butler receive me but also calls us both to another council in the captain's cabin. The navy will set sail in a few hours, and the decisions that are made at that meeting will be crucial for the conduct of the campaign.

They interrogate me, and I give them a true but exaggerated version of the situation on the island. I tell them that the islanders aren't prepared for the attack of troops by land, that the campaign could be a stroll in the park. On the other hand, I warn them that they shouldn't land in Santo Domingo because the San Jerónimo Fort has long-range cannons—which is true—that could destroy the entire fleet. I suggest landing farther to the west. Penn agrees. Venables hesitates but, since he trusts me, ends up agreeing. After all, he is proud to have discovered a fellow traveler loyal to the Puritan faith. Finally, they decide that the attack on the island will begin in the shallows of Haina, where Drake landed long ago. I am pleased, remembering Aguilar's words about the Haina River currents that will push the ships toward Nizao.

We set sail the next day. From the aftercastle, I contemplate the sails of countless ships of war. For all its disarray, Cromwell's fleet, the lord protector's Western Design, constitutes a truly menacing force.

After sailing for a few days, when the sun is high in the sky, we catch sight of the coast of Hispaniola. The navy starts lining up at the mouth to the Ozama. I imagine the confusion and terror running through the city. I abandon myself to contemplating the reddish walls under the noonday sun, the forts, and in the distance, the thick vegetation. She is there somewhere, perhaps watching the ships. Rodrigo de Alcalá, beside me, points out the Alcázar de Colón, the Casas Reales or Royal Houses, and the cathedral. But I'm only thinking about Len. We move forward slowly, deploying the ships far from the cannons of San Jerónimo Fort, San Gil Fort, and the fortress. The hours go by, and night falls. Along the coast, lights go on in the houses.

We don't remain in front of the walls for very long. As soon as day breaks, we weigh anchor and sail along the rocky coast for Haina. Finally, we reach the shady beaches where we should land. But, as Aguilar told me in Santo Domingo, the currents at this time of year pull us farther to the west. From the port bow, I can make out the beaches, mango groves, wooded areas, and cliffs. Hernando de Montoro tells me the names of the places we are passing: Los Norios, Palenque, and finally, a bay with a large gray beach lined with palm trees: Nizao. Through flag signals, I indicate to Sir William Penn that we are reaching a good place to drop anchor. From one ship to the next, the order to go ashore spreads. Just before landing, in the officers' cabin of the patache, I meet with Hernando de Montoro, Íñigo Zudaire, Cosme de Azúa, and Rodrigo de Alcalá.

"Montoro and I will guide the English troops toward the capital," I inform them. "When we reach the Dominican lines, I'll turn myself over to the Spaniards, and Montoro will return to you."

"This double-dealing is dangerous!" Rodrigo de Alcalá exclaims anxiously.

I observe him, thinking how much affection there is in the old bonesetter. But I shouldn't let myself be distracted; the most delicate part of the campaign is beginning.

"Yes," I affirm. "It's dangerous, but not only for me and Montoro. It's dangerous for everyone. It's important that you not stay with the English for very long. Sooner or later, they will suspect something. As soon as Montoro returns and you see an opening, you should steer the *Indomitable* to the north, toward Samaná. Depending on how things go, we will meet either in the capital or at Montoro's plantation."

We all embrace, knowing that we may never see each other again. If everything goes well, these men will once again be subjects of the Spanish Crown, with full legal rights, and I will take sanctuary under their flag and no longer be an outlaw. If things go wrong, we could end up hanged, either by the English as traitors or by the Spaniards as enemies.

We don't have time to say anything more. One of the sailors has appeared. Azúa is left in command of the *Indomitable* while Montoro and I set sail in a tender, which is crowded with English combatants and is under the command of a Scottish officer. We row forward toward the shore until we hit the sandy bottom. Around us, a cloud of small boats come and go between the coast and the ships. They are transporting weapons, troops, provisions, and even horses. Everything is piled on the beach; later, it will be transported inland to an improvised camp.

Suddenly, two unexpected enemies make their presence known: the torrid heat and the mosquitoes. Robert Venables wants to attack as soon as possible, but Sir William and Commissioner Butler have suggested it would be better to build a trench. Though Venables doesn't agree, since he doesn't think the soldiers should spend so much time at this place without water, the trench is finally dug. Then the two commanders battle it out again; the admiral has decided to return to the comforts of his ship's cabin, together with his lovely wife, leaving the troops under the general's command.

The next day, Sunday, the Puritan pastors harangue the army. They sing the psalms of Israel, which say that God is with them and they will devastate the enemy. Coleridge and I, with our hats in hand, exchange ironic looks.

When the prayers have ended, Venables orders a regiment of soldiers to march toward the city and explore the terrain, and he orders Montoro and me to guide them.

The Creole, a regiment captain, and I mount our horses in front of a battalion of foot soldiers. After marching several hours down dusty roads, the men, discouraged by the heat and mosquitoes, begin to complain and fall behind. Only the three of us, in our saddles, reach an esplanade with tall grass.

A party of Dominicans comes out to greet us; knowing which way the enemy would come—thanks to me—they have set up a guard on the road to La Haina. The English soldiers are too far away to help us. We engage in combat. Their musket fire kills the regiment captain and wounds Montoro in the shoulder. They knock me off the horse and take me prisoner. I let them tie me up, and when I see that Montoro is trying to come to my aid, I order him to flee. He has no choice but to escape and ask the regiment of English infantry for help. I am led away, a prisoner of the Spaniards.

This wasn't the plan. I was supposed to turn myself in to the Spaniards, to show my good will. I speak to my captors along the way, asking them to contact Morfa or the governor, saying that I know them. The troops look at me in surprise, but dismiss my words as lies.

They rush me along, and when they cross paths with someone, I hear them say that they have a good catch: a prisoner to interrogate in Santo Domingo.

53

THE INTERROGATION IN THE ALCÁZAR DE COLÓN

Santo Domingo, April 1655

I return to Santo Domingo as a prisoner. Today, the streets are congested with people and wagons with clothes, beds, and furniture. Everything is permeated with dust and noise. The locals are fleeing from the capital. Some houses have been locked up tight, while in others, I can see inhabitants peering out at the captive, the first enemy to have entered the town.

The troops shut me up in a military prison. There at least I am cool, safe from the tropical heat. I fall on the floor and prop my back against a wall, closing my eyes and trying to rest. I can't think about anything. A few hours later, they come looking for me to take me before the principal judge.

He awaits me seated behind a somber desk, in a room faintly illuminated by a deep window. The office opens to a courtroom. The judge is a man with a big-boned, inexpressive face and a prominent bald patch that makes his face look even longer. He is dressed rigorously in black, with an old-fashioned collar, a neckerchief, a long black cape, and a sword at his waist. An usher announces him as Don Juan Francisco de Montemayor y Córdoba de Cuenca. I can't find any resemblance to

Len, except for the deep-set eyes, common among Spaniards. Telling him I know Don Juan de Morfa does not seem to improve his impression of me. And when I say I am working for Governor Meneses, Montemayor looks wary, thinking I am making fun of him, and he sarcastically asks if I'm also buddies with King Philip.

He interrogates me about how I arrived in the Caribbean. When I tell him I am an Irish Catholic nobleman, he isn't satisfied and asks me several times about my family, trying to find some contradiction in my account. I tell him a masked version of my past, omitting the last three years or so, when my life was wholly incompatible with the rectitude that the judge radiates. Still, I realize I'm not persuading him of my good intentions. He clearly distrusts me.

They take me back to jail. Night falls, and my sleep is troubled; I wake up thinking about Len. Her uncle didn't believe me. Will he even let me near her? After pacing the cell a thousand times, I sleep until dawn, when a rooster's crow awakens me. Within a few hours, they call for me again, but this time I'm led to the Alcázar de Colón.

Among those present are Governor Meneses, Aguilar, Don Juan de Morfa, and Montemayor. When he sees me, Morfa looks happy and asks them to untie me, insisting I can be trusted. But even though Meneses and Aguilar agree, Montemayor categorically refuses. The governor doesn't say anything; I sense that he feels intimidated by Montemayor.

For now, my possible liberation is set aside because they are all anguished by the arrival of the enemy. The terror of the invasion has spread through the streets and houses to such an extent that it has overwhelmed judges, military officers, and other city authorities. It seems that the memory of the terrible looting by Francis Drake still lives on. They bombard me with questions, while I am still shackled, about the size of the enemy forces, how many men have landed, and what their plans are. I quickly summarize the situation. They look at each other, worried.

"We shall have to resist," asserts Aguilar, "until the reinforcements arrive from the north."

"It's possible that the Englishmen won't advance for a while yet," I tell them. "I expect they're still digging trenches and getting organized on the beaches of Nizao."

"Have they all landed?" Aguilar asks.

"Yes. Except for the sailors in charge of the boats, all the rest are on land. They were bombarded by mosquitoes and very annoyed by the heat."

"No doubt," says Montemayor with a laugh. "They couldn't have landed in a worse spot!"

Then Don Bernardino intervenes again in my favor. "Precisely. And we owe that to Captain Pedro Leal! He has risked a great deal, playing a very committed role. He has managed to get them to land where we wanted."

"I beg that you grant him his liberty," Morfa requests again.

"We have to try him first! We are at war. We can't let a foreigner run free," Montemayor insists.

"His actions are judgment enough," Meneses points out.

"He's a privateer for the Spanish Armada," Morfa asserts.

"Who has named him so?" the judge asks mistrustfully. "A privateer needs a letter of marque from the Crown."

"Don Gabriel de Rojas enlisted him for the attack on Tortuga," Morfa explains. "On his ship, there is an endorsement signed by the captain, who had the legal authority to do so. Without Don Pedro, the pirates' island would never have fallen."

"But we never heard anything further about Gabriel de Rojas, and I have no guarantee that all of this is true. The only one vouching for the prisoner, so far, is you. And your testimony has no value; you are a foreigner."

Don Juan de Morfa gets indignant. "I'm a field marshal in the army of His Majesty the Catholic King!"

But Don Juan Francisco de Montemayor is undaunted. "No. He'll go to jail. If Don Gabriel de Rojas appears and bears out your story, we'll set him free."

"I don't think this solution is appropriate, Don Montemayor," Don Bernardino de Meneses objects. "Captain Rojas could take months to appear. He could be dead."

The face of the principal judge contracts with sorrow at the possible loss of Rojas, though he immediately recuperates his self-control.

"Mr. Leal may stay at my house; I would take responsibility for him," Morfa suddenly offers.

Montemayor begins to protest, but Meneses orders, "It is my will as governor that the gentleman Don Pedro Leal be set free, without charges."

"I don't agree, my esteemed count. We don't know who this man really is."

"I order you to obey!"

"In that case," Montemayor responds angrily, "all the responsibility falls on you. We shouldn't allow foreigners to do as they please on this island without being duly investigated."

"This foreigner," Morfa repeats, "will be welcomed into my home."

Don Juan Francisco holds my gaze.

"You will be my neighbor, then." His expression is still unfriendly, but in his voice there is a hint of irony.

Meneses tries to ease the tension with an invitation. "My wife is worried about the state in which the colony finds itself. She has organized a gathering for the noble people remaining in the city. It will take place tomorrow; I would be very pleased to count on Your Honors' presence."

He looks first at Aguilar, whose perplexity suggests that he thinks a party absurd in such a moment of crisis, but he accepts with a nod. Then Meneses addresses himself to Montemayor, more in confidence, but I can hear what they're saying.

"My wife would like it very much if your niece, Catalina, came with you to the luncheon."

"My niece has had a setback these past few days."

That startles me. Is Len sick? I try not to reveal my concern.

"What's wrong with her?" Don Bernardino asks.

"She has fallen victim again to a deep melancholy; she says someone is coming and is anxious."

She's waiting. She's waiting for me, I think. She knows I'm coming; perhaps she senses it. The voices reach me as if in an echo; I hear the conversation between the governor and Len's uncle as if it were off in the distance.

"Perhaps the young lady is lonely."

"She is always accompanied by . . ." The judge's voice is nearly inaudible.

"I assure you, my wife would be delighted to receive her. Perhaps being around more people will cheer her up."

"I don't know. I'll try."

I'm confused. I should have come sooner. I've been trying to reach her for a year and a half, redeeming myself for her sake, but perhaps Len doesn't need a redeemed man. She just needs me.

Meneses has turned toward Juan de Morfa and says, "Mr. de Morfa, I'd also be happy to count on your presence and that of your charming wife, if her condition allows."

The man thanks him again and confirms that they will attend.

Then I hear, "Mr. Leal, you, too! I'd love to introduce you to the members of this colony."

I wonder if perhaps Meneses is a parlor dandy who doesn't know what he's getting himself into. Eight thousand men have landed a few dozen miles away, yet he's carrying on his social life as if he were in the court in Madrid. The city will soon be under attack; many will be fleeing. Perhaps he wants to give the impression that everything is normal. I nod my head in agreement. "Thank you, sir."

54

BEATRIZ DÁVILA

I go out with Morfa onto the large esplanade in front of the Alcázar de Colón. He tells me his house isn't far. We pass in front of the Casas Reales, where just a few hours ago I was held prisoner. Then he leads me up the beautiful Calle de las Damas, with its whitewashed houses and cobblestones. The heat and humidity are intense. There are puddles of water on the ground from the recent rains.

Since an edict forbids women from going out of the house as long as the enemy is so near, we only pass a few soldiers and bureaucrats in dark suits. They all greet Don Juan de Morfa; one even stops him to ask what he thinks of the enemy.

"They think highly of you here," I tell him.

"I've been on this island for several years. A while back, I used my earnings as a coast guard to acquire an ancient *encomienda*. It is a sugar mill near Nizao, the place where your compatriots have landed and where I lived for a time. Thanks to the good sugar harvests, I managed to arm several ships and keep fighting as a privateer for the Spanish Crown. Now I belong to the Windward Fleet, and they even named me field marshal and cavalier of the Order of Santiago. Still, though, Montemayor and some of the judges consider me an outsider."

"But the title of field marshal—"

"It's more honorific than real. In Spain, it would indicate that I command a regiment, but here there are no regiments. The previous governor, Don Andrés Pérez Franco, granted it to me when he began to plan the attack on Tortuga and I offered him ships. Since Pérez Franco died under suspicious circumstances, my situation has become somewhat more insecure. Montemayor doesn't trust foreigners."

"I've noticed."

"The real reason many folks in the city respect me is because my wife, Doña Beatriz Dávila, is a Creole from a family prominent since the Conquest. Now, since my wife is expecting our first child, we have returned from Nizao and settled near her mother." Morfa smiles with pride. "I was able to acquire a house in the best part of the city, on Calle de las Damas. It's called that because it was here that Doña María de Toledo, wife of the first governor, Diego Columbus, would go walking with her entourage."

We pass in front of a baroque church. He says it belongs to the Jesuits, and my uncle Andrew's kind face flashes through my mind. A bit farther along, Juan de Morfa points out a house with a large stone door and a shield on the façade. "And this is the house of Don Juan Francisco de Montemayor."

This is where she lives! I think. But her uncle worries me.

"He seems a very rigid man," I say to Morfa. "He didn't believe anything I told him when he interrogated me."

"He is overly solicitous with what he considers his duty. As interim governor, he has governed the colony with a heavy hand and has managed to bring order. As I told you, the previous governor had planned the assault on Tortuga. When he died, we all thought it would come to a halt. But Don Juan Francisco saw the plan through and has conquered the pirates' island. Don Gabriel de Rojas was his right-hand man." He lets out a sigh. "If Rojas has died, it will be terrible for us all."

"For me, too. I would lose a friend and the only man who could explain my history to the judge, who distrusts me so."

"As I said, he distrusts all foreigners. A few years ago, a fellow named Richard Hackett passed himself off as an ally of the Crown against the English, but was finally found to be a double agent. Hackett tried to bribe Montemayor, who is beyond reproach. Not only did Montemayor refuse to be corrupted, but he expelled the man from the island. Since he had fallen for Hackett's ruse at first, he felt that his honor had been compromised. Ever since then, he is very careful, perhaps excessively. Above all, he rejects foreigners with any relationship to England. You and I are judged by the same yardstick as Hackett."

"Fortunately, you have nothing to worry about. I, on the other hand, could be in danger. You haven't been a—" I'm about to say *pirate*, but Morfa stops me.

"You should forget about the past. Rojas and I trust you completely. And, goddamn it, Don Gabriel has to show up sooner or later. Don't you worry!"

I shake my head. "It isn't just me I'm worried about. I'm worried about the sloop's provisions. If I fall, my men will fall along with me. My crew has abandoned a lucrative life because they trusted completely in me. I owe it to them to see that they get what was promised them on Tortuga, and I don't know if Montemayor will do it."

That incorruptible judge, cold and severe, is the gatekeeper to my future in every possible way, and most importantly, to Len. Might Morfa know her? I stare at the stone door, the only thing now separating us.

"A lovely residence. I heard he has a niece. Does she live with him?"

"Yes, Doña Catalina de Montemayor y Oquendo. She arrived a while back. A lovely young woman with golden hair, but she never leaves the house. Everyone says she lost her mind, that she isn't all there."

My heart is wrenched. What has happened to her during all this time? What suffering has she had to endure?

Morfa goes on. "Apparently, she lived too long in that heretical country." He realizes that my expression has changed. "No offense, Mr. Leig—Leal."

"Years ago . . ." My head is still a whirlwind of images and thoughts; I speak without thinking. "Years ago, she was full of life and happiness. She was always laughing. I promised her we would be together."

"You know her?" he asks with surprise.

We have stopped in front of what I suppose to be his house.

"She is all I have left of my people. My whole family died in the war."

Morfa looks at me with curiosity and compassion. "Let's not stand out here. Come into my house, and you can tell me."

He pushes open the enormous door, and we go into the entrance hall. A woman with black hair and white skin comes out to greet us.

He presents her with pride. "Doña Beatriz, my wife." And he introduces me. "Don Pedro Leal. Many years ago, he saved my life."

I bow low, uncovering my head. She curtsies.

"My husband has spoken to me about you." When he explains the reason for my presence there, she responds, "We'll put you up in the guest room overlooking the Ozama River. You'll be comfortable there."

Doña Beatriz's gaze is lovely; her figure, rounded by maternity, emanates sweetness.

I thank her for her kindness.

They summon a servant, who accompanies me to the ample, well-prepared room with dark wood floors and shining whitewashed walls. In the middle is a bed with a canopy and mosquito net. To one side there are a washbowl and a pitcher of water. While I am freshening up, I hear a knock at the door. They bring me clean clothes, perhaps from

Don Juan de Morfa himself. I change and go down to lunch; they're waiting for me.

At the table, we converse about different matters. Doña Beatriz is a cheerful, bubbly woman. With bright irony, she laments that the city has to be under siege in order for her husband to spend a few days at home. Morfa laughs.

After I take a much-needed nap, she offers to show me her house. With great pride, she tells me about the state it was in when they bought it and the improvements they have made. Her husband accompanies us, smiling, and only adds an observation every now and then. Behind the house, there is a large waterwheel that irrigates a back garden containing fruit trees and vegetable gardens. It is constrained by a wall along the Ozama and is connected with the neighbors' orchards. The one on the right, she says, belongs to Don Juan Francisco de Montemayor, and one more past that is her mother's house.

"Maybe later I'll pay a visit to Doña Catalina, to see how she's feeling today," she tells her husband. Then she turns to me to explain, "She is the niece—"

"He already knows who she is."

Doña Beatriz observes me with surprise.

"My friend, why don't we go inside?" Morfa says. "We can speak privately there."

I agree; I know he won't betray me. When I realize that his wife is discreetly stepping away, I ask her to join us. I will need her help as well.

In a spacious sitting room, the hours go by while I speak to them of Len, of our years at Oak Park, of my promise to her in the cave. When I finish, I look at Doña Beatriz. "I need a favor, my lady."

She encourages me with her sparkling dark eyes.

"I must talk to her."

"Perhaps I should tell Josefina," Doña Beatriz whispers, as if to herself. "The slave can let me know if it's the right moment."

"I beg you to show the greatest discretion; don't tell anyone I know her. My life depends on it! Your husband's honor, too."

She nods, very serious, and sits there thinking. Finally, she stands. "Wait here. I'll bring her to you."

55

In the Courtyard with the Wrought Iron Trellis

Golden light spreads across the Ozama as I pace the Morfas' vegetable gardens. Doña Beatriz has promised me that Len will come. The sunset seems interminable, waiting impossible. In a nearby window, a candle burns. The sun descends over a horizon with no sails. The war is far away still, on a distant beach.

Here there is peace, interrupted only by the sharp cry of the seagulls.

The creak of a rusty gate makes me jump and spin around. A shadow approaches.

It floats toward me and whispers, "Piers?"

I can make out a large woman with very dark skin. It's unnerving to hear a name no one must know on the lips of a stranger.

"You know my name?"

She nods. "I am Josefina, and I take care of her. Ever since you arrived on the island, my lady dreams at night and shouts, 'Piers, Piers!'"

"She . . . they tell me . . ." The words catch in my throat. "They tell me she has lost her sanity. Is that true?"

"Ah! You should have come sooner." The black woman wags her head. "But you're finally here! I prayed. I asked the good Lord for you to come. Only you can help her."

"That's the only thing I want. But tell me, how is she?"

"She began to seem content, perhaps too much so, Señor Piers. But now she is melancholic again, shut up inside herself. Oh! When they wound you, as they have wounded me and my lady, it never leaves you. I know, I know it well, I'll say—"

"But how is she?"

"You will see for yourself. When I started to take care of her, she was always silent. She would only cry; sometimes she was delirious. Not long ago, she began listening to what I told her, and little by little, she began to speak. She had to endure much suffering! She needs to tell you herself, but I don't know if she'll be able to. Señor, I beg you to be restrained, to listen to her, to tell her about your suffering also. She regains her strength when she snaps out of herself. Don't be impatient! She loves you, but she has wounds. Yes, many wounds in her soul. She says she is guilty."

"Of what?"

"There are demons." She looks at me with frightened eyes. "There are demons of sadness. Malignant spirits who slip into our souls. Only love can save her. Yes, Señor Piers, you can save my lady."

I'm startled to hear such words on the lips of an uneducated woman, a slave.

She goes on. "But I warn you: when we are sad, we only see blame. There's no pity, even for ourselves. Doña Catalina has not forgiven herself." She falls silent and smiles kindly. "You should speak with Don Juan Francisco. He is a good man, very just."

I shake my head. "I need to see her first, alone. We are from countries at war with each other; I have to warn her not to give away my presence."

She sits there pensively and finally nods. "I'll go get her. Oh señor!" she murmurs as she takes the first step. "How do I tell her you're here without her dying on me?" Then she pauses. "Not here."

She leads me by the hand to the courtyard of the judge's house, where we won't be seen. There, she motions for me to wait. Before I can say anything, she has disappeared.

I am more nervous than I ever was during the most difficult assaults. Since I saw Len's name in the Spanish captain's log, I've been filled with doubt, fearing and longing for this moment. Could she still love me? Will she accept me when she knows about my past? She is sick, and I'm afraid I have arrived too late. But how could I have come any sooner? At least now I'm a man of honor; a future opens before me that I can offer her. This courtyard is surrounded by four whitewashed walls with grillwork; in one of them, there is a wrought iron gate leading to the house. Vines partially cover the bars and the walls; the large tropical flowers exhale a sweet, aromatic fragrance. I walk up to the gate and realize that it is open. I wait there, lost in my memories.

And I don't hear her arrive.

Suddenly she stands before me, not a shadow, not a ghost from another time and place, but someone real. She isn't the young girl I left in England, but a very pale woman with eyes filled with suffering and anxiety. Still, she is as lovely as ever. She stands there quietly, looking at me without blinking.

"Who are you?"

"Len, it's me," I tell her in a clear, but gentle voice.

"Piers?"

"It's me," I repeat.

I take a step forward. I want to hold her hands, to press her against my chest, to kiss her. But something in her expression holds me back. She observes me rigidly, without reacting. Only the tears running down her cheeks reveal her intense emotion. After a few seconds, which seem interminable, she speaks a few words in English.

"Piers, where have you been?"

"Out to sea."

"I thought you were dead."

"And I thought you were."

"The *Defiance* sank!"

"But I wasn't on that ship," I say gently.

"I had no more news of you."

"In a news sheet in Dublin, I read that my mother and the three of you had been executed."

"Executed?" She shakes her head. "No, only Lady Leigh; your sisters died in a different way . . . but they all died because of me. Yes, because of me," she repeats to herself, lowering her eyes.

"No, Len." I try to lift her chin, but she turns her face and takes a step backward. "You weren't responsible for anything. I am the guilty one. I should have protected you all."

"You? No!" she exclaims. "You saved me! The Spanish ambassador told me a young sailor had spoken with him."

I remember that day, and I'm swept with a wave of consolation. If I couldn't help my mother and Ann, at least I was able to help Len.

"I wasn't sure. Ambassador Cárdenas told me he couldn't do anything," I say, almost to myself.

"Well, he did, eventually. I spent a lot of time in Bridewell, a time erased from my mind."

Len looks at me with those enormous, translucent blue eyes that I thought I would never see again. How beautiful she is, with a more mature and spiritual beauty. How I long to embrace her! But she has started pacing nervously.

Finally, she whispers, "Piers, you're alive, but . . . but I'm not worthy of you."

I lift a hand to caress her face, but she backs away and leans on the bars. She looks at me warily.

"I'll tell my uncle. I'll tell him you're here."

"Listen to me, Len, you can't do that. You must act as if you don't know me."

"Why?"

"I also am ashamed of something. Something that has kept me away from you."

"What is it?" Her eyes have opened wide with horror.

"It's no longer the case," I assure her, "but over the past few years, my life has taken a . . . dark course."

"What course?"

"One of robbery, of dishonor. I was a privateer, and then . . ." I falter.

"I know: a pirate."

Hearing it on her lips, now I'm the one who steps away. "I'm not worthy of you."

She reaches out a trembling hand; her index finger brushes against my forehead and starts to move down my nose, as if wanting to make sure I'm real. Her expression is full of bewilderment, but also tenderness.

"Yes, you are. You're my Piers."

Her finger has reached my mouth, and I try to hold back her hand.

"No, Len, not anymore. I'm a killer, a thief, a pirate. I've acted against everything I was taught during my childhood. I deserve to die."

"No! You can't die! Now that you're here, no!"

Once again, she steps back from me. She looks at the lights on the other side of the river, the stars that have begun twinkling in the sky.

Then, as if to herself, she says, "There was a time when I also wanted to die. I was about to throw myself into the sea, to sink forever and stop suffering. I'm the killer, the guilty one."

"How can you say that? You were just a victim of—"

"No!" she interrupts me. "I was a coward. I disobeyed. Because of me, Uncle Andrew died the worst possible death."

"I don't understand."

"The Roundheads surrounded Oak Park on a night with a full moon. Someone betrayed us—"

"It was Ruthven. He is the guilty one."

"No, it was my fault!"

"Len, how can you say that?"

"Because it's the truth. Piers, let me speak, I beg you."

Tears bathe her cheeks as she accuses herself of Uncle Andrew's death as he was trapped in the cellars. Suddenly, I understand, and I realize I should have found her sooner, much sooner, to have helped free her from this weight. I tell her how I arrived at Oak Park and how I found him in the tree.

"I cut the rope and buried him with my hands. It wasn't your fault! It was them, the fanatics! Don't cry, Len. That was his fate; ever since Andrew was a child, he wanted to die like Edmund Campion. He was a martyr in the midst of the civil war, and you shouldn't punish yourself for that."

"But that's not all! Piers, they caught us because I disobeyed by running back to Andrew! Your father used to say that my disobedience could lead to death for you, me, and others. I didn't listen to Lady Leigh. I know you will hate me, but your mother, Margaret, and Ann died because of me. All that was left of your family!"

I try to hug her to calm so much pain, but she doesn't let me. I don't know what to do. She runs to the garden next to the Ozama, goes up to the wall, and leans on it, staring at the dark river. I go and stand next to her, and I wait.

Finally, she breaks the silence. "Forgive me, Piers!"

"I don't forgive Ruthven! I don't forgive the unleashed hordes! But Len, I have nothing to forgive you for. In fact, please forgive me, for leaving you in that prison, for not returning to you sooner. We have to keep moving forward. Together, you and I!"

I can see I have reached her. She turns around, sits on the wall with her back to the sea, and looks into my eyes.

"We will forget the past!" I tell her.

"I don't know if I can."

"I'll help you!"

She shakes her head, gets down from the wall, and walks toward the house. I follow her.

"You say you want to help, but how? You can't take the memories out of my mind!"

"You're right. I can't." I remember what Josefina told me. "Then I only ask one thing of you: that you help me."

She turns around, surprised. "How?"

"Help me like you did when they expelled me from the navy, and I came back home. Like when they assassinated my father."

"I didn't do anything!"

"You understood my fury. You wrapped me in those eyes of yours, full of sweetness, and you cried. You calmed me. If you're by my side, I can be a good man. I can overcome my years of violence and dishonor."

The expression on her face reminds me of how she looked before we parted.

"I can do that." And for the first time, she smiles faintly. "I can cry. That's all I've done for the past few years."

There is a noise; the vegetation moves, and we are separate from each other. A kind face appears.

Josefina speaks in a low voice. "You should come back inside, my lady. Your uncle is asking about you. Tomorrow, there will be a gathering at the governor's palace, and he wants to ask you to go."

"I'll be there, too!" I say. "We can see each other again."

Len doesn't answer; Josefina is leading her away. She casts one final glance at me; in her eyes is deep love and, at the same time, intense suffering.

I head toward Juan de Morfa's house, my heart overflowing with a bittersweet joy. Len is no longer the lively young woman I knew, but a soul tortured by memories, and I realize that I love her now even more than before. A woman who loved me once, but who now pulls away. Someone I must conquer again.

56

In the Alcázar de Colón

I greet Doña Alberta Josefa de Mendoza with a bow. She is the wife of Governor Meneses, a spirited lady from the harsh lands of Castile. Stocky and mustachioed, she doesn't strike me as charming, but I have to recognize her strength. Despite the curfew and though just a few miles away the enemy lurks, Doña Josefa didn't hesitate to gather what is left of the colony for a party. The resolute lady is trying to support her husband with a gesture of encouragement toward the men and women trying to defend the city of Santo Domingo.

In response to my greeting, she smiles at me with her irregular teeth. Her ample skirt, spread over a silly farthingale, takes up nearly the width of the stairway leading to the reception room.

The lady waves us up. Don Juan de Morfa, his very pregnant wife, and I walk all along the Renaissance balconies. Doña Beatriz walks slowly, leaning on her husband's arm.

The guests are milling around and uneasily peering out the windows overlooking the Ozama.

"Despite Pimentel's proposal, there are plenty of people," Morfa remarks to me.

"What did he propose?" I ask.

"To send the women away," Doña Beatriz explains. "But Don Juan Francisco insisted that, if they left, their husbands would follow them, and the city would be left undefended."

"Our new governor has been more . . . accommodating." In Morfa's voice there is a hint of criticism. "Don Bernardino has allowed many of the wealthy people to flee the capital."

"What?" I cry. "If the enemy takes the capital, the whole island will be theirs, and it won't matter where those good people might be hiding. Pack of cowards! They should stay and help with the defense!"

"That's what I think, too. That's why my dear wife hasn't left Santo Domingo."

Beatriz holds her husband's arm with one hand, while with the other she touches her stomach. "Nor would I dare venture out, when I'm this far along, down those dusty roads full of potholes and mud."

While we await the call to dinner, Morfa speaks to me in a low voice about this person and that, explaining to me who they are. He knows the whole colony.

I overhear someone lamenting that the most dashing members of local society are missing. Morfa, with a sigh, clarifies that the whining lady is his mother-in-law, Doña Luisa Dávila. With her are two smiling young women, Doña Beatriz's sisters. Everyone is speaking too loudly, nervous about the English attack. I'm tense too, but mostly about facing Len again.

I hear someone beside me say, "Montemayor is here."

I turn and am filled with the sensation that the room has darkened, and it is she who illuminates everything. I'm in a daze. Last night, I saw her by starlight. Now, in a room lit by the afternoon sun, her beauty and fragility move me. I realize how much she has changed.

"Let's go," Doña Beatriz says quietly.

She motions for me to follow her. An usher has invited Montemayor to sit at a place of honor, near the governor, so he left his niece in the care of Doña Luisa Dávila. Doña Beatriz goes into action, walking up to her mother and making the introductions. Len acts as if we have never set eyes on each other; she doesn't even look my way. I don't understand what's happening. Her chest is heaving with rapid, anxious breaths. She doesn't speak. As Montemayor walks away, I realize that he is looking at me warily and with contempt, as if wondering how it is possible that I could share a table with respectable people.

The guests are taking their places at the long table set with Talavera pottery. Len sits between Doña Beatriz and her mother. Morfa and I sit across from them. The meal begins, but I can't stop watching Len. I respond vaguely when spoken to. Every now and then, Len looks up at me with anguish. She responds in monosyllables to those who speak to her. I feel happy just to behold her. What more do I need, now that I have found her again?

When dinner is over, we hear the strumming of a guitar and a lute. Don Álvaro de Aguilar leans over to one of the Dávila sisters. Some couples begin to dance. I walk up to Len and bow, remembering that long-ago dance on the stairway at Oak Park. She blushes, curtsies, and takes a step forward. Don Juan Francisco turns his head precisely at that instant and is surprised to see the look on his niece's face.

The music is very different from that pavane we danced to as children. At one point, my hand rests on her waist. Len turns rigid, as if a mysterious force emanated from my hand, making her recoil. There are pearls of perspiration on her brow. What's wrong with her? My darling Len! When we move apart, she recovers, but during the next movement calling for me to touch her, she is flustered again.

When the dance ends, Len goes back to the ladies. Don Juan Francisco crosses to her and says something very serious. I can't stop staring at her, nor she at me. No other gentleman dares invite her to dance. Perhaps they are afraid of the dumbstruck young woman with enormous eyes.

When the lady sitting next to her gets up to dance, I go over and sit in the vacant chair.

"My uncle has warned me about you, Piers," she tells me in English.

I answer in Spanish. "Speak to me in your language. And don't say my name; I can't allow anyone to recognize me."

She looks upset. "You won't leave me again? I'm afraid of losing you! And even so . . ."

"What?"

"I don't know." Her eyes turn glassy. "Sometimes you have a dream of happiness, and my dream was you. Now you're here, and I don't know what's wrong with me. I feel glad but also sad, and, somehow, I'm afraid of you."

"Len!" I protest. "I only want to make you happy."

"I know," she says, and more passionately adds, "and I, you. When I received the medallion, I don't think I've ever been so happy in my life."

"You received it?"

She touches her hand to her neck and shows it to me.

"Who gave it to you?"

"Don Gabriel de Rojas."

"What the devil?" I can't hide my surprise. "Where is he?"

"Sick with malaria in the Hospital of San Nicolás. But you mustn't tell anyone."

"My Lord!" I exclaim, impatient. "I have to go see him. Everything depends on him."

"He's very sick; he might die."

At that moment, we hear a far-off explosion. The music stops. Some people rush out onto the balconies.

Someone shouts, "The English are attacking the city!"

The confusion inundating the city reaches us through the windows.

Len grabs my hand, and we follow people to the large terrace overlooking the Ozama and the sea. We hear another explosion to the east and make out the glow of a fire. She is trembling.

"Just like before!" she says. "That horrible noise. Like at Oak Park, like when they burned down the house and—"

"Easy! Nothing is going to happen. I'm here with you."

Gently and firmly, I lead her away from the balcony, and once we are inside, I force her to look at me. She returns to reality.

"Yes," she says more serenely. "Next to you, nothing will happen to me. I'm safe if you are here."

We hear a commotion behind us. I turn and realize that very near us, a stocky, tall man with an unfriendly face and a thick beard is watching Len and me with thinly veiled curiosity. Farther away, one lady is crying, and another is screaming with fear. We hear more explosions.

"There is no immediate danger!" The voice of Governor Meneses resounds through the great room, as he tries in vain to calm everyone. "The explosions are at San Jerónimo Fort, more than a league from here. Still, it's a good idea for the ladies to go home."

Doña Beatriz finds us and tells Len that Montemayor has asked her to take Len home.

"I don't want to leave you. When will I see you again?" I ask her.

Len grips my arm; she doesn't want to be separated from me, either.

Doña Beatriz murmurs, "We have to go, but I'll try to arrange for you to see her sometime tomorrow."

As the guests are leaving the room, the governor calls for his military authorities. Juan de Morfa and Don Álvaro de Aguilar both agree that I should stay.

"The English are now very near the walls of the city," the governor explains.

"All the women and clerics should be ordered to leave the city," says a gentleman dressed in black with an elegant white ruff.

Don Juan de Morfa whispers in my ear, "That's Pimentel, Rojas's enemy."

I scowl. He was the one eavesdropping on Len and me a moment ago.

Morfa adds, "A scoundrel. He only looks out for his own interests."

"What are those interests?"

"Well, if we evacuate the city, Doña Inés will leave the protection of the Convent of Las Claras, and he can do whatever he wants to her."

I observe Pimentel warily; his expression is that of a wolf sniffing its prey. While Morfa and I were speaking, Montemayor has confronted him.

"Why will you not desist from this, Don Rodrigo de Pimentel?" Montemayor looks angry. The circles under his eyes are even darker. "If they leave, some of the troops will have to accompany them, morale will be worse, and the city will be more unprotected than it is now."

"The enemy is very powerful. We must be prudent!"

"Prudence? Cowardice, I would say!"

"Please, gentlemen—" Don Bernardino de Meneses intervenes.

"What I am saying is elementary," Montemayor continues indignantly.

"There is no time to argue. The situation is critical," Don Álvaro de Aguilar says.

"We must attack as soon as possible!" exclaims Juan de Morfa.

"There are eight of them for every one of us," Pimentel replies with something like a smirk.

What a nasty man, I think. And, worst of all, what he has said is totally true.

"We must attack them, but it is already too late in the day," Aguilar decides. "We will have to wait until tomorrow."

Only when I go out with Don Juan de Morfa, to the plaza in front of the palace, do I have a chance to tell him what Len has revealed to me about Gabriel de Rojas.

He grabs my arm. "It's crucial that we speak with him."

57

THE STORY OF GABRIEL DE ROJAS

Inside the thick walls of the Hospital of San Nicolás, we can hear piti-
ful cries and moans of pain. The shells fired by English ships have
wounded many in the neighborhoods near San Jerónimo. The good
friars are busily tending to patients as we stumble along amid the rough
beds. There is hardly any ventilation, and everything is in darkness,
with only a few candlesticks lit.

One of the friars bumps into us and spills his washbasin full of
water.

"This is no place to be wandering around," he snaps.

"Brother Alonso," says Morfa, "we're looking for a sick man."

"Really?" he says, looking at all those surrounding us. "That's what
we have too much of here, sick and wounded people."

"We're looking"—the Irishman lowers his voice—"for Captain
Rojas."

Brother Alonso turns pale and starts to back away from us. "I don't
know anything!"

Morfa follows him. "You do know, of course you do."

"No."

I grab the man's shoulder. "Brother, you have to help us! We are friends and only want to help him. If you don't take us to him, we'll turn this place inside out, and we'll call in the aldermen."

"Who did you say you were?"

Juan de Morfa quickly answers, very annoyed. "You know me perfectly well, Father. Don Pedro Leal"—he gestures to me—"is a good friend of mine and the captain. Enough, Father! Tell us where you've hidden him!"

He has grown so impatient that he has placed his hand on the handle of his sword.

Brother Alonso realizes he has no way out, so he says, "All right. Wait here."

We start to follow.

"For pity's sake! I'll be right back."

We wait for him uneasily, a bit queasy from the odor of putrefaction and blood. After a while, the cleric reappears and signals for us to follow him. He says Don Gabriel has agreed to see us.

We rush through the hospital church full of saints and candles. We climb up to the presbytery and from there to a sacristy, which leads to the cloister.

Friar Alonso pauses in front of a small cell. Before opening the door, he warns us. "Now his fever has gone down, so you can talk to him. If it starts to rise again or if he gets worked up, I beg you to leave. Every bout of fever takes him closer to the grave."

We enter the tiny chamber. Lying on a rickety old bed of dry leaves is Rojas, pallid and emaciated. A candle flickers dimly at his side, casting shadows on the wall.

"How?" he asks in a weary voice. "How did you find me?"

"The medallion reached its owner," I respond. "She told me where you were."

"But what has happened to you?" Juan de Morfa asks, alarmed. "How did you end up here?"

"Shortly after we said our farewells, a great storm came up . . ."

Rojas tells us very slowly, pausing frequently to catch his breath, about his travails. His ship was dragged by the hurricane to the north of Hispaniola, where it crashed into the rocks along the coast. He came to badly injured, with his legs broken, in a camp of buccaneers who, though outlaws, treated him with great care. They recognized him as commander of the fort and, fearing he might denounce them to the judges, wouldn't let him leave. After his legs finally healed, he did escape, but on the way back to Santo Domingo, he came down with terrible fevers that nearly killed him. He arrived in the city half crawling and headed for San Nicolás, hoping Brother Alonso could keep him safe from Don Rodrigo Pimentel until he recuperated his strength.

"Are you so fearful that he'll try to kill you again?" I ask. "Even while you're in the city, under Montemayor's protection?"

Rojas is silent for a long moment. "I must tell you that, in Tortuga, Monsieur Renard spoke of Don Rodrigo as someone who had 'dealings' with the Brethren, ever since the times of Levasseur. Furthermore, he said that the judges were involved. I didn't want to believe him, at least not so far as Don Juan Francisco de Montemayor is concerned, but what if it is true?"

"That's impossible!" Juan de Morfa declares. "I may not get along with him, but Montemayor is the most honorable person I know."

"Appearances can sometimes be deceiving." Captain Rojas wipes a hand across his eyes. "Pay no attention to me, my friend. It's these fevers devouring me; I see ghosts where there aren't any. I've become so paranoid that I even came to think that"—a sad smile slips out—"he had bought you, too."

"The worst thing about dishonest men," Morfa reflects, "is that they scatter their shit, even over honest people, and make us distrust everyone."

Don Gabriel remains silent; he looks exhausted and weak. After a while, he says, "I think that much, if not all, of what Renard said is true. Don Rodrigo Pimentel is not only a contrabandist, as everyone suspects. He is an out-and-out pirate and a criminal, even if it can't be proven."

"Why do you say that?" I ask.

"The buccaneers, who know everything that goes on here, revealed to me what he has been doing with his fleet. We know he is licensed to act as a privateer, but he doesn't just attack enemy ships—he attacks ours, too. And even worse. They told me he was behind the death of Governor Pérez Franco." Rojas pauses, exhausted. "It makes sense. Don Juan, don't look at me like that. The governor planned to conquer Tortuga, and that would have put an end to Don Rodrigo's business, so he got him out of the way. What he didn't foresee is that Montemayor and I would take over the mission. That's when he tried to do away with me, and I ended up"—he looks at me—"on the sloop you took prisoner."

"So, it wasn't all because of Doña Inés," I say.

"No," he responds, "it wasn't just because of her."

"Are you really sure about all this?" Morfa asks.

"I have no proof, but Renard and the buccaneers concurred in all details. They described Pimentel as someone far worse than you and I ever imagined. If you think it over, as I have done, you'll realize how he has manipulated us all. You, my friend, he has slandered for years, especially to Montemayor, claiming you can't be trusted, that you're a pirate in disguise."

"And there's nothing worse he could tell Montemayor about me," Morfa confirms.

"As it turns out, Alderman Pimentel is accusing you of being what he himself is!"

"The shameless bastard!"

"But we must be careful, very careful. Pimentel is smart. From what Monsieur Renard told me, he has surely bought off other aldermen and judges, but maybe not Montemayor." Rojas has been talking for too long; he is exhausted, very weak.

"What can we do for you?" I ask him.

"You must put a stop to it."

Juan de Morfa exclaims, "We have to explain all this to the principal judge. He respects and will listen to you. He is the only one who can act against the alderman. He has been trying to prosecute him for months, without success."

Brother Alonso, who has stood by, looks scandalized by what has been said in this small cell. He steps forward now to agree with Morfa.

"Sooner or later, he will find you here, Captain, and I fear we won't be able to protect you," Alonso tells him. "It would be wise to appeal to the principal judge; he is a fair man. You will be safer under his protection than here."

"Yes," I agree. I look at the friar. "Will you go to him? He will believe you."

I need Don Gabriel to speak with Montemayor; he's the only one who can redeem me to him. Brother Alonso fixes his dark, penetrating eyes on me.

58

AT THE HOUSE OF THE PRINCIPAL JUDGE

After leaving Rojas in the care of Brother Alonso, who has assured us he won't leave his side until we return, we set out from the Hospital of San Nicolás late at night with one objective: to see Montemayor.

In just a few minutes, we reach his house. A servant has us wait in a large patio with a fountain in the middle. Don Juan Francisco appears shortly. He looks unkempt: he isn't wearing a ruff, his shirt is open, and his fingers are stained with ink. He must have been writing.

"What do you want at such a late hour?" he asks brusquely, without even greeting us.

"We have found Rojas," Morfa responds.

The judge's face lights up. "I thought him dead," he mutters. Then he quickly asks, "Where is he?"

"Very sick, in the Hospital of San Nicolás."

"Why hasn't he let us know?"

Morfa briefly shares Don Gabriel's story, along with his suspicions about Pimentel. They don't seem to surprise the principal judge.

"As God is my witness, Pimentel will end up on the gallows! For the past few years, I've been keeping an eye on him, but I've never been able to prove anything. I tried to prosecute him for smuggling, but the case was halted because of the attack. With Captain Rojas's testimony—thank God he is alive!—we can demonstrate that Pimentel tried to kill him."

"He fears for his life and doesn't trust anyone."

"And he's right to do so! He must be extremely careful! That damned alderman is a scoundrel who fools everyone with his clever words. We must get Don Gabriel out of the hospital; he isn't safe there."

"But where can he go?"

"I think the only place Don Rodrigo wouldn't dare enter is this house."

"He will need constant care," Morfa warns him.

"Josefina will look after him, and my niece can also help. We can't waste any time; tomorrow may be too late. Vicente!"

He asks the servant who comes running to bring his hat and cape, then turns to us.

"Perhaps I'll have to change my opinion of you both," he confesses.

Vicente returns and helps his master dress. I turn to look behind me. At the top of the stairs, Len is watching us; I feel transfixed by her gaze and greet her with a touch of my hand to my hat. Don Juan Francisco, who is ready to leave, turns and notices his niece's presence, the expression on her beautiful face. Len, startled, disappears into the gallery of the first floor.

Wasting no time, Montemayor hurries down the street. After a few blocks, we reach the Hospital of San Nicolás. When we open the door of the cell, we find that the sick man's fever has gone up, and he is delirious. He won't stop shouting Pimentel's name.

Brother Alonso quickly stands and waves us in; then he goes away, leaving us with Don Gabriel. It surprises me to see the wiry, sullen judge kneel on the ground next to Rojas's bed.

"Old friend, what have they done to you?" he muses.

When he hears the judge's voice, Don Gabriel calms down. He stops shouting and closes his eyes, falling into a soft lethargy.

With the help of two young friars, we discreetly transfer Don Gabriel to Montemayor's house in the silence of dawn. Vicente is waiting for us, along with Josefina and also Len. They are accompanied by only a few trusted servants; we have to keep news of the sick man's arrival from getting out.

We carry him to a small room with good ventilation overlooking the mouth of the Ozama. Len and Josefina make him comfortable. Len's elegant hands plump pillows, smooth covers, rest on Don Gabriel's forehead. She is very quiet, but her face is serene. Morfa catches me staring. He tugs at my sleeve, suggesting we leave. We withdraw to his house next door. It has been a long night.

59

IN THE CATHEDRAL

I'm awakened by explosions. I hurry out of bed and open the window; there are clouds of smoke in the distance. I get dressed and run down the stairs to the entrance hall. Morfa is speaking with a frightened young man who has come on behalf of Don Álvaro de Aguilar. The English ships are once again bombing the defenses at Santo Domingo. For the moment, the castle of San Jerónimo, the forts of El Matadero and La Puerta Grande, and the wall overlooking the sea are holding up.

After gulping down some food under the close supervision of Doña Beatriz, we put on our capes, hats, and swords, and the Irishman hands me a musket. Along the way to the plaza, he tells me that the greatest concern of those who know the terrain is the part of the wall adjoining the countryside; it's little more than a fence. Apparently, a few months back, Montemayor ordered ditches and trenches dug to prevent the enemy from coming in, but the work hasn't been finished.

The young man who came looking for us, a soldier from the fort, explains that at dawn that morning, Governor Meneses went in person to inspect the northern part of the defenses, but as he was doing so, he received word that several enemy regiments were advancing on the city. That's why he gave orders to the fort's commanders, Don Álvaro de Aguilar and Don Damián del Castillo, another alderman, to gather all men of combat age in front of the cathedral. They were to go into battle with every musket and lance they could get their hands on.

In the streets, there are sounds of military bands and trumpet calls. When we turn the corner leading to the plaza, we see a crowd: merchants, artisans, peasants, northern landowners, and a good number of slaves who have been promised freedom in exchange for fighting. Both the new recruits and veteran soldiers await orders in the shade of the great basilica or under the trees, avoiding the burning sun that is rising. Juan de Morfa greets people here and there. The tone of the conversations is very loud; everyone is both swaggering and worried. They want to defend against the common enemy and save their belongings and their families from an unjust attack. We hear all kinds of rumors, some exaggerating the enemy forces and others underestimating them.

We are waiting for Don Álvaro and Don Damián, who will lead the defense. Someone claims they are at the fort, stocking up on weapons from the arsenal; others laugh, saying the captains are stuck to their bedsheets since they are nothing but cowards.

Tired of waiting, I lean my heavy musket against a tree and pause to observe the distinguished silhouette of the cathedral truncated by Drake seventy years ago. The solid walls, made of luminous limestone, glisten in the clear sunlight.

Before long, down a side street, I see some veiled ladies going to Mass. Today, despite the bombardment, they don't expect a direct attack on the city and have allowed the women to go outside. I recognize Doña Beatriz from her advanced state of pregnancy and her deliberate walk. Beside her, I think I recognize another, slender figure, as well as the slave Josefina. I follow them inside the temple.

As I cross the threshold, I remove my hat, overwhelmed by the sense of the sacred when I see the great central nave, its arches pointing to the altarpiece.

Morfa, who has followed me, points to a side chapel and explains that Christopher Columbus is buried there. I don't hear the rest of what he says because the doors of a great balcony have opened to the right of the altar, and several ladies have appeared, among them Len. She is so beautiful I can't take my eyes off her.

An elderly lady beside me whispers, "She's Montemayor's niece. Very pretty, yes, but they say the poor thing is mad."

I'm irritated by her intrusion; I feel like slapping her and telling her Len isn't mad but has been beaten by a painful past. I don't respond, nor do I take my eyes off Len. She is kneeling and praying with devotion. After a while, she lifts her dark eyelashes and scans the faithful who fill the basilica. When she sees me, her blue eyes stop.

Seeing her so alive, so beautiful, something is purified inside me. I can't bring myself to pay attention to the prayers. I go through the motions of the rituals. The service seems endless, and due to my lack of sleep, I start to nod. I awaken to the shot of a musket outside. Morfa elbows me, indicating we should leave. I say farewell to Len with a gesture; she smiles with the warmth of other times, amused perhaps at seeing me fall asleep.

We go out to the plaza, where I retrieve my musket. Don Álvaro and Don Damián have arrived, and soldiers from the forest are handing out weapons to the recruits. Aguilar names me captain of a little battalion of rural militia. He briefly explains our mission and assigns us a local guide. I examine the men making up my squadron: rough farmworkers, hunters, vaqueros, and a few slaves. I ask each man his name and where he is from. Since most of them are from the northern part of the island, I ask them if they know Hernando de Montoro. An enormous black man says yes, but he ran away years ago. I miss Coleridge, my second mate, as well as his complaints and barbs; we parted ways several days ago. He probably hasn't had time yet to run away from the English fleet, as we planned. I hope nothing terrible has happened.

Aguilar moves from group to group, explaining the strategy, which is to harass the enemy through ambushes on the sides of the mountain, down paths and shortcuts.

Before preparations for the march are finished, the service in the cathedral ends. I make out Len, walking along, listening distractedly to Doña Beatriz and other ladies while searching for me in the crowd. They stop under one of the trees shading the plaza, near a large statue of Columbus. I'm glad to see her like this, among other young ladies. She looks better today, less melancholic, and I let myself hope I might be responsible for the change.

I step away from my men and manage to approach her. I whisper in her ear that I'm leaving. We're off to the front lines, but I'll soon return, and then nothing will separate us again. She turns pale. I hear the lilting voice of Josefina, who has come up beside us.

"My lady, he will return. Don't you worry."

Len regains her composure. The slave tugs her arm gently and leads her off down a side street to Calle de las Damas. Once again, Len turns to look at me.

I meet again with the new recruits they have assigned me: good people, capable of fighting. More than half are vaqueros, and they remind me very much of the buccaneers I met on Tortuga. They stand out, in their loose pants and black shirts tied by strips of rawhide with knives dangling from them. Their rough shoes are cowhide or pig hide, made in one piece, and tied to their feet. They carry high-caliber short muskets. Some of them wear caps with pointed visors. They look somewhere between savage and sinister, but when I hear them talking, I understand that they have left behind wives and children, land, and plantations. They are frightened, despite their rowdy appearance.

The plaza feels packed, but there aren't more than two hundred and fifty men here. The English outnumber us by many times. Yet no one is discouraged. These poorly armed men are fighting for their loved ones against foreign domination. They're spirited and courageous. They're used to the climate, this humid tropical heat that's so hard for someone not born here. Also, they are familiar with the island's trails and paths, its vegetation. Even so, I wonder if there is any hope of victory; it seems nearly impossible. I know my countrymen to be strong, disciplined soldiers, people who fought in a war not so long ago.

Of course, I don't reveal the misgivings that crowd my soul; rather, I urge my men on. As a pirate, I wasn't afraid of dying; death came to seem like a liberation. But now that I have found Len, now that I can demonstrate to Montemayor that I'm not a traitor, now that I am fighting alongside decent men who are honorable heads of households, I am overcome with fear. I want to go on living with dignity and rescue Len from her melancholy, to see her smile again, as she did so long ago.

60

AMBUSHES

La Haina, April 1655

The two hundred fifty men in the plaza march in a long formation down the dusty streets. We will leave from the northern sector, which borders the countryside and is where the enemy is expected to arrive. Before we cross the city limits, another infantry company joins us; they look much braver than the men who have been entrusted to me.

Shortly after we leave Santo Domingo, the road has thick vegetation. It's hot, and everything feels heavy: the weapons, our clothes, the scarce food we carry with us. Within two hours of marching, we are surrounded by mosquitoes; we have entered the area around the Haina River. Despite everything, I take time to converse with the men with whom fate has united me. They confide in me their fears of the enemy, infidels, and heretics; they've been told the English are like demons. I listen to them, alternately amused and uneasy.

The regiment begins losing troops because, every now and then, Don Álvaro and Don Damián send battalions peeling off down trails and paths; from there, they will attack the enemy and stop their advance on the capital. The group of soldiers preceding us takes a path heading south. We continue along the main road, which is now crossing through some thick woods; the vegetation nearly covers the trail of sand and dirt. Amid the tree branches, I see enormous, unsightly iguanas. When we reach a small path, Don Álvaro indicates that I should follow him, and he asks our guide, a young boy, to lead us to the other side of the mountain. From there, we are to stand guard over the road from Nizao so that we can attack the enemy from above.

My men tell me the names of plants we pass: *guayacán, cambrón, baitoa, candelón*. When we descend the mountain, we reach a dry, thorny hill; we can see the road where the enemy must pass. I imagine my compatriots thirsty, without water, under the scorching sun.

At sundown, we reach our lookout point and take up positions. We can hear a nightingale cooing as the sun sets. Later, the moon rises, creating phantasmagoric shadows.

My men take shifts, but I barely shut an eye. At dawn, through the tree branches, I can make out Aguilar's battalion on the other side of the mountain. Our strategy is a good one; whoever comes down that road will be caught in the crossfire.

When everyone is awake, I address my men, simple folks who have probably never killed a man before, but who are brave and spirited.

"My friends, soon we will go into combat. We are fighting for our honor and for our families, for our faith, for what we love."

I see them swelling with ardor, eager to confront the invaders.

"Don Pedro," says a vaquero, tall, strong, with an olive complexion, "don't worry. We know how to shoot."

Soon, a guard alerts us that a company of enemy soldiers is approaching; they are proceeding slowly, dragging heavy cannons. The officers' helmets glisten in the weak morning light. I signal to everyone to load their weapons. Once we have them within range, we start firing. From the other side, our other battalion is also letting them have it. When we run out of munitions, we rush down to the road, armed with lances and swords. The combat is fierce. The vaquero has not only shot well, as he promised, he has also fought with bravery. But he isn't trained in hand-to-hand combat. An English soldier is about to cut him down, so I run over to help.

By some miracle, we defeat the enemy, despite being outnumbered. The sun is high in the sky when they flee to their trenches, leaving some dead and wounded men. We manage to capture a few of those left behind.

I recognize one of the captives as my friend Coleridge. His face lights up when he sees me. I speak to Aguilar, asking him to let me set him free. The captain shakes his head, with a touch of condescendence, and tells me that the matter is beyond his jurisdiction. Nothing can be done until we return to Santo Domingo and he goes before the judges. It makes me angry, but I have to resign myself as they tie good Richard to some trees. He looks furious.

Once night falls and everyone is asleep, I am able to get near him and ask about my men. He tells me that Hernando de Montoro returned to the sloop and deserted that same night. The English spotted him and began to shoot at the rigging, but he managed to escape with the whole ship. Unfortunately, when Admiral Penn found out about Montoro's betrayal, it was Richard he began to distrust. Following a harsh interrogation, he forced Richard to march at the front of the combat line to demonstrate his loyalty to the English army.

"So, here you have me, Piers, tortured by the damned Roundheads and then taken prisoner by the papist pigs." He says it in good humor.

I squeeze his shoulder and assure him I will have him freed.

"It looks like things are going better for you," he says. "They even gave you a command."

"Good folks."

"Bah! Vaqueros and buccaneers."

"I see you're still a snob."

"Pardon me! A gentleman! Hey, could you find me something to drink? I need to wet my whistle."

In the morning, while we're getting ready to return to Santo Domingo, I approach Don Álvaro and again plead on Coleridge's behalf, but he sticks to his guns.

On the road back, Richard tells me that there are some cases of dysentery in the English camp and that the sick men are in bad shape. In the shallows of Haina, there is no potable water, and they are dying of thirst.

61

LIFE AND DEATH

Santo Domingo, April 1655

The next morning, after leaving the prisoners of war at the penitentiary, I decide to go look for Don Juan de Morfa to figure out how to free Coleridge. The streets of the capital are packed; reinforcements have arrived from all over the island, from Puerto Plata, Monte Cristi, and Samaná, and a company has just come in from Santiago de los Caballeros: one hundred medics, most of them lancers. They march in a disorganized fashion.

Suddenly, I hear a hoarse voice.

"Captain Leal!"

It's Hernando de Montoro, along with a dozen of my sailors from the *Indomitable*. They surround me, interrupting each other to tell me in fits and starts how they deserted and managed to reach Samaná, near the Montoros' property. The sloop has remained there, somewhat damaged by bullets, under the command of Field Marshal Cosme de Azúa and with part of the crew, including artilleryman Kerrigan, who wasn't convinced they wouldn't hang him if he showed up in Santo Domingo.

I'm so happy to see the little Valentín de Torres, Zudaire, the helmsman Blas de Alcolea, the grumpy bonesetter Rodrigo de Alcalá, the cook Domingo Rincón, and all the rest that I embrace each of them, heartily slapping them on the back.

"You can't imagine how happy I am to have found you, Don Pedro!" Montoro tells me, grinning from ear to ear. "I've been terribly worried about what happened to you since they took you prisoner. But I see you're free and looking good!"

I look for Don Álvaro de Aguilar, who is dividing up the reinforcements, and I ask him to let me add my men to my battalion. He refuses; he's going to need them to reinforce the trenches in the northern zone. I don't like being separated from them again, but I have to obey orders. Before taking my leave of them, I promise to do everything I can so they can join me later. I leave them eating the grub several women have prepared for the soldiers at the Casas Reales, which has now been turned into the city barracks. Montoro is talking with Alcalá, and Domingo Rincón is flirting crudely with a large black woman, who slaps him. I can't help but laugh; my men haven't changed.

Finally, I reach Morfa's house, landing in the middle of a true domestic storm: Doña Beatriz has gone into labor.

Her mother, Doña Luisa Dávila, has taken over. The house is overflowing with noise and shouts, with women rushing around, busy and nervous, bringing and carrying away clothing, cloths, washbasins, and bandages. The birth is progressing slowly. Morfa gives a sigh of relief when he sees me. His nerves are shot, and he can't stand his meddlesome mother-in-law.

We go out to the garden, where I plead with him passionately to intercede with Don Álvaro de Aguilar and the judges so the men from the *Indomitable* can fight with me and so Coleridge can be freed.

"Don't worry. We'll speak with Montemayor."

"Will he listen to us?"

"Since Rojas is at his house, everything has changed. It's as if he's been freed from prejudices and—"

A loud scream interrupts him. He hurries into the house and stops one of Doña Beatriz's sisters, who is coming down the stairs.

"Amalia! What's wrong? Is Beatriz all right?"

"Bringing a child into the world is painful," the young woman answers with an air of self-sufficiency reminiscent of her mother, as if she knows everything there is to know about childbirth.

Doña Luisa Dávila peers over the railing of the upper floor.

"You should leave, Don Juan. It's not polite for you to stay here, nor to have a stranger running around the house at such a time." In her voice, there is a hint of disdain.

We walk next door. Although the whole city is in disarray, in the principal judge's house, tranquility reigns. Don Juan Francisco is attending to some officials, giving them orders, but he is serene and level-headed. When he finishes, he greets us with a benevolent look, much friendlier than yesterday. We sit down, and I speak to him about Coleridge, about my men, about Tortuga, about the promise that Don Gabriel made to me.

"I'd like to corroborate with him what you are telling me."

He stands up calmly and invites us to follow. We silently walk up the marble staircase, then along the balcony ringing the central patio, which all the rooms open up to.

Before entering Captain Rojas's room, Montemayor warns me in a low voice, "He has gotten worse over the past few days. His fever rose again, and he barely responds to Josefina's attentions."

Despite his words, I'm shocked by Don Gabriel's appearance. He is totally consumed, all skin and bones. His face is nearly bloodless, translucent, with large blue rings under his eyes. Sitting next to him, a slender figure mops his forehead with a kerchief. She is wearing an orange skirt and a bodice of the same color, which opens in slits on the sleeves, exposing her white blouse. Len. She stands up when she hears us come in, and her eyes open wide, fixing her gaze on me. She blushes and smiles softly.

He smiles weakly at Don Juan de Morfa. "Good-bye, my friend."

Morfa nods his head, unable to speak.

Then Rojas turns to Montemayor.

"Dear Don Juan Francisco, I beg you to take care of and protect my Inés."

When Brother Alonso and Doña Inés come in, he is still conscious, but fading. To our surprise, he solemnly asks the monk if he will marry him and Inés, joining them in matrimony before it's too late.

He calls her to his side and whispers, "I'm going to die! Don't cry, darling. You're what I have loved most in this world. What I regret the most is leaving you, because I love you."

Inés wails.

"But if I'm dying, at least—at the very least, my señora—you will be free. We will be husband and wife in this life, as well as in the next one. I will thus free you from Don Rodrigo, who will have no power over you anymore."

He looks again to the principal judge. "I want to testify that every-thing that is mine goes to her, and you will administer it. Inés will live at peace, under your guardianship, Montemayor, my friend."

Don Juan Francisco nods.

Shortly afterward, in front of us all, Doña Inés and Don Gabriel become husband and wife. After the nuptial blessing, a notary who has been called records the dying man's last wishes.

We leave them alone, closing the doors of the room behind us, where happiness and suffering are intermingling. After some time, the new bride comes out asking for help. Don Gabriel's fever has begun to rise, and he is delirious again. He repeats the name *Pimentel* furiously and that of Doña Inés with love. Then he slips into a placid drowsiness.

At sunset, he opens his eyes for one last time and stares at the light flowing through the window. His strong heart stops beating; on his face, there is peace. Inés de Ledesma embraces his body, crying.

We leave the room in silence, respecting the widow's grief. The sky turns deep cobalt, and the stars are beginning to come out. We wait a long time in silence, while inside, Josefina and Vicente Garcés wrap a shroud around Don Gabriel de Rojas, captain of the Armies of His Majesty King Philip, a man of honor.

Shortly afterward, a servant comes looking for Don Juan de Morfa. A baby boy has been born in the house next door.

Morfa, his voice breaking with emotion, exclaims, "His name will be Gabriel. And I hope he will be as worthy as the man who gave it to him."

over the deceased, sometimes saying prayers together. A wailer, brought
for the purpose, sobs disconsolately. Every now and then, I get up and
walk out to the patio, where Josefina and the servants bring me something to drink, hot chocolate or coffee. Then I return. Len and I watch
each other from opposite sides of the room. The coffin separates us.
The torches illuminate Captain Rojas's waxen face. I reflect that it is
thanks to him I have reached Len.

At dawn, Len stands and leaves the room. Shortly afterward, I follow her and find her sitting on the wall overlooking the Ozama. The
temperature has dipped, and she is wrapped in a pastel-colored shawl;
there is something magical about her figure, illuminated by the dawn.
I stand behind her, looking out at the estuary.

"Are you all right?" I ask her.

"Yes. I feel bad for Doña Inés."

"Why?"

"I had to convince her to come. She was afraid of being taken
prisoner by Pimentel." She pauses, then turns to face me. "If I knew
you were dying, I would run to your side, even if all the scoundrels in
the world were chasing me. She didn't. Don't misunderstand; she is sincere. She has told me she admires Don Gabriel, she was grateful for his
love and loyalty, but what she loves the most is her own freedom. She
wants to be able to live her own life without a husband, and now Don
Gabriel has given her that chance; he must have known her well. The
single woman is beholden to her legal guardian, the married woman
to her husband. A widow is free; by law, she can administer her own
patrimony. Inés will be able to live however she likes at last."

"Would you live alone? Would you be able to live without me?"

"No, Piers. Never. Without you, there's no light in my life."

"So?"

"I'm locked in a prison."

"What do you mean?"

"I'm not free because the past imprisons me. Something happened that . . . that won't let me love you as I would like. I'm dirty!"

"How can you say that?"

"I am, ever since that night."

She falls silent, and I sit down beside her. Like a few nights ago, we don't look at each other. Our eyes are fixed on the open sea.

"Piers, I'm impure. They abused me in Oak Park, me—and the others, too."

I grip the edge of the wall until my knuckles turn white; pain suffocates me. I think about Margaret, Ann, my mother. "Savage beasts!"

I control myself so I can listen to Len, who confesses nearly in a whisper, "In a way, I was happy when I heard your ship had sunk since that meant I would never have to tell you what I'm telling you now. It wounds my soul."

A knot forms in my throat. A few instants go by when I can't swallow.

"Don't torture yourself!" I beg her. "You, for me, are purity itself, the clean life of a happy past. Nothing that happened matters to me. Oh Lord! I'm the one who is dirty. I wasn't able to protect any of you or even get you out of prison. Only Elizabeth is left, and she is partly responsible for our misfortunes."

She looks at me in surprise. "Elizabeth? You're wrong. Piers, she died."

"Elizabeth died?" I'm startled. "But how?"

"When I was still at Bridewell, she arrived. Ruthven brought her there; I don't know what horrible crimes he accused her of. She didn't tell me; she didn't speak to me; she was as proud as ever. Then Don Alonso rescued me. I asked him to do something for her, but it was impossible. Before I left England, the ambassador told me that Elizabeth had wasted away from desperation and grief. You are the only one left of the Leighs, of your family—of our family. You will have to remake yourself, just as I will. I must do it because I love you, but I ask that you give me some time. Don't force me to kiss you; don't caress me. I want you by my side. I don't want you to go away or to be far from me again, Piers, but—I can't bear it when you touch me!" She looks at me with her eyes glistening with pain. "Do you understand?" She takes a few steps backward, against the wall, without taking her eyes off me.

The sun has risen now over the Ozama, and it tints the water red. In the Montemayor house, a bell rings. I hear Morfa's voice calling me.

"I understand and will respect your wishes. We have each other. You and I are all that is left of Oak Park. I'll never leave you! No matter what happens, I'll stay by your side."

Vicente Garcés makes his way through the plants in the garden and is surprised to see me alone with the principal judge's niece; it isn't proper. He informs me that they are waiting for me to help take Captain Rojas's remains to the cathedral.

With a bow, I take my leave of Len. On the patio, there are several soldiers from the fort. They shut the coffin, and together we carry it on our shoulders. It seems strangely light. On the street, people remove their hats as the funeral procession goes by.

The coffin is placed on a catafalque in the middle of the central nave, under the main altar. I hear the murmur of the old women's prayers, their sighs, the gentlemen's firm steps, the delicate step of the ladies filling the church.

Doña Inés, dressed in rigorous mourning, but now without her nun's headdress, enters the temple, accompanied by Len. They walk up to the balcony above the north door of the cathedral; the young widow is the center of everyone's attention. She doesn't look at any-one; her eyes are fixed on the coffin. I think about what Len has told me, that thanks to Don Gabriel, Inés has achieved her freedom. Len still isn't free from herself and from the past. But her face glows with a newfound peace.

63

THE BATTLE OF THE CRABS

Santo Domingo, May 1655

The light of dawn bathes the cupola of the cathedral and Plaza de Colón. I'm weary after several nights with hardly any rest, but I'm optimistic about the future. Len seems more and more serene. Last night, we were talking under the starlight on the patio with the wrought iron trellis and flowers. I didn't try to take her hand or kiss her, though there is nothing I would have liked more. We talked, not like we did in the old days, but as the people we are now: a man and a woman who love each other, though the past may chase us still.

I'm also pleased because Don Álvaro has given in and placed the crew of my sloop under my command. I found them fed up with digging trenches and anxious for combat. Together with Coleridge, on whose behalf the principal judge finally interceded, we walk the streets today, passing time before leaving the city.

I hear Montoro shout, "Why don't ships in the Royal Navy carry life preservers?" He answers himself: "Because shit floats."

People laugh.

Richard, who is walking beside me, looking very serious, responds, "I think you are insulting me."

The pilot Zudaire tries to reassure him, saying, "Oh no, sir. Not at all."

"Mr. Coleridge," I add, "it's nothing but a joke. Don't try to make it a question of honor."

"One does not joke about honor," he replies.

I manage to calm him by ordering Montoro to apologize. We keep walking all day, down paths and hills, without further incident. Then Don Álvaro de Aguilar sends us to the battle front with equipment and reinforcements.

On the beaches of Nizao, I introduce my crew to the rest of my battalion. The islanders greet me with shouts of joy; I hear them saying in their soft Caribbean accent, "Captain! Captain! How wonderful that you've returned!" They extend this trust and camaraderie to my sailors, and the newly enlarged battalion gets on better than I'd dared hope.

Two days after we arrive, they call the battalion commanders to a council of war. Apparently, Governor Bernardino de Meneses has ordered that the troops be concentrated for a military offensive. At dawn, we will directly attack the enemy in place, that is, in the trenches. Don Álvaro de Aguilar is the one who brought us the orders. Of course, he doesn't say anything during the meeting, but he later confides in me and another trustworthy commander that he doesn't agree. He tells us that, when Montemayor heard the plan, he called it insane.

"Then Montemayor said, 'It's a mistake to attack the enemy when they're in the trenches and when our forces are inferior to theirs. It would be better to provoke them to come out, as we have been doing until now.' And he's right. What is the governor thinking? Hell, we're walking straight into the lion's den!"

And in fact, the attack turns out to be almost suicidal. The English repel us, and we can't touch them. We return to camp without achieving anything; ten or twelve of our soldiers are dead at the foot of the enemy bastions, along with a captain who was a friend of Don Álvaro. The furious commander returns to Santo Domingo to let them know.

Then our spies tell us about an English counterattack directed at the fortifications surrounding the capital. It seems that defeating us at the trenches has given the enemy renewed courage. However, they haven't dared to take the inland route to Santo Domingo and are following a road near the coast, which takes them right in front of San Jerónimo Fort.

Don Álvaro de Aguilar has returned now, and he directs us to get ahead of them. The Dominicans guide us down hidden jungle trails. We overtake the English and, before long, reach a place very near the fort where we hide in the vegetation and wait. Soon, we see them coming, dragging their muskets. What follows is a real massacre. We rout them so badly that we capture eight flags, more than four hundred men fall, and we take numerous prisoners.

After our victory under San Jerónimo Fort, the enemy is forced to retreat. We have suffered some casualties of our own, so we take refuge within the thick walls of the fort to regroup. In the central patio, Aguilar, Damián del Castillo, Morfa, some other captains, and I debate our next move.

Suddenly, Montoro comes running. "The spies report that the enemy is retreating along the coast road to La Haina," he informs us.

"We can't waste another moment!" Aguilar exclaims. "We need to head them off and destroy them before they can shelter in their trenches once more. But first we have to do something to distract them and delay their march."

Montoro, who knows Hispaniola well, says, "There's a little path, a shortcut, and we could use it to overtake them. It crosses the narrow mountain passes high up, and then it leads directly to La Haina."

Aguilar narrows his eyes. "I know it, too—it's the smugglers' path."

Montoro nods guiltily and lowers his head, but Aguilar doesn't press the matter.

"It's settled: you'll guide Don Damián del Castillo's lancers down that path," Aguilar orders. "When you reach La Esperilla, you must delay the enemy's arrival as much as possible. That will allow us to take the royal highway and set up the muskets, cannons, and culverins pointing at the trenches. You must delay the English as long as possible. We can only claim victory if we manage to knock out the trenches of La Haina."

Don Damián del Castillo protests. "We are just a few men, and soon it will be night."

Suddenly, I remember something I heard a long time ago, a ruse the Royalists practiced against the Parliamentarians.

"I need some tarred ropes," I tell Aguilar.

Surprised, he asks me what for, and I quickly explain.

"A daring idea," he agrees. "It will allow Captain Castillo to reach the trenches before they do."

Then he spells out the plan in detail and concludes, "Captain Leal, as soon as you carry out this maneuver, you will head to the beach in Nizao and await the enemy there."

I put each man in my battalion in charge of heavy rolls of rope that the quartermaster of the fort supplied. I explain to them that our mission won't be to fight the enemy, but to distract them. If we do it well, we can turn fortune to our side. I harangue them about the importance of stealth and speed in this matter. They joke that they aren't pack mules, but they obey.

We set out for Montoro's shortcut, which crosses a low, wooded hill. From our positions, we can make out the lights of the enemy down below. They are advancing slowly, dragging cannons and wounded men, and we pass quickly up above. A few leagues farther, in a place where our adversaries are forced to choose between two paths, we hang the tarred ropes from the trees over one of the paths. We station guards to let us know when the enemy troops arrive. Night falls. When we receive word that the enemy is approaching, we set fire to different parts of the cords. I burn my hands in the process. The forest lights up with the little flames, creating an eerie effect in the blowing wind. It looks like men with torches are moving among the tree branches, as if there were many troops hiding in the depths of the forest.

When the British arrive, they are startled by lights and phantasmagorical shadows in the grove, and at the fork in the road, they take the one we want, leading them away from the trenches and directly toward Captain Castillo's lancers. The lancers attack them with verve and kill more than eighty men. While this combat is taking place, Don Álvaro de Aguilar manages to reach La Haina. He attacks the trenches and the English soldiers guarding them.

The battalion under my command continues down Montoro's shortcut directly to the beaches of Nizao, where the enemy can connect with their ships anchored in the bay.

As we are approaching, Montoro seems to remember something. He breaks into an ironic smile and tells me, "On the beach, at night, we can count on some unexpected help to frighten the English."

"What's that?"

"The crabs."

Laughing, he tells me an old story from the times of the pirate Drake, which has been handed down in his family.

I smile. "Let's find some palm leaves."

In the sands of Nizao, a few enemy soldiers are standing guard. Crawling along the beach, our knives in our teeth, we sneak up on them. We place our knives at their throats, then disarm and gag them, tying them to one another.

Next, we gather palm leaves, while Montoro eggs us on. "That's it, friends! Just wait till you see!"

We scatter the palm leaves all over the beach; the full moon facilitates our task. In the distance, we can hear muskets and cannons bombing the trenches. The enemy comes running, but there on the sands a new surprise awaits them: the crabs.

Montoro has told us that, on the beaches of Hispaniola, especially in the south, large crabs are abundant. They hide in the woods during the day and come out of their dens at night for something to eat. There are so many of them that their legs knock against each other as they walk, making a sound like maracas. Using the smoke from some green palm leaves we've set fire to, he teaches us how to goad the crabs out of their dens. The bizarre animals begin overrunning the beach, making a terrific racket. The noise is so unnerving that even we, who are expecting it, are shocked. The British all run away, thinking it the sound of soldiers' bandoliers. Some of them leap into the sea. Others run for their boats.

Cromwell's army loses the battle, along with the island of Hispaniola. The retreat happens so rapidly that they leave weapons, baggage, bombs and blunderbusses, scales, and horses scattered all over the beach, along with all sorts of implements of war. When the troops of Santo Domingo arrive, they are delighted by the booty. We stay there a long time, shouting and firing at the boats that are retreating. We insult them, calling them cowards, chickens, eunuchs, lily-livered, and other pretty things.

Afterward, Aguilar orders some of our troops to return down the road to La Esperilla and collect our wounded, who have remained behind. Damián del Castillo wisely warns us not to assume all danger has passed. He decides to organize an improvised camp on the sand to ensure the enemy fleet doesn't attempt to land again. The beach fills with campfires and singing. After a while, there is no longer any doubt: the lights of the English ships are receding.

"We've won!" Aguilar exclaims.

Damián del Castillo is reluctant to celebrate because the fleet pauses a bit farther out. But the next day, it disappears over the horizon. Hispaniola has been saved.

64

VICTORY

The journey back to the capital seems short. The battalion walks along, singing military marches. When we arrive, the city has a festive air and, more than that, an air of bravado. Everywhere, people are celebrating the victory. Those who had fled are starting to return, and the streets are once again crowded. Among those from my sloop, there is an even more festive atmosphere because they realize that the victory is astonishing and that, both for them and for me, it means a new life.

The troops scatter through the streets, filling bars, taverns, and bordellos, but I can't stay away from Len any longer. I arrange to meet Montoro and Coleridge at the port the next day, and I bid farewell to my men. I hurry up several blocks, cross the packed plaza with the cathedral, and head down a side street to Calle de las Damas.

At Montemayor's house, Vicente Garcés lets me in. I ask him about Doña Catalina, and he tells me she is in the garden. Paying no attention to his questions, I cross the patios separating me from the back of the house. There, in the meadow overlooking the Ozama, Len and Doña Inés are reading a book together. Josefina, who has done so much for them both, is there also, smiling contentedly. I rush to Len, who turns when she hears my steps. Her face fills with happiness; she jumps up and stretches out her hands to mine.

"You're back! You're all right!"

When she squeezes my hands, she realizes that they are burned; she lowers her head and kisses them.

This is the moment when Don Juan Francisco arrives, perhaps notified by Garcés. Len and I immediately separate. Nevertheless, the principal judge doesn't react to his niece's gesture, so improper under rigid Spanish customs.

"Mr. Leal, congratulations. Don Álvaro has told me about your intelligence and courage. Just a few weeks ago—what am I saying?—a few days ago, people in this city thought it would be impossible to defeat the enemy, but clearly what we have here is a great deal of military spirit, of courage and bravery. We all know there is something providential in the assistance that you and Don Juan de Morfa have given us. I beg of you most humbly to forgive me for doubting you and your honor. I would be very pleased to have you share my table today."

"I would be honored to do so."

Over lunch, Don Juan Francisco expresses himself with great distinction and propriety. Len participates in the conversation quite naturally, and Doña Inés turns out to be an exquisite and charming woman. The principal judge observes Len and me with veiled sympathy as we converse. It's clear that he loves her dearly. The conversation ends when a servant comes to say he is needed at the Audiencia.

We go outside together, and before we separate, he tells me, "Don Pedro, I appreciate the attention you pay to my niece. Ever since you started visiting, she is much changed."

We say farewell and I head next door to Don Juan de Morfa's house. There, I am greeted warmly by my friend, who returned from the front the previous afternoon, and his wife. Doña Beatriz proudly shows me her son, a chubby baby with a dark complexion and eyes of an indefinite color who does nothing but sleep and breastfeed.

Shortly before nightfall, I cross the orchard again and walk to the wall. I let my gaze wander to that infinite sea stretching before me and wait. Before long, Len is at my side.

As if the turbulent years had vanished like smoke, there is once again that gentle complicity that united us in the past. She asks about my wounds. I tell her about the battle in great detail, the songs on the beach at night, and how, the next morning, the English ships disappeared over the horizon. The Battle of the Crabs, as she baptizes it, makes her laugh, and in order to hear her laugh again, I tell her the story again, exaggerating and acting it out. When I imitate the movements of the crabs' legs over the palm leaves, I grimace with pain. She grabs my hands and gently caresses the burns.

Then she lowers her head. I see her blonde hair shining in the last rays of sunlight. I move to embrace her, but she gently moves away, trembling slightly.

Nevertheless, she doesn't drop my hands, and she asks, "You won't leave me ever again?"

"Never. I'll always be by your side."

Holding hands, we sit there without talking for a while.

"Len . . ."

"Yes?"

"At the wharf in the cave, you told me that you loved me. Do you still?"

"More than ever. You're all I have, all I want. But even if that weren't so, even if nothing had happened, I would love you, and even if the world ended, I would keep on loving you. As a little girl, I loved you more than a sister; then I loved you as a woman loves a man. Now that you have returned from the dead, I know that I'll love you forever, even beyond this world."

It moves me to hear her speak this way. Perhaps I can't embrace her, but it's enough to have her near, to know that she loves me.

"Do you remember that I asked you to be the Lady of Oak Park? It no longer exists, so now I can only ask that you be the lady of my heart, that you marry me. Would you be my wife?"

She drops my hand and stands up. "You know I can't be your wife."

"Didn't you just say that you will love me forever?"

"I—Piers, I won't be able to give you what you will ask me for one day."

"That doesn't matter."

"Today I'm all right, but tomorrow, sadness could grip my heart again. There may be days when I won't be the happy companion you're looking for."

"And there may be days when I'll become angry and let regret consume me. But you're the only one who understands me, and when my temper gets the better of me, the only one who can calm me."

"Oh Piers! I can't."

"Yes, you can; you know you can. You told me yourself; without me you can't go on, and I can't live without you. I swear I won't ask you for the thing you deny me now. I'll be patient, and one day you may come to me."

She comes close again. We are standing, facing each other. Softly, she grasps the backs of my hands, puts them together, and kisses them. The moonlight envelops us. I lean my forehead against hers, and we stay that way, united, while night falls and the stars emerge against the blackness of the horizon.

Josefina arrives, telling us that it's late and that Don Juan Francisco is looking for Len. But now I know that our separation will be brief. We will be together; nothing will separate us ever again.

Before she goes inside, I tell her that, the next day, I will speak with her uncle, to ask for her hand in marriage. Len blushes.

65

A Request and Some Farewells

In the morning, I knock gently at Don Juan Francisco's door. Happiness, together with a certain uneasiness and impatience, fills my heart.

A dark-skinned servant with a broad smile opens the door; I ask to speak with the principal judge, but he has gone to the Audiencia, to the Casas Reales. I ask when he might be able to receive me.

"He generally receives visitors in the afternoon, first thing."

I don't want to see Len, not until everything is resolved with her uncle. So, I take a walk along the shore, looking at the sea and letting the warm breeze caress my face. I walk as far as the port, and there, I catch sight of her from a distance. I stare affectionately at her silhouette, as if reencountering a dear old friend: the *Indomitable* rocks on the water, all her dents repaired, her sails folded, and her hull gleaming with a new layer of paint. As I approach, Cosme de Azúa and Kerrigan greet me from on board, and, shouting, tell me they arrived the previous afternoon from Samaná.

I go aboard and find that Rodrigo de Alcalá, Montoro, and Richard are also there. I suspect that Domingo Rincón and other sailors won't surface until the victory celebrations are over. After chatting with everyone for a while and confirming that the deck is shining, I invite Richard for a glass of rum in my cabin.

Once we are alone, I ask him to stay with me, to work for the Spanish Crown. As he did once before, he tells me that he is an Englishman, a nobleman, and that he will never renounce his country. He has fought against Cromwell's army, and he considers the man a tyrant for attacking the Caribbean, but—he drains the glass of rum and then says something that really surprises me.

"Through some men in Admiral Penn's navy, I found out that the Royalists have some new endeavors under way."

"The Royalists, my dear friend, have shown themselves to be little more than a bunch of dandies," I say. "That Charles II won't rule the British Isles."

Richard frowns. He wants to return to the world we left behind. I argue that a true restoration of the monarchy is highly improbable and that returning to the old world, governed by the hereditary nobility, is totally impossible.

"You haven't heard me: the situation is changing rapidly," he insists. "Apparently, Cromwell is in poor health; he won't last forever. And when he dies, there's no one capable of taking charge of the government. His son, who has been named his successor, has no backbone. I'm telling you, a restoration isn't impossible, not at all!"

"I'll never return to England," I tell him. "What for? Everyone is dead. It would be too painful."

He shakes his head. "Well, I haven't lost hope. And I won't fight with the Spaniards anymore. You heard Montoro that day. They make fun of us!"

"It was a joke! You're so stubborn!"

He takes a sip from his glass, which he has refilled, and looks at me intently. "Piers, today I'm leaving for the island of San Cristóbal. I've arranged for Beltrán to meet me there in the patache, provided he can run away from the navy."

"Why didn't you tell me sooner? Richard, do you really trust that character?"

"Beltrán's not a bad sort, just a little annoying. And he's taken a liking to me. I don't know why he hates you."

I don't, either, but I know that I deeply dislike my former pilot, Juan de Beltrán.

"So far, he has always been loyal to me," Richard goes on. "I'm confident that he's waiting for me there. I've found a boat that can take me, and I'm eager to rejoin my crew."

I propose that he join us with his patache.

"Piers," he laughs. "You know my men; they had the chance to sail on the *Indomitable* with you, and they weren't interested in an honorable life in the service of the Spanish Crown. I sincerely doubt they've changed their minds; they're already bored enough after spending months with Admiral Penn. To tell you the truth, I don't understand what keeps you on this sweaty island."

For the first time, I tell him about Len, that I have found her, that this very afternoon I am going to ask for her hand. He listens without interruptions, taking sips from his glass, not acting surprised or offering me useless advice. At noon, we go down to eat at a tavern in the port, and then I accompany him to the end of the pier, where the small ship that will take him to San Cristóbal is anchored. With his immutable equanimity, Richard bids me farewell as if we might meet again soon. But I fear it is the last time I will see my friend and that my next-to-last link to England and my past is breaking forever. I watch him board the ship, wave his hand, and then sit down. He doesn't turn around even once.

I note the position of the sun and decide it's time to go to Montemayor's house. I breathe deeply, feeling both nervous and excited. As I cross the plaza, someone calls to me. I turn and see some of the locals who fought in my battalion. They are about to go home and wish to say good-bye.

"Don Pedro," one of them tells me, "I hope these damned Englishmen never return, but if they do and we have to defend ourselves again, I'd like to fight with you. And not just me, I think that's true of all of us."

The others nod and smile.

I can't find the words to say how moved I am by the trust of these generous, strong people. We slap each other on the back, and they leave.

I again knock loudly at the door of Len's uncle's house. They show me in to his office. It takes a few minutes for him to arrive, but each minute feels like hours.

When the judge comes in, he wears his customary frown, but his gaze is friendly. I explain the reason for my visit, and he listens silently. I am overwhelmed with worry that he might suspect I'm not what I seem to be and that's why he is observing me so circumspectly.

"What can you offer my niece?" he asks at last.

"You know that I have a license from Don Gabriel de Rojas himself allowing me to act as a privateer in wartime and as a coast guard for the Spanish Crown in times of peace. In Tortuga, I received my share of the spoils that you so graciously ordered distributed among the troops. With that, I can provide for her until I begin my work."

Don Juan Francisco looks at me for several long moments. "I must tell you that I have never been in favor of allowing privateers in the Spanish Crown," he says softly.

I sit paralyzed, gripped with anguish. But before I can speak, he goes on, "But I'm the only one, I'm afraid. Don Bernardino himself defends it. And when I look at you, Don Pedro, I see an honorable man and not the privateers I've known up to now."

"I swear to you that I will always take care of her! I know I can make her happy. At another time, I could have offered her everything; I am a good man."

Montemayor interrupts me, repeating, "A good man."

"I assure you," I exclaim emphatically, "I am a gentleman. I give you my word."

He fixes his eyes on me again with a strange gleam. "Yes. You say you are a gentleman." He sits quietly for a moment. "I can't answer you without speaking first with my niece."

"But what do you mean?"

"Come back tomorrow."

He hasn't denied my request, but he also hasn't accepted it. I leave feeling anxious and weighed down by what might happen.

66

DON JUAN FRANCISCO DE MONTEMAYOR'S REVELATION

I finally get up at dawn. I've spent the whole night tossing and turning in bed, the shameful memories of piracy filling my mind. Has Montemayor found out about my past? Will he arrest me and take me to prison? He didn't even ask me for my real name to corroborate what I was telling him. And what would I have done, if he had asked? Why was it so important for him to speak with Len?

I tiptoe downstairs and out onto the back patio. Through an open window I can hear the wails of an infant and then Doña Beatriz's voice, trying to calm her son. His bawling stops; perhaps she is feeding him. Then I hear Don Juan de Morfa calling to his wife; I hear them laughing. I walk away from this intimate moment, the life of a decent family, like what Len and I had in our childhood and might someday recuperate. But do I deserve it? I killed and robbed; I broke all the promises I made to my father. Sooner or later, the principal judge, all the judges, will find out about my past. I feel like running away. And yet, I can't imagine life without Len.

Lost in thought, I've reached the wall. Warm, cleansing rain begins to fall. I no longer feel rage, just remorse. The rain stops as suddenly as it began; the clouds part, and sunlight shines on this brilliant blue Caribbean Sea, so distant and so different from that other, silvery sea that bathed the coast of Essex. I tell myself we're in a new world, totally different from the one we have left behind. I can't imagine any other future than Len, an honorable life next to her, and I'm going to fight for it.

I hear footsteps behind me. Len has come looking for me.

"My uncle told me. Piers, I'm not worthy of you."

"How can you say that?"

She steps away and leans on the wall. She is trembling, afraid to tell me something. Then, with a strand of her hair fluttering in the soft breeze, she tells me every detail of her conversation with Don Juan Francisco.

Apparently, right after I left, her uncle had called for her. He was waiting for her at a large oak desk, a terribly serious look on his face. He set down his pen.

"Have a seat, Catalina. I need to tell you something that has been weighing on my conscience. I have endeavored to always conduct myself in an irreproachable manner, but when you came to this island, sick with melancholy, I couldn't bring myself to tell you something that you have a right to know. But now, thanks to that foreign sailor, you have recovered the will to live."

"Yes," she had whispered. "Thanks to Don Pedro Leal."

"Good. Don Pedro just came to ask for your hand. I see you are blushing; did you know he was planning to? You don't need to answer or feel guilty for not telling me. But since he wants to marry you, it's my obligation to reveal certain aspects of your past. Then you can decide, once you know the facts."

Len's uncle had fallen silent; he fixed his eyes on the table and drummed the fingers of one hand. Then he looked up and said, "Remember when I told the story of your mother and my brother the governor, hoping you would overhear? Almost everything I said was true, but—there were things I left out. My brother, Don Pedro de Montemayor, didn't ask to be posted to the Indies in hopes of getting rich and winning over your mother. He did it because Doña Isabel broke his heart. She told him she couldn't marry him, because she loved another man.

"Two years later, when my brother found out they had granted him a posting here, in Santo Domingo, he decided to say farewell to her. Deep down, he still harbored the hope that Doña Isabel may have changed her mind. But when he reached the Oquendos' home and asked to see the daughter of Admiral Don Antonio, the servant threw him out, saying she didn't live there anymore.

"He asked around in the village, but they refused to answer him. Finally, someone told him where to find her: in the Oquendos' ancient country house on the side of Mount Ulia. There, he was able to see her. She was holding a baby girl in her arms, just a few months old. You, Catalina."

"Me? But what are you trying to tell me?"

"That you aren't my brother's daughter."

Len had just stared at him, baffled.

He continued. "Doña Isabel de Oquendo was a strong-willed woman, too much so, I would say, and she was not ashamed. She admitted that the child was hers and that her aunt had thrown her out while the admiral was away. She claimed—though she couldn't prove it—that she had secretly gotten married to the man she loved, a young, penniless ship captain. Your father, Catalina."

"My father . . ."

"He apparently died before you were born."

"But my mother always told me—"

"Your mother always told you the story she and my brother decided on. Pedro believed her and asked her to marry him. He told her he would consider you his own daughter, that he would give you his name. And this time, she accepted. They got married in town, and he left, promising to send her the money for both of their tickets as soon as he could raise it. It took a while, but he did it. My brother was a man of his word."

Don Juan Francisco had fallen silent another instant, while Len, stunned, was trying to absorb it all.

"Because of what I promised my brother on his deathbed, and because of the affection I've come to feel, I've treated you as if you were my legitimate niece, as if there were no stain on your past. Nevertheless, due to my faith and to my honor, I can't allow you to deceive anyone. Don Pedro Leal thinks you are someone you're not."

Finally, Len had dared to ask, "Do you know the name of my true father?"

"No. My brother didn't know it; your mother didn't reveal it to him."

"I'll never know who he was."

"No. But Catalina, you must tell Don Pedro Leal. He doesn't need to swear it to me; I recognize a gentleman when I see him, and if he hides his true name from us, I'm convinced that he has his reasons. But I beg you, he needs to know the truth about you; a marriage can't be founded on a lie."

Len's voice dies out. She is confused and depressed about finding out that she is as much of a stranger in the judge's house as I. It grieves me to see her like that; I'm afraid she might withdraw into herself again.

Then she tells me, "Piers, I can't marry you. I'm not a lady. I'm not the daughter of a gentleman, as I always believed. I don't know who I am. I'm not worthy of you."

"The devil—" I'm about to curse, but I control myself.

I take a deep breath and tell her that nothing Don Juan Francisco has revealed matters to me.

"Dear Len, I'm the one unworthy of you, not the other way around. I care nothing about that father—I, who am a ship captain myself. Nothing matters to me except having you."

"You'll never be able to have me entirely. I'm incapable of loving, and perhaps someday you'll throw it in my face that I am not a lady, just a—" She breaks into a horrified sob.

I'm lost, unsure how to help her forgive herself for things that aren't her fault at all. Then I remember my father and mother, who raised her as a lady because they considered her to be one, and Uncle Andrew, who didn't hesitate to take her to Oak Park.

"Len! You may not know who your father was, but you do know who you are. Do you remember what Uncle Andrew told us? You're the great-granddaughter of Don Miguel de Oquendo, a heroic sailor, a friend of my own family. You yourself explained to me that old Matt had spoken to you about him. And above all, you are the only woman I will ever love. I'm asking you again: marry me."

She nods and bursts into tears. I embrace her tenderly, caressing her beautiful hair, and we stay that way for a long time while the splendid morning sun makes the waters of the river and sea sparkle.

67

THE COAST GUARD

Santo Domingo, June 1655

After I overcame Len's objections, we talked to her uncle—since we continued to see him as that—and set a date for the wedding. From that moment on, the principal judge's house became a hive of activity. Doña Inés and Doña Beatriz and her sisters wore Len out with their conversations about clothing, flowers, and dishes for the celebration, which would take place in a few short weeks. Len would look at me, both amused at their attention and begging me to free her. But those industrious women pushed me aside. I was merely the groom, necessary for the ceremony but marginal to the preparations.

I took refuge in the house next door, where Don Juan de Morfa was putting up with a similar fuss since his annoying mother-in-law invaded constantly to see baby Gabriel and dictate how they must care for him. In both houses, the women overcame us. The pandemonium reminded me of when Elizabeth and my sisters planned the ball at Oak Park, but the memory was a painful one, as their deaths still torment me.

Fortunately, not long afterward, the governor, concerned about the security of the island, ordered Morfa and me to sea as coast guards in the service of the Spanish Crown. I set out with relief on the *Indomitable*.

I now have new sailors among the crew since some of those who sailed with me have sought new lives. That was the case with Hernando de Montoro. The Audiencia pardoned his sentence for smuggling in reward for his invaluable assistance during the English attack. He has returned to his family. During these days of smooth sailing, when Morfa and I are near Samaná, we drop anchor and go visit him. I enjoy seeing him surrounded by his patient wife, who waited for him for so long, and his children and grandchildren. The pirate's life we once shared now seems like a fading nightmare to us both, though I suspect that he still dabbles in business dealings with dubious characters.

After the most recent of these visits, we are heading back to the high seas. The watch's shout, "Ship ahoy!" brings me running out to the bow. Morfa and I both steer our ships close since it isn't a smuggling vessel or an enemy English ship, but a small brig without a mast that's on the verge of capsizing. They are refugees, people who fled Jamaica following the British conquest of the island, so we begin the work of transferring the crew and passengers to our ships.

Hours later, the deck of the *Indomitable* is crowded with ragged children, women nursing babies, peasants, mulattos, Taíno Indians, and black slaves. The captain of the brig explains to Don Juan, who has come over from his ship, and me that the formidable English squadron had appeared one day, surrounding Morant Point. The English cannons commenced battering the forts, and as soon as the troops landed, the Jamaicans had to abandon their garrisons, overwhelmed by the numerical superiority of the attackers. The next day, the capital fell, and General Venables decreed that the people must leave their island within ten days, under penalty of death and confiscation of all property.

The captain adds that a plantation owner, Francisco de Proenza, had rebelled and plans to put up resistance in the mountains and forests of the island, and he begs us to bring him before the governor of Santo Domingo. We do so as soon as we arrive in Hispaniola.

In the Alcázar de Colón, Bernardino de Meneses receives the three of us. Also present is Don Juan Francisco de Montemayor, who is no longer the principal judge because he has received a new posting in Mexico City.

Although Len's uncle argues in favor of defending the Spaniards rebelling on Jamaica, Don Bernardino doesn't want to tarnish the glory of his brilliant triumph in Santo Domingo with a doomed campaign in Jamaica. Morfa and I exchange looks, our skepticism of this dandy renewed. Montemayor doesn't criticize the governor openly, but his disagreement is likewise clear. Finally, the governor agrees to send Morfa and me, with the captain of the sunken brig and some of his sailors, to the neighboring island to gather information and take a few supplies. Once we are there, there is little we can do aside from delivering the gunpowder and munitions, which are insufficient to wage a long campaign.

Back in Hispaniola, to the southwest of the island, we board a ship loaded with mahogany that doesn't have its documents in order. We impound it and take it to the capital, where its cargo is confiscated. Since mahogany is a semiprecious wood of great value, my crew celebrates, thinking about the share of the booty they will receive when it is divided up. I do, too; that will allow me to keep my promise to Montemayor to support Len with dignity.

I have spent several weeks away from her, and I hurry to Calle de las Damas. When she hears my voice on the patio, Len looks over the second-floor balcony and greets me cheerfully, then comes down the staircase with her eyes shining. I whisper that, tonight, we will meet in the usual place. Then I greet her uncle, who has been notified of my arrival and is walking toward us. He wants me to explain to him what happened in Jamaica; I do so in his office, with the two of us alone. I end up telling him about the seized ship as well. He shakes his head thoughtfully.

"Did you say mahogany, Don Pedro?"

"Yes."

"You're going to have a hard time recovering your reward."

"Why?"

"Because it's possible, though I'm afraid I can't prove it, that it's one of Pimentel's contraband ships. They say he controls the mahogany business on the island. He'll surely pull strings to recuperate his cargo without his name getting out. It pains me to say so, but he will have the help of some of the new judges Don Bernardino brought with him. I suspect he has bought them off."

"The judges? But there are laws arbitrating all this!"

"The laws of the Spanish Empire depend more on the honor of the judges than anything else. Anything can be distorted. Years ago, a judge had to be a model citizen, someone whose decisions were guided only by truth and justice. The profession came to be seen as a sort of priesthood; they even advised us not to marry, but it's not that way anymore. Because of the expensive wars that plague the empire, public offices are now bought and sold to the highest bidder."

Sitting up straight in his armchair before the table covered with papers, with a deep crease in his forehead, he laments, "I'm a scholar, a legal academic who loves his profession. But increasingly, it is being debased by greed. Don Pedro, it will be corruption, not enemy ships, that will take down this kingdom!"

I don't know what to say in the face of this stalwart man's pain. Don Juan Francisco lets out a sad sigh and changes the subject.

"You have made Doña Catalina very happy, and I am deeply in your debt. I'm relieved that you aren't concerned about the obscurity of her origins. You are a man of honor."

It makes me ashamed to hear him speak like that; it pains me to hide my past from such an honest man. I fear that someday it may all come to light.

"I'll do everything in my power to look after your niece as she deserves."

"I trust you will. And I imagine you're eager to talk to her! Go, go, and I beg you to stay for supper afterward."

Don Juan Francisco calls Vicente Garcés, who leads me to the second floor, where Len is seated at a certain distance with Josefina. She shows me the trousseau that she has embroidered with our initials over the past few weeks. It pleases me to see her like this, happy, chatting about fabrics and clothing.

Over the days that follow, I try to arrange for payment for the cargo. But, as Don Juan Francisco warned me, my words fall on deaf ears. Every time I see Pimentel, he looks at me with a sardonic glint in his eye. My only consolation is spending time with Len. I see her frequently during the day, with Josefina. But many nights, we meet alone next to the wall overlooking the Ozama.

We are the happiest we've been since our shared childhood, though not knowing who her father was has only increased her sense of impurity. Once, when I tried to steal a kiss, she burst into tears, saying we shouldn't get married because she can't give me what I want. I assure her I will wait for as long as necessary, that I am far less worthy than she. I love her just as she is. In a way, I also feel unworthy of her love.

On the day of our wedding, longed for all these many dark years, as I see her walking down the aisle, I feel the presence of my family, my parents, Thomas, and my sisters. In the face of the priest who is marrying us, I think I recognize Uncle Andrew.

The Cathedral of Santa María la Menor is filled to the brim with the curious since the principal judge's niece is marrying a foreign sailor. But there are also the friends who truly wish to share our happiness:

Don Juan de Morfa and his lovely wife, Doña Beatriz; Doña Inés; Doña Berta and Doña Amalia; Captains Álvaro de Aguilar and Damián del Castillo; Hernando de Montoro and his family, the physician Rodrigo de Alcalá; the pilot Zudaire; the rest of the crew of the *Indomitable*; some of the men who fought alongside me in Nizao and in La Haina; Josefina; and, of course, the imperious Doña Luisa Dávila.

68

THE ROYAL ORDER

Santo Domingo, August 1656

A gentle but constant wind allows us to approach the north coast of Hispaniola, palm trees swaying on the beaches. Next to me, Rodrigo de Alcalá enjoys the view in silence. When we round a cape, the watch gives out a cry of alert. We are in front of a cove where a moderately sized brig is anchored. The physician and I exchange glances.

"The devil be damned!" he exclaims. "Smugglers!"

When they make out the *Indomitable* bearing the standard of the Spanish Crown, the men on the brig try to flee, but it's too late. They surrender without a fight, and I board it with some of my men. In the holds, we find a large quantity of silk, porcelain, and spices. The captain, a man with blue eyes and thinning gray hair, is an Englishman, as are some of the crew. I speak to him in Spanish, and he indicates he doesn't understand. Then, I hear him speaking to his second mate; he is devastated by the loss of the cargo.

"We're going to have problems with the fat man," he concludes.

They go on talking in low voices about that "damned alderman" in Santo Domingo, who has convinced them to make this trip, and I realize that it can be no other than Pimentel. Later, I mention it to Alcalá.

We all know that the smugglers have a collaborator in the capital, but it's the first time I've heard them refer directly to an alderman.

We return to Santo Domingo with the brig and its precious cargo. My crew is content once more, already thinking about their shares. The coast guard seems to be an excellent business, letting us do the work we did as pirates, but now under the protection of a flag, entirely legitimate.

As we approach the mouth of the Ozama, I smile to see my home. A year has gone by since Len and I became man and wife. Although I spend a lot of time at sea, I now have a place where someone is waiting for me, where I'm always eager to return.

After the wedding, I moved into the house of Len's uncle. Our rooms are a little drawing room and a bedroom on the second floor. They look out over the river, and every evening, they are flooded with soft, warm light. We share meals with Don Juan Francisco. The rest of the time, he takes refuge in his office, writing and organizing papers. His grim face always softens when he sees us together. A new life has opened up for us and also for him. When he finishes the judicial review that will conclude his mandate in Santo Domingo, the *juicio de residencia*, or Trial of Residence, he will leave for his new posting. For the moment, we are all enjoying the present.

Once we have turned over our catch to the port authorities, I hurry up hill, eager to see Len. We are gloriously happy together, but the imposed abstinence does sometimes weigh on me. At night, I hear her soft breathing as she sleeps beside me, and my fingers ache to caress her. Courting her as patiently as she needs has become a game and a challenge, which renders her even more alluring.

I stride through the door and head for the courtyard, where I see Len chatting happily with Doña Beatriz and Doña Inés. They are sewing together and sharing a gourd of hot chocolate. Josefina sits nearby. I stop before they can see me, and I listen in.

"There are many men who would like to court you," Doña Beatriz is saying.

At first, Doña Inés, to whom she is speaking, doesn't respond. Then she says in a low but clear voice, "I'll never marry again."

"Do you mean you'll return to the convent?" Doña Beatriz asks, surprised.

"No. That isn't my life, either. Don Gabriel gave me my freedom, and I will not give that up."

"They'll criticize you! In fact, they already do."

"I know."

Doña Inés has recuperated the manor house that belonged to her family, and she devotes her life to works of charity. Her beauty, her fortune, and the legend surrounding her all make her highly desirable, but she pays no attention to her suitors.

At that moment, Len spies me; she drops her sewing and stands up. Kissing me softly on the cheek, she excuses herself with a gesture from her friends and leads me by the arm into the house.

"My uncle asked to speak with you as soon as you got here, Piers," she whispers, coming close to me. I try to kiss her, but she slips away, laughing.

"Don't be silly! This isn't the time!"

"It's never the time!" I complain without thinking.

When I see the sadness clouding her eyes, I regret having been so brusque.

Len swallows and keeps on walking. "I think it's something important. You'll find him in his office. Meanwhile, I'll have them prepare supper and say good-bye to Doña Beatriz and Doña Inés."

I knock firmly on the thick wooden door.

"Come in!"

As I go inside, Don Juan Francisco stands, walks around the large oak table, and comes up and warmly rests a hand on my shoulder. "Don Pedro, I regret having to share some bad news with you."

He looks even more serious than usual. I freeze, wondering if he has found out about my life as a pirate, if I've made some mistake.

"What is it?"

"While you were away, our new governor, Don Félix de Zúñiga, received a royal order dated shortly before Cromwell's navy attacked Santo Domingo; I don't know why it took so long to arrive. In any case, what it says is very important to you. The employment of privateers and, of course, foreign coast guards is now categorically forbidden."

"That can't be! What about the license Don Gabriel de Rojas gave me?"

"Just a scrap of paper. I can't tell you how sorry I am. You'll have to change professions."

"And Don Juan de Morfa?"

"It doesn't affect him. He is part of the Windward Fleet."

"Couldn't I—?"

"No. Don Juan has been recognized by the Council of the Indies. They wouldn't recognize you as part of the army of the Spanish Crown for several more years."

"But my sloop? My crew?"

"You can sail as a merchant marine, but if you attack anyone, even a smuggler, you will be accused of piracy. I must insist that, for the time being, you don't sail. You and I have enemies in the city who would like to discredit us both. I beg you not to provoke them."

"Just yesterday, we caught a brig smuggling in one of the coves up north. In fact . . ."

I recount the conversation between the smugglers, and he listens closely.

"Be careful," he warns me. "Without proof, you mustn't accuse him. Pimentel is a bad enemy to have. Don't worry, Don Pedro. You can sail as a merchant marine; it will take a while to arrange it, but it is a solution, unless you want to work on land. By now, you have earned enough to establish yourself somewhere on the island."

I leave the office downhearted and walk out to the wall. The sun is setting, and in the distance, I see a galleon with its sails partially folded. I absentmindedly calculate the size of its crew, how many pounds it weighs, and where it might be coming from.

I sigh. Sailing was my first passion, and even now, I love it as much as I love Len. Yes, I could be a merchant marine. My family did that for generations. But the crew of the *Indomitable* may not want to sail with me. They aren't commercial sailors; they're men of combat and action. And so am I.

That night I wake up to Len saying my name in a frightened voice. She tells me I have been thrashing in my sleep.

"Piers, what's wrong?"

"Oh Lord," I groan. "I can't bear the thought of a landlocked life. I need the open sea, calculating the shot, firing the ship's cannons, combat . . ."

I curl up into a ball, and Len begins tenderly stroking my hair. She kisses my neck sweetly, and her soft hand moves down my back, comforting me. I look up; she has never done this before, caressed me in this way, and she goes on more and more intensely, going further and further. I'm burning with desire, but I wait. This must come from her. I let her continue, and suddenly she is covering me with her kisses. For a while, I forget about everything. All I want is for this to continue, being loved by her. Then I kiss her, and she doesn't turn me away. I gradually make my way to the forbidden place, and she lets me. I continue slowly, and when I see her become tense, I pause, gaze into her eyes, whisper words of love in her ear. Then she turns to me, with gestures and caresses; she goes forward and encourages me to follow. We reach the zenith of love, each at our own rhythm, each in our own way, without insisting, forcing, rushing anything. I would like to abandon myself, but I manage to control my instincts and proceed with exquisite tenderness. Despite the passion, my mind is clear because I know our happiness is at stake, and I want Len to recover.

Dawn finds us awake, holding each other after a night when we have finally become husband and wife. That night will not be the only one. Len loves me, and what began as a way of consoling me ends up beginning to heal the trauma inflicted years ago in the Norman Tower. We are united as never before; we are truly lovers.

69

THE ACCUSATION

Over the following days, I try to convince Don Juan Francisco to appeal to the Council of the Indies to accept me into the Windward Fleet. He barely has time to see, though. I realize how immersed he is in his *juicio de residencia*, which is dragging out. I decide to appeal to Don Juan de Morfa.

At the house next door, Doña Beatriz greets me; she is expecting their second child. She shows me to a room where her husband is poring over maps and nautical charts.

I explain my situation and ask him to intercede on my behalf. He listens kindly but shakes his head; it's not within his power. When I complain that Montemayor isn't helping me, he explains that the *juicio de residencia* has become complicated. It is a mechanism of control, making officials account for everything that happened under their mandate before letting them transfer to a new post.

"That should be no trouble! Don Juan Francisco is the most honest man here."

"Yes, but he has enemies, and they have been speaking to the visiting judge, who is in charge of the inspection and gathering all possible information. He is also requesting reports from the different colonial institutions and reviewing the books of the local Royal Treasury and the city treasury."

"But that's been going on all this time! How much longer can it take?"

"As long as they deem necessary. Montemayor has complained to the Council of the Indies, and Governor de Zúñiga supports him. But neither of them can elude this process. You see, Don Pedro, the *juicio de residencia* is a way of assuring that civil servants of the Crown behave appropriately. They're looking into each of his actions in detail, seeing that nothing stains his record. There's nothing he can do for you now."

Weeks go by, and this eats away at me. Finally, the visiting judge completes his inspection, and they deliver the charges to Don Juan Francisco.

At his hearing, Don Juan Francisco argues that his fortune is the same as before he began, that he has never committed a dishonest act, and that he has never allowed himself to be guided by favoritism. He describes the Tortuga campaign in heroic terms and describes how he acted in the island's defense.

The other judges then read a deposition in which they say that he was a good governor and a clean and fair official. They also point out a few small defects, like his sullen character. Len and I, who are in the room along with many others, exchange a smile. The sentence has been favorable, but now begins the public portion, where anyone can speak in his favor or against him.

No one imagines that the upright Don Juan Francisco de Montemayor y Córdoba de Cuenca might have the least problem, but suddenly, a respected friar stands up. He asks them to investigate the former principal judge regarding a misappropriation of funds from the booty obtained after Tortuga was taken.

Len and I keep her uncle company during the resulting investigation over the next days. Morfa mentions that, for months, Don Rodrigo Pimentel has been rumored to be circulating an exaggerated list of what was captured on Tortuga, spilling his venom into insecure minds. Don Juan Francisco, however, is able to present all the documents and demonstrate that a proper inventory was made and every *maravedí*, or coin, distributed according to the law.

It seems that the last stumbling block has been overcome, that the *juicio de residencia* has concluded, when a voice is heard.

Don Rodrigo Pimentel himself stands up and calls the judges' attention. He, the alderman of Santo Domingo, also has an accusation to make against the former principal judge: that he protects pirates. They ask him for proof, and he responds that he will present it the next day.

An expectant murmur runs through the courthouse of the Audiencia.

70

THE PIRATE

Santo Domingo, November 1656

Len and I return home while her uncle stays at the Audiencia. He didn't seem concerned; Pimentel's accusation struck him as ridiculous. Len observes my alarm, but doesn't say anything until we are safely away from the Casas Reales.

"Do you think Don Rodrigo might know something?"

"How could he? Here in Santo Domingo, the only ones who know about my past are Don Juan de Morfa and the crew of the *Indomitable*. None of them would betray me. Len, should I tell your uncle?"

"No!" She stops in the middle of the street. "Piers—there's something I should tell you."

I look her in the eye. "That you despise me for having been a murderous pirate?"

"Don't say that! It's something else. I wanted to wait until I was sure, but maybe you need to know it now."

I stare at her blankly.

"I think I'm expecting a baby, our baby."

Her face radiates happiness. I don't react at first to the news, which disconcerts me. My mind is still on the grave accusation against Montemayor, which might involve me.

Unaware of my distraction, she goes on. "We'll have a son who will continue the line of Lord Leigh, of Lady Leigh, of my mother. He will look a little like each of us."

This new responsibility frightens me. Still, seeing her so happy, I smile and joke, "And if it's a girl, she might look like my sister Elizabeth."

"Yes, she was very beautiful," Len says. "But I think I'd prefer that she look like Ann or Margaret."

"Yes, me, too."

Len grips my arm firmly and looks at me with her eyes shining. "Piers, if the worst comes to pass, if you're found out, please, don't leave me."

"No, I won't."

We keep walking in silence, and when we reach the front door, I tell her, "Go on in. I'm going to notify the men from the *Indomitable*."

Since we haven't been able to sail, some of the sailors have scattered, but the core of my old crew is still in the city. We gather at a tavern in the port. I warn them that they are in danger if I am discovered, and I order them to take the ship and go to Montoro in Samaná. Rodrigo de Alcalá and Cosme de Azúa look at me, worried.

"Captain Leal," says the bonesetter, "come with us! If they find out, they'll hang you."

"I can't leave right now. And maybe nothing will happen!"

Before going home, I stop to see Morfa. He also advises me to leave, until the accusation in court has been clarified. "Go to Samaná with your crew."

"No, I can't leave my wife now or Don Juan Francisco. Whatever happens tomorrow, I will accept it. Maybe it's time for me to pay."

"To pay for what?"

"My crimes."

"What crimes? A war in which you fought, like any other soldier? In which you saved people's lives, including mine?"

"Piracy."

"Rojas told me you were forced to become a pirate."

"Yes, but then I kept at it—and I enjoyed it."

"My friend, life in these latitudes is complex."

But I've made my decision. I won't abandon Len and the child she is expecting, and above all, I won't act dishonorably, not even one more time. What's more, I can't leave Don Juan Francisco alone if the truth comes to light. Perhaps the time has come to atone for all I did. When I finally manage to fall asleep that night, my dreams are filled with terrible images.

The next morning, around noon, the doors of the Audiencia open. Shortly afterward, the witness Don Rodrigo will introduce is called to testify.

Into the room walks a tall man with dark eyes and greasy gray hair. I recognize him immediately.

"Your name?"

"Juan de Beltrán."

"Profession?"

"Ship's pilot, trained in the University of Seafarers of Seville."

"Do you know this man?" The judge who is presiding points to Montemayor.

"No."

"Then?"

Beltrán turns to the audience and points at me, sitting in the first row.

"I know that other fellow."

"From where?"

"I served under his command."

"On what ship?"

"On the sloop the *Indomitable*."

"Under what flag?"

"The pirate flag."

"What is his name?"

"His real name is Piers Leigh, and for a while, he was known on these seas as the Englishman."

The room fills with whispers, and Len squeezes my arm. I hold her hand, trying to calm her.

"Are you saying, and let me remind you that you are testifying before God our Lord, that this man claiming to be Pedro Leal, married to the niece of the judge under examination, Don Juan Francisco de Montemayor y Córdoba de Cuenca, was a pirate?"

"Yes."

"Did Don Juan Francisco know?"

"I couldn't say."

"What we're hearing is very serious." Don Rodrigo Pimentel's haughty voice resounds throughout the courtroom. "The honorable Don Juan Francisco de Montemayor has shared his home with a pirate, without denouncing him."

"Don Pedro," Len's uncle says in his own defense, "was vouched for by Captain Gabriel de Rojas, in whose honesty everyone present trusts, and since he has been on the island, he has behaved honorably and in defense of our interests."

"Yes, but can you deny he was a pirate?" Pimentel responds sarcastically. "Because that's what we are discussing here."

"I know nothing about that." Montemayor looks at me, shocked and wounded.

I can't look at him. I take a deep breath and stand up. "Don Juan Francisco de Montemayor knows nothing about my past, whatever it might have been. When I met him, I was already serving the Spanish Crown."

The presiding judge stands up. "What we have heard is sufficient. There is a grave suspicion that this man, the so-called Don Pedro Leal, is really a pirate known as the Englishman. An investigation will be opened, and if he is found guilty, he will be sentenced to death. Bailiffs, arrest him."

I hear Len moan beside me. The guards stride over to take me into custody. Len clings to my arm, not wanting to let me go. I have to remove her hands gently, and embracing her, I whisper, "Don't you worry. Take care of yourself and of our child."

I leave the courthouse a prisoner followed by the murmurs of stupefaction and disapproval of everyone present.

71

THE JAIL

I return to the same jail where they held me after I landed with the British. I spend all night thinking about Len and about my child, who probably won't ever meet me. I think about generous and good Montemayor, whom I have compromised terribly. I think about my men, worried that they, too, might be taken to the gallows. But in an odd way, I feel liberated, freed from the burden of hiding.

In the morning, the cell door opens, and Len comes in. Behind her I see loyal Josefina, looking distraught.

We embrace. Len sobs on my shoulder.

"What will happen now?" she asks me in a voice choked with worry.

"They'll have to prove what Juan de Beltrán has said. None of my men will betray me, I know, but there are others, like the pilot, who know about my past. If they can find them . . ."

"You can . . . you can explain to the judges what you told me, how they forced you to become a pirate. They'll understand!"

I smile, though I know they wouldn't. She steps away and touches her hand to her neck, as if she has had a revelation.

"My mother's medallion," she mumbles. She takes it off, kisses it, and hangs it around my neck. "When you were far away on the open sea, it protected you. Now that you're a prisoner, it will protect you again."

Len moves me, as she always has. I take her by the shoulders and softly whisper in her ear, "Don't worry, my love."

A guard comes in and makes her leave. I hear her sobbing as she walks down the stone stairway to sun and liberty. My heart breaks.

From that moment on, I'm allowed no more visitors. If they didn't give me bowls of food, I would scarcely know whether it was day or night. Time goes by slowly in that cold, dark prison cell.

Finally, they transfer me to a larger cell with some other prisoners. Not only am I locked up, but now I have to live with delinquents and rascals, some of whom have lost their minds. We are like animals, eyeing each other with distrust, and I retreat inside myself.

One day a potbellied, sweaty man, noticing I haven't touched my rations, pounces on me; grabs my shirt and tears it; slugs me, knocking me to the ground; and takes the bowl. Another prisoner, taking pity, comes over with a grimy piece of cloth and tries to staunch the blood gushing from my nose.

I thank the old man for his gesture. He sits down next to me and points at the tin medallion, which is now exposed.

"Was somebody in your family also on the expedition against England?" he asks me with a toothless grin.

"I don't know what you're talking about."

From inside his shirt, he pulls out an identical medallion.

"They were given to everyone who sailed with the Great Armada," he says with pride. "My grandfather fought in the expedition against England. He gave the medallion to my father, and my father gave it to me."

I sit there thinking for a long while and then, for the first time since coming here, I smile to myself. Because in my mind, a distant memory has reappeared of the happy times at Oak Park, when Len and I had no cares.

I hope I'll have the chance to explain it to her before they take me away to the gallows. I'm astonished at how intertwined our paths have always been.

Epilogue

JOSEFINA

Mexico City, October 1658

When they put Don Pedro Leal in prison, my señorita Catalina, who had been cured of her melancholy, fell sick again, and, once again, stopped speaking.

Don Pedro was a very good man. She called him Piers, but I was the only one in the house who knew. No one thought it right that they were going to hang him because of Don Rodrigo's shady dealings. The soldiers and vaqueros who had fought alongside him came to protest to the judges. It wasn't fair for them to lock him up when he had done so much to save us from the invaders. There were many who spoke in his favor, but the alderman paid some to tell very bad stories about my lady's husband. A rumor ran through the city that he had killed and robbed.

So, as I was saying, my lady got sick from her nerves. I worried so much about her and about the child she was carrying. I thought if things went on that way, she might lose the baby. I had seen it happen to other women who got sad, and their little ones weren't born right.

Ay, señor! It was all Don Rodrigo's fault. What a despicable man! The worst part is that he's one of those people who thinks he's good because he prays a lot and gives to charity. They think that alms will send them to heaven, despite their evil lives. But I know the real reason he helped the poor was so the powerful priests and nuns would be on his side. Ay! I feel such sadness, thinking about all this! Because I don't think it's right, not at all, that those who serve the good Lord use him for their wicked ways. Because the good Lord saved my life. I would have died in Cartagena de Indias when I was bleeding to death after my daughter was born. But a priest, one who truly was a man of God, saved my life. I'll never forget him.

The holy man from Cartagena, the great port for trafficking in black people, called himself the slave of the Negros. He took care of us and came to our poor hovels to visit us, and when we were sick, he took us to the San Sebastián Hospital. That's what he did with me, when my daughter was born. It's because of her that I love my lady so. She is like the daughter I had but who is no longer with me. They're about the same age, and my child might have had the same light-colored hair because the man who made her had hair that color. Also, my lady was raped, which also happened to me, first on the slave ship, and then in Cartagena. That's why I love her so very much. Some white men say we don't have a heart or soul, but we do. I love my lady, and everything that happened to her felt like it happened to me.

What was I saying? Oh yes. It was only when the trial began, in the great courtroom at the Casas Reales, that my lady saw Don Pedro again. I liked that place because it was cool and bright, but not blinding.

Don Pedro came in. They pushed him, tied up, and made him climb onto the witness stand. He had always seemed to me a handsome man, but since he had been in jail so long, his skin had turned milk-white, and his eyes were sunken and had dark rings under them. Señorita Catalina told me Piers was an Englishman, which surprised me because his hair was dark, and I knew that Englishmen's hair is yellow. That man who abused me was English, and his hair was yellowish, nearly white. When I think about that, my past comes back and hurts me. Yes, a lot, it hurts a lot.

My memories of Cartagena return, one on top of the other, there in the New Kingdom of Granada, where the business with the yellow-haired Englishman happened. Even though lots of men forced me, he stayed with me and liked to beat me. At that time, I wasn't like you see now; I was slender. The Englishman would charge men a lot of money to be with me. But then he stopped charging because the demon of jealousy got into him, and he wouldn't let other men come near. He would get drunk and shout that I was a bitch, that I went with everyone. I don't have words for how bad it was. He was so crazy that he locked me up in a shack outside the city and put a horrible guard dog at the door. He was the one who abused me the most, and he got me pregnant. Yes, he made a little girl with me.

The blond slave trader really liked rum; he drank more and more and went mad. He used to see strange things, bugs everywhere. Sometimes he would foam at the mouth, as if he had a demon inside. He died like that, shouting strange noises and with spasms all over his body. I buried him myself because I thought they would accuse me of killing him, even though I didn't. He died from madness because he ran out of rum.

From working so hard to dig the grave, my birth pangs began, and I gave birth to a little girl, a beautiful child, but weak because she was born too soon. She wasn't black like me; her skin was white, like her father's, and her eyes weren't brown like mine, but gray. After the birth, I started bleeding and lost consciousness. My little girl was crying; someone heard her and notified the priest.

I spent the happiest months of my life there in the San Sebastián Hospital. I watched my beautiful daughter get chubbier every day and helped the priest look after the sick. I learned many things from him and from the other black people who helped him. But that happy time didn't last. My daughter's father had a lot of debts, and his creditors, who knew he had a beautiful black woman worth her weight in *maravedises*, or gold coins, came looking for me. The good priest couldn't stop the slave traders, and they took me with them, me and my little girl. I was so upset that I had no milk. I've known such suffering in this life, but when my daughter died, something broke in my heart.

Years later, they auctioned me off at the market in Cartagena, and a man bought me and took me to Hispaniola, where he finally gave me to Doña Luisa. When I remember everything I went through in Cartagena, my mind wanders. Yes, at times I get distracted and the past returns to me. What was I saying? Oh yes, I was terribly worried about my lady, my Catalina, when they put her Piers on trial.

On the witness stand, Don Pedro looked at Señorita Catalina with great devotion, the way the devout look at the Virgin in the cathedral. She couldn't stop looking at him, either. And I couldn't take my eyes off the two of them. My lady was so sad, and he, such a gentleman, was trying to hide his suffering from her. The trial lasted several days, and my Catalina withdrew further and further inside herself, sinking into a well that she couldn't climb out of.

But the day before they were going to pass sentence, she went into Don Juan Francisco's office and started to talk again, like a madwoman. Her words are etched into my head. She told him that she was alive thanks to Don Pedro's family, that he was a good man, that he was her husband, that she couldn't live without him. Don Juan Francisco, angry, responded that Don Pedro had deceived him and passed himself off as a man of honor. She said that circumstances had forced Don Pedro to become a pirate, but that now he was a gentleman again. Her uncle didn't give in, and my lady began to cry and say she was going to throw herself into the river if they hanged her husband. Don Juan Francisco tried to console her. He might seem very harsh, but I know he is a man with a good heart. She begged him, again and again, to do whatever he could to free Don Pedro, and he told her, again and again, that it was out of his hands. Finally, he promised her he would try. That seemed to calm her somewhat, but that night she didn't sleep a wink; I know because I slept at the foot of her bed. Her uncle didn't sleep, either; the lamp in his office burned into the early hours of the morning.

So, the next day, the three of us went to the Casas Reales again to hear the sentence. During the previous days, that fellow Don Juan de Beltrán had spoken; I couldn't look at him without my insides churning. But another witness appeared, too. A man who said his ship had been captured by pirates, and he recognized Don Pedro as their captain, but he said Don Pedro had treated them with great humanity and had set them free to return, safe and sound, to Hispaniola. You could tell he was grateful, but in the interrogation, they twisted everything he said. He finally had to acknowledge that, though he was a good man, Don Pedro was a pirate. That is what did him in; that morning, they sentenced him to death. Then Don Juan Francisco stood up and, citing many laws, offered what he called extenuating circumstances, and he demanded that the sentence be ratified by the tribunal in Seville. The judges agreed the case could be transferred to the other side of the ocean, but they warned that the death sentence couldn't be appealed. If they didn't hang him in Santo Domingo, they would hang him in Spain.

When they announced the sentence, there was a great fuss in the room, and the head judge had to call for order. Then he said that everyone who had sailed with Piers Leigh would be condemned as pirates, too. When he heard that, Don Pedro stood and spoke in defense of his men, saying all they had done was obey his orders. The head judge spoke with the other judges, then he ordered the search and capture of all those who had ever sailed with the pirate Leigh. Don Pedro looked like he'd been struck. Ay, señor! Even if he was a pirate, he was a good man!

We went home, and my lady kept begging to see her husband until Don Juan Francisco had to give in. That same afternoon, I went with her to see Don Pedro.

They had put him in a cell by himself again. He was sitting on a pallet, his head on his chest, oblivious to everything. His unruly chestnut hair fell over his forehead. He looked up, and he must have thought I was bringing him a message from Doña Catalina. I quickly stepped aside, and when he saw her behind me, his face lit up. They embraced and kissed so passionately that I felt embarrassed to be there. Then he put a hand on her stomach, which was now showing a lot. He told her not to worry about him, that maybe he deserved what was happening, that he was paying for his crimes. When I heard this, I burst into tears, but they only had eyes for each other. She repeated that she couldn't live without him, and Don Pedro said she needed to take care of the child she was carrying, who was all that would be left of their family.

I remember how a ray of sunlight filtered through the little window in the cell, making my señorita Catalina's golden hair shine.

"We'll meet in another life, my love," he told her. "There, we'll be reunited with my father, with my mother, with"—his voice broke—"with all the people at Oak Park who died."

His speech didn't fool me. Of course he wanted to live and be with her. He was just saying that stuff about being with his family in heaven because he couldn't bear to see her cry so. Then he must have remembered something because he touched his hand to his neck, to that old tin medallion, which I took to my Catalina one day and it cured her.

"Many years ago," Don Pedro began, "when we said good-bye at the cliff, you gave me this medallion. You told me it belonged to your mother, and that a long time before, your father had given it to her. Your real father. I think, my Len, that I know who he might have been. I've learned that all the men in the Great Armada had a medallion just like this."

My lady looked at him in surprise. "Piers, have you met a sailor from the Great Armada?"

"Yes," he said, excited, "and so have you."

"Who?"

"Old Matt! You're the one who told me so."

My lady opened her eyes wide. "Matt? Yes, I remember, but—"

"Remember how Matt spoke to you about his son, saying he was a sailor? He became captain of one of the merchant ships belonging to my family because he was a brave man and a man of the sea. Perhaps it was he who carried Uncle Andrew back and forth between Oak Park and the Basque coast. Maybe that's how he met your mother! The old sailor, you told me, had given this medallion to his own son."

She fell silent, thinking. "Matt always had a special affection for me. Once, he told me something I didn't understand."

"What?"

"How beautiful it seemed to him that stories that begin in youth end in old age. Piers, do you think he was my grandfather?"

"I suspect he was. And I think my father and Uncle Andrew also knew. Didn't you ever think it strange that they didn't try harder to find your supposed father in the Indies?"

"I was so little when I arrived, and then I was like part of your family, so I gave it no more thought. When he told me about his son's death, Matt mentioned that he had saved the life of 'the priest.' Do you think he was referring to Uncle Andrew?"

"I do."

My lady kissed the medallion, and through her tears, she forced a sad smile. Then she embraced Don Pedro, and he embraced her. Some time went by. All I could hear were noises from the street and a prisoner asking for water. After a while, we heard footsteps in the hallway, then a key turning in the lock. The guards came in, and the two of them stepped away from each other, as if embarrassed. Don Pedro begged the jailors to let us stay a moment longer, but the men refused.

We had to leave. Still, my lady seemed more at peace since she had spoken with him, and they both had remembered long-ago times. She caressed her stomach and sang a lullaby to their child. It moved me to see her like that.

Over the coming weeks, Doña Luisa took the opportunity to reclaim me. The old gossip told Don Juan Francisco she was delighted to have me take care of his niece, but later, she beat me, saying I was neglecting the sick people who paid her so many *maravedises*. So, I had a lot of work those days. What happens is that, when I do my curing work, I use my hands and all my energy, but I also think a lot. And so, I started thinking, figuring out how to help my Catalina and her Piers. I thought about Don Juan de Morfa, the one they say is an Irishman and who was so fond of Don Pedro.

I put on my cloak, so no one would recognize me. I escaped from Doña Luisa's house and, crossing through the orchards, reached Doña Beatriz's. I found her sitting outside, cradling her newborn baby. I told her that Don Pedro might die, and she looked at me with eyes full of worry and said, "There's nothing that can be done."

"Yes, of course there is," I told her. "Don Juan knows pirates and people from the sea, so he can get them and save Don Pedro."

She looked at me with her eyes very wide, half amused and half annoyed.

I repeated it. "Don Juan knows pirates, pirates who are friends of Don Pedro. They can save him."

I repeated it many times, "the pirates can save him," each time louder and more nervously. Then Don Juan de Morfa arrived.

"What does the black woman want?" he asked his wife.

He didn't mean any offense. I know perfectly well when there is contempt and when there isn't.

Doña Beatriz repeated it to him, with a sad smile. Don Juan looked pensively at the river and at the sea shining in the distance. In such a soft voice that we almost didn't hear him, he said, "The slave might just be right."

He took me aside. "Josefina, your idea is a good one. Maybe we can still do something to help Don Pedro."

"Yes!" I exclaimed.

"I can't leave the city to let his former men know——"

I looked at him, disappointed.

"But," he went on, "no one would suspect a black slave woman. Go to Samaná, find Don Hernando de Montoro, and hand him a letter that I will give you."

"Doña Luisa will whip me if I go that far away."

"Don't you worry. My wife and I will make your excuses. But go today."

I can't remember everything I did. I only know that I spent two nights and two days walking almost constantly until I arrived in Samaná, dirty and tired, with sores on my feet. There, I looked for Don Hernando de Montoro and gave him the letter from Don Juan. A strange smile crossed his face when he read it. Then he told me not to worry about anything, that Don Pedro had more lives than a cat and that he had gotten out of worse scrapes before. He laughed, handed me some coins, and ordered one of his servants to take me back to Santo Domingo. Once I was in the cart, he thanked me for everything and told me good-bye.

So, I returned, content because it was clear that Don Hernando was going to help my Catalina's husband. Also, I liked the trip in the cart, not having to walk so much and being able to watch the fields full of sugar cane and the faraway mountains turn green.

When I reached the capital, everyone was out in the street, as they usually are when ships are leaving to join the fleet of the Indies in Havana.

I recognized Don Pedro in the line of condemned men headed for one of the ships. They were already taking him away, to that country on the other side of the ocean, where other judges would ratify the sentence they gave him in Santo Domingo, and they would hang him by the neck until he was dead.

Following the prisoners, I found my Catalina, crying and not caring who saw her. I ran to her; I didn't like her to expose herself so much because the people in the capital are wicked; they make fun and laugh at other people's suffering. My lady, whose pregnancy was pretty far along, wanted to get on that big ship with Don Pedro, but of course, they didn't let her. I stayed with her at the port until the ships disappeared over the horizon. Then I took her home and put her to bed. I gave her laudanum, to stop her from suffering, and she fell asleep.

Then I left because I couldn't stand so much sadness anymore. First, I went to the Hospital of San Nicolás, where they bandaged my feet and gave me some new sandals. Then I roamed around the city, which is what I liked the most. Also, I was afraid to return to Doña Luisa's house.

After nightfall, though, I had no choice but go back to my mistress. She gave me the worst beating I can remember, for running away for days without saying anything to her. She left my back flayed. May God in the heavens someday give her what she deserves! My cries could be heard from next door, and finally Don Juan Francisco appeared. He told Doña Luisa that he needed to buy me to take care of his niece, and he offered her so much money she couldn't refuse, that greedy woman! Then Don Juan Francisco told me that, as soon as his niece had given birth—oh, and I knew it would be a boy, by the way. I can tell by looking into a pregnant woman's face whether she's carrying a boy or a girl. Anyway, once she had given birth, he said, I would be free to go wherever I wished. They were leaving for the lands of New Spain, Mexico City, where he would be a judge and hear more important cases than in Santo Domingo. I told him that all I wanted was to be with my darling girl, Doña Catalina, and to stay with him since he was a good man. I was so happy at not having to see Doña Luisa again that I was crying, and also because my back burned so from the whipping.

Days went by and my lady was still sad, even though I told her about my trip to Samaná. Then some serious news reached the island. Pirates had attacked the ships that were going to join the Indies fleet, near the canal of Tortuga, and it had shipwrecked the one carrying prisoners. Most of the men were rescued by the other ships, but some had been lost, including Don Pedro. Don Hernando de Montoro, I thought, hadn't managed to get there in time. Don Juan Francisco ordered that nothing be said to his niece, and when Don Juan de Morfa arrived the next day, asking to speak with her, the judge wouldn't let him in.

The time of childbirth soon arrived, and as I expected, my Catalina gave birth to a little boy. She wanted to name him Pedro because she somehow sensed that her husband had drowned. But I told her it was bad luck, and she should give him another name. Then she decided he should be named Mateo for that grandfather who gave her the medallion. My Catalina was delighted with the baby, and though she always talked about her Piers, she didn't cry as much, and she sang a lullaby in that lovely language I don't understand. She called it Basque.

A few months later, we set sail on a large galleon: Don Juan Francisco, my lady Doña Catalina, her son, Vicente Garcés, and I, Josefina, who felt very, very content because I liked freedom and doing whatever I wanted, and what I wanted was to be with Don Juan Francisco and my lady.

From the beginning, the crossing seemed eternal, what with all the rocking of the boat. I got very seasick, and my Catalina did, too. When the sun had set and risen I don't know how many times, a ship started chasing us. When it got close, it raised its flag, and everyone screamed in horror; it was a pirate flag.

Don Juan Francisco de Montemayor asked the captain to surrender so as not to endanger the lives of the passengers. The scowling sailor agreed. They boarded our ship, and one of those who jumped on deck was Don Pedro. My señorita Catalina was beside herself with joy when she saw him. He was, too, because he had found her, and she was holding their baby in her arms. The pirates spoke English, like my lady and Don Pedro used to between them, and their captain was a young, balding man who introduced himself as Ricardo Colerich. He informed the Spanish captain that they would be taking only Doña Catalina and not to worry, they wouldn't bother them anymore. My lady and Don Pedro Leal stepped aside and spoke for a moment. I watched them from afar with some sadness because I knew what was going to happen. Then they walked over to where I was standing, holding their son, and asked me to go with them. My lady embraced me again and again. But I knew that they had each other, and that the one I had to look after was Don Juan Francisco, who would be left all alone.

Don Pedro thanked me for taking care of his wife and for making that long walk to Samaná, when I flayed my feet. He explained to Don Juan Francisco that, thanks to that walk, Montoro had received the letter from Don Juan de Morfa telling him when the ship carrying prisoners would leave Santo Domingo and asking him to find Ricardo Colerich so the pirate could intercept it.

Then he reassured his wife's uncle, telling him that he would never again be a pirate but would return to England with Ricardo Colerich. There was a tyrant there who wouldn't last much longer, and they would soon have a new king. They would rebuild the house where he was born and that had burned down. Near it was a tree they called the oak.

They left on the pirate ship. They took their son with them, and I stayed with Don Juan Francisco so I could look after him and help him. He cried to see them go. We arrived in Mexico City three months ago, and now I am content here because I do as I like, and I take care of Don Juan Francisco, an honorable man who doesn't mistreat me. In fact, he's grateful for what I do.

Last night I dreamed about them, my lady and Don Pedro. They lived in a beautiful house, surrounded by fields and hills opening up to a sea that wasn't blue like the Caribbean Sea, but gray, like the sky. There was a big tree and a green pasture leading to a cliff. Yes. I dreamed about my lady, about my darling little girl, Doña Catalina.

Piedralaves, 11 February 2016

Fiction and Reality

This novel was born one summer in Manchester, when, after finishing *El astro nocturno*, I was faced with the challenge of leaving the Visigoth world to plunge into a different era. At that moment, I had read Hugh Thomas's book, *The Golden Empire: Spain, Charles V, and the Creation of America,* and I was thinking of doing something in depth with Spanish America in the seventeenth century. Since I love the places related to literature, I went with my family to visit nearby Lyme Park, one of the English mansions where the BBC filmed the adaptation of Jane Austen's *Pride and Prejudice* in 1995. We hoped to reencounter the settings and characters of that wonderful novel from the Georgian era. But something very different happened to me.

As I walked through the house that members of the National Trust so kindly show people, I discovered the history hidden behind those ancient walls. That seemed more fascinating to me than the BBC series or Lizzie Bennet's visit to Pemberley. What the guide told us transported me to the seventeenth century, a time of war between Parliament and King Charles I, when Lyme Park was a place of Royalist conspiracies involving its owners, the Leigh family. In the eastern part of the house, there is still an office, a mixture of a smoking room and library, with wood-paneled walls, paintings of the Stuart kings, and some large windows overlooking the park. Apparently, that's where the plots of the Royalists were hatched. During the visit, the guide told us that, in the cellars, they had found the corpse of a Catholic priest who had died, trapped there during those times of persecution. All these stories of conspiracies, of cellars with corpses, not to mention the beauty and enchantment of the place, unleashed in me the creative process that has culminated in *Open Sea*.

Nevertheless, Lyme Park currently has little in common with a seventeenth-century mansion, the setting of the novel I was planning, because its original Elizabethan design was modified to simulate a nineteenth-century Italian palace. After looking into various locations in the British Isles that could help me travel to the appropriate period, I finally ended up at a mansion near Dublin, smaller than Lyme Park and not as closely related to the English Civil War, but that conserved the structure and furnishings of the seventeenth century. Malahide Castle, stately and ancient, with crenellations and towers, revealed itself to me as the place where Piers and Len would have played as children. It still has a hole in the wall in the main sitting room, accessed by way of the servant hallways and covered by a tapestry, and in its gardens, you can see the ruins of an ancient abbey.

The scenery surrounding the fictitious mansion in *Open Sea*, which I called Oak Park, is inspired by the cliffs of Essex, specifically the Naze peninsula and the nearby village of Walton-on-the-Naze. These are not the white cliffs of Dover, but outcrops of sandstone that are slowly crumbling, so every year the coast recedes a little. When I saw the silver-gray sea from there and discovered that the cliffs had receded more than a hundred meters in recent centuries, I started thinking that they were like the ones I had imagined. Perhaps, centuries ago, there might have even been a cove there that has now disappeared. I should say that Horsehead Cove is also fictitious, though the rock in the middle is inspired by one near the Galician coast, which in fact looks like a horse from a chess game and is covered by water at high tide. It is located on the Ría de Pontevedra, the place my family vacations in the summer.

The protagonists, Len and Piers, are products of my imagination. From the Leighs of Lyme Park, I only borrowed the name. On the other hand, the Oquendos did exist. They were a clan of Basque sailors who, from out of nowhere, rose to belong to the *hidalgería* or petty nobility, and even to the nobility, of the Spanish Empire. Apparently, the patriarch, Don Miguel de Oquendo (as one of the characters, Matt, explains in the novel), was the son of a modest rope maker and participated in the Indies run. He may have increased his fortune through smuggling and commerce, and he came to own his own fleet. Later he fought in different naval campaigns with the poorly named Invincible Armada, causing his death.

It's one of the most studied episodes in naval history of the sixteenth century. The confrontation between the English and Spaniards didn't quite reach the proportions of a naval battle, though it was a Spanish defeat due to the climatic conditions and poor planning. Everything in the chapter "Invincible" is historically documented. The Armada crossed the Bay of Biscay and the English Channel, and it placed itself along the coast of Flanders. The objective was to pick up the Tercios, at that moment the best prepared army in Europe, to invade England and overthrow Elizabeth I. The confrontation between the English and Spanish navies took place not far from what is today the coast of Essex, where Oak Park is situated in the novel. Here we enter the realm of fiction; it's not impossible that one of those ships, pushed by the storm that came up after the brief combat, might have taken refuge there while the rest of the Armada returned to Spain, sailing down the English, Scottish, and Irish coasts on a journey in which many ships sank.

Don Miguel's son, Admiral Antonio de Oquendo, participated in various battles, like the defense of the empire's possessions on the coasts of Brazil and many other missions. He died after participating in the Battle of the Downs. He had two legitimate sons, who died before receiving an inheritance, and one illegitimate son, Miguel Antonio, who was also a sailor. Miguel Antonio ended up with all of the Oquendos' fortune after marrying a cousin, who was the one who finally inherited. The story of that bastard son, his wife, and her mother—the Aunt Juana mentioned in *Open Sea*—could have been the theme of another novel. One character who is fictitious is Isabel de Oquendo, Len's mother; I've allowed myself to play with the possibility of a third legitimate child of Don Antonio.

I began to immerse myself in the history of England at that time. For the atmosphere of London in the seventeenth century, I had the invaluable assistance of Hazel Forsyth and Sally Brooks of the Museum of London. They helped me document the prisons, walls, palaces, and location of the embassy of the Spanish Crown in that epoch. If you visit the city, don't miss that interesting museum, located very near the center.

For most of the events that occur in *Open Sea*, I depended on many books and articles. The seventeenth century is a fascinating period that the British historian Geoffrey Parker has nicknamed "the cursed century." Several factors came together—the Little Ice Age, which caused poor harvests and famines; the tremendous religious wars, like the Thirty Years' War; and, above all, the one that interested me here: the fierce English Civil War, which, in the words of the British historian Martyn Bennett, "invaded people's fields, patios and kitchens, taking away their beds and the mirrors on their walls" (*The English Civil War: A Historical Companion*, 2013). Some two hundred and fifty thousand men and women died, nearly seven percent of the total population of England. That was the terrible consequence of the confrontation between Charles I and Parliament, which opposed a monarch with absolutist ambitions. But it was also a war between opposite ways of understanding faith.

In the novel, I describe the fratricidal conflict through the misfortunes of the Leighs. Everything I say about the war is rigorously historical, including the Battle of Naseby, which is recounted in one chapter;

the rape and killing of women who followed the Royalists; the assaults by Parliamentarian troops against houses of Catholic nobles; and the horror of the siege of Colchester during the summer of 1648. Thomas's letter is inspired by an authentic one written by a Royalist gentleman.

The trajectory of the Royal Navy, which sympathized with Parliament during the first Civil War and in the second Civil War allied with the king, is a complex story. It is eloquently described by the historian John Rowland Powell in his interesting book, *The Navy in the English Civil War*. There, he relates another event that is also crucial to the novel: when Captain Swanley gave the order to execute Irish soldiers by throwing them into the sea, tied back to back.

The English Civil War must also be understood in the broader context of the religious wars that assailed Europe during the seventeenth century. European Christianity, which had been more or less united during the Middle Ages, had divided in two during the sixteenth century, with moments as dramatic as the Massacre of St. Bartholomew's Day, and the two sides became increasingly opposed.

Perhaps for the current epoch, when agnosticism and atheism have become the currency and when Protestantism and Catholicism have softened many of their positions, it is difficult to understand the radicalism and importance of religious ideas for the men and women of that time. Those in power used religion as a political weapon, while the lower class looked for an escape in it. Life expectancy was lower than today; there were great famines, and plagues desolated the population. The living conditions of the humble classes were very harsh, and in England, wealth was in the hands of some three hundred noble families. Because of all this, man in the Middle Ages thought about the next life in order to forget this one, and he moved around in codes of eternity, damnation, and salvation. Protestantism, and especially Calvinism, believed in the idea of predestination, so someone could be designated by God for perdition (as Mademoiselle Maynard tells Len in the novel). We watch pirate movies, and it seems picturesque that they sprinkle their conversation with *hell*s and *damnation*s. Those of Protestant origins knew themselves to be predestined for hell, so if salvation was denied them, they had to enjoy this life without any restrictions. Those of Catholic origins sought salvation through last-minute conversion or some sacrament that would save them, like just another amulet. One example of this, the episode of the blasphemous Mass described in *Open Sea*, is historical, and the French pirate Alexandre Olivier Exquemelin recorded it in a famous autobiography.

Yes, the seventeenth century was an epoch of religious extremism and *autos-da-fé*, of inquisitions, of summary executions of Catholics as traitors in the England of the last Tudors and Stuarts. Both on the Catholic side and the Protestant there were many deaths, martyrs to their own beliefs. Some women labeled as witches were publicly burned, becoming sacrificial goats for the conflict. One consequence of the ruthless English Civil War is that afterward, England imposed religious tolerance.

There was also the Jesuit mission of England. Convoked by the pope, young Englishmen of Catholic origin were educated in Jesuit seminaries in Catholic Europe, among them the Royal College of St. Alban, also known as the College of English, in Valladolid, founded in 1587 by Robert Persons, an English Jesuit. Then they returned to Great Britain. Some of these priests were executed through bloody martyrdom, like Edmund Campion, who is described in the novel.

After my immersion in the conflictive and passionate history of England, I returned to what had been the starting point when I began planning to write the new novel: the Spanish Empire. I must thank my family for their patience; they accompanied me to the Caribbean, and instead of resting on the beautiful Dominican beaches, they found themselves being dragged to ruins and museums, the places where the action would unfold. We stayed in a hotel on Calle de las Damas, right in the center of colonial Santo Domingo. Calle de las Damas ends in a great esplanade, where the Alcázar de Colón is situated. It was built by Don Diego Columbus, and his wife, Doña María de Toledo, lived there. She was from the powerful family of the Dukes of Alba. I saw the street, which conserves its colonial charm; it is ornamented by various churches as well as by houses from the epoch, and it ends at the Casas Reales, the former Audiencia of Santo Domingo.

The back of one block of houses on Calle de las Damas overlooks the Ozama River, and at that time, they were joined together by small orchards along the wall. I have imagined one of them to be the house of Don Juan Francisco de Montemayor y Córdoba de Cuenca, Len's uncle. I gave him good neighbors: on one side, the Dávilas, an old Creole family, and on the other, the Irishman John Murphy and his young wife.

Don Juan Francisco de Montemayor really existed. He was a jurist educated in Huesca who, through a series of circumstances, became principal judge of the Audiencia of Santo Domingo. During a couple of key years, when the governor was absent from the island (the previous one had died, and they were awaiting the arrival of the next one), he occupied the position of interim governor. We must keep in mind that the Audiencia of Santo Domingo at that time legislated, judged, and governed most of the Caribbean and what are today Venezuela and Colombia. Montemayor wrote numerous works of Indian law, and in one of the most important of them, he speaks of the division of booty. He did it to defend himself against the accusations made against him during his *juicio de residencia*: he was accused of having unfairly distributed the booty captured during the taking of the island of Tortuga.

The *juicios de residencia* or governors' trials further demonstrate the control that the Spanish Crown had over their subjects in the New World. All the civil servants posted to the Indies had to submit, at the end of their posting, to a trial to determine whether they had acted honestly. Anyone could give an opinion about the person on trial. It was a very useful mechanism of control for the administration of the Indies to prevent officials from exceeding their limits.

Montemayor was also behind the attack on Tortuga, which was a nest of pirates, privateers, and buccaneers. Two men led the action: Gabriel de Rojas and John Murphy. We have little documentation about Captain Rojas, so everything described in the novel is fictitious, except his involvement in the assault. John Murphy Fitzgerald Burke, whose Spanish name was curiously Juan de Morfa Burco y Geraldino, was an Irishman. He may have been a privateer for the Spanish Crown who came to the defense of the Indies against the actions of the English and Dutch. Apparently, in the seventeenth century, on the island of Hispaniola (today Haiti and the Dominican Republic) there was an Irish colony, which was crucial to the resistance against the English attack.

The episodes of piracy described in *Open Sea*, though fictionalized, are inspired by true events. Privateers, pirates, and buccaneers, undesirable people, populated the Caribbean, a stopping place for galleons and other ships loaded with riches.

During Montemayor's term as interim governor, Tortuga, the pirates' island, was recuperated at the end of his stay in the Audiencia while Oliver Cromwell's attack on Hispaniola, part of his Western Design, also took place. It is documented in three sources: the account written by Montemayor; that of Bernardino de Meneses, governor of Santo Domingo; and finally that of Sir William Penn, commander of the Royal Navy. The fight between Penn and Venables and the lack of cohesion between the sailors and the ground troops, which was one of the causes of the English defeat on Hispaniola, were true. The episode of the Battle of the Crabs, on the other hand, is based on a Dominican legend.

In the Dominican Republic's *Bulletin of the General Archives of the Nation*, I found the names of military officers, clerics, aldermen, and other bureaucrats of the era, which I have used. Among them, one that stands out is Don Rodrigo Pimentel, a curious character that we know was a smuggler associated with pirates, who controlled governors and judges in Santo Domingo, and who bought the position of alderman.

It seems that he received religious instruction and had a lover he gave refuge to in the convent of the Clare Sisters. That woman, Doña Inés de Ledesma, was involved with the captain that Pimentel tried to assassinate. He was tried and sentenced to death, but he died first of natural causes. He is buried in the Santa Clara Convent in Santo Domingo.

But I have used all this interplay of reality and fiction only as a background for the story that I really wanted to tell: that of Len and Piers and to a certain extent that of Josefina. Their lives are eventful, and like everyone, they have to depend on their own attitudes toward life, on their strength, in extreme circumstances. I have used a war to temper my characters and see if they are able to live up to the challenge. My experiences as a physician have taught me that being human requires overcoming one's own emotional wounds.

Suggested Reading

Open Sea is a novel that seeks to entertain readers and immerse them in the lives of fictitious characters. It's not a research project or doctoral thesis, so although I have incorporated over a hundred references, both books and articles, I don't think this is the place to give a full bibliography.

For those who would like to explore the history behind the story of Len and Piers, I would suggest some places to start. To become familiar with the America of the sixteenth and seventeenth centuries, I believe that Hugh Thomas's *The Golden Empire: Spain, Charles V, and the Creation of America* is fundamental. The general atmosphere of decadence in the court of Philip IV is depicted in the classic book by Martin Hume, *The Court of Philip IV: Spain in Decadence*, published in New York by G.P. Putnam's Sons in 1907 (republished by Espuela de Plata in 2003).

On life in the Caribbean, I recommend the works of Esteban Mira Caballos, *La Española, epicentro del Caribe en el siglo XVII* (Academia Dominicana de la Historia, 2010), and of Frank Moya Pons, *La vida escandalosa en Santo Domingo en los siglos XVII y XVIII* (Universidad Católica Madre y Maestra, Editora Cultural Dominicana, 1972). The latter reveals that the houses on Calle de las Damas were connected by orchards in the back.

To understand the complex international politics of the Spanish monarchy in the seventeenth century, I recommend a stupendous book edited by Enrique García Hernán and Davide Maffi, *Guerra y política internacional en la monarquía hispánica: Politica, estrategia y cultura en la Europa Moderna, 1500–1700* (Editorial CSIS, 2006), particularly the essays by Professor Porfirio Sanz Camañes of the University of Castilla–La Mancha. Regarding piracy and privateers in the Indies, I recommend *El combate a la piratería en Indias: (1555–1700)* by Oscar Cruz Barney (Oxford University Press, 1999); *Historia general de los robos y asesinatos de los más famosos piratas* by Daniel Defoe (Valdemar, 1999); *Los bucaneros de las Indias Occidentales en el siglo XVII* by Clarence H. Haring (Renacimiento, 2003); *Piratas, corsarios, bucaneros y filibusteros* by Manuel Lucena Salmoral (Síntesis, 2006); and *La vida de los piratas* by Stuart Robertson (Crítica, 2008).

To learn about the Oquendo family, see the brief review published by Manuel Gracia Rivas, "Los Oquendo: historia y mito de una familia de marinos vascos" (*Itsas Memoria. Revista de Estudios Marítimos del País Vasco*, no. 6, Untzi Museoa-Museo Naval, 2009); it can easily be found on the internet at http://um.gipuzkoakultura.net/itsasmemoria6/699-724_graciasrivas.pdf. Closely related to the history of Don Miguel de Oquendo is that of the Invincible Armada, which is retold by a variety of sources, though I would especially recommend *La Gran Armada: La mayor flota jamás vista desde la creación del mundo* by historian Geoffrey Parker and marine archeologist Colin Martin (Planeta, 2011). For the story of Inés de Ledesma and Gabriel de Rojas, I based my description on the chapter "Aproximación jurídica a los derechos de la mujer en los contratos matrimoniales" by Petra Neurkitchen, included in the collection *Historia de la mujer e historia del matrimonio*, edited by María Victoria López Cordón y Montserrat Carbonell i Esteller (Servicio de Publicaciones de la Universidad de Murcia, 1997).

Finally, I found Don Juan Francisco de Montemayor in an article by Maria Luisa Rodríguez-Sala and Miguel B. de Erice, "Juan Francisco

Montemayor y Córdoba de Cuenca, abogado, oidor y recopilador del siglo XVII" (*Anuario Mexicano de Historia del Derecho*, no. 9, 1997), which is available on the internet.

There are many publications about the English Civil War, most of them in English. Among them are two excellent general histories: *A Brief History of the English Civil Wars: Roundheads, Cavaliers, and the Execution of the King* by John Miller (Robinson, 2009), and *The English Civil War: A Historical Companion* by Martyn Bennett (History Press, 2013). I would also recommend a book by an Australian historian who is currently a professor at Oxford, Diane Purkiss, *The English Civil War: A People's History* (Harper Perennial, 2007), which gathers anecdotes, documents events, and talks about the lives of many characters from different social origins of that period. Regarding the trajectory of the Royal Navy during the Civil War, you should consult a now-classic book that describes all the naval events year-by-year and nearly day-by-day: *The Navy in the English Civil War* by John Rowland Powell (Archon Books, 1962). And if you are interested in the travels of the fleet commanded by Prince Rupert of the Rhine after fleeing from Ireland, I recommend the open-access website of the BCW Project, British Civil Wars, Commonwealth and Protectorate 1638–1660 at http://bcw-project.org/military/third-civil-war/prince-ruperts-voyages.

Historical Dates in the Novel

1577: Antonio de Oquendo, father of Isabel de Oquendo, is born.

1581, December 1: Edmund Campion dies.

1588, May to July: The Spanish Armada begins the mission called the English Enterprise.

End of September: Miguel de Oquendo dies upon his return from the English Enterprise.

1589: The Royal College of St. Alban (College of the English) is founded in Valladolid.

1605, November 5: Gunpowder Plot.

1610, January: San Pedro Claver, the "slave of the Negro forever," is posted to the New Kingdom of Granada.

1620: Juan Francisco de Montemayor y Córdoba de Cuenca is born.

1620: Antonio de Oquendo, who had been punished and imprisoned in Fuenterrabia the previous year, is transferred to the monastery of San Telmo on Mount Urgull (San Sebastián).

1639, October 21: Antonio de Oquendo fights in the Battle of the Downs.

1640, April: Charles I convenes the Short Parliament.

June 7: Antonio de Oquendo dies in La Coruña.

November: The Long Parliament begins.

1641, May 12: Thomas Wentworth, Earl of Strafford, is executed.

November 22: The House of Commons presents the Grand Remonstrance.

November 23: Charles I rejects the Grand Remonstrance.

1642, January 4: Charles I appeals to Parliament to arrest five Parliamentary opponents.

January 10: Charles I abandons London and goes to Hampton Court.

April 23: Charles I goes to Hull and is rejected by Sir John Hotham. He loses control of the navy.

May to June: Robert Rich, Earl of Warwick, secures the navy for Parliament.

August 22: Charles I rises up in Nottingham; the first English Civil War begins.

October 23: Battle of Edgehill; Charles I wins, with the cavalry of Prince Rupert of the Rhine, his nephew.

November: Royalist troops loot Brentford.

1643, January: The Royalists make Oxford their headquarters.

June 30: The Royalists defeat the Parliamentarians at Adwalton Moor.

July 26: Charles I takes Bristol and recuperates some ships.

September 20: First Battle of Newbury is fought; no winner.

1644, July 2: Charles I is defeated at Marston Moor, and the Royalist army is exhausted.

October 27: Second Battle of Newbury is fought; the battle is a draw.

December: Cromwell enacts legislation prohibiting Christmas, which was enforced until 1660.

1645, February 17: Parliament creates the New Model Army under the command of Sir Thomas Fairfax.

June 14: The Royalists are defeated at the Battle of Naseby.

August: Bristol falls to the Parliamentarians.

1646, April: Charles I leaves Oxford to negotiate with a Scottish regiment, which turns him over to the English Parliament. He had already sent his son Charles, Prince of Wales, to France for his protection.

June: Oxford falls to the New Model Army. Charles I surrenders, ending the first English Civil War.

1648, March: Southern Wales rises up in support of Charles I. Royalists rise up in Kent.

May: The navy changes sides and becomes Royalist.

May to June: The Royalist navy sails along the coast of Essex in rebellion against Parliament.

June 11: Royalist ships set sail for Hellevoetsluis (Netherlands) in search of the Prince of Wales.

June 13 to August 27: The siege of Colchester.

July 17: The navy leaves Holland for Yarmouth with the Prince of Wales.

Middle of July to end of August: The Royalist ships are along the coast of Essex.

August 25: The New Model Army under the command of Oliver Cromwell is victorious in the Battle of Preston. End of the second English Civil War.

August 28: The defenders of Colchester, Sir Charles Lucas and George Lisle, are executed.

August 30: The Royalist and Parliamentarian fleets maneuver in the Thames but are driven in opposite directions by bad weather.

1649, January 1: Prince Rupert of the Rhine and his brother, Prince Maurice of the Palatinate, set sail with the Royalist ships for Ireland.

January 30: Charles I is executed.

March 30: Juan Francisco de Montemayor is named principal judge of Santo Domingo.

May to August: The Royalist squadron, under the command of Prince Rupert of the Rhine, carries out raids against Commonwealth shipping from its base in Kinsale (Ireland). Then, driven away by Commonwealth General-at-Sea Robert Blake, he sails to Portugal.

August 2: Oliver Cromwell's campaign in Ireland begins.

1650, March: Robert Blake blockades Prince Rupert's squadron in Lisbon, until, in October, he manages to escape.

1650: Juan Francisco de Montemayor reaches the island of Hispaniola.

1652: François Levasseur, governor of the island of Tortuga, is killed by irate taxpayers and is replaced by Baron de Fontenay.

May 9: Prince Rupert of the Rhine's squadron, which had remained within the Mediterranean, the European Atlantic coast, and the African coast until then, leaves Cabo Verde headed for the Caribbean.

May 29: The squadron of Prince Rupert of the Rhine arrives at the island of Saint Lucia.

September 13: A storm sinks the *Defiance*. On board is Prince Maurice of the Palatinate.

October: Prince Rupert of the Rhine returns to Europe.

1653, August 18: Andrés Pérez Franco, governor of Santo Domingo, dies and is replaced by Juan Francisco de Montemayor as interim governor.

December: Oliver Cromwell takes his vows as Lord Protector of the Commonwealth.

1654, January to February: Gabriel de Rojas and Juan de Morfa (John Murphy) conquer Tortuga.

December 25: Cromwell's navy leaves England for the Caribbean.

1655, April 10: Juan Francisco de Montemayor ceases to be interim governor of Santo Domingo with the arrival of the new governor, Don Bernardino de Meneses, Count of Peñalba. Juan Francisco de Montemayor is posted to New Spain.

April 13: The Royal Navy appears in front of Santo Domingo.

April 17 and April 24: British assaults begin against Santo Domingo.

April 24: Curfew is proclaimed in Santo Domingo.

Early May: The British and the Dominicans fight, and the British begin to retreat.

May 4: The English retreat definitively.

May 10–17: The English arrive in Jamaica. Jamaica surrenders.

1656, end of January: Governor Bernardino de Meneses is transferred to the Royal Audiencia de Charcas (Sucre) and is replaced by Félix de Zúñiga.

1656, January: The royal writ prohibiting Spanish privateers, promulgated on March 2,1655, arrives in Santo Domingo.

1658, March 27: Juan Francisco de Montemayor arrives in Veracruz.

1658, September 3: Oliver Cromwell dies.

1659, May 29: Charles II arrives in London.

1660: The English monarchy is restored.

Acknowledgments

First, I would like to thank Natividad Lorenzo Gil for her marvelous stylistic work and her editorial suggestions. These encouraged me a great deal when the text was still in a preliminary state.

From when the first sketches of *Open Sea* emerged, up to its final pages, Lourdes Álvarez Rico has accompanied me, and her ideas, her friendship, and her invaluable recommendations helped in so many literary tempests.

To my brother José María, who introduced me to the world of piracy.

I have returned to Pilar de Cecilia, an expert literary critic, on many occasions. Thanks to her, I began in this world of literature, and all my novels are—in one form or another—daughters of hers. To Ángel Pozuelo, doctor of history and efficient consultant in the many aspects of naval history included in the novel, I owe my thanks for his expert historical corrections.

Margarita Sánchez, one of the people who knows the most about the situation of women in the Americas at the times of colonization and the empire, was of great assistance in understanding the society and customs of Colonial Latin America.

Porfirio Sanz Camañes and José Gregorio Cayuela Fernández of University of Castilla-La Mancha (UCLM) have provided important bibliographic suggestions.

I am grateful to Pilar Latasa, professor of Latin American history, for the patience she showed me that Saturday morning when we got lost in the bibliographical depths of the university.

My sister Ana, my brother-in-law Hossein, their children, and my aunt Felisa have been priceless companions on my travels in search of documentation.

Hazel Forsyth and Sally Brooks, of the Museum of London, have been of invaluable help in re-creating the atmosphere of that city in the seventeenth century. I am grateful for their brilliant suggestions and their patient work.

I also want to thank the members of the Neurology Department of the HGUCR, especially the head of the department, Dr. Julia Vaamonde; my senior colleagues, María Ángeles del Real, Amalia Hernández, and Ramón Ibáñez; and all the rest, who, with their patience and help, have supported me in so many moments.

And to Lourdes de la Torre, who drew the maps for the novel. Finally, I am grateful for the patience that my editor at Grijalbo, Mònica Tusell, has always shown, and for the constant support of Ramón Conesa of the Agencia Literaria Carmen Balcells, who has negotiated all nonliterary aspects involved in the publication of a novel.

About the Author

María Gudín is the author of the acclaimed novels *Queen with No Name*, *Sons of a Gothic King*, and *The Night Star*. A doctor specializing in neurology, she lives in Ciudad Real, Spain, where she practices at the general hospital and teaches at the university. She devotes all her spare time to reading and writing. For more information, visit her website at www.mariagudin.es.

About the Translator

Photo © 2018 Carolyn Cullen

Cynthia Steele, who received her PhD in Spanish literature from the University of California at San Diego, is professor of Comparative Literature, Cinema, and Media at the University of Washington in Seattle. She has published numerous translations of fiction and poetry by Spanish-language authors, including José Emilio Pacheco, Sergio Pitol, Inés Arredondo, and Elena Poniatowska. She is also the author of two books of literary criticism, *Narrativa indigenista en los Estados Unidos y México* and *Politics, Gender, and the Mexican Novel: Beyond the Pyramid.*